SHADOW DEEP

PROF CROFT 10

BRAD MAGNARELLA

THE PROF CROFT SERIES

1

Sixteen years earlier

"I can't do this anymore, Everson."

The room hardened around me: words on a page, open book, cheap desk. My hand held a pen, its tip resting on a notepad scrawled with notes—my own, but I could barely remember writing anything.

"Did you hear me?" the voice asked.

Blinking moisture into my eyes, I straightened and craned my neck around. The figure standing in the doorway of my dorm room sharpened into focus. My girlfriend. Her brunette hair, normally straight, fell in thick ringlets over the shoulders of a black evening dress that hugged her in all the right places.

"Wow. You look amazing."

"Do you want to know why?"

I searched my memory, but it was still misty. The book was a thick tome on Norse myths that I'd been lucky to find—and from which I'd yet to entirely emerge. The parallels to

Greek mythology were incredible. When Jennifer sighed harshly through her nose, I realized my gaze had begun wandering back toward the book.

"It's our six-month anniversary," she said, answering her own question. "We had a reservation for dinner."

Dammit!

I shot up, trying to remember if I'd showered that day. It didn't matter. There wasn't time. At the closet, I pulled out my lone suit, which I kept in a plastic garment bag. I struggled with the zipper until the bag burst open, spilling a clutch of ties I'd draped across the hanger.

"Yeah, yeah, all right," I stammered, scooping them up. "Just give me, like, three minutes?"

"The reservation was for an hour ago."

"An hour ago?" I straightened, the arm holding the ties falling to my side. "Why didn't you say anything?"

"About a reservation *you* made?"

"I did make the reservation, didn't I?" I muttered, everything coming back now.

She faced me, her purse hand pressed to her cocked hip. "We had this conversation last week. I told you that we never do anything together. You said, 'What do you mean we never do anything? We're doing something right now.' And I said, 'Watching you read isn't doing something.' And you said, 'We're studying.'" I nodded hurriedly to tell her I remembered, but once Jennifer got going, she was impossible to derail. "I pointed out that I'd stopped studying almost two hours before and that you *always* do this. You get so wrapped up in your books that you forget I'm even in the room, let alone your *life*."

"That's not true."

"You asked me what I wanted to do, and I said, 'Our six-month anniversary is this Saturday. Let's go out for dinner and a movie. No books. No research. Just the two of us enjoying ourselves.' And you said, 'I know the perfect place.' And now look at you." She gestured with her purse toward my book-heaped desk. "Doing the same thing you always do. And this isn't even for school!"

She was right about the not-for-school part. I'd taken to browsing the old bookstores in Greenwich Village, allowing certain titles to call to me. This particular title had used a bullhorn. That had been around eleven this morning. The hands on my bedside clock now pointed to five past eight.

I opened my mouth, then closed it. I couldn't explain to myself, much less her, how it happened. I wasn't just reading the words—I was seeing the stories, inhabiting them, strange forces shifting deep inside me...

When I felt my gaze being drawn back to the book, I stepped forward and rubbed Jennifer's bare shoulders. "Look, I'm sorry. I got absorbed, I guess. But we can still go out. We'll just go somewhere else."

We'd had a few versions of this argument during our six months together. Once Jennifer had her say, things were usually golden again. But she remained taut in my grip. And now she was shaking her head, sending the bangs she'd obviously spent considerable time fixing back and forth across her brow.

"Not this time."

"What do you mean?"

"I like you, Everson. I *really* like you. But this isn't working for me."

My heart sank. I really liked Jennifer DeFazio too. Jersey born, she possessed a solidity I hadn't known in many girls. And where I was an absent-minded muser, she was a crack observer. We fit. We made each other laugh. We may only have been nineteen, but weren't those the bedrocks of *till death do us part*?

"What do you want?" I said, then caught myself. "I mean, what can I do to make this up to you?"

"A month."

"A month?"

"You box up all of your mythology books, and I put them somewhere for a month."

Her proposal left me feeling strangely empty. "Why? I mean, I don't see how that—"

"Because I need to see what you're like without them. I need to see what *we're* like without them."

"Jennifer, mythology is my degree field."

"Which is still two years away, and you've read enough for the next twenty." Her lips twitched up at her own observation, but she set her jaw again. "One month."

"Isn't that being a little extreme?" I chuckled. "I mean, why don't we—"

"Look, I'm hungry," she said, cutting me off again. "I'm going to my room to order a pizza. You're welcome to join me, but only if you agree to the one month. It's ten after eight. If you're not there by nine, I'll take that as your answer, and I'll appreciate it if you never contact me again. I'm not trying to be a dick. Under the circumstances, I think I'm being incredibly fair. Nine o'clock," she repeated and left.

I looked at the closed door for a moment, then snorted. *Definitely extreme.*

But I would do the month for her sake. Maybe I'd learn something about myself too. Because if I was being honest, the whole-soul absorption, not to mention the missing time, had been bothering me. No matter how much I enjoyed mythology, that couldn't be normal.

I took a quick shower, then dressed in my suit. Yeah, it was pizza delivery in a dorm room, but it would make Jennifer laugh, and it was the least I could do after standing her up. I picked the tie she'd gotten me for my birthday, knotted a passable Windsor, and brushed off the lapels. I was reaching over to snap off the desk light, when I caught the spot in the mythology book where I'd left off.

Don't, I warned myself.

I saw myself killing the light and hustling to Jennifer's dorm, getting there with fifteen minutes to spare. We'd laugh, we'd eat pizza, we'd fool around. And at the end of the month, I'd know a lot more about myself, about us.

But my gaze lingered on the enchanting words.

Just to the end of the paragraph, I decided, a sensible compromise.

But when I finished the paragraph, I saw that the section ended in only another page and a half. And when I finished the section, I flipped ahead. Only four more pages to the end of the chapter.

I glanced at the clock. *Plenty of time.*

I went from propping a knee on the chair to lowering myself all the way down. And then I was at the book's appendix, my suit jacket slung over the chair back, tie hanging loosely from my neck.

What in the...?

I blinked and twisted toward my bedside clock. It was after eleven. Heart pounding sickly, I called Jennifer.

She didn't answer.

2

Central Park, present

"It's Alec DeFazio," the young man standing before me said, "and I'm actually fifteen."

He'd first appeared in my classroom two weeks earlier, posing as my student and introducing himself as *Sven Roe*. Argumentative, he'd also displayed an acute understanding of mythology. I'd taken him on as a graduate assistant only for him to demand I teach him magic. He then booby-trapped the door to my office with a fire rune. A manhunt ensued for Sven Roe, who wasn't enrolled at the college, it turned out, and whose name was just a rearrangement of the letters in *Everson*. When I caught up to him, I learned he'd come from the shadow present, a probable reality that paralleled our own. He was also carrying a powerful artifact, the Tablet of Hermes, which had bonded to him and boosted his innate magic. I enlisted Sven to transport me back to the shadow present to stop a cult operating out of an old explorer's club, the Discovery Society. Its president, Eldred, was hellbent on summoning the Greek god Cronus, leader of the Titans, to bring about a new order. He ended up severing his own head with Cronus's scythe. Only later would I learn that the essence of Hermes had recruited Sven and me to stop Cronus's return.

Sven had promised to tell me his true name when that was all over, and true to his word, here he was.

Alec DeFazio, I repeated to myself.

As I shook his hand, my mind started making associations: *DeFazio... Jennifer DeFazio... my girlfriend from college.*

My flip phone hummed. While hunting for *Sven Roe,* the Sup Squad had been searching for facial matches, but the software had only returned some close hits based on morphology. There was one in particular they'd wanted me to see, and the hum told me it had finally uploaded to my primitive device. I opened the phone to find my faculty photo from Midtown College staring back at me.

Huh?

"I'm your son," Alec said now.

When I looked up, it was as if the young man were caught in an afterimage of my faculty photo. I honed in on Alec's eyes. Frank, intelligent eyes, like his mother's. *Jennifer's eyes set inside my face.*

"My son," I echoed.

"Well, not technically speaking," he said, fidgeting with the sleeve of his hoodie shirt. "Your son over there."

He meant the shadow present, where he'd come from. Even now, he seemed a part of the shade where we stood, with his dusky features and gray attire. I stared, unable now to unsee Jennifer's eyes set inside my face.

I remembered the book on Norse mythology from sixteen years earlier, a book I still owned. Jennifer had given me an ultimatum—my mythology books or our relationship. Years later I would understand that my magic had chosen for me, plunging me deep inside the Norse myths until it was too late for me to go to Jennifer and alter my path to wizardhood. But had there been another path in which I'd resisted my magic?

"Don't worry," Alec said. "I'm not suggesting you have any responsibility for me. I promised I'd tell you who I was, and this is who I am."

"How is she?" I asked, finding my voice. "Jennifer?"

After that night, she hadn't returned my calls. The few times I saw her on campus, she would respond to my lame wave with a stony glance before walking away. When she transferred to another college, I kept up with her doings through a mutual friend long enough to know she'd gotten engaged her senior year.

Of course, that had all been in the actual present.

"Not terrible, all things considered," Alec replied with a shrug. "She's a nurse at General, a unit manager. She's survived a few rounds of layoffs, but they've cut her salary and benefits to the bone. She's pretty stressed, but we both know she's lucky to have a job. For now. Sorry, too much information."

"No, no, I wanted to hear it."

"It sounds like you knew her here?" he said. "I wasn't sure."

"We dated in college. Not for very long, but I ... Well, I liked her. Great person," I added weakly.

I could see the question in his eyes: *What happened, then?*

"Was I ever in your life over there?" I followed up quickly.

"Until I was about three, but I don't remember anything. You went overseas and something happened. An accident of some kind. My mom never went into the details. At first I thought it was to spare me a horrible truth, but as I got older, it became obvious she just didn't want to talk about it."

The timing would have lined up with my trip to Romania when I'd gone in search of the *Book of Souls*. I very nearly hadn't made it back, but I was comparing actual to probable. In the shadow realm, I could have gone to any number of places for any number of reasons and gotten into any number of jams.

"So, it's just been you and her?" I asked.

"Yeah, pretty much."

As I watched him will the somberness from his eyes, a sympathy for this young man who was and wasn't my blood surged up and threatened to pummel me. I extended an arm as if to pull him into a hug—I knew about growing up father-less—but it felt too soon. I gripped the strap of his backpack instead.

"How are you doing with this?" I asked, giving it a shake.

His pack held a powerful box and the Tablet of Hermes. Even before the father-son revelation, I'd been concerned about the tablet's hold over him.

"Fine," he answered. "I mean, it's not strangling me or anything."

I checked the shimmering threads that bonded him to be sure. "Any more changes? Or intense dreams?"

After destroying the Scythe of Cronus, I'd hoped the tablet would release Alec, but either the Hermes essence had become too comfortable in his body or the threat wasn't gone. Either way, I needed to keep an eye on him.

"No," he replied, but his look suggested he was with-holding something. Or maybe he was just uncomfortable from having revealed so much.

We stood in silence for a moment, my mind scrambling to

find the words appropriate to a revelation I'd never seen coming. I came up empty.

When Alec peered past my shoulder, the rest of Central Park seemed to return to living color. Music wailed from the mayor's much ballyhooed "Concert on the South Lawn." I followed Alec's gaze across the green grass and vibrant crowd to where my wife, Ricki Vega, eight months pregnant, was reclined against Mae's picnic basket with a plate of food. Bree-yark, who had just proposed to Mae, was returning with her from their walk. Ricki's son, Tony, jogged from a pickup soccer game to catch up to them.

"C'mon," I said, clapping Alec's shoulder. "I want to introduce you to my family and friends."

But the young man remained planted in the shade of the surrounding trees. "How would that work?"

"What do you mean? I'll tell them what you told me."

"If it's all right, Professor Croft, I'd like to keep this confidential for now."

By formally addressing me, he seemed to be trying to put space between us. But I wasn't having it.

"It's Everson," I said. "And is there a reason you don't want me telling anyone?"

He hiked up his pack and studied the grass at his feet. "It's just that I'm still getting used to the whole thing myself. And look, I don't want you treating me any differently now that you know about this." He gestured between us. "That's not why I told you. The *you* here has nothing to do with the *me* there."

"Well, you're wrong about that part. We have plenty to do with one another. In fact, we should probably work out a schedule."

He looked up. "A schedule?"

"For training. You're in possession of something powerful, and I want to make sure you can handle it as well as your own magic. That's not just coming from me, but the senior members of my order."

His spine straightened slightly. "Yeah?"

"How do Saturday afternoons work for you? Two to four?"

"Where?"

"Midtown College. Do you remember how to get there?"

He'd attended my first summer-term class, where we'd debated the definition of a trickster. *Our first father and son argument,* I mused now.

"I remember. I'll be there." He glanced at our picnic setup again. "Well, I should probably get back. I don't want my mom to start worrying."

"Does Jennifer know about me? Here, I mean?"

He snorted a laugh. "Sounds like a good way to get me committed to Manhattan Psych. No, she doesn't know about any of this."

"Welcome to the life of a magic-user." I smiled sadly, remembering my first years of wizarding.

Alec lingered, appearing to weigh something, before unshouldering his pack and bringing it around. From the small pocket, he pulled out a photo and held it toward me.

"I brought it in case you needed proof."

I took the small portrait photo. The toddler was clearly Alec. He was sitting on the lap of Jennifer DeFazio, who had cut her long hair into a bob. And then there was the man beside them, hugging Jennifer to his side and smiling over Alec's head. I'd grown my hair longer, and I was wearing an argyle vest—no doubt a present from a well-meaning wife. I searched my eyes. They looked tired but content.

"Wild, huh?" Alec said.

Unreality spiraled through me. "Just a little."

I handed the photo back, and he stowed it in his pack. With a small wave, he withdrew into the shade.

"Hey!" I said, before he could translocate back to the shadow present. "Do you still have my schedule at the college?" I'd passed out the syllabi for my summer term that first day, and he'd taken one.

"Yeah?" he said.

"Our meetings don't have to wait till Saturday. Drop by my office whenever you want, for whatever reason. I mean it."

He nodded in a way that was hard to read and disappeared.

3

"Your son?" The bed shifted as my wife propped herself onto an elbow, her eyes picking up the glow from our bedside clock. "How is that possible?"

"Sorry, let me try again." I needed to use fewer *here*s and *there*s this time. "I knew his mother here, in college. We broke up. Evidently, the shadow us didn't, and that probability played out there. Alec was the result."

"So, he's your shadow son?"

"Well, the son of my shadow, yeah."

I was breaking my promise to Alec from that afternoon, but there was no way I could keep the info from my wife. I'd waited until Tony was in bed, though. I was going to have a hard enough time explaining this to an adult, never mind an eight-year-old. Especially since I'd yet to fully process the revelation myself.

"That explains why you were so quiet after the picnic," she said.

"Well, it was a lot to digest. Bree-yark's fermented anchovies probably didn't help."

"I feel even worse now for shooting the poor kid."

She was referring to her shadow self, who'd engaged Alec when he tried to pull me from the shadow realm following my battle with a shifter. The way she said it made me chuckle, but her face remained serious.

"That wasn't you," I reminded her.

"But she's a probable me, right? It's what I would have done if I'd been in her situation."

"The city over there is *much* different than our version, danger factor off the charts. I mean, there was a giant Cerberus on the loose that night, and I was running around chucking lightning grenades at squad cars."

"It still doesn't make it right."

I hadn't expected our talk to take this turn, but I understood her concern. It was the idea that she held the capacity to harm—possibly even kill—an innocent boy. And in this case, an innocent boy who'd turned out to be the son of my shadow. Before I could reassure her, she tilted her head and squinted slightly.

"I can see it."

"What's that?" I asked.

"The resemblance between you guys."

"Yeah, me too. So much so that I never even thought to question his claim."

"Should you?" she said, the thought appearing to occur to her for the first time.

"He brought a family picture from when he was a toddler, one of those studio shots. It was definitely me." I shook my head in disbelief. "Surreal doesn't even begin to describe it. Apparently, something happened to me when he was three, some sort of accident. That's why I'm not there anymore."

When she remained quiet, I looked over to find moisture standing in her eyes.

"Hey, are you all right?" I snapped on the bedside lamp and twisted back toward her.

She lowered her gaze, her face vulnerable in the sudden light. "Yeah, sorry. It was just the thought of something happening..." She snuffed out a laugh as she wiped her eyes and palmed her swollen belly. "My hormones are all over the place. I was the same way when I was pregnant with Tony."

I stroked her midnight hair behind her ear.

"I know this is a helluva time to be dropping this on you," I said. "It won't change anything with us."

That was probably why Alec had wanted me to keep the news between us, because he didn't want my wife to consider him a threat to our family.

"I feel bad for him," she said.

"Who? Alec?"

She nodded. "Tony spent his first seven years without a father, and I know that was hard on him."

Alec had made a point of telling me he wasn't looking for a father, and I'd taken him at his word, but I had only to look at my own experience to know how naïve I was being. I'd spent my first thirty years wondering about my dad. Our reunion had been one of the most monumental experiences of my life. Getting to see who he was, finally; getting to work alongside him, an advanced magic-user. All the way up until our last moment, when he'd sacrificed himself to repel Dhuul the Whisperer.

"I told Alec I'd meet with him on Saturday afternoons for training," I said. "I need to make sure he can control his magic. It's also a way for me to keep an eye on the Hermes tablet. I hope that's all right with you."

She nodded. "Of course."

"Thanks for understanding."

"And if you want to be a dad to him, I'd understand that too. He's welcome in our home anytime." She probably mistook my silence as I considered how fast things were moving for doubt because she added, "Hey, us Puerto Ricans are all about big, extended families. The more, the merrier. And after the dad you've been for Tony, how wrong would that be if I couldn't be a mom to Alec?"

"He's not actually my son," I reminded her.

"But he needs a role model, someone who understands him."

I touched my forehead to hers, and we kissed. When we separated, concern lines returned to her face.

"You're not still hung up on your shadow, are you?" I asked.

"Police officers aren't trained to shoot extremities. That was a center-of-mass shot gone wide."

"Our probable selves have done all kinds of things we wouldn't be proud of. I mean, it's a fluke you even know about that encounter. And that wasn't you," I repeated for emphasis. "Ricki Vega in the shadow present is an independent entity."

She gave a slight nod, her pensive gaze recalling her shadow version. I couldn't help but wonder what had happened to that Vega after I'd left the basement of the Discovery Society. Her team would have found her near the decapitated body of Eldred, who had been harvesting organs to summon Cronus. And if Eldred was as influential a figure in that version of the city as I'd come to believe...

"What is it?" my wife asked from beside me.

I relaxed my brow and cleared the thought from my head. We already had enough going on.

"That downstairs unit I told you about?" I said, changing the subject. "I'm going to make an offer on it tomorrow. The space needs work, and the sooner I can have it ready, the better." It was a pledge I'd made to Ricki at the picnic earlier —to store anything potentially dangerous in a separate space —and it was the right move for our family. Our little girl would be arriving next month.

"You're not planning to build the space out yourself, are you?"

"Actually, I have someone else in mind."

4

Bree-yark frowned as he strolled around the basement efficiency, then frowned some more.

"What's the verdict?" I asked at last.

"Hate to break it to you, Everson, but this is gonna be a major project."

"Really? The building owner made it sound like he'd done the heavy lifting and the space just needed finishing. He even said we could use his material." I nodded toward some cans of primer and a sagging roll of carpet.

Grunting a laugh, my goblin friend shook his head. "Heavy lifting? If anything, the joker gave us a bigger job."

"How so?"

He stalked over to a wall half-mounted with drywall and ripped out a fistful of exposed insulation. "This stuff might be fine for Nashville," he said, "but a New York winter? Fuhgedd-aboudit."

"Aren't you supposed to handle that with gloves and a mask?"

He sniffed the wad of fiberglass and tossed it aside before

snapping off an entire section of drywall. Inspecting the edge, he released a snort. "Quarter inch at best. Yeah, he was doing this on the cheap."

He dropped the drywall and gave it a pair of stomps.

"Hey, maybe we should leave everything intact until we know—"

"Even the framing's suspect," Bree-yark grunted. He swung a stubby leg into the exposed wall, fracturing a two-by-four.

"All right, all right," I said, moving between him and the damaged wall. "I get the picture. How much would we be talking for a basic renovation? Remember, this is just going to be a space for me to store volatile items and perform certain spell work. I don't need it to be a pimped-out man cave."

The ridge over Bree-yark's right eye cocked upward. "You sure? I mean, it could be kind of nice. A pool table here." He walked over and mimed the table's placement with his hands. "A keg fridge in the corner. Pair of Barcaloungers right over there. The facing wall would be perfect for a mounted flatscreen."

"Doesn't leave room for much else."

"We'll find the room. Priorities, my friend."

"I noticed you mentioned a *pair* of Barcaloungers. Is this for me or for you?"

"I'm just saying that married life can get a little heavy sometimes, and having a place to yourself—all right, to *our*selves—could help."

"Not having second thoughts about Mae, I hope."

My mentor, Gretchen, had tried her best to insert herself between Bree-yark and Mae, even using a shaved bugbear as a "boyfriend" to stoke his jealousy. But Bree-yark proposed to Mae, and Gretchen fled to Faerie to recover from her humiliation. I hadn't seen or heard from her since, and I feared now that she was resorting to subtle enchantments, but Bree-yark quickly put the concern to rest.

"No way, buddy. Asking for that woman's hand was the best thing I've ever done. Doesn't mean I'm gonna stop hanging with the boys, though." He punched my shoulder. "And seeing as how you have your own pad now..."

"You're welcome here anytime, but for now let's not set our sights any higher than a minifridge and a collapsible card table. I want this main area devoted to shelving, storage, and casting. Sound good?"

"Hey, you're the boss."

"And you're all right with something of this scale? I thought it was just going to be a patch-up job, but if it's a major project, I don't want you to feel obligated—especially with your wedding coming up. I'm sure I can find someone else."

"And end up with more shoddiness?" Bree-yark shook his head. "Nah, if you want this done right, you hire a goblin. We're talking some of the best builders and engineers in the world. It's in our gristle."

"And you've built out something like this before?" I asked to be sure. "You, specifically?"

He shrugged. "More or less."

Not exactly confidence-inspiring, but before I could press him further, he produced a small notepad from the pocket of his overalls and began scribbling on it. As he muttered, I picked up something about subflooring and concrete screws.

"We're looking at around fifty bucks a square foot," he said at last. "That would put the entire project at roughly..." He scribbled some more. "Let's just say twenty thousand even. Friends and family discount."

He ripped out the piece of paper and handed it to me. It was an illegible list surrounded by illegible calculations. All I could make out was the "20" at the bottom, underlined twice.

"And this is for a finished job?" I asked to be sure.

"Yup, the whole meal, roots to grubs. Oh, it's gonna be nice, Everson."

"We should be able to swing that," I said, handing the paper back. "When can you start?"

"How about today? In fact, I should make my first run to the hardware store before it gets too late. Wanna come with?"

"I'd love to, but I need to head over to the college."

"On a Saturday? What for?"

"You remember that kid I told you about?" I said. "Sven Roe?"

"Oh, yeah. Blew up your office and sent us on that wild goose chase for—what was it—red tanzanite?"

"Same kid, but he ended up being a good guy, remember? His real name's Alec DeFazio. I'm going to be training him, helping him develop his magic." A small bolt of pride shot through me, and I suddenly wanted to tell Bree-yark about the boy being my shadow's son. But I'd made a promise that I'd already had to break once. Anyway, Bree-yark was back to inspecting the unit with a critical frown.

"Just don't let him send any fireballs your way," he said absently.

"No, we'll work up to that." I lifted my satchel and slung it over a shoulder. "Need anything else to get started?"

"Just an account at the hardware store. Got a credit card handy?"

To be safe, I chose the one with the lowest credit limit and handed it over. "Call if you think you might go over budget."

"I'll be purchasing bulk rate, not to mention flexing my

haggling muscles. Something else goblins are known for. If anything, I'll come in well under. Just watch."

"And we're clear on this being a basic buildout, right? No man caves."

"Heard you the first time. Basic buildout." He'd resumed frowning around the space, no doubt lamenting the vast potential I was throwing away. "Well, better get started," he said, snapping to.

"Thanks again, Bree-yark."

I'd just ascended to the ground floor when I heard what sounded like a wall collapsing, followed by a burst of angry swearing. I started back down before deciding, for better or worse, my wizard sanctum was in his hands.

"Been waiting long?" I asked.

Alec rose from the bottom step to the college's west entrance. "Not very. Five minutes?"

"I wasn't sure if you were a coffee drinker, but I grabbed an extra."

He hiked up his pack, accepted the paper cup, and took a sip. "Not bad."

"Colombian dark. There's a guy with a cart just a couple blocks south of here in Bryant Park. Roasts and grinds his beans right there. Some of the best coffee in the city, and about half what you'd pay at the chains. I've been a loyal customer since college. The start of my addiction," I added with a chuckle. Realizing I was talking too much, I took my own sip.

For a moment, the unreality of the week before, when Alec had shown me our family photo, returned in a spiraling wave. I was having a coffee with my probable son, a kid who carried half my DNA. When our eyes met, I gave him a self-conscious smile. Alec returned it before looking away.

"Well, shall we?" I said, breaking the awkward silence.

I led the way up the steps, unlocking the door and holding it open for Alec.

"Is anyone going to have a problem with us being here?" he asked as our footsteps echoed in tandem down the empty corridor.

"No. I chose the college partly because it sits on an intersection of ley lines but mainly because it's closed weekends." Producing another key, I unlocked my classroom door and snapped on the lights. "It also gives us more space."

"Yeah, if it weren't for all the desks," he said.

"Funny you mention them. The desks are your first assignment."

"You want them moved?" When he started to lift the closest one, I pressed it back down gently.

"With a force rune," I said. "Line the desks up against the wall, all except for mine. I want to see your control."

He blew out his breath. "You're talking *serious* control."

"Don't overthink it. I just want to get an idea of where you are."

"Mind holding this?"

I took his coffee cup and set both of ours on my desk along with my satchel. By the time I turned back, he was hunkering in the middle of the room, his backpack swung around to his front. From the pack's pocket, he produced his silver-flecked grease pencil and began rendering a symbol on the floor.

"I can take your pack too," I offered, but he acted as if he hadn't heard me.

As he worked, I tuned into his ethereal layers. The threads bonding him to the Hermes tablet in his pack quivered into view. I couldn't perceive complex bindings as well as Claudius, but I could see well enough to know there were at least a couple more threads since I'd checked him out the week before. If they were bothering Alec, he gave no sign. Still, it wouldn't hurt to have Claudius take a look.

I returned my focus to Alec, who had completed the basic circle and was now adding various lines and sigils. He looked up periodically, gauging the desks and their relative distances from the walls. I recognized the look in his eyes, the whole-soul absorption. It was the same absorption that would possess me whenever I used to read books on mythology and later, arcane tomes. He was his father's son.

"Well," Alec said, straightening. "If it's not right, it's as close as I'm going to get."

He angled his head, giving the rune a final assessment. The circle and fundamental elements looked sound, but he'd overdone the sigils. That was to be expected. In his inexperience, he was trying to account for every possibility. With time and practice, he would learn the value of elegance, accomplishing more with less.

"Ready?" he asked.

"Why don't you stand here with me?" I said, backing behind my desk.

To be safe, I gathered some shadows over the door's window so no one could see inside. Alec paused at my desk for another shot of coffee before arriving beside me. He gave me a furtive glance before returning his attention to the rune, a coaster-sized rendering in the room's center. Magic hummed between the flecks of silver.

"Don't be nervous," I said. "Trust your rune. Only give it as much as it needs."

"Okay." Shaking out his arms, Alec released his breath and lowered his lids to half-mast.

My ears ached slightly as the pressure in the room dropped and a connection took up between Alec and his creation. I adjusted my grip on my cane and readied a shield invocation. For just in case.

Without warning, the rune flashed green and the desks blasted out in all directions. My shield was around us in an instant, but before the desks and chairs were reduced to shrapnel, they stopped. They then waddled the final foot before coming to a rest in a neat row along the sides of the room. The pressure on my ears eased, replaced by a fantastic silence.

"Holy shit," Alec whispered, echoing my very thought.

I dispersed the shield from around us and walked the perimeter of the room. I'd been expecting something much messier, but the legs of each chair and desk were in perfect alignment with their neighbors on either side. When I arrived at a chair that was a little out of place, it seemed to notice too. Rocking to attention, the chair scooted back in line.

Alec let out a surprised laugh.

"I think it's safe to say you passed," I said.

I'd meant it as a joke, but the words came out grave-sounding.

Alec, who was dragging a hand through his hair, didn't seem to notice. "But it was just a force rune. I didn't..." He gestured around at the desks, his expression incredulous. "How in the heck did I make them walk like that?"

"See these?" I said, crouching beside the dimming rune and pointing out the angular components.

"Yeah, control sigils," he said. "I added them at the very end in case the forces got away from me."

"Is that a technique you learned from a book?"

Alec started to nod, then stopped, his eyes pinching in thought. "More from intuition, I guess."

Which meant the sigils had come from his bond to the tablet in his pack. "They may be control sigils," I said, "but they belong to the Hermes essence—a trickster god, as you know. I think he was having a little fun."

Alec laughed again, then looked up. "Does it still count?"

The question, posed in perfect innocence, made me chortle. "Of course. Well done, Alec."

But as I considered what I'd witnessed, my smile shrank again. The manifestation, which had taken and channeled Alec's raw power through Hermes's design, had gone off flawlessly. But would there come a point when the Hermes essence would demand more control of that power? More control of Alec?

"What's next?" he asked excitedly.

5

My tests for Alec progressed from having him demonstrate his vagueness rune, to rendering a defensive shield, to casting a controlled fireball. The basic components of each rune were his, but by Alec's own admission the sigils came to him spontaneously. In other words, from the Hermes essence. The results might have lacked the flourish of walking desks, but they were no less impressive.

During the vagueness exercise, I had to cast a reveal spell to locate him. His defensive shield held up to my moderate assault. And his fireball carried an extra oomph that shook my own shield.

He shouldn't have been able to do any of those as a fifteen-year-old novice who'd only discovered his magic in the last year. But I kept that to myself. With each exercise, I told him "well done," and with each "well done," I could see his confidence growing. I also felt his emotional guard coming down.

"Need a break?" I asked him.

"Why?" His smile turned prankish. "The old man having trouble keeping up?"

"All right, no need to get cocky," I said, grinning back. "Let's revisit the defensive shield."

"No problem," he said, hopping into the circle he'd rendered earlier.

"Actually, let's make a fresh one. And I want the sigils to be your own this time."

He'd pulled his grease pencil from his back pocket, but now he hesitated. "What do you mean? They are my own."

"Not the ones that come to you. The ones you practiced before finding the Hermes tablet."

"But these are the ones I draw now," he said, his voice hardening.

"And I'm telling you to go back to the old ones."

"What's the point?"

"I want to see something."

"But those old sigils are crap."

"Alec," I said sternly. "When I'm training you, you'll do as I say."

He exhaled, sounding every bit his fifteen years. "Fine."

As he rendered a new rune, I watched, arms folded. He started out hastily, as if determined to have the final word by just going through the motions. But soon the whole-soul absorption took hold, and he smoothed out what he'd drawn before completing the rest of the rune with care. I noted the absence of angles that were the signature of the Hermes essence, but I wanted to be sure the work was really his.

He rose and stood in the center of the rune. "Ready?" he asked without enthusiasm, but I picked up an angle of determination in his eyes. He'd given the rune his best, and he was anxious to put it to the test.

"Go ahead," I said.

As he pushed power into it, his design glowed to life. A column of force rose around him, distorting his image. I sized the shield up. It would repel a punch or moderate blow from a blunt object, but not much more. He eyed my cane, waiting for me to draw my sword as I'd done the last time, but I kept it sheathed.

"Good," I said. "And take it down."

As the column dropped back into the rune, he nodded morosely. "That weak, huh?"

"It wasn't bad, but your shield's strength wasn't the test. How did you feel when you were drawing the sigils?"

"Like I knew what I *should* have been drawing, but I did them the way you wanted."

"Was that hard? Going against how you thought they should have been drawn?"

"A little." He peered between his two defensive runes. "You're worried about the tablet's hold on me?"

"I am," I confessed. "I wanted to see how... insistent it would be."

"It didn't put up too much of a fight, if that's what you're asking."

"Did you feel anything when you resisted? An emotion, maybe?"

"Besides my own annoyance?" He allowed a smile. "No. And it's cool. I understand now what you were doing."

"It's something we need to keep close tabs on. For homework, I want you to draw one of your own runes every night. Keep track of any pushback. If it feels like it's getting stronger, let me know right away."

"All right, cool. Is that all for today, then?" he asked, his eyes betraying his disappointment.

"Yeah, I should probably—" I consulted the time and did a double-take. How was it already after six? Alec looked equally surprised when he checked his own watch. Our loose relationship with the hours and minutes was another quality we shared, apparently.

"I told my mom I'd be home thirty minutes ago," he said.

"I told my wife the same. C'mon, we better get going."

As we left the classroom, I sent Ricki a text to tell her our training session had run over, but that I was on my way home. Alec didn't have the same luxury, his mother existing in an alternate reality.

"Where will you cross over?" I asked.

"Not here," he said, looking around apprehensively. "In my city, the college has been shuttered for years. God only knows what's living in these classrooms now. I use some bushes in Dewitt Clinton Park. Good concealment, and it's only a couple blocks from our apartment."

"Dewitt Clinton, huh? I didn't realize you guys were on the West Side."

He glanced over as if he'd revealed too much. "It's not *Upper* West, but yeah. We're getting by."

"I was planning to grab a cab, so you've got yourself a ride."

"Thanks, but it's not far. I don't mind walking. I prefer it, actually."

Now that our training session was over, I could feel Alec drawing into himself again.

"I wasn't asking," I said as we exited the college and I locked the door behind us. "A cab gets you home a lot quicker, and you don't want to worry your mom."

For a moment, I had this strange sense that Jennifer and I were sharing custody of Alec—which in an odd way we were, except that she knew nothing about the arrangement. My phone buzzed as Alec and I approached the street.

No worries hon, Ricki texted back, *but please hurry. Your cat is driving me crazy!*

Welcome to the club, I typed with a snort.

"My wife," I told Alec.

"Where did you tell her you'd gone?"

"Today? I told her the truth. That's how it goes with spouses, but don't worry. She's cool with everything."

"I thought it might be kind of weird for her—you know, me being the son of your shadow."

"Well, it's different, but she's supportive. She also feels bad about the shooting last month."

Alec rotated his shoulder where the bullet had gone through. "That wasn't her. It's all healed up, anyway."

I'd tried telling my wife the same thing, but beneath her toughness, she was a sensitive soul with a strong moral compass. Something told me the same was true of shadow Vega. I started to hail a cab, then lowered my arm.

"Hey, has there been any news about what happened at the Discovery Society?" I asked. "You know, about Eldred's death? Finding the victims' remains in the basement? Anything about an investigation?"

"I've been wondering the same, but there hasn't been a single mention—and I've been looking. Of course, the Discovery Society in my New York was a weird place that no one ever really talked about to begin with."

That was true enough, but if Eldred's role in the murders was being actively covered up, that couldn't mean anything good for shadow Vega. I raised my arm again, and Alec and I were soon climbing into a cab. We arrived at Dewitt Clinton Park a short time later.

"This is me," he said, gesturing to a mass of shrubbery.

"Great session today. Don't forget about your homework."

"I won't." With one foot on the pavement, he twisted around to face me. "Thanks for, you know... taking me on."

He had risked a lot by telling me he was my shadow's son, and he was thanking me for not dismissing him. I also heard an apology for his earlier defiance when I'd had him render his own defensive rune.

"My pleasure, Alec. Next Saturday?"

"Next Saturday," he confirmed and swung the door closed.

The cab was pulling away when my phone rang. I checked the caller, half expecting it to be Ricki asking me to grab something for dinner on my way home, but it was her partner.

"Detective Hoffman," I said. "To what do I owe the pleasure?"

"Hi, yourself," he said gruffly. "Got something we want you to take a look at."

"A case?"

"Plural."

"Can it wait until after dinner? I'm on my way home."

"If it were me, I'd say *bon appetit,* but the mayor's asking."

No wonder he sounded cranky. Whenever the mayor intruded on one of his cases, Detective Hoffman acted as if he were undergoing small bowel surgery. But if Mayor Lowder wanted me, something big was happening.

"Where do I need to be?" I asked.

6

A t the Homicide unit of 1 Police Plaza, a curmudgeonly task sergeant met me at the elevators and led me down a remote corridor. At the far end, he rapped twice on a door. The door cracked open, and a slice of Detective Hoffman's portly figured appeared. His right eye cut from me to my escort and back.

"Thanks, Beats," he grunted.

He waited for the sergeant to head back to his post before opening the door enough for me to pass. There was something very "secret club" about the whole thing.

"What is this place?" I asked him.

"Just get in here."

As he closed and bolted the door behind me, I looked around. We were in a windowless room roughly half the size of my classroom. At a large table covered in laptops and stacks of files, a man and woman looked back at me.

The man was big, built like a linebacker, but his salty manbun and goatee suggested his full-contact days were behind him. The black woman across from him was young-looking and petite, her hair in a curly perm reminiscent of the 1980s. Though the two couldn't have appeared more different from one another, they were both detectives. They had that overworked aura I'd come to know and respect from my wife.

"Welcome to the Special Task Force," Hoffman said. "This is Rousseau and Knowles," he said of the woman and man. "Better known as 'Rules' and 'Know-it-all.'" He snickered, but the detectives' frowns suggested they weren't as taken with their nicknames. "And this is Everson Croft, our wizard consultant."

They made no move to stand and greet me. I returned the man's slight nod with one of my own.

"Task force on what?" I asked.

When the two exchanged disgruntled looks, Hoffman sighed at them. "We've been over this. Mayor's call." He turned to me. "Missing persons."

"I thought the NYPD had a division for that."

"We do," he said. "That's where Rousseau and Knowles are from. But hot cases are up. Way up. More than fifty percent year to date."

"Sixty-two, in fact," Knowles said, frowning from his goatee.

"Yeah, anyway," Hoffman continued, "the mayor wants an explanation."

"He also wants to keep this need-to-know," Rousseau said. "So anything we tell you doesn't leave this room."

"My wife's a homicide detective," I said. "Hoffman's partner, in fact—"

"So I've heard, but she's not on the task force," she interrupted. "When we say nothing leaves this room, nothing leaves this room. Understood?" I immediately appreciated her nickname—"Rules." She was also acting as if she were speaking to a grade-school student, and by some stubborn defect in my character, it only made me want to act the part.

"Oh, are you saying nothing leaves this room?"

She glared at Hoffman. "Do we really need this joker?"

"Mayor's call," he repeated. "And, yes, he understands. Just nod your head, Croft."

"Sure," I said, circling my hand for someone to get the show going.

Hoffman limped to the front of the room, an ortho boot still encasing his fractured right foot, and rotated several whiteboards that had been facing the wall. Writing covered all except the center board. The large male detective snapped on a projector connected to one of the laptops, and a map of the city appeared.

"Hot cases are the unsolved disappearances most likely to be abductions versus voluntary runaways or relocations," Hoffman began. "These are last year's hot cases through June." He indicated the black dots on the map. "And this is year to date." A constellation of red dots broke out over the map like a rash. The discrepancy was immediately apparent, the red dots exceeding the black by a good fifty.

"And you think there's a supernatural explanation?" I asked.

"Mayor does," Hoffman said. "Or at least he wants to rule it out. That's the reason for the task force. Which I'm leading, I should add." He puffed out his chest importantly.

"What do we know so far?" I asked.

Hoffman nodded at the male detective. "Why don't you start with the stats, Know-it-all?"

As the detective stood, I sized him up at six-foot-six, easy. And solid. Beside Hoffman, he looked like a tower. As if deciding it best to keep the man he'd just insulted at a distance, Hoffman backed off several feet.

"We have missing persons data going back decades," Knowles began in a deep but mild-mannered voice. "They climbed in the nineteen seventies and eighties, dropped in the nineties, went up to their highest levels in the decade following the Crash, then fell just as steeply following Mayor Lowder's eradication program."

"Thanks to this man you call a *joker*," Hoffman said to Rousseau. "Croft here practically authored the program."

Hoffman going to bat for me? That was new. But it appeared I'd been wrong about his annoyance. It wasn't coming from the mayor's involvement; it was coming from having to work with these two.

"The trend remained downward for the next couple years," Knowles continued. "It had all but plateaued, and then in March, boom. Unsolved disappearances shot up and have been on an upward trajectory ever since. If it continues, we'll be at a hundred percent over last year by October."

"Are murders up too?" I asked.

"That's the funny thing," Hoffman said. "Not at all—or at least that we know of."

"Marginally, but in no statistically significant measures," Knowles corrected him.

Hoffman grumbled, but I was looking between the distribution of black and red dots. "Patterns?"

"The distribution is interesting." Knowles used a remote to return to the first image. "If we just look at last year, it's what we'd expect. The cases are concentrated in higher-crime areas with a random distribution throughout the rest of the city. But when we overlay this year's numbers, look what happens. The high-problem areas stay roughly the same. It's the distribution in the rest of the city that changes."

"Higher concentration in the lower half of Manhattan," I observed.

"Exactly. But the data's imperfect."

"How so?"

"These are last-known whereabouts. Could be where the person was last seen or where we were able to recover location data from their devices. In cases where the info is lacking, we use addresses of residence."

"Which may or may not be near where the disappearance happened," I said in understanding.

"We're going through the city-wide security cameras in search of facial matches," Rousseau said. She'd remained sitting at the table, arms folded as if determined to block me out, but her partner had made that impossible by this point. "We need to place them all as close to their locations of disappearance as possible," she continued. "Best case, we capture the moment they actually went missing."

"Anything yet?" I asked.

"Nothing on the cameras," she replied, "but we have one eyewitness account."

"Which touches on the other way the data's imperfect," Knowles put in. "The witness observed one of the disappeared, a young woman, getting into an unknown vehicle. But we don't know whether her case falls within the normal or the abnormal pattern of disappearances, only that it happened in Lower Manhattan."

His mention of a young woman got my cogs turning.

"Any patterns among the victims?" I asked. "Age, gender, hair color?"

"Nothing obvious," Knowles replied. "The demographics

run the gamut, and regression analysis hasn't spit out anything promising yet."

That seemed to cripple my idea that we might have been looking at abductions for ritualistic purposes or to create vampire spawn. In both cases, victims tended to fall within the young-adult bracket.

"So now you know the essential info," Rousseau said abruptly. "What can you tell us?"

"Going on that alone? Not much."

"Aren't you supposed to be an expert?"

I held up a finger and turned to Hoffman. "Can I have a word with you?"

With a sigh, he unbolted the door and led the way into the corridor. "What is it?"

"Do they know what I can do?"

"I'm sure they've heard the stories. Whether or not they believe them…?" He made a dubious face, which was what I'd been afraid of.

"Look, I'm always ready to help the city, but if most of my job is going to be dealing with pushback from them, I can't promise I have it in me. With my summer teaching term in full swing and a baby on the way, I've got a ton on my plate." Not to mention training my shadow's son and keeping tabs on the Hermes tablet. "Maybe it'd be better if I consulted unofficially, outside the task force."

"Nah, I get it," Hoffman said, surprising me. "They haven't been so accepting of me either. They think the only reason the mayor assigned me lead was to bring you in. As if I'm not one of the most senior detectives in Homicide."

I nodded, even though Rousseau and Knowles were probably right. I'd delivered for the mayor enough times that he'd become convinced I could fix anything in his city. And if securing my participation meant putting Hoffman in charge —someone I'd just worked with on the organ-harvesting case —he would have made the call.

"The thing is," Hoffman continued, "if you're outside the task force, I can't share any case info with you. They'll make damn sure of that." He cocked his head toward the door. "Especially Rules."

"Did the mayor say why he's keeping this so hush-hush?"

"Didn't have to. The stats are heading in the wrong direction."

"And leaders are judged by their numbers," I said, completing the thought. "But aren't the crime statistics public record?"

"Sure, but they can be finessed so they're not so obvious. You know, spread over several categories."

"Is that what's happening?"

"Hey, not my department. But that'd be my guess. Someone nosy enough could put it together with a little digging, get the actual figures, but it hasn't happened yet. Doesn't mean it won't."

"And the mayor wants to be on top of it well before it does," I said.

"Which is where me and you come in. And this feels big, Croft. Let me worry about the other detectives. I actually have a little experience when it comes to being a skeptical ass, so I'll know how to handle them."

I couldn't argue with him there. "All right," I conceded.

We returned to find Rousseau and Knowles huddled in their own private conference.

"Can you help us?" Rousseau asked me as they separated. "Or is this just going to be a time-wasting sideshow?"

I aimed my cane at the empty chair beside her. With an

uttered Word, I jerked my cane back, and the chair skittered across the floor. I caught it by the backrest and took a seat, casually crossing my leg.

"First, I'm going to need some material from the missing," I said. "Anything that holds their essence works best—hair, sweat, skin cells, that sort of thing. I can also work with objects of emotional significance. Journals, personal letters, and so forth. Through them I should be able to pinpoint some of the victims' whereabouts."

I'd be lying if I said I didn't savor Rousseau's stunned look.

"Of—of course," she stammered. "Hoffman said you might need those."

She nodded at Knowles, who lifted a cardboard file box from the end of the table and carried it over. As he handed it to me, he peered back at the empty spot where the chair had been. He then walked a circle around me, as if checking for trick threads. I wasn't sure whether my invocation had convinced them of anything, but it would give their skepticism some pause going forward. Maybe that was all I needed.

I hefted the box onto my lap and began sifting through it. It held a few dozen plastic bags tagged with victim ID numbers. The bags contained everything from a plastic comb to a vintage pipe.

"This looks good," I said. "I—"

My voice caught in my throat as I uncovered a bag with a baby's shoe. I lifted it out.

"Belongs to the youngest victim," Hoffman said. "A one-year-old girl. Emma Crain. She and her mother disappeared while out on a walk, stroller and all. Her father gave that to us."

I looked over the little white shoe. So small. My earlier

concerns about Knowles and Rousseau dwindled to ridiculous insignificance. I set the bag gently back inside the box and replaced the cardboard lid.

"There's quite a bit of material in here," I said quietly. "Probably best if I do this back at my lab. It'll take some time, but I'll get started on it right away."

I made a mental note to grab a bag of Colombian dark roast on the way home. It was going to be a long night.

7

"Well, this is nice to come home to," I said, tossing my bag of coffee onto the kitchen counter. I kissed my wife, squeezed Tony's shoulder, and took a seat at my place in front of a steaming plate of pasta. "Thanks for waiting."

"*Most* of us waited," Ricki said.

I followed her critical gaze to Tabitha, who was licking her chops, an empty plate at the foot of her divan. She stopped when she saw us all watching. "What?" she demanded. "Everson's social calendar does *not* dictate my meal time. Not that the meal was anything to talk about," she added in a mutter.

Ricki's look told me Tabitha had been doing that all day. I nodded sympathetically. After seven years, I knew my cat's mood swings better than anyone.

"So, how was your day otherwise?" I asked her, changing the subject.

"I got some organizing done and ordered a few more things for the baby's room. I hope that's okay."

An image of the little girl's shoe flashed in and out of my

mind's eye.

I forced a smile. "Hey, I trust your maternal instincts a lot more than mine. Plus, you have prior experience, and this kid turned out alright." I hooked a thumb at Tony. "How was engineering camp, buddy?"

Ricki's son had hit a recent growth spurt and was inhaling his pasta as if it were air. He nodded to give himself time to chew and swallow.

"Good," he said at last. "We have an egg drop competition next week, and I've been working with my partner on the design."

"Egg drop?" I said. "Like the soup?"

He laughed. "No, we're building something to put an egg inside of, then we'll drop it one level at a time from a parking tower the camp uses. The team whose egg survives the highest drop gets the prize."

"Well, that sounds idiotic," Tabitha said.

"What happens if there's a tie?" I asked over her.

"Lightest design wins."

Ricki looked at him sternly. "You didn't tell me any of that when *I* asked."

Tony shrugged and went back to shoveling calories into his growing body.

"Kids," I remarked.

She allowed a small smile as she shook her head. "Speaking of engineering, how did it go with Bree-yark and the basement unit?"

"He's up for the job," I said. "In fact, he started work today."

"That might explain the detonations I heard earlier."

"Detonations?" I'd meant to check the unit on my way up, but I'd been running late.

"Are you sure he knows what he's doing?" she asked.

"No," I admitted. "But I'll keep a close eye on his progress."

"Please do. I don't want us being responsible for an accidental demolition."

I nodded, even though she would have been surprised at what this building had withstood during my early years of wizarding.

"How was the rest of your afternoon?" she asked. "Everything go okay with Alec?"

"About as well as could be expected. The kid is scarily adept, and that worries me. He's beyond where anyone at his age should rightfully be. The Hermes tablet is guiding him, taking his raw power and alchemizing it into advanced manifestations."

Concern grew in Ricki's eyes. "Are you worried he'll lose control?"

"Yeah, but more of himself than the manifestations. I've started him on some exercises that should help us track that."

"Can Claudius do anything?"

"He can monitor the bindings, but he can't remove them without trapping Alec here."

"Right, and Alec has a mother in the shadow present," she said, seeing the problem. Though she didn't voice it, the idea that the mother in question was my ex-girlfriend was probably as awkward for her as me. "What does it want with him, the Hermes tablet?"

"Good question. It originally bonded to him to prevent Cronus's return. Mission accomplished, which means the Hermes essence either believes there's still a threat, or it's become comfortable with the idea of Alec as a vessel. As long as the relationship remains symbiotic, I think Alec will be okay. My job will be teaching him when and how to use his magic and, more importantly, when to put a cork in it."

I looked over at Tony, who was still in the dark about my relationship with Alec, his mother and I deciding it best for now. I slid the basket of garlic bread toward him, and he plucked out two pieces.

"I'll keep Mae in the loop too," I said. "The bindings have nether qualities, and she was able to soften their hold on him the last time."

"We should have them all over for dinner one of these nights."

"I think that would be good for Alec," I said. "I'll ask him the next time I see him."

"What did Hoffman want?"

"Oh, the mayor called a special task force and—"

She showed a hand. "Say no more. I've been on a few of those, and I know the confidentiality provision."

"I was only going to speak in generalities."

"Better you don't. If either of us are ever asked, we want to be able to honestly say that you told me nothing. The city takes special task forces *very* seriously."

"Fair enough."

"Is that what the box is for?"

I looked between her and the cardboard box I'd set beside the coat rack. "Am I allowed to tell you?"

"As long as you don't say what's in it. I won't ask any more questions, I promise."

"Then, yes. In fact, I need to head up to the lab after dinner to do some spellwork. I'll be late getting to bed."

"If you're going to empty the box, can you let me know?" Tabitha called. "I might want to spend some time inside it."

We ignored her, Ricki's dark eyes fixing on mine. "That

serious, huh?"

The image of the girl's shoe returned, and I nodded. "That serious."

———————

I removed the shoe from its plastic bag and turned it gingerly in my gloved fingers. It was a classic walking bootie. The outer material was white leather, the inside padded with wool around the ankle.

Good absorptive medium.

I was trying to remain objective, but my efforts were already wobbling. As I swallowed back my emotions, I found myself thankful for the confidentiality provision. I didn't want Ricki to know about the child victim.

Hang in there, I thought at little Emma Crain.

I placed her shoe sole-down in the center of a casting circle I'd built on my lab table. Then, incanting, I stepped inside the protective circle in the floor. As the circle enclosing the shoe began to glow, I moved my staff in slow figure-eights, my incantation becoming the words for a hunting spell.

Shortly, a light mist drifted from the wool inside the shoe —remnants of Emma's cells—and entered my staff's opal. For a moment, I caught or imagined a faint gurgle, innocent and good. A toddler's laugh. I refocused on the hunting spell, watching my cane for a reaction.

Give me something, dammit.

My jaw trembled as I pushed more power into the spell, but it returned nothing. After another minute, I broke it off and paced the lab. My spell hadn't met resistance or a barrier. Emma was gone.

Doesn't have to mean dead, I told myself. *Could be in another plane. The Fae realm, for example.*

I stopped in front of my cabinet of tinctures, removed a purple vial, and rolled it back and forth between my fingers. A special nightshade essence. Two droplets, and I could narrow down the child's fate. Then again, it could also inflict permanent damage if it remained in my system too long.

Risky, but if the alternative was abandoning her...

I winced as the droplets bit like acid into my tongue and sent up thin curls of smoke. Eyes leaking, I hurried to my casting circle and tapped back into the hunting spell. If the poison wasn't enough of a worry, I would be extending my magic's reach across the boundary between life and death: the In Between realm.

Before I could second-guess myself, the staff jiggled in my grip. I made small adjustments, my tongue feeling as if it were being attacked with razor blades. I struggled for each syllable, all the way to the final Word.

Where are you, kid?

The staff tugged, and an impossible weight collapsed around me. Stunned by the force and an indescribable cold, I lost my breath. Pain gored my lungs as my body went into full-system shock. In the next moment, I was staring around a luminescent darkness of shifting shapes and roaring energies.

The In Between realm.

Shadows veered toward me, resolving into a pair of cloaked gatekeepers. I struggled to invoke, but I couldn't shape a single sound. If they mistook me for dead, they would seize me. And if they seized me, they'd carry me over.

As the gatekeepers loomed nearer, I managed to move the fingers of my right hand, forming a small sign. A gatekeeper reached forward just as energy broke through me. The In

Between dispersed as the hunting spell came apart and my lab returned to form. But I wasn't out of the woods yet.

I stumbled from the casting circle, mouth throbbing, and activated a neutralizing potion from my premade stock. I swished it around my mouth before swallowing. The nightshade's potency thinned, and I sat hard in my desk chair. I'd been playing with hand-signing as a substitute for basic incantations, and that was the first time I'd put it to the test. The sign had come through, but there was no celebration in me.

The little girl was gone, presumably along with her mother.

I eyed the small shoe somberly, then dropped my gaze to the box with the remaining items. Without post-mortem cellular material from the actual bodies, I couldn't scry into their final moments. In the child's case, I wouldn't have wanted to. There were some things you never recovered from, and I was certain that feeling her last vulnerable breaths before the light left her forever would have been mine.

I'm so sorry.

I wouldn't be going that deep again—even my luck quotient had its limits—but I could still hunt for the living. The spell on the next item returned nothing, most likely signifying another death. I jotted this down in my notebook before unbagging the third item, a woman's diamond engagement ring. Within moments, essence from the band was drifting into the opal end of my cane.

The cane kicked, then pulled. I called Hoffman one-handed while restraining my cane with the other.

"Yeah?" He answered, snorting the sleep from his sinuses. "What is it?"

"I got a hit on one of the disappeared."

8

"Diana Parfait," Hoffman said, slapping a file that had been slipping around the dashboard.

He'd picked me up in his sedan, and we were racing east, police colors strobing between his headlights. I took the file, opened it, and studied the photo in front. It was a close-up of a young woman with long brunette hair and a self-conscious smile that suggested the photo hadn't been her idea.

"Twenty-six years old," Hoffman said. "Tied the knot just last month. Husband is going out of his head, calling us ten, fifteen times a day. When we asked for something personal, he fetched her engagement ring, no hesitation. Has to be worth at least ten thou. She was the one the eyewitness saw climbing into a van."

"Forced in?" I asked, leafing through the file.

"Looked voluntary, like she knew the person."

"Description of the driver?"

"Tinted windows. The wit couldn't ID the van's make, either. Just said it was dirty white, no windows on the body.

From the traffic cams, Rules and Know-it-all were able to pick out a few white vans around the same time and location. They cleared four of them, but a fifth had mud covering the plate."

"Well, I've got her hooked pretty good," I said, closing the file and adjusting my grip on my tugging cane. "The ring was a powerful object. That's what emotional potency, oil residue, and a precious-metal medium will do."

"I'll take your word for it," Hoffman muttered.

Though he'd come around to the supernatural, he had no interest in how any of it worked. His priority was clearing cases. If my magic could help him, great. If not, I was as useless to him as tits on a bull.

To his credit, he'd arrived at my apartment fifteen minutes following my call, wearing the same crumpled suit from that afternoon, his wreath of brown curls in bed-headed lumps. He'd even foregone brushing his teeth, popping a couple pellets of nicotine gum as I got in. He smacked the gum loudly now.

"Did you arrange backup?" I asked.

He barked a laugh. "And make a jackass of myself again? No, thanks."

He was referring to our last case, when I'd directed him to a murder scene only for his SWAT team to come up empty. It turned out that my scrying spell had seen into the shadow present, where the murder had actually happened. Hoffman broke his foot that night rage-kicking a file cabinet. I was about to explain to him how this was a different spell before realizing it would be like speaking Coptic.

"Did you at least clue in Detectives Rousseau and Knowles?" I asked.

"They're good at crunching numbers and following policies and procedures, but that's about the extent of it. How do you think they got their nicknames?" When he saw my concerned expression, he said, "Look, when we get a location —a *confirmed* location—I'll call for backup, and we'll go from there."

The hunting spell took us through Chinatown and over the Manhattan Bridge. As we descended toward Brooklyn, the pull grew stronger. Hoffman cut the police lights, and I called out turns until we were in a mixed-use section of northern Brooklyn. We circled a block of respectable-looking businesses before I had him park curbside.

"She's in there," I said.

Hoffman lowered his head to take in the inconspicuous façade. A sign for LOOSEY'S glowed over a low-slung doorway.

"A club?" he said.

"That's where the spell's pointing."

"Yeah, we'll see about that," he muttered, opening his door.

"Wait, what's the plan?" I asked.

"We check it out."

"Just walk in?"

"It's a club. People walk in all the time." Pulling out his phone, Hoffman tapped the keypad. "Look, they even have a review page. Four stars. 'Charming little dive,' this one lady wrote. 'Try the Loosey Goosey cocktail.' This place doesn't know us from Adam. We're just a couple guys out for a late drink."

It was quarter after one—normal business hours for a club, I supposed, but I still didn't like it.

"I could down a stealth potion," I said, patting my coat pockets. "Slip in through the back door."

"You could, but we're going in through the front, and I don't want you *stealth* anything. We're going to treat this place as a legit business until it gives us a reason not to."

"A place that's holding Mrs. Parfait?"

"That *might* be holding Mrs. Parfait. Has it occurred to you that she could've left the mister of her own volition?"

I started to answer, but stopped. "No," I admitted.

"I'm just saying it's not outside the realm of possibility. I've had enough contact with Missing Persons to know that sometimes spouses just leave. Believe it or not, I've been doing this police thing for a while."

I had a couple zingers I could have fired back, but I restrained myself. "What do we do when we see her?"

"*If* we see her, we watch," he said. "Check out who's with her. Get a sense of her mental state. If it doesn't look like she's in danger, we talk to her. See what's going on. If she left by choice, case closed. We take her off the board."

"Fair enough."

But I was still going to treat this as a potential kidnapping, possibly even a supernatural one. That was why the mayor brought me in. As we walked down the sidewalk, my senses rang with vigilance.

"Can you do something about that?" Hoffman said.

He meant my cane, and he had a point. It was jerking up and down like a fishing rod.

"Sure, if you spit out your gum," I countered. His smacking was getting on my nerves, and I could always resurrect the hunting spell.

He grumbled, "You're worse than my wife."

As I spoke a dispersal, he hawked his wad of gum into a

planter. My cane went inert, and I tapped it along the side-walk. At the club's entrance, a massive doorman rose from a stool set in a recess.

"Carrying any weapons?" he asked, lifting a detecting wand.

Before he could pass it over me, Hoffman stepped forward.

"NYPD," he said, showing the shield at his belt. So much for a couple guys out for a late-night drink.

The doorman lowered the wand. "I'm very sorry, sir. Do you need to talk to someone? The owner's left for the night, but I can call a manager." Though the doorman was just shy of ogre proportions, he was courteous in a wide-eyed way. He didn't strike me as a henchman for a kidnapper, anyway.

"Nah, nothing like that," Hoffman replied. "End of shift. We just want to unwind a little before heading home."

"I hear that," the doorman said. "The cover's ten bucks, but it's on us. For all you do."

I didn't know the ethics of the police accepting gifts from the public, but Hoffman was clearly chuffed at being able to keep his ten. "Thanks, kid," he said, jerking his head for me to follow.

I searched the doorman's eyes just long enough to confirm he wasn't hiding anything. "Thanks," I echoed.

"Enjoy the show," he said.

Loosey's featured a bar at one end and a stage at the other, the walls in between plastered with fliers for past performances. Though the stage was presently empty, every chair facing it was full, with another half dozen or so people standing. A banner below the stage announced that it was comedy night.

I was searching the crowd for Diana Parfait when the lights dimmed and a single bulb illuminated the stage.

"Over here," Hoffman called from the bar.

I joined him as he was ordering two beers from the bartender, a young woman with blond dreads and colorful tapestries down both arms. I shifted to my wizard's senses as I watched her pour, but like with the doorman, nothing appeared off. So far this place looked like one of any number of businesses that had been sprouting up during the recovery. The mayor called them his "green shoots."

Hoffman tugged my coat until I was sitting on the stool beside his, then elbowed me around so I was facing the stage. A woman with sheared bangs and a strong Brooklyn accent was up there, introducing the next act.

"I see her," Hoffman whispered. "Far left."

I followed his nod until I saw her too. Diana was sitting at a small table with a man who looked a good twenty years her senior. She was in a red evening dress while he wore a gray formal jacket, shirt open at the collar. Both of them were smiling. If I hadn't known she was missing, I would have thought she was on a date with her boss. Hoffman gave me a knowing look and sipped his beer.

"Hey, aren't you on duty?" I said.

"Relax, it's light beer. We should get *something* for driving all the way out here."

I shook my head and returned my attention to Diana, who was watching the stage expectantly.

"...to Loosey's," the emcee was saying. "So put your hands together, ladies and gentlemen, for Mr. Funny!"

The crowd responded enthusiastically and a few whistles went up. A portly figure appeared from a side door and jogged up on stage. The stage lights revealed a middle-aged man with mussed brown hair and a glum smile. He was dressed in pinstripe pants supported by red suspenders and had on one of those "I heart New York" shirts. He pumped his clasped hands to one side and the other. My first impression was that this guy was cornier than Iowa, but maybe that was part of his schtick.

"All right, all right," he said into the microphone. "Settle down, you yahoos. So, I'm driving into the city the other day, and I'm thinking to myself, 'Boy, there's a lot of traffic.'"

I waited for the punchline, but he looked around expectantly as if he'd just delivered it.

"Traffic, right?" he said, laughing at his own non-joke. "Zoom, zoom, zoom, every which way? And don't get me started on the buildings. It's like, how many buildings does a metropolis need? And do they have to be so tall? Yeah, I went there. But I'm just saying what everyone's thinking. They're tall and everywhere, am I right?"

"This guy's as funny as a kidney stone," Hoffman grumbled.

The audience concurred by remaining silent, but I remained fixed on Diana. I tried but couldn't isolate her aura —too many people around her. She leaned toward the man beside her and whispered something. He whispered back. Discussing their exit strategy, if I had to guess. Hoffman, who was also watching, nodded and cut his eyes toward the door, telling me that when they got up, we'd follow and talk to her outside.

On stage, Mr. Funny continued his act, unfazed.

"As you might have guessed, I'm not from around here." He snapped his suspenders and waited for another reaction that never came. "In fact, do you know what we call *suspenders* where I'm from? 'Stretchy things that whack your nipples every time you do this.'" He snapped his suspenders again. "Ow!"

I was doing everything in my power not to cringe, and I was failing badly. This guy couldn't be serious. When he was greeted by more silence, his glum smile faltered above his slumping shoulders.

"All right, I can take a hint," he said. "You're not feeling me."

"Ya think?" Hoffman muttered.

"But what you don't know," he said, straightening slowly, a devilish grin stretching his lips, "is that I knew this would happen, and I brought something special. A secret weapon, you might call it."

I tensed as he reached into his back pocket, an invocation on my tongue. But when his hand reappeared, he was holding a slide whistle. He proudly displayed it back and forth, which got a couple laughs. He blew into it, working the slide to produce one of those dipsy-doo sounds, which evoked more laughter.

"So, where was I?" he said. "Oh, right. I was shopping with my wife the other day, and she said, 'Did you remember to put the toilet seat down?' When no one reacted, he produced the whistle and gave it another blow. The audience erupted now, including Diana and her date. "Wives and toilet seats, right?" he said.

"Did these people start drinking at four?" Hoffman asked, incredulous.

It was a great question. I could understand deliberate awkwardness as humor, but I didn't think Mr. Funny was being deliberate, and the audience's reaction was *way* over the top.

I focused on the slide whistle now. An enchanted object?

When I shifted to my wizard's senses, nothing supernatural appeared around it. There was nothing I could see around the comic, either. His act went on like that for ten more minutes, each bit ending with a laughter-inducing blow on the whistle.

"Hey, you guys have been great!" he said following the audience's loudest response. He understood that aspect of comedy, anyway. "I'm going to make like a properly inflated ball... and bounce. But remember the name. It's Mr. Funny." He produced the longest, most loopy sound on his whistle yet. The crowd rose to their feet, cheering as he left the stage and backed through the side door, blowing them kisses.

"Where in the hell am I?" Hoffman asked.

Yeah, something wasn't right, but I couldn't put my finger on what. As the lights swelled and the jukebox kicked in, the bartender announced last call. When I turned, she was wiping down the bar with a completely straight face.

"What did you think?" I asked her.

"Besides being the lamest shit I've ever heard?"

"Thank God I wasn't the only one. Was this his first time here?"

"Unfortunately, no. Our last couple comedy nights, he's been the closer. What can we do? He fills seats."

"It's not normally this crowded?"

"We're doing well when we're at half capacity," she said, then lowered her voice. "If you ask me, he's uber wealthy and paying them off."

"Does he always use the whistle?"

"Every freaking time," she said with a grimace.

"C'mon, she's splitting," Hoffman whispered at my shoulder.

I turned in time to catch Diana and her date filing out the front door.

"Go ahead," I told him. "I want to have a word with Mr. Funny before he leaves."

"What for?" he asked.

"Not sure yet."

9

I slipped through the door beside the stage and into a narrow corridor lined with boxes of supplies. The corridor soon opened into a break room with a littered table, a three-tier stand of metal lockers, and a small bathroom. The club must have let the comics hang out here before their sets, but Mr. Funny had left the building.

I made for the rear exit door, still trying to figure out what I was going to say to him. More than anything, I wanted a closer look. My instincts were suggesting a connection to Diana's case—a woman who disappeared only to show up in this guy's audience, laughing at his non-funniness.

My hands were on the push bar when I sensed motion. I turned to find a pair of men in greasy shirts moving around opposite sides of the breakroom table. They could have been brothers with their wiry frames, hatchet faces, and identical mats of dirt-colored hair. The man on the left breathed with a crackling wheeze, while his partner stared from a pair of twitchy eyes. There was probably a decent "an emphysemic

and an epileptic walk into a bar" joke here, but where had
they come from?

"What're you doing back here?" Wheezy demanded.

"I was hoping to catch Mr. Funny before he left."

"Why?" Twitchy asked.

"Just wanted to talk comedy. Is that a problem?"

"We saw you in there, you know," Wheezy said.

"Yeah," Twitchy added, his eyes convulsing independ-
ently of each other. "Noticed you and your tubby friend
weren't laughing."

They stopped a couple feet in front of me. As a magic-
user more than capable of defending myself, I was more
annoyed about being stalled than anything. The interrogation had gotten interesting, though. Why did they care if we'd
laughed or not? Were their loyalties to the club or to the
comic? I decided to find out.

"That would have required him to be funny," I said.

"Well, maybe you weren't *listening*," Wheezy hissed.

"Oh, I was listening. He made the bombing of Pearl
Harbor seem tame. And what was with the stupid whistle?"

The two looked at one another. As if coming to a silent
accord, they began to circle around my sides. It seemed I had
my answer.

"Anyway, nice chatting," I said, invoking quietly as I
backed toward the push bar.

In a flash, Wheezy darted behind me, his wiry arms
bracing my torso in a grip that was way too strong for
someone whose lungs sounded as if they were drowning in
phlegm. Twitchy moved to my front.

"Next time you come to a Mr. Funny show," he seethed,
"you'll *laugh*."

His eyes stopped twitching and began to glow a sickly

yellow. The shadows it cast across his face made him appear rat-like. When a scurrying force explored my mental defenses, I knew what I was dealing with.

"Respingere!" I called as I drove my forehead into the center of his face.

Twitchy's nose crunched just as the form-fitting shield around me detonated. He left his feet and crashed into the lockers. Behind me, the invocation blasted Wheezy against the push bar and out the exit door.

I was dealing with wererats.

Twitchy rebounded from the lockers and sprawled amid the breakroom furniture, a hand to his busted nose. I could finish him in any number of ways, but I wanted him for questioning. His jittery eyes found mine as I advanced.

"Entrapolare," I said.

Light glimmered around him and hardened into a sphere, but I'd only captured his discarded clothes. Something scurried past a fallen chair. He'd transformed, dwindling to a rat, and was making for the boxes in the corridor.

"Nope," I said, enclosing him in a second invocation.

Two of the lockers had swung open from his earlier collision, giving me an idea. I shaped his confinement into a tube and aimed it at one of the open lockers. With a force blast, I shot him like a potato from a homemade cannon. It was as fun as it sounds. As his rat form thumped into the back of the locker, I slammed the door and sealed it with a locking spell.

Now for his buddy.

Out in the alley, Wheezy had made it to his hands and knees, where he wavered drunkenly. He'd suffered a collision with the wall opposite the alley, and the blood running down his face was dripping into a puddle under his chin. When he saw me coming, he morphed into a rat the color of his hair and staggered toward a storm drain. I stopped him well short, and moments later he was Twitchy's neighbor.

Unable to shift back to their human forms in the small enclosures, they went into a fit of screeching that registered like needles in my eardrums. I sent a sleeping potion through the vents in the doors, finishing up as my phone rang.

"Where are you?" Hoffman asked.

"Back of the club," I said. "I lost Mr. Funny, but I grabbed a couple of his henchmen. Are you with Parfait?"

"Yes and no. She and her date joined a group getting into a pair of white vans, one with a mud-covered plate, just like the witness described. And guess what? I recognize several in the group from the missing persons files. We've stumbled onto something big here."

"No kidding," I said as the rats' screeches softened to sleepy squeaks.

"I want to follow them," Hoffman said. "Could lead us to more of the missing."

"All right, wait for me."

By the time I ended the call, the wererats were fast asleep, Wheezy's breath cycling in thin gargles. I searched their discarded clothing, retrieving a pair of phones and clips of cash. No IDs. For weapons they had been packing blades and low-caliber revolvers. I stowed everything in my coat.

Taking the alley to the street, I spotted the vans Hoffman had mentioned idling in front of the club. Hoffman was parked on the corner. I cased the street, but there didn't appear to be any more henchmen. No sign of Mr. Funny, either.

"Wererats," I said, getting into the passenger seat. "I've got two knocked out and secured in lockers."

Hoffman's face scrunched up. "Were *whats?*"

"Beings that can change between rat and human. Some have powers of mind control—the ones I encountered, for example. They wanted me to *laugh* the next time I saw Mr. Funny."

Hoffman's face managed to express confusion and understanding at the same time. "So they're working for that clown," he said. "And the whole point of these kidnappings is to give him, what, an appreciative audience?"

"That seems to be part of it, anyway."

"So who's Mr. Funny?" he asked. "The rat king?"

"Not sure. Did he come out this way?"

"If he did, I didn't see him. I've had my eye on *these* guys." He nodded at the pair of vans still in front of the club.

"I took the rats' phones, cash, and weapons," I said, emptying my haul onto the dash. With a nod, he opened a compartment and was placing the items inside when one of the rats' phones lit up.

"It's a text," Hoffman said. "It says, 'You coming?'"

He thought for a moment before tapping a response. "'Go ahead,'" he murmured. "'We'll catch up.'"

No sooner than he'd hit send, the vans pulled away from the club. Hoffman grinned, proud of himself, and waited several beats before following.

"Hang back as far as you need to," I told him. "I can still call up the hunting spell on Parfait."

"I know how to tail a suspect. Even tailed you a couple times back in the day when I was still trying to figure you out."

"You did?"

His grin broadened. Ahead, the vans had a block lead on us. Their course led us southeast, deeper into Brooklyn. After another mile, the streetscape changed to abandoned cars and hollowed-out buildings. We were almost to Queens when the lead van suddenly dropped from sight. The second van followed.

"Shit," Hoffman grumbled.

I rose in my seat. "Where'd they go?"

"The Hole."

"The Hole? Wait, that sunken neighborhood?"

I'd heard rumors of the place but had never seen it in person. It wasn't exactly a tourist destination.

"The name fits and not just 'cause it's thirty feet below grade," he said. "I used to get called out here for decomps. Some were mob jobs, but not all. If we'd known you back then, we might've had you take a look at a few of them. Place was wild as shit. Anyway, the calls stopped, but it wasn't because the bodies went away. The residents did. Cleared out, and I can't say I blame 'em."

"Good place to hide the disappeared, then," I said as Hoffman switched off his headlights.

When we reached the point where the vans had vanished, the street ramped down into what looked like a pond, moonlight rippling over its surface. *Flooded street,* I realized. We arrived fast, whooshing through two feet of water crowded by reeds and cattails. On the other side, rows of ravaged lots appeared. A few single-family homes remained standing, but none looked habitable. Ahead, the second van was turning.

"Think I know where they're going," Hoffman said.

Instead of following them onto the same street, he continued for another block and turned down a pitted dirt road.

"There's a small farm back here," he said.

"In Brooklyn?"

"I told you this place was wild. The owner was one of the

last holdouts in the Hole. He put up metal fencing, guard towers, had an arsenal like something out of a movie. Place looked like Fort frigging Knox. But at some point he decided enough was enough. Sold his horses and moved to Florida. That was ten years ago, but the stables are still standing. We should assume the towers are manned."

Hoffman pulled over between two clumps of brush. "I'm gonna go ahead and call backup," he said. "Does the Sup Squad need anything special for these wererats?"

"Composite rounds will do the trick, but have the team hang back. I don't want Parfait and the others getting caught in any crossfire."

He gave me his *I know my business* face as he made the call. When he finished, he accessed a map on his phone. Tilting it toward me, he indicated an empty area just north of our position. "The Farm," he said. Switching to the map's satellite view, he zoomed in on the buildings that comprised the complex.

"The main gate is up here," he said, showing me with the edge of a fingernail. "The only gate, in fact. Big enough to drive vehicles in and out. You hear that?" He raised his eyes. In the distance, metal clanged, followed by what sounded like a heavy chain being dragged through an eyebolt. "Must be locking up for the night."

"So," I said, readying my cane, "how do you want to do this?"

10

I hunkered behind a pile of brush, flames spreading the length of my blade. When it verged on molten, I pressed the tip against the metal fencing. The contact sent up a thick coil of smoke, and half the blade plunged through. From there it was like working a hot knife through taffy. Upon finishing, I recalled the fire, slotted the blade back inside my staff, and downed a stealth potion. I then slipped through the opening, easing my way along a narrow stretch of muddy ground behind the stables.

As I emerged onto the edge of an overgrown yard, I spotted the two white vans we'd been tailing, parked now and dim. Beyond them, the main gate was closed and secured. Two towers loomed above the complex, but both looked vacant.

Where were the weres? Under different circumstances, I might have appreciated the tongue-twister.

Cries sounded from an enclosure. I edged forward until a battered mobile home slid into view. Beyond the open windows, wererats moved in a haze of smoke. Though in their human forms, I recognized the scrawny, pointy-faced looks. The home shook, producing more cries—no, cheers, I realized. A pair of grappling shadows appeared beyond the screen door before tumbling into another room.

Some sort of fight breaking out.

"C'mon, Tubbs," a rat shouted. "I've got twenty bucks riding on your ass."

More like a wererat version of Fight Club, I amended.

Above what sounded like a fist pummeling a face, another rat shouted, "And Tubbs is out like a light. We have a winner!"

The announcement was met with a mixture of cheers and jeers, and money changed hands.

The mobile home had a good view of the stables, but I was fully cloaked now, and it sounded as if the rats' fight night was just getting started. The next combatants were barely announced before dollar amounts were being shouted back and forth. Moments later, the home began to shake again.

I cut my gaze to the stables' closed doors.

Has to be where they're holding the disappeared.

I texted Hoffman: *Checking stables.*

Stowing my phone back in my coat, I moved toward the large building and tested the front doors. The right side opened, and I sidled through, keeping an eye on the mobile home. The stable was just shy of pitch black and carried a shut-in smell thick enough to saw in half. I cast a weak locking spell on the door to alert me if anyone tried to enter, then called light to my cane. A long line of stalls glowed into view. I peered inside the closest one. On a stripped-down cot, a heavy man lay flat on his back in boxers and a sleeveless undershirt.

Good god.

It took me a moment to recognize him as the older guy Hoffman and I had mistaken for Diana's date back at the club. The rest of the stall had been converted into a very rustic dorm room. A five-gallon bucket and toilet paper sat near the bed. A second bucket held gray water, a couple rags hanging from hooks in the beams.

Toilet and bath, I thought grimly.

The suit the man had worn that evening was draped over a rail, while a nearby milkcrate contained some other clothes. Back on the bed, the man was staring up into the rafters, still under the rats' mind control.

I continued down the line of stalls, taking a head count. Fifteen were occupied. Diana Parfait was among them, along with several others I recognized from the club. What bothered me were the four stalls that looked as if they should have been occupied—buckets, rags, clothing, crates—but no people.

Executed? Or maybe instead of fight-clubbing amongst themselves, the wererats were pitting their captives against one another. I turned toward the faint burst of cheering. That would place at least four inside the mobile home.

Dammit. I called Hoffman.

"Where are you now?" he asked.

"Inside the stables," I whispered, and proceeded to update him on my findings.

He swore too. With innocents inside the mobile home, raiding it with an armed force had become too risky.

"You sure about those four inside?" he asked.

"Ninety percent."

"Little rat shits," he seethed.

"We have another option. I can wall in the mobile home

and fumigate it with sleeping potion." I patted my pocket to ensure I'd packed enough. "Drop everyone into la-la land long enough to extract the victims. Should take me about ten minutes."

"Go ahead. I'll move the Squad in closer."

I'd just returned the phone to my pocket when the door to the stable shook. I killed my light and scattered the locking spell. A moment later, the door shot open. Overcompensating for what the wererat believed to have been a stuck door, he stumbled backward, dropping his beer bottle. I sidled up to a pillar as he swore and recovered his footing. His scrawny figure soon bisected the rectangle of moonlight coming through the door, beady eyes glowing pale yellow as his night vision kicked in.

From behind him, a mean voice called, "Grab a pair of ladies this time! These dudes fold too easy!"

"Yeah, no shit," the approaching wererat grumbled, suggesting he'd been on the losing end of at least one bet already.

He staggered down the line of stalls, peering over doors. He paused at Diana's, seeming to mark her, and came to a full stop at the next stall, which held the largest woman. He released a sniveling laugh.

"Oh, you'll fetch good odds," he said. "But what if I have insider info?"

When he produced a blade, I guessed his plan. Cripple the favorite with a sly cut and bet heavily on Diana. To this point, my own plan had been to stay put, wait for the rat to return to the mobile home with his new combatants, and then proceed to fill the joint with sleeping potion. The blade changed things.

"Rise and shine, hoss!" he called as he opened her stall door.

Before he could disappear inside, I uttered a Word. The distance between us crackled with mystical energy, and the rat stopped suddenly, grasping the sphere of hardened air that now encased his head. His shrieks were faint, barely audible. With no time to wait for him to drop unconscious, I upped the pressure. His glowing right eye bulged before filling with a network of ruptured vessels. The left eye followed.

The knife fell to his feet. A moment later, his body stopped jerking and he collapsed to the ground. If I hadn't killed him, I'd come close. Even with his regenerative abilities, he'd be a long time recovering from the brain trauma. But I had to move quickly before the rest of the rat nest missed him.

At the main door of the stable, I peered out, then quickly retracted my head. *Crap.* Several of the wererats were spilling from the mobile home and relieving themselves around the yard.

"Hey, Buck!" one of them called. "Are you having a tea party in there or what? Bring 'em out already!"

"By the hair if you have to!" another one added.

"We can't hurt them," a third wererat cautioned.

"The boss said *we* couldn't hurt them," the first one fired back. "Didn't say nothing about them hurting each other."

As they broke into drunken laughter, I wondered if the boss in question was Mr. Funny. But I had more immediate concerns. The second they emptied their bladders, they'd be making their way to the stable.

I called Hoffman again.

"Change of plans," I whispered. "The rats are all over the

yard. I'm going into the home to secure the four captives. Send in the Squad. Tell them to shoot any vermin that moves, human or otherwise."

"You sure?" Hoffman said. "We're gonna need info, and dead rats can't talk."

"They also can't mind-control Squad members," I pointed out. "We'll still have those two at the club."

I caught the sound of a zipper refastening outside. "Dammit, Buck," a rat complained. "If I find you passed out in there..."

"Gotta run," I told Hoffman.

I stepped from the stable and sealed the door with a locking spell. My recent invocations had burned through my stealth potion, thinning its effect, but even as the approaching wererat fixed on me, I didn't slow.

"We got an intrud—!" he started to shriek.

A force blast sent him into the bushes he'd just been urinating in.

I took the front steps of the mobile home in a single leap, a shield hardening the air around me. With a lowered shoulder, I broke through the flimsy screen door. The rats inside scrambled, some for cover, others for the small arms they'd set on tables and countertops. I sent a blast from my shield, scattering wererats and weapons, then made a circuit of the living area before hustling down a short corridor.

At the end, I burst into a master bedroom, where the bloodied combatants had been dragged and deposited. I counted them quickly—*one, two, three, four*—and sealed the door an instant before a wererat collided into it.

"Hang tight, guys," I said to the unconscious men, growing the shield around all of us.

Small arms fire cracked from the hallway, sending bursts

of particle-board from the door, but the shots were wild. I adjusted my sword grip, ready to decapitate anything that came through. Within moments, the sharp cracks were being answered by deeper *pop-pop-pops*, coming from outside.

The Sup Squad had arrived.

11

I remained with the captives during the shootout that followed, the snaps of small-arms fire becoming drowned out by the Squad's growing semi-automatic assault. A few rat cries went up, but they were short-lived.

While the battle raged, I knelt beside the closest man, his arms still overhead from having been dragged into the room. In his forties, he possessed the muscular build of a regular gym-goer. Probably why the rats picked him as a combatant.

I peered into his eyes. One was swelling shut and the other was bloodshot, as if his opponent had stuck a thumb in there, but both were equally vacant. When I tuned into my wizard's senses, I picked up a sickly yellow hue around his mind—the wererats' influence. The same thing I would have discovered on Diana had I been able to get close enough to her at the club.

I positioned the end of my staff in front of the man's face.

"Look into the stone," I commanded in my wizard's voice.

His eyes flicked toward the opal inset in the wood—a good sign.

"Liberare!" I said.

The opal flashed, scattering the rats' control. He squinted away and curled into a fetal position, hands grasping his battered head. The normal response to a sound beating. I spoke a few words of reassurance before moving onto the next victim. By the time I finished clearing them all, the shooting had stopped.

Pounding shook the door. "You in there, Croft?"

I recognized the voice as belonging to Trevor, leader of the Sup Squad.

"Yeah, me and four of the disappeared," I replied.

"The site is clear and secured."

I opened the door and found Trevor with a small team ready to stack and enter. "Thanks for coming," I said.

"No problem, bro. You all right?"

"Fine, but these guys are going to need medical attention." I indicated the four, who lay in various states of consciousness. "There are fifteen more captives in the stable, but I need to release them from their mind control before they're moved. It's a wererat thing," I added, not sure I'd given the creatures more than a mention in the manual I'd designed for the Sup Squad. "How's your team?"

"Casualty free," he said. "The weres folded like cheap suits. No survivors. And the two who turned into rats? Nothing left of them but paste."

When a pair of medics arrived, Trevor and I left the back room. I skirted several dead wererats en route to the front door, smoke still floating above their bullet wounds. Against the superior training and firepower of the Sup Squad, they hadn't stood a chance. But what was the point of this place? And who was in charge?

"So I understand your pyro ended up being a good guy," Trevor remarked.

I looked over before realizing he was referring to our last case. "Oh, yeah. 'Sven Roe,' actual name Alec DeFazio."

"Weird about the facial recognition returning your mug as a close match."

Trevor was the one who'd messaged me the image, just as Alec was telling me he was the son of my shadow. "There's actually a story behind that. I'll tell it to you someday over a couple beers."

"Hey, I'll go for the beers alone," he chuckled.

Outside, The Sup Squad had opened the main gate to the grounds, and now idling personnel carriers waited to extract the victims. Hoffman had pulled his sedan inside as well and was shining a flashlight into one of the white vans.

"I'll join you in a sec," I told Trevor, releasing the locking spell on the stable doors.

While he and some Squad members entered the stable, I went to check in with Hoffman.

"A lot messier than you promised," he said of the operation as he snapped off his light. "But at least you got the right place this time." Though we were on better terms, Hoffman still knew how to get under my skin.

"Don't mention it," I said flatly.

"When we finish up here, we'll swing by the club for those rats you detained," he said. "Then we're all gonna meet at the task force room for a debriefing. Just got off the phone with Rules and Know-it-all. Talk about a couple sourpusses. Said we should've called the minute you got a hit on Parfait."

"Just how sour are we talking?"

Hoffman gave a self-satisfied snort. "Expect some fireworks."

"Great," I muttered.

It was after three a.m. when Hoffman and I made it up to the task force room at 1 Police Plaza. The Missing Persons detectives were already there. I'd barely closed the door when Rousseau shot to her feet. She might have stood shy of five feet, even with her big hair, but the severe angles of her cheekbones looked capable of cutting diamonds while her eyes could have torched a small village.

"What in the fuck are you doing?" she demanded. "It's one thing to horn in on our case, but take it over entirely?"

Hoffman gave me a smug look. "What'd I tell you?"

"There was *no* reason you couldn't have called us tonight," she went on. "None."

"She's right," Knowles put in, standing from the opposite side of the table. "That was unacceptable."

Though Knowles was more than twice his partner's size, at the moment, he was the less imposing of the two.

"All right, all right, loosen your man-bun," Hoffman told him. "Look, Croft got a possible hit on one of the disappeared, Diana Parfait. It wasn't a slam dunk, so we checked it out. It led us to a club. Still nothing to call in—Parfait looked fine. About the time I recognized more of the disappeared at the club, Croft got jumped by a pair of wererats in back. Next thing we know, we're on the other side of Brooklyn raiding their farm. We called the Sup Squad because they're trained for that stuff—unlike you two. No offense. And in case you've forgotten, the mayor made *me* lead on this."

"It's still our case," Rousseau said.

"*Our* case." Hoffman circled an arm to indicate the entire

room. "That includes me and Croft, and he'll confirm everything I just told you."

I was so bleary-eyed, I only wanted to collapse onto one of the chairs and sleep for a solid ten. After freeing the remaining victims of their mind control, I returned with Hoffman to the club. We'd contacted the owner ahead of time, and she met us to let us inside. While Hoffman pressed her for info about Mr. Funny, I removed the sleeping rats from the lockers and placed them inside my coat pockets. At IPP, I happily transferred them to a pair of special cells I'd prepped to detain supernatural beings. Under the power of the cells' wards, the weres reverted to their human forms, and we got them into prison scrubs. The guards were under orders to alert us the minute they awakened.

It took me a moment to realize everyone in the task force room was watching me, awaiting my response to Hoffman's prompt.

"Listen, guys," I said tiredly. "If Hoffman promises to call you from now on, can we get started on the debriefing? I'm not going to hold out much longer."

Rousseau looked between us with compressed lips. "I'd like to hear it from him."

"Fine," Hoffman sighed. "I'll call you. But now that we know we're dealing with supernaturals, you two are gonna need to study the manual Croft gave the department. How big is that thing?" he asked me with a smirk. "Eight hundred pages?"

"Something like that, but I can point them to the relevant parts."

That soured Hoffman's smile, but I could easily have shared that he'd never read the manual himself.

"Are we good?" I asked Rousseau.

Without nodding, she said, "I'll have the intern bring us some coffee."

———

For the next hour, Hoffman and I debriefed them on the events of the night, starting with my hit on Parfait. Though all was far from forgiven, Rousseau and Knowles settled into detective mode, taking notes and asking follow-up questions. For his part, Hoffman dropped his smug, I'm-task-force-leader attitude.

"So, that's where we are," he finished. "The victims are at General being assessed and treated. When the docs give us the go ahead, we'll start interviewing, see what they remember. In the meantime, we've got Rat One and Two down in the Basement. Croft thinks they'll be awake enough to talk in the next couple hours."

"What are the protocols for interrogating wererats?" Rousseau asked me.

"For everyone's safety, it will need to be done in the cells. The wards negate their mind-control ability."

She raised a questioning eyebrow.

"Why don't you let Croft and me handle them," Hoffman said. "You two can get started on tracking down this Mr. Funny, obviously not his real name. According to the club owner, he started booking slots at her place last month. She never actually talked to him, just chalked up his crowds to some sort of cult following since the guy wasn't funny. She's going to message her staff tomorrow, see if anyone knows him."

"We'll contact every club in the five boroughs that hosts comedians," Knowles said. "He might have a circuit."

"Good thinking," Hoffman conceded.

"Do we even know he's connected to the rats?" Rousseau asked.

"The ones I met in the back of the club sure acted like it," I replied. "And here's the thing about wererats: they're terrible organizers, super impulsive. For a kidnapping-and-control operation of this size, someone must have been directing them. I don't know who this Mr. Funny is, but he's no were himself."

"We're writing up a pile of requests on the phones we gathered at the Funny Farm," Hoffman said, pleased with the nickname he'd given the compound. "We'll know soon enough if there was any chatter with their organizer. I'm also getting an order to point some surveillance cameras at the Farm in case he shows up there."

"I know a judge," Rousseau said.

"Congratulations," Hoffman said. "So do I."

"I've heard about your judges," Rousseau shot back. "I want warrants that can't be picked apart by a good attorney."

"Let me worry about that," Hoffman snarled.

Before another melee could break out, one of the phones on the table rang. Knowles answered it and snapped his fingers for our attention. *Mayor,* he mouthed. "Yes, sir," he said into the phone. "I'll put you on speaker."

"Can everyone hear me?" Mayor Budge Lowder asked. His normally boisterous voice was subdued, and I pictured him propped up in bed, the cowlick that was perpetually dropping over his pudgy face in disarray.

"We're here," Hoffman said loudly, stepping toward the phone.

"Croft too?"

Before I could answer, Hoffman gripped my shoulder and

hugged me to his side. "He's right beside me, Mayor." The
move was discombobulating, and not only because it drew
me inside a stale cloud of coffee breath. Hoffman had never
been this affectionate with me. When he smiled at Rousseau
and Knowles, I understood why. He was making it clear that
he was the connection to the mayor's prized asset, not them.

"Okay, good," Budge said. "I heard about the raid and
rescue. Where does that put us with the numbers?"

"We were just going over that," Hoffman replied, releasing
me. "Detective Knowles, can you fill the mayor in?"

The large detective hunched over his laptop and, with a
studious frown, began tapping away. "Thins it out some," he
said at last. "But it doesn't appear to alter the distribution in
Lower Manhattan."

"No clear pattern?" Budge asked anxiously.

"Not to the naked eye. I'll put the updated data through
the algos."

"At least those nineteen are safe," Budge said. "Where are
we now, about thirty hot cases above normal?"

"Thirty-six," Knowles said.

Hoffman cleared his throat. "We have two rats in holding,
possibly with more info on other kidnappings. That would
take the numbers down more, maybe enough to fulfill the
mandate of your task force."

"Love to hear that," Budge said. "Keep up the great work,
everyone."

As the mayor signed off, Hoffman turned to me. "Those
dead you mentioned when you did your hunting spell. Think
any of them were rat victims?"

I thought of the little girl's shoe and my brief visit to the
In Between. I couldn't speak to the other victims, but I knew
the girl hadn't met her fate at the hands of a rat. Her death

had arrived like a cold weight, a pitiless force of nature. The phone rang again, giving me a moment to collect myself.

"It's the Basement," Hoffman said, hitting the speaker. "Are our prisoners awake?"

"They are," came a guard's voice, "but something's wrong. They're convulsing all over the place."

The shrieks and gargles in the background jolted me upright.

"Don't open the cells," I said. "We're on our way."

12

I arrived in the Basement with Hoffman and the duo of Rousseau and Knowles at our heels. The guards and a small group of Sup Squad officers were in front of the cells, peering in. As I approached, they created an opening.

"They're not looking good," the lead guard said.

I arrived at the first cell. Beyond the window, the wererat I'd nicknamed Twitchy was kicking around on his back as if performing a spastic dance. Beneath his bugged-out eyes, pink foam poured from his mouth. Next door, Wheezy wasn't faring any better. If anything, his movements looked weaker.

"Cover me," I said, opening his door.

I'd thought maybe the wererats were putting on an act to lure the guards inside—a very wererat move—but this was no ruse. Something was killing them. As I knelt beside Wheezy, my eyes began to sting and my throat to close. An effervescent mist was rising from the foam coming off his mouth.

"Stay back!" I shouted over a shoulder. "Shut the door!"

Holding my breath, I produced a small vial from one of

my coat pockets—a purification potion. A rapid incantation brought the potion to a bubble. Drawing a quantity into the dropper cap, I plunged it into the corner of Wheezy's mouth and squeezed. Almost immediately, the foam thinned and stopped misting. But the wererat had gone still. I shook him, then started into chest compressions. He convulsed and belched out a torrent of dark red blood before going limp again, his beady eyes rolling back into his head.

Swearing, I stood and waved to be let out.

"What the hell's going on?" Hoffman asked.

"Poison of some kind," I said, gasping in the fresh air and taking a drop of potion myself. "I neutralized it, but too late."

Drawing a deep breath, I plunged into the cell holding Twitchy. He was still kicking around, which was promising. I squeezed a dropper full of the purification potion into his mouth, jerking my hand back before his snapping incisors could shear off a finger. While the foam thinned, I launched into an incantation. Light grew from the opal end of my cane, enveloping his body in a healing aura.

I backed from the cell to catch my breath.

"Think I got to him in time," I panted. "We'll know in a minute."

"Hope so," Hoffman said, "'cause he's our most solid lead on Mr. Funny."

"His buddy's a goner," the lead guard said, staring through Wheezy's window. "Looks like he puked out his weight in blood."

Rousseau and Knowles remained back, observing the spectacle of dying wererats in stunned silence, but Hoffman was right. Twitchy was our best lead on the mastermind, and I couldn't take any chances with his life.

"Hold your breath and give me a hand," I told him.

Back inside the cell, I lifted Twitchy under his armpits. After a moment, Hoffman followed me and gripped him behind the knees. Together, we carried him out of the cell and set him down on the floor. Twitchy's body had gone limp, but that was courtesy of my healing magic. He was breathing.

Rousseau followed but remained back a safe distance. Knowles arrived beside her and gazed down at the wererat soberly.

"Wasn't he more secure in the cell?" Rousseau said.

"The wards on the cell are designed to dampen his powers," I replied. "Powers that include enhanced healing. If we want him to recover so we can talk to him, his chances are much better out here."

Hoffman, who was still catching his breath, nodded and pointed at me as if to suggest he'd been prepared to say the same thing.

"How long will that take?" Knowles asked.

"Not very," I said, picturing my magic combining with the wererat's to close the ulcers that had dissolved his buddy's insides. "In fact, you may want to get your cuffs ready, Hoff. Could be any minute."

"Should I put them on now or—shit!" Hoffman exclaimed.

As if jumpstarted by a defibrillator, the wererat thrashed upright. A semicircle of guards greeted him with aimed weapons. As Twitchy stared at them, I noticed his tongue poking around the insides of his cheeks as though in search of something. Not finding it, he narrowed his eyes and coiled to spring.

Oh, no, you don't, I thought, flattening him with a wall of hardened air. His arms and legs flailed helplessly.

Hoffman, who had ended up on the floor, pushed himself upright with a grumble.

"Looks like he's ready to talk," I said.

I stood off to one side as Hoffman sat across from Twitchy, who was cuffed to a table in an interrogation room. Outside, Detectives Knowles and Rousseau watched on a closed-circuit television.

"Some night, huh?" Hoffman said to Twitchy with a snigger.

"What am I doing here?" the wererat asked in a reedy voice, his eyes bouncing between us.

"Well, you attacked an associate, for one." Hoffman cocked his head at me. "At the club."

"Bullshit. He attacked us."

"You're also connected to a group that abducted and wrongfully imprisoned at least nineteen individuals."

"Prove it."

"Won't be hard with your phones."

Twitchy set his narrow jaw but lost his stare-down with Hoffman. His beady eyes dropped to the table, which wasn't surprising. Wererats were pretty gutless.

"Why don't you start by telling us your name and where you're from," Hoffman said.

"Mickey. From Orlando, Florida."

"Oh, I get it," Hoffman said dryly. "Last name *Mouse*, right? Funny guy."

"Unlike his boss," I remarked. "I'm still recovering from that awful set."

The anxious way Twitchy's eyes shot toward me confirmed once more that he'd been connected to Mr. Funny.

"Earlier tonight, we busted up the Farm in Brooklyn," Hoffman said. "Where else are you holding people?"

Twitchy's defiant gaze returned to the table.

"What's your boss's name?" Hoffman pressed.

When the wererat remained silent, Hoffman's grin crumpled at the edges. "Like it or not, we're your best friends right now. Play nice, and this could turn out all right for you. You're a small-time rat, and we're after the big cheese. Help us find him, and we'll work something out. You might not even do time on this."

Twitchy's lips drew into a sneer. If he'd been ready to die —first by self-poisoning, then by cop—I doubted he was looking for clemency. But maybe that was the key to getting him to open up.

"What were you eating back there?" I asked him.

He must have had a mouth pouch, something I would need to add to my notes on wererats.

When he remained silent, I said, "The question I have is whether your boss gave you the poison, or you picked it up yourselves—maybe to avoid a less pleasant punishment for screwing up? Though it would have to be *a lot* less pleasant, considering what the poison was doing to your insides."

Hoffman squinted from me to our suspect, trying to figure out where I was going with this. But the anxiety written across Twitchy's face was my answer—it was the second. He'd self-administered the poison out of fear. Now we had something to leverage.

Stepping beneath the closed-circuit camera, I grew my aura out until a pair of electrical pops sounded. The tentative knock on the door that followed confirmed that I'd successfully disabled the feed. I returned to the table and leaned over Twitchy.

"Tell us what we want to know," I said in a lowered voice, "and we'll let you out. Stay quiet, and we'll keep you alive. We'll even make it super easy for your boss to find you."

"Hey, uh, maybe we should discuss this outside," Hoffman said, but I ignored him.

"You have to decide now," I told the wererat. "Because once that door opens, the offer's off the table."

The knocking resumed. "Hoffman?" Rousseau called from the other side.

Twitchy's breathing sped up, his eyes shifting between the door and my face.

"I'm guessing you have about two seconds," I said.

The knob turned. *"All right,"* Twitchy hissed.

I straightened as the door opened and Rousseau's head appeared. "The CC just went out."

"Oh, yeah?" Hoffman said, sliding me a look. "Let's take him next door, then. Our friend here was just getting ready to help us out."

As Hoffman secured him to the table in the neighboring interrogation room, Twitchy narrowed his eyes at me as if to say, *You better keep your fucking word, pal.* I nodded and stood back to give Hoffman the floor.

"Name?" Hoffman asked.

"Stan Kriebel," Twitchy answered.

"Address?"

He shrugged. "Nothing permanent. I move around New York and Jersey picking up the odd job."

I'd read that wererats were itinerant, many with drug and alcohol problems—something to do with a chemical imbalance. Stan's convulsing eyes and trembling fingers seemed to support that. And given their craven nature, wererats were more likely to commit petty crimes than major offenses. Probably why I hadn't encountered any in my work to date.

"How did you end up at the Farm?" Hoffman asked him.

"Don't know. Just turned up there."

Hoffman frowned. "You call that cooperating?"

The wererat shrugged his narrow shoulders. "I think it was like that for all of us. We don't usually hang around our own, but there was plenty of food in the fridge, playing cards and bags of gambling chips, places to sleep. Over the course of a week, one or two of us would show up each day."

"Then what happened?" Hoffman asked.

"Middle of the night, this strange dude dropped in. Not a rat, though. We could see that right off from his suit—expensive, tailored. We thought maybe he was lost. We surrounded him, and the next thing I knew, I was on the ground with what felt like a boot on my throat. Couldn't breathe. Couldn't fight or shift, either—hell, couldn't even get up. None of us could. I started to think that this dude had set up the place to draw us in, and now he was taking us out in one go, like some fucking exterminator."

When fear seized his jittering eyes, he didn't try to hide it.

"Then the choking stopped." He snapped his fingers. "Just like that. The dude came to us one by one and helped us to our feet, shook our hands like a proper gentleman, and introduced himself. But the whole time, he had this fake smile, like it'd been plastered on, and his eyes looked like a graveyard. "

"His name?" Hoffman asked, a pen poised over his pad.

"Mr. Funny."

"How about a real name?" Hoffman growled.

"That's how he introduced himself, I swear. 'Mr. Funny.'

We called him 'Fun' for short, but never to his face," he added. "Anyway, a rat named TJ got spooked, made a dash for it. Fun looked over at him—that's all he did, looked at him—and the flesh ripped clean from his body, outta here. TJ went down like a sack, writhing on the floor in his own blood and hair. He was regenerating, but every time he got close to healing, more flesh blew off him. It kept happening, and the mess around him kept getting bigger. A couple of the rats lost their dinner. Finally, TJ was just a puddle of chunks. 'Would anyone else like to leave,' Fun asked us."

I was racking my brain for what sort of being Mr. Funny could be—Demon? Dark fae?

"'Course no one took him up on his offer," Stan continued with an edgy laugh. "That was when he said he had work for us. Paid well, but we had to do exactly what he said. We agreed. After TJ, what the hell else were we gonna do? So he started going down the list. Wanted the stables cleaned and prepped for 'the guests,' he called them. Then he described the kinds of guests he wanted—New Yorkers, adults, respectable looking. Next morning, a pair of panel trucks were sitting in the yard."

"How many guests?" Hoffman asked.

"Ten at first."

"Were there other sites?" I asked. "Other kidnapping teams?"

"Didn't hear nothing about any."

"All right, so you get the ten to the Farm," Hoffman said. "Then what?"

"Then Fun showed up with this silly whistle. He wanted us to make it so his guests laughed every time he blew it. It was nerve-racking, 'cause he didn't just want them laughing, but laughing in a certain way. Loud, but sincere. Like I said, after TJ, we didn't ask questions. Took a long night of trial and error, but we finally got them laughing how he wanted. That Saturday, he told us to clean them up and drive them to this place in the city. Some club. We had no idea what it was all about until he showed up on stage wearing suspenders and telling the worst jokes I've ever heard."

Hoffman grunted in agreement. "My opinion of you just climbed a notch."

"Yeah, he was bad," Stan continued. "You could've heard a cricket fart. But once he started blowing that whistle, he got his laughs. He looked pretty pleased with himself until he realized no one else was joining in. He was after a trigger effect, I guess. Get enough laughing and the rest of the crowd would join in. Didn't happen, though. And there was nothing *fun* about him when we got back to the Farm. He did to Dent what he'd done to TJ, except the sorry bastard didn't die till the next morning."

That explained why he and Wheezy had been so upset Hoffman and I hadn't been laughing at the club. Their lives depended on it. It also explained the poison. The wererats might have kidnapped and held "the guests," but they were captives of Mr. Funny and his homicidal mood swings.

"So he had you add more guests," I said.

"Yeah, two at a time till we got to twenty. In some venues it was enough, in others, it didn't quite reach that wall-to-wall effect he was after."

"We only recovered nineteen," Hoffman snarled.

"That shit was Larry's fault," Stan said defensively. "He tried to possess an old man in the Upper East Side. Went in too hard, and the dude had an aneurysm, dropped dead on the street. He was the only one we lost, though."

"Are you sure Mr. Funny didn't off anyone during one of

his tantrums?" Hoffman pressed. "'Cause we've still got a lot of disappearances to account for." He was speaking as the task force leader now.

"No," Stan said emphatically. "Fun made it clear that he didn't want us hurting them."

"Is that why your buddies had them fighting each other when we showed up?" I asked.

"Fighting?" Stan said in surprise before his mouth drew into a scowl. "Probably another one of Larry's bright ideas, the dumb shit."

"How did this Mr. Funny communicate with you?" Hoffman asked.

"He'd just show up."

"No phone calls or texts?"

Stan shook his head. "I don't think he even owned a phone."

"Besides the vans," I asked, "did he ever give you anything or leave anything behind at the Farm."

"Money. He was always good about the payments. He also kept the place stocked, but no one saw how he did it. One day the kitchen would be down to scraps and crumbs, and the next day it'd be full again."

I made a mental note to talk to the team processing the site to see if they'd recovered anything I could cast on.

"That's really all I know to tell you," Stan said before looking pointedly at me, his twitchy stare watery and desperate. He still intended to end himself before Mr. Funny could do the deed his way.

"We'll book you for now," Hoffman said. "We might have some more questions."

Stan's eyes, which remained fixed on mine, beat furiously. "Hey, man, you promised me!"

"The cell is protected with a dislocation sigil," I said. "No one will be able to find you inside."

"That fucking psycho will!" he screamed.

———

Pebbles of guilt rolled around my gut as a squad car drove me back to my apartment sometime after four a.m. I'd broken my promise to Stan, but with the other rats dead, he was the only informant we had. He was also a victim of Mr. Funny's coercion. Though I was sure Stan's list of misdemeanors ran a mile long, he would never have kidnapped and held those nineteen people otherwise. Wererat or not, he didn't merit a death sentence.

As we transferred him back to the cell, I'd assured him it would just be for a little longer, even suggesting that we might apprehend Mr. Funny in the meantime. He launched into such a fit that I had the guard switch off his speaker so I didn't have to hear his crazed shrieks of "Liar!" and "Goon!" as I left.

Now, sitting in the squad car, my thoughts turned fully to the figure who'd inspired that terror in him. *Mr. Funny summons the wererats to the Farm, controls them through violence and fear, sends them on a kidnapping spree...*

But I was back to the question that had plagued me earlier.

...all so he can have an audience who will laugh at his jokes?

I was beginning to wonder if we were dealing with a deity. Comedy gods and muses relied on laughter for sustenance. But I couldn't come up with a single god of comedy who also fit Mr. Funny's penchant for torture and killing. Demon, then? But no comedic demons came to mind, either. This was going to take research—on top of my other duties to the task force. Though the problem-solving part of my mind was primed to get started, my eyes could barely focus out of the window.

I needed to catch up on a little sleep first.

13

The next week had me on two pots of coffee a day. When not teaching, I split my time between casting on personal items from the remaining disappeared and researching all manner of gods, demigods, demons, nephilim, and cambion in search of our Mr. Funny.

The research had yet to bear fruit, but I was getting some results with the casting. One item led us to a boy who'd been abducted by his grandmother. Judging from his methed-out parents, she'd clearly been in the right, and Hoffman turned the case over to Child Protection. Another hit ended with a high-speed car chase. The "disappeared" in that case was a husband who'd left his family and was waiting on a forged passport to skip the country with a Brazilian drag queen he'd fallen for. They weren't supernatural cases, but with each one we were able to take another disappeared off the board.

In the meantime, the task force interviewed the nineteen victims the wererats had abducted. All were recovering, even the ones who'd participated in Fight Night, but their memories were shot. They recalled some version of a scrawny man with a narrow face approaching them, in most cases to ask directions, but everything that followed was a void in their memories. That would have been the moment the wererat mind-controlled them.

The wererats' phones revealed local chatter, coordinating Mr. Funny's orders. No communication with other wererats who may have been holding more disappeared, and none with Mr. Funny himself. Neither did the boss turn up on the surveillance cameras we'd aimed at the Farm. The only visitor of note was a ghoul who climbed the gate one night. A Sup Squad unit was dispatched to eliminate him.

That Friday, we reconvened as a task force at 1 Police Plaza.

"So where are we with tracking down Mr. Funny?" Hoffman asked the room.

Rousseau cleared her throat. "*Knowles* and I," she began, emphasizing her partner's actual name, "contacted every club in the city with a comedy stage. Got almost a dozen hits. In every case, Mr. Funny signed up, performed a set with his whistle, the crowd responded with excessive laughter, and he left. Never disclosed his real name and barely spoke to the staff. Several managers used the word 'vanished' to describe his exit."

"Pretty much my experience," I said, remembering how he'd disappeared out of the back of Loosey's.

"The earliest date we could find was last month," she continued. "A poor outing, according to the manager. Mr. Funny was jeered off stage. But what stood out for the manager was the way he looked at the audience before leaving, like he wanted to murder them all."

"Let me guess," Hoffman said slyly. "He didn't because it

would've *killed* his comedy career." He snickered at his own punchline.

"So he went out and kidnapped an audience instead," I said over him.

Rousseau continued as if neither of us had spoken. "As far as upcoming dates, it looks like he booked out about two months in advance. The next date is tomorrow night. A club in the Village called The Spot. We'll need a team on it." When she looked at me, it was as if she had to force the words that followed. "Croft should probably be there, too."

"I'm happy to have my presence tolerated," I said. "But let's not get our hopes up. He's lost his audience, and getting a reaction was the whole point of his sets. He's not going back to being jeered off stage. So he's either retired from comedy or suspending his tour until he can rebuild his guest list."

"The club is still our best lead," Rousseau said.

"I'd have to concur," Knowles added in his mild voice.

Shocker, I thought, but the duo wasn't wrong. The club was our *only* lead.

"How are you coming with your research?" Hoffman asked me. "Any hits yet?"

"Well, no candidates that I'm confident in," I said, ignoring Rousseau's critical look. "If we're dealing with a minor god or demon, I may be able to summon him, trap him in a casting circle. But I can't rush something like that. The last thing we want is to call up a being that has nothing to do with anything. We have enough on our plate."

"Keep at it." Hoffman turned back to Rousseau. "What else? Any info from the security cameras?"

"Actually, I finally located one of the disappeared the night he went missing." She rotated her laptop so we could all see. "Demarcus Ward, age thirty-six. He left for a jog at around nine p.m. I picked him up here, on the Hudson River Greenway. His wife confirmed those were the clothes he'd been wearing when he left." The screen showed a black-and-white image of a lone man in a sleeveless shirt and bright running shoes. He advanced the width of the screen in staccato hops spaced about a second apart.

"The next camera was out," Rousseau continued. "A vandalism job, probably. The camera after that didn't pick him up. Of course, he might have turned before then, but it narrows his disappearance location to somewhere in this area."

"Can you play that back again?" I asked.

As Rousseau did, I watched closely. Something was bugging me, but I couldn't put my finger on what. After the third playback, Rousseau raised her eyebrows to ask whether I'd seen enough. I nodded.

"I've updated the location information in the system," Knowles said.

"How does the distribution look after this week?" Hoffman asked him.

"Still no obvious patterns. The ones the algo returned are weak, don't hold up to cross-pattern analysis."

"I'll take your word for it," Hoffman grunted. "So we're at, what, thirty hot cases above normal?"

"Thirty-four," Knowles said.

Hoffman ambled the length of the room on his ortho boot, sucking his teeth in thought. "I'm betting this Mr. Funny has more people stashed somewhere, probably enough to get our numbers down to the averages. What do you think, Croft?"

As much as Hoffman prided himself in being task force leader, he was under pressure to close this out, and he had a bad habit of clinging to his favorite theory despite mounting evidence to the contrary—something he was doing now. It felt more important, though, to keep our alliance intact against Rules and Know-it-all.

"Possibly," I hedged, "though my hunting spells haven't returned any hits."

A number of my spells had suggested death, though—that horrible, empty feeling when my cane went inert. Perhaps it was a lingering effect of the nightshade essence, but with several, I picked up the cold weight I'd felt with the little girl. Though I marked them "likely deceased," I placed them in a special column that I chose not to share with the task force. I wanted to know what it meant first, if anything.

"Nothing, huh?" Hoffman made a dour face. "Then staking out the club tomorrow is probably our best bet. If I'm right and he's got another audience out there, maybe he'll show and we can wrap this thing up."

Rousseau frowned. "I just said that."

"Oh, and then there's rat boy," Hoffman continued, referring to Stan Kriebel, who remained in holding. "The judge gave us an extension, but come Sunday noon we either have to charge him or kick him loose."

"Let's see what happens tomorrow night," I said. "If Mr. Funny doesn't show, let Kriebel go."

Rousseau looked around in alarm. "What? Why? At the very least he's an accessory to kidnapping and unlawful imprisonment."

"Under coercion," I said.

"According to him," she shot back.

"Right, and he bluffed us all by popping a poison capsule that killed his friend." I took a calming breath. "Just hear me out. He's terrified of Mr. Funny—so much so that he'd rather off himself in one of the most agonizing ways possible than face him. If we set him loose, I can track him. If Mr. Funny is as vindictive as Kriebel fears, he'll find Kriebel before he can pop another capsule. I'll be there."

Rousseau looked over at her partner, who gave a slight nod.

"Sounds like a plan, then," Hoffman said. "Stake out the club tomorrow night, kick Kriebel loose the day after, and then wrap up this shitshow in a pretty bow."

14

The next morning, Saturday, I was awakened by a minor earthquake. I squinted at the bedside clock: 9:20 a.m. A folded piece of paper leaned against it—a note from my wife, reminding me that she and Tony were going to her brothers' for the day. It ended with, "You need to talk to your friend about his work hours."

Bree-yark, I thought with a groan.

I rolled over and closed my eyes. It had been another late night in my library/lab, and I needed more than four hours sleep, but the shaking resumed, making that impossible. After another minute, I got up and shuffled from the bedroom. Tabitha greeted me from her divan with flattened ears and a scowl.

"You need to talk to him about—"

"—his work hours," I finished. "I know. How long's it been going on?"

"Since seven, at least, and it's doing *horrid* things to my insides."

Though Tabitha tended to exaggerate her maladies, I was

starting to feel a little queasy myself. I could also feel a migraine coming on. Back in the bedroom, I pulled on a robe and stepped into a pair of slippers.

"I can't believe you're only noticing now," Tabitha said as I reemerged.

"Well, I was in a deep sleep. That's what work does," I made a point of adding.

Tabitha responded with a grumpy face as she adjusted her mass on the divan. I couldn't remember the last time she'd patrolled outside, and she was putting on weight. Now I wondered if it would even be safe for her to navigate the ledge. Still, I didn't like her playing diva on her divan all day.

"Plans for today?" I asked as I prepared a pot of coffee.

"It's Saturday, darling. A day of rest."

"Sounds an awful lot like the other six days of your week."

"And tomorrow is *the* day of rest," she continued, "so there's my weekend."

"I didn't realize you'd found religion."

"You shouldn't presume to know *anything* about me. It's not as if you ever bother to ask. No, it's *so* much more entertaining for you if I remain the fat, foul-mouthed ginger with no inner life of my own."

"Fine. Are you religious now?"

She stared at me from hooded lids. "I'm a succubus once removed from a demon. What do you think?"

"Glad I asked," I muttered.

The apartment shook again, this time making the double-story windows ring.

"Oh, for *fuck's* sake," Tabitha snapped. "Are you going to talk to him or not."

"Going now," I said, abandoning my brewing coffee. "I expect a clean mouth when I get back."

"Then expect to be disappointed."

All week long, Bree-yark had been working on the unit in fits. I'd gone down to check on his progress, but he was out each time, and below a construction sign that he'd affixed to the door, a thick padlock blocked my access. Not sure whether it was meant for public safety or to keep me from peeking, I'd left it intact.

As I descended the staircases now, the shaking became more violent. On the basement level, I emerged into a corridor littered with building supplies and heaps of debris. I picked my way toward the door, which was rattling on its hinges—much like the teeth in my gums. Beyond, a motor pounded above a series of sharp cracks.

Is he running a jackhammer in there?

I covered my ears until there was a break in the cacophony and pounded on the door. "Bree-yark!" I called.

Something heavy hit the floor, and a moment later, the door cracked open on my goblin friend. He was wearing a pair of yellow-tinted goggles and a wooly set of earmuffs.

"Thank the gods it's you," he said, pulling the earmuffs down to his neck. "Thought it was gonna be another one of your neighbors coming to give me grief."

"You've already had visitors this morning?"

"Just a few," he said, barking a laugh. "It's a wonder I'm getting anything done."

I made a mental note to pick up some wine baskets to give out as peace offerings.

Above Bree-yark's dust-coated face, I made out a dim wedge of my just-purchased apartment. It looked like a bombed-out pit. When Bree-yark caught me squinting, he sidled out and closed the door behind him.

"What's going on in there?" I asked.

"What're you talking about? I'm doing your buildout."

"Well, it feels like the whole building's about to come down."

"Oh, that. Yeah, when I ripped out the flooring, I wasn't happy with what I saw. The concrete subflooring is a moisture sponge. Starting to crack in places. Better to jack it all out now and replace it before I install any materials."

"How much more jacking are we talking?"

He shrugged. "Two, three hours? That gonna be a problem?"

"Is there any way you can wait until later in the day and do it in intervals?"

"No can do, chief. Got some fresh cement on order that'll be here this afternoon. I leave it out front, and it'll be pinched like that. We're talking primo stuff." By his grin, I guessed the cement in question was an unanticipated expense. He confirmed it with his next words. "Oh, reminds me. I had to up the budget a little. It's one of those 'ounce of prevention' type things. Didn't think you'd mind."

Under-slept, absent my morning coffee, and my head still throbbing from the mini concussions of Bree-yark's jackhammering, I could only nod vaguely. Concern lines sprang over his leathery face.

"Hey, you all right?" he asked. "You're as pale as a banshee. Here, have a seat."

He pulled over a bucket of plaster, then took a seat on a paint can facing me. The simple act of removing the weight from my legs helped immensely.

"Thanks," I said. "Just been burning the midnight oil a few too many straight."

"Got a new case or something? 'Cause if you do, I'm there." He tugged off his work gloves, a sign that he was ready to drop everything and join me. "The buildout can wait. I'm serious. I'll tell 'em to warehouse the cement till I'm ready for it." He had his phone halfway out before I showed him a hand.

"I really appreciate that, but this is more of an investigation. Something I'm working on with the NYPD."

He hesitated to make sure I didn't need him before replacing the phone in his pocket. "What's it about?"

I was bound by the task force's confidentiality agreement, but Bree-yark wasn't tied up with the NYPD like Ricki, and he wasn't going to run out and blab. Neither was the agreement personal, like the one I'd made with Alec. Speaking of whom, we had a two o'clock training session that afternoon.

"It has to do with disappearances in the city," I said. "The numbers have been well above the norm. We busted an operation involving wererats and recovered their captives, but the ringleader is in the wind."

"Skeevy sons-of-vermin," Bree-yark muttered of the weres.

"That accounts for a chunk of the disappeared, but here's the thing. I think there's a second supernatural threat out there. One that's not just taking people, but killing them." It was the first time I'd voiced the suspicion aloud.

"How many people we talking?" he asked.

The separate column I created for the deceased who carried the cold, crushing weight was nearly to the bottom of the page now.

"Thirty-two," I said. "So far."

"Holy thunder. Any ideas what it is?"

"None," I confessed. "Only that it's heartless. Probably soulless."

When Bree-yark's thick hand gripped my shoulder and patted it gently, I realized I was choking up.

"It took a little girl," I managed. "A one-year-old."

The emotions heaved around inside me. I hadn't been able to talk to my wife because of the agreement. And Hoffman, even this chummier version of him, would have said something about those kinds of cruelties coming with the job. But as a soon-to-be father of a daughter myself, this one cut too close to the heart. All week, I'd been needing to open up, to process it with someone else.

"Oh, man," Bree-yark said.

The yellow of his eyes deepened, telling me he got it. And that was enough to anchor my emotions.

"Yeah," I managed. "It sucks."

"What can I do, Everson? And don't tell me nothing."

His readiness to help warmed me and made me smile. "I'll let you know. For now, keep on building and send any future complainants to me." I wasn't going to take up the issue of the noise with him—that was between me and my neighbors. Anyway, I had an idea for a potion.

"You got it, buddy." Bree-yark gave my shoulder a final clap and rose with me. "The jack-hammering will be the worst of it, I promise. After that, it'll be mostly drilling and regular hammering."

"Can I take a look inside?"

"Well, uh, it's not going to look like much of anything right now. Once I get the subflooring sorted, I've gotta cover it over and reframe the walls. Give me another week or so, and it'll start looking like a studio."

I nodded, even though his initial stammer had me wondering if he really did know what he was doing.

"Can I at least get a key to the padlock?" I asked, as insurance.

"Oh, yeah, meant to make you a spare. I'll, um, I'll do that this week." He lifted his earmuffs back in place before I could respond. "Well, back to the job." Opening the door behind him, he backed through the wedge and closed it again.

"Let me know when I can help!" he called.

The jackhammer started up again.

———

After preparing a noise-dampening potion, which I emptied into a dehumidifier and carried back to the basement, I spent the rest of my morning in my lab, reviewing the items for the thirty-two people I'd classified as "special deaths." But "special" how, exactly? That was the million-dollar question.

Using my wizard's vision, I examined the personal items for clues, even casting variations of hunting spells to see if my go-to spell had missed something. Finally, I sent the list to Detective Knowles without explanation, asking him to check for patterns. An hour later, he called me back.

"I looked at that subset you sent, and nothing leapt out. Sorry, man." With his mild-mannered voice, I never would have guessed there was a six-and-a-half foot giant on the other end of the line. "But why those? Seeing something unusual?"

I was really tempted to tell him about the special deaths, but I withheld at the last moment. If it didn't make sense to me, how would it make sense to him?

"Not really," I said. "Just exploring all avenues. I appreciate you taking a look."

"That's what I'm here for. I don't even mind the overtime,

to be honest. Helps with the alimony and child support." I made a noise of interest, an invitation for him to keep talking if he wanted, but he apparently wasn't looking for a sympathetic ear. "See you at seven this evening," he finished.

He was referring to our meeting for the stakeout at the club. Right now, though, I needed to get to my session with Alec.

"See you at seven," I echoed, and ended the call.

At my library, I drew a book that had been on my reading list—a tome on forgotten gods—that I'd yet to go through. I would skim it in the cab, but what I really needed was an assistant. I started to insert the book in my satchel, then stopped. It was a long shot, but if I played my cards right...

Downstairs, I jostled Tabitha's divan with my foot. She had fallen asleep in such a way that her belly was hanging off the edge like a beanbag. It swayed when I jostled the divan a second time.

"What?" she moaned.

"It's time for you to get back to work."

"I told you, today is my rest day."

"You owe me like two-hundred hours of patrol time."

"Fine, darling. I'll start back Monday." Her eyes had remained closed, and now she smacked her mouth lazily. "First thing Monday morn..." The word trailed from her skewed jaw as she drifted back to sleep.

"Well, I'm cutting your food portions in half until you do."

Her eyes snapped open. "What?"

"Look, I've given you the last month off while you adjusted to Ricki and her son moving in. And by all appearances, you've adjusted just fine... and then some. You can't keep lying around all day amassing calories."

"So you go straight to starvation?"

I snorted. "What you call 'starvation' is more than I eat on a good day."

"Well, my metabolism is different from yours. But you can't be serious, darling. This is just, it's..." She gathered her stomach with her front paws as if safeguarding something precious. "*Vicious.*"

Good, I was getting the desperate reaction I'd wanted.

"Well, there's an easy solution." I said, nodding toward the ledge.

Tabitha's bright ochre eyes cut from me to the cat door and back. With a moan, she released her belly, letting it all spill out again. "I tried, darling," she wailed. "And I... I can't fit through it anymore."

I stifled a laugh as I pictured her attempting to cram herself through the opening.

"It's not funny," she pouted. "It took an hour of wriggling before I could back myself out."

When my chest started to convulse, I coughed to cover it up. I had her right where I wanted her, and I couldn't afford to blow it now. "No. No, it's not," I agreed, resetting my jaw. "All the more reason to go to half portions. In the meantime, I'll talk to Bree-yark about installing a wider door."

Tabitha gave me her most miserable look. "Have a heart, darling."

I started to turn away, then stopped as if an idea had just occurred to me. "Unless you'd be willing to do something else for me?"

She narrowed her eyes suspiciously. "What?"

I produced the tome from my satchel. "Some light reading?"

With Tabitha grudgingly agreeing to go through the tome, I caught a cab to Midtown College. I'd made a list of Mr. Funny's most salient qualities and instructed Tabitha to note any close matches. How thorough she'd be was another question, but I suspected she'd put in enough effort to extend my clemency.

As the cab pulled up to the college, I spotted Alec at the bottom of the steps where he'd been waiting the week before. But he wasn't sitting this time; he was pacing back and forth. When he spotted my cab, he veered toward me, his pack bouncing with each herky-jerky step.

My paternal instincts fired up. Something was wrong. I broke into a jog to meet him halfway. When he arrived in front of me, his face was ashen, the skin around his bloodshot eyes pinched with anxiety.

"What's up?" I asked, my heart pounding.

"They—" He choked on the word, as if about to get sick, and started again. "They've taken my mom."

15

———

"I want you to tell me everything that happened," I said. "From the beginning."

We were in my classroom, Alec sitting at one of the front desks with a bottle of water I'd given him. Outside, he'd managed to share a few desperate fragments before he began to clutch his chest and hyperventilate. Now, under the calming influence of my healing spell, his breathing was steadier, his eyes more focused. But he was still freaked out. For my part, my heart continued to hammer.

"First, you have to promise not to get mad," he said.

I lowered myself onto the edge of my desk so I wasn't looming over him. "All I want to know right now is what happened so I can help you."

He nodded and took a shaky sip of water. "I'd been thinking about what you asked me last week, if there'd been any news about the Discovery Society. Like I said, I've been wondering too, and I guess my curiosity got the best of me. I went over there—just to look," he added hurriedly. "I stayed across the street. I just wanted to see what kind of people were coming and going. That's all."

I had half a mind to shake him, but the most important thing right now was finding out what happened.

"Were you using your vagueness rune?" I asked.

"Absolutely. I almost never hit the streets without it on. Anyway, a few people went in and out the first day, most of them in suits. Could've been anyone. The next day, a few guys in bulky uniforms joined the traffic, all armed. I couldn't tell if they were police, private security, or what. Either way, it spooked me. I took off. A couple blocks later, bam. Something hit me in the back, flattened me."

"What was it?"

"No idea, but all my muscles seized up. Someone heavy straddled my back and pulled up my sleeve. I felt a prick in my shoulder, and the next thing I remember is being at a table in a small room."

"In the Discovery Society?"

"Maybe. It felt like an interrogation room, possibly because this big guy was staring down at me, two of the thickest arms I've ever seen folded across his chest. A couple more people were off to the sides. The first thing the big guy said was my name; 'Alec DeFazio.' He wasn't asking. He knew who I was."

Alec paused to take another shaky sip of his water.

"He wanted to know what I was carrying in my pack. He meant the Hermes box, but I lied and said it was my late grandmother's jewelry box. He asked if I'd stolen it, and I told him no. Then he said, 'Funny, because an artifact fitting the box's description was stolen from a private residence in Tribeca.' So he knew about that too. He said I was in a lot of trouble."

No kidding, I thought, but here Alec was with his pack.

"Then out of the blue, the big guy said, 'I know you're working with—'" Alec broke off before restarting again. "'I know you're working with Everson Croft.'"

I rose from my desk. "What?"

"Yeah. I tried to play dumb, act like I had no idea what he was talking about, but then one of the other men came forward with a tablet showing security footage from that night you and I went to the Discovery Society. It was shot from a distance, probably the street, but you could make us out in the alley behind the building. When I denied it, he pulled up another video—a live feed, he said. It showed my m-mom in a holding cell."

Alec wiped his eyes fiercely.

"The big guy told me to listen to him very carefully. My mom was being held on suspicion of stealing and selling narcotics from the hospital—which is a fucking lie. She'd never do that." I nodded and waited for him to collect himself. "In the video she was in scrubs, so they must've gotten her after her shift. The big guy said she was looking at twenty-five years minimum, unless I did exactly what he said."

Oh, boy, here it comes.

Alec took a deep breath and raised his guarded gaze. "He wants me to bring you to him. 'Straight-up swap,' is how he put it. You for my mom. He'd even forget about the theft of the box. That's why he released me. He returned my pack when I told him it was the only way I could get to you."

I paced toward the window and stared outside. The afternoon heat shimmered over the brick walls behind the college.

"I—I'm so sorry," Alec said from behind me. "I screwed up."

For some reason, the heat-distorted view recalled the night I turned thirteen—just two years younger than Alec was now—and snuck into my grandfather's forbidden study. He'd found me and sliced my finger with his cane sword. In that shocking moment, I'd felt a similar unsteadiness, like the world I'd known was coming apart. *You are curious,* Grandpa had said in his stern German accent, *but you must not be foolish.*

"What you said earlier about curiosity getting the best of you?" I turned from the window. "I'm pretty sure that's in our DNA." And in Alec's case, I didn't doubt the Hermes influence was contributing.

"I should never have gone there, *dammit,*" he seethed.

"Don't beat yourself up. It sounds like these people were looking for you. They would have found you eventually."

"Who are they?"

"Society of Cronus goons if I had to guess."

"Can they really have my mom arrested and charged?"

"They could well be bluffing," I said, but I was thinking about the organization's strong ties to the NYPD. "Where are you supposed to deliver me?"

"The guy gave me an address for a parking garage. No weapons, and you're supposed to wear this." Alec unzipped his pack and pulled out a billowy shirt and pants, both made of a semi-transparent material. "He also wants you shackled." He produced a pair of cuffs that looked thicker than standard issue.

I walked over and took them in my hands to inspect. The cuffs hummed with energy, but not from magic. When I ran a finger around the inside of one, a faint current wobbled the aura around my hand.

Magical inhibitors?

"They glow blue when they're locked," Alec said. "He showed me."

"Be very careful with them," I said, replacing the cuffs in his pack and stuffing the clothes in after them.

"The second we get there, I'm supposed to surrender my pack. If we try any 'cute shit,' he said they have special weapons for that. They'd also see to it that my mom got the harshest sentence. But we—we can do something, right?" His voice broke on the last word, and I watched him struggle to steel himself again.

"Well, I'm not putting on those see-through pajamas." When I cracked a smile, he snuffed out a small laugh.

"Yeah, that could be awkward," he said.

"How much time do we have?"

"Till midnight tonight. At 12:01, my mom gets booked."

With a knuckle to my chin, I mulled our options. Turning myself in would mean death—not only for me, but Alec, and with no guarantee his mother would be freed. After all, they'd had no problem hacking up three perfectly healthy adults for their organs and a fourth for his blood. So, yeah, we'd table that for now. My other idea would take time to execute, and the deadline gave us less than ten hours.

"We first need to find out where they're holding your mother," I said. "And to do that, we'll need to find her here."

Alec looked around. "Wait, *here* here?"

"Here here," I said, pulling my phone from a pocket.

Ricki, who was still at her brothers' place, answered on the tail end of an exchange with someone. "Hey, hon," she said.

"How's it going over there?" I could hear the clamor of nieces and nephews above the lower murmur of adult conversation.

"The kids are building a rollercoaster," she said.

"An actual rollercoaster?"

"Well, a household version—guys, watch the plants!"

"Tony's idea?" I asked as a collective thrill-scream sounded in the background.

"Yeah, he's really taking to this engineering," she said. "How's work going?"

"I'm actually at the college with Alec, and something's come up. I need a hand."

"Hold on a sec." The background noise diminished, then cut out. "All right, I had to go into a bathroom to hear you. What's up?"

"I need an address on someone."

"Does this have to do with the task force?"

"It's a long story, but no."

"Name?"

"Jennifer DeFazio."

She hesitated. "Your ex-girlfriend?"

"Yeah, but it's to help Alec's mother over there. It's urgent."

"Fine, but while we process the search, you're going to tell me what's going on."

"Deal. I have Jennifer's date of birth and two colleges she attended. Oh, and the last name of the guy she married. Will that be enough?"

"Unless she's gone into witness protection. Know if she's still in the area?"

"I hope so." Because if she'd moved to Idaho, our ten-hour window wasn't going to cut it.

"All right, I'm ready," she said.

I gave her the information, then waited while she called it in.

"Jaden says he'll have it for us in five or ten," she said when she returned. "What's going on with Alec's mother?"

I told her the story he'd told me, even the part about the group's demands: handing me over in exchange for his mom. Though every instinct in me wanted to shield Ricki from the truth, she was my wife, not to mention a veteran detective. I may have had an excuse to keep the little girl's death from her, but not this.

"Jesus, Everson," she said when I finished.

"Yeah, not how I was planning to spend my Saturday."

"How's he doing?"

I could hear the mother in her asking. I glanced over at Alec, who had pulled his notepad from his pack and was sketching a runic design.

"Keeping it together."

"What's your plan?" she asked, her tone changing over to concerned wife.

"Do you remember the final victim in the organ-harvesting case last month, Ludwig? Well, when I cast a hunting spell on his hair here, it led me to his shadow version over there. I'm going to try the same with Jennifer. See if I can locate her there. Should give me a better idea of what we're dealing with."

"Do I want to know how you're planning to get her hair?"

"Not sure yet, but yeah, it might involve a little misdemeanor-ing."

"Hold on, it's Jaden," she said, taking the call. She returned a few moments later. "You're in luck. She's right across the river in Jersey City."

"Yes," I said, pumping a fist. When Alec looked over, I gave him a thumbs-up.

"If I didn't know you," she said, "I'd be a little worried about that reaction to finding your ex."

"And that's why you're the best."

"I'm texting you her address and number now."

My phone buzzed as they arrived. "Got 'em."

"Two years ago, her last name went back to DeFazio," she said.

"Divorced?"

"Looks that way, so remember your vows, buddy. No children listed, either. Unless there's a roommate or live-in parent, she should be *sola*."

"Good to know. Thanks."

"Anything else you need?"

"Not right now. I'm heading back to the apartment to pick up some things from the lab. I'll see if Bree-yark can drive us over to Jersey." I was also going to need to call Hoffman about the stakeout that night.

"I want updates," she said sternly. "Lots of them."

"Will do. Love you, too."

16

Bree-yark swore and downshifted toward the river of brake lights filling the Holland Tunnel. "It's Saturday, fer cryin' out loud!" he barked. "Who in their right mind is taking a weekend trip to North Jersey?"

"Well, they do say the turnpike is lovely this time of year," I joked.

Bree-yark's low chuckle turned into a muttering growl as we came to a complete stop. I'd managed to catch him at the apartment before he started prepping the cement. He'd rented an industrial mixer, another unanticipated budget item. But even though the mixer was costing me by the hour, I was grateful for Bree-yark's company. He had a grounding effect on me. Usually.

"Move, you lame brain!" he shouted, shaking a fist out the window.

"Are you sure you're up for this?" I asked.

"Yeah, if these dipshits would learn how to drive!" Catching himself, he peered at Alec in the rearview mirror. "Pardon my French, kid."

"No worries," Alec said. "I'm fifteen. I've heard worse."

Bree-yark laughed. "I keep forgetting how fast you guys develop. At fifteen, your typical goblin is still being weaned."

I winced at the image, but Alec scooted to the center of the backseat. "Really?"

"Oh, yeah. We don't get our first set of adult teeth till we're twenty-two, twenty-three."

"That's wild."

"Hurts like the devil too."

Though traffic remained gridlocked, Bree-yark's annoyance softened beneath Alec's show of interest. Never lacking for stories, he started into one about the time he tried to teethe on a boar's tail and was dragged for over a mile. I hadn't had time to call Hoffman at the apartment, and now seemed a good time.

"What's up, Croft?" he answered.

"I don't think I'm going to be able to make tonight's stakeout at the club."

"Why the hell not?"

"I have to take a trip to the shadow present." Before he could start grumbling, I said, "Remember how our organ-harvesting case ended at the Discovery Society over there? There's been some fallout."

"So?"

I turned my head toward my door and spoke so Alec couldn't hear me. "The kid who helped us? His mother's been kidnapped."

"Sorry, Croft, but I still don't see the problem."

Just because we were on better terms didn't mean Hoffman had stopped making me want to ulcerate on the spot.

"They need my help," I said. "How's that so hard to understand?"

"Isn't the whole point of that place that it never really happened?"

I opened my mouth to answer, then closed it again. In a way, he was right. There were multiple probable realities, some more substantial than others, but this one involved the widow and son of my shadow. How could I abandon them to their reality? Especially with Alec sitting two feet behind me?

"We have a chance to nab an *actual* kidnapper," Hoffman continued. "And if you're not there tonight, I'm calling it off. This Mr. Funny sounds beyond us, and I like my flesh where it is, thanks. Which means you're coming."

Alec laughed at Bree-yark's arm-waving account of being yanked from his feet by the boar's tail.

"Why didn't you just let go?" I heard Alec ask him.

"I tried, but a baby tooth was lodged in the danged sinew!"

"I can't promise anything," I said to Hoffman.

"I don't get you, Croft. You've got a wife, a kid on the way. Why do you want to piss-ass around over there?"

Another fair point. The previous three times I'd gone to the shadow present, I'd had a rough go—first from a shotgun blast to the face, then from a Cerberus shifter, and finally from Cronus's scythe. Was I doing Ricki and our future daughter a disservice by tempting fate a fourth time? But what was the alternative? To tell Alec, *Sorry buddy, you're on your own*? Shadow present or not, I couldn't do that.

"If I get back in time," I said, "I'll go straight to the club."

"Well, you sure as hell better be back by Sunday noon when we spring rat boy."

"Oh, definitely. I feel like that's our best shot at Mr. Funny, anyway."

"Without the stakeout, it's gonna be our *only* shot," Hoffman reminded me.

By the time we ended the call, traffic was moving again, and Bree-yark was wrapping up his story. Before he could start into another one, I turned to face Alec.

"Since we didn't get a training session in today," I said, "I want you to propose a plan for when we get there. Employing the most efficient use of time and magic, how do we access Jennifer's apartment, obtain hair samples, and leave without being detected?"

His smile straightened. "I'm leading this?"

"You're making a proposal," I said. "We'll adjust it as needed."

I had a plan in mind, of course, but I'd felt bad sidelining him back at my apartment. With the time crunch, I couldn't talk him through the potion prep. Instead, I left him downstairs with Tabitha, who was at least pretending to read the tome I'd given her. When I finally returned from my lab, pockets heavy with vials, I found Alec gazing at one of our family portraits of me, Ricki, Tony, and Tabitha. Even without a scowling cat, the photo had to seem a bizarre contrast to the one he carried in his pack.

"A proposal," Alec repeated now, blowing out his breath. "Okay, my mom—or this version of my mom—needs to be out of the unit. So I go into the building using my vagueness rune and wait outside her door. You call and pretend to work for the building, tell her she needs to move her car."

"She might not have a car," I pointed out.

"Okay, then you tell her that she needs to sign for a delivery."

"That would work," I said. "But I'd first back up and use a listening rune to make sure she's alone in the unit."

I was fully aware that I was teaching my probable son to break and enter.

"Right, right," he said, becoming immersed in the exercise. "Okay, I've done that, and she's alone. The minute she leaves her apartment, I'm in. She may not even lock her door, but if she does, I'll have an opening rune ready. Once inside, I'll look for something with her hair. A brush, her pillow, maybe." He squinted toward the ceiling for more candidates. Not only did he think like me, but he made the same thinking expressions.

"Shower drains make good hair repositories," I said. "And while you're in there, go ahead and grab her razor."

He made a face. "Seriously?"

"Better to err on the side of too much material than not enough."

"Then that should be it," he finished. "I slip back out of the apartment with her hair. How does that sound?"

I turned to Bree-yark. "What do you think?"

"If he can do all that before she gets back, sounds grand."

"Agreed," I said. "But do you really want to be the bagman?"

"It'll be good practice," Alec said. "Plus, I want to see how she's doing here."

I nodded, knowing that if it had been my mother, I would have wanted to see the same. It also felt less intrusive for the son of her shadow to be searching her apartment than her ex-boyfriend. Less creepy, too.

Twenty minutes later, Bree-yark found a parking spot near the front of her building, a twenty-story apartment complex in the Liberty Harbor neighborhood.

"Nice," Alec said of the building.

"Are you still sure about this?" I asked him.

He nodded quickly, as if to override any lingering indecision. By prior arrangement, Bree-yark handed him his phone.

"Text me when you're in position," I said. "I'll text you back once I've made the call."

"Got it," he said, closing his eyes in concentration. I felt ley energy collapse around the vagueness rune he'd had tattooed on his thigh. The next moment, he was gone. The Hummer's backdoor opened and closed.

"Gods almighty," Bree-yark muttered.

"Yeah, he's good," I said apprehensively.

Alec had assured me he'd done his assignment that week, that he'd been able to draw his own runes without the Hermes essence forcing his hand or pushing back. Even so, I wanted Claudius to examine him. The threads appeared a little stronger in my own sight, but concern could have been influencing my perceptions.

"So, you wanna tell me what's really going on here?" Bree-yark asked.

"What do you mean? I'm responsible for Alec, and now his mother needs our help."

"Everson, this is a goblin you're talking to." He tapped his nose. "He smells just like you."

I sighed. "He didn't want me telling anyone."

"That he's your son?"

"The son of my shadow, but yeah."

"I knew it!" Bree-yark pumped a fist and shook my shoulder. "You're a papa! This calls for some celebrating. Open the glove compartment, there should be a couple stogies in back. They might be half-smoked, but—"

"Let's hold off on that," I interrupted, moving my knee in front of the glove compartment as he reached for it.

The enthusiasm in Bree-yark's eyes dimmed, and I immediately felt bad.

"Not that I don't appreciate the thought," I said, "but we should wait until he's ready."

"Nah, I get it. But why doesn't he want anyone knowing he's your son? What's the big deal?"

"Son of my shadow," I amended. "He knows I have a life here, and he thinks he's upsetting it. He's not, but it's going to take more than me telling him that to convince him. He feels especially bad now with this situation with his mother."

Bree-yark nodded, but his smile returned. "Even if you didn't smell alike, I would've guessed it from the way you two are with each other."

"And how's that?"

"You've got that combo of pride and concern going, and he's got that mix of admiration and approval-seeking. Classic father-son stuff."

"You saw all of that? I'm impressed."

"I've gotten more observant in my retirement. But you need to be careful with him." His face turned serious. "He may be on his adult teeth, but he's still at a sensitive age. Take it from someone who had a chieftain for a father: everything you tell him right now is gonna stick. *Everything.*"

"No pressure, right?"

"Hey, I'm just saying you need to pick your battles."

My flip phone buzzed with a message from Alec that he was in position.

"Time to phone the ex," I told Bree-yark, my heart already pounding with the idea. I entered a three-digit code to hide my number and then dialed hers. The line intoned four times before someone picked up.

"Hello?"

It was her, the Jersey accent collapsing the sixteen years between the night she left my dorm room and the present.

"Jennifer DeFazio?" I asked in a deep voice.

"Who's this?" Always straight to the point.

"We have a delivery down here that you need to sign for."

"Okay, I'm actually downstairs now. Are you in the lobby or outside?"

Bree-yark tapped my shoulder and pointed past me. I followed his finger to the woman who had stopped ten feet outside my window, a phone to her ear. Her hair was now shoulder-length, but I knew the stance and profile.

"Shit," I whispered.

"Excuse me?" she said.

I slid down the passenger seat, but my cane was angled such that it stopped me halfway. Bree-yark reached over to move it, but his attempt only drove the handle into my crotch. I let out a low grunt.

"Where are you?" Jennifer demanded.

"Lobby," I said breathlessly. *"The lobby."*

Giving up on my cane, Bree-yark used the steering wheel to push himself upright, accidentally blaring the horn.

There was a moment of silence and then, "Everson?"

"No," I replied into the phone, but Jennifer hadn't meant the caller. When I peeked over, she was staring straight at me. I averted my gaze and lowered the phone.

"Drive," I whispered to Bree-yark from the side of my mouth.

"I would, but there's an actual delivery truck boxing us in. Damned karma."

In my peripheral vision, Jennifer grew larger. A series of hard taps sounded on the glass. When I looked over this time, she was making the lower-your-window gesture. I complied, frowning in confusion.

"Yes?"

"It is you," she said.

"It's me, who? Wait..." I fashioned my expression into one of dawning realization. "Jennifer? Jennifer DeFazio? Wow, what are you doing here?"

She held up her phone. "Is this you?"

"Um, no," I said, blindly searching for my off button. I mashed the keypad instead, the tones sounding through her speaker.

She returned her phone to her purse and crossed her arms.

I grinned. "Wanna grab a coffee?"

17

"Your iced latte," I said, placing the cup in front of Jennifer.

I took the chair opposite her at a small corner table in a coffee shop one block from her building. Jennifer sat back and crossed her legs. She was dressed for summer: shorts, sandals, and a plum-colored blouse. Sixteen years had drawn out the angles of her face and threaded her hair with a few silvery strands, but her eyes hadn't changed. Intelligent and striking, they were a dead ringer for Alec's.

"Still with your Colombian dark, huh?" she said.

"Old habits," I chuckled. Other than the obligatory "you look well" and "how have you been?" we hadn't really talked on the short walk over. The bizarreness of the encounter probably had a little to do with it. "Hey, do you remember that guy in Bryant Park with the coffee cart?" I said. "He's still there, believe it or not."

"Hmm." She took a swallow of her latte, eyes watching me over the rim.

"Look, I know this is…" I circled a hand in search of the right word.

"Weird as shit?"

"That works. There's actually a reason I came."

"That involved pretending to be a delivery service?"

"I wanted to get you alone."

More like *out of your apartment,* I thought, guilt wiggling inside me. At that moment, Alec was stalking around her unit in search of hair samples. *It's for a good cause,* I kept trying to remind myself.

"Asking me to meet for coffee would have worked." Jennifer said. "Crazy, huh?"

When I nodded in accession, she cracked a small smile. At nineteen, the same smile would dimple her cheeks, but now it looked hard.

"I live alone," she said. "Divorced two years ago."

"Oh," I said, feigning surprise. "I'm really sorry."

"Don't be. He was a jerk."

"I'm sorry for that, then."

"I see *you're* officially devoted." Her eyes dropped to my wedding ring.

"Yeah, married this past spring," I said, thumbing the silver band.

"Congrats. Fellow academic, I assume?"

"NYPD detective, actually. Homicide."

"Really?" She combed a hand through her hair and gave me a searching squint. "I would never have guessed. So, it sounds like you stayed in the city?"

"Yeah, I'm teaching mythology at Midtown College."

"Now that *doesn't* surprise me," she said with a wry smile. "At all."

"How about you?" I asked.

"I'm a judge here in Jersey City. Municipal court. Why are you looking at me like that?"

"No, no, that's awesome. It's just that for some reason I pictured you in healthcare."

A small light kindled in her eyes. "Really?"

"You must have mentioned it at some point."

"Not back then. It wasn't until my junior year that I started thinking nursing. I was undecided between that and law school. I finally said, 'screw it' and flipped a quarter. It came up heads: law school. Some days I wonder if I made the right choice," she said, her eyes dimming again.

"I've stood at a couple of those crossroads. It's not like we can ever know."

But even as I said it, I wondered if in the shadow realm her coin had come up tails.

She gave a resigned nod before taking another swallow. "So what did you really want to talk about?"

"Well, um…" I rotated my coffee.

What was I going to tell her? That a probable version of her was in danger and in order to locate her I needed her hair? Oh, and by the way, we got married over there and our kid is presently tossing your apartment?

"I'm sorry about that night," I said, the words just falling out.

"That…? Oh, pizza night." She rolled her eyes, then narrowed them. "Is this part of some twelve-step program?"

"No, not at all. It's just something that's been on my mind."

"It's been over fifteen years, Everson. I got over it."

"Better late than never?"

"Dumped for mythology." She smirked. "I cried for a whole week, you know."

"It wasn't intentional. I only planned to finish the chapter that night and—"

"You got lost," she finished for me. "I used to see you do that all the time. I actually admired your devotion, even after we broke up. Envied it. You always knew exactly what you wanted to do."

"Some things choose us," I said, thinking of my magic.

But how true could that be when in the probable reality I'd chosen her?

"For a long time I wondered if shutting you out had been the right decision," she continued. "But it's like you said, there's no way of knowing. You could have turned out to be an even bigger jerk than my ex."

"Most likely," I laughed.

We had been falling back into something like our old familiarity, but the last sixteen years had changed us in ways such that the familiarity no longer fit. When Jennifer flashed her most genuine smile of our meeting, I believed she was coming to the same realization, a relief for both of us.

"Your driver's here," she said, peering past me.

I turned, surprised to see Bree-yark sitting on one of the plush chairs, licking a wad of chocolate from his thumb. A thick wedge of cake rested on the table beside him. He was supposed to have waited in the car for Alec.

"Is that your son?" she asked.

"*Him?*" I said before realizing her gaze had shifted from Bree-yark to the entrance, where Alec stood just inside the door.

He'd stalled, his eyes cutting between Jennifer and me. I could only imagine the scene from his point of view: his mother and father in casual conversation over coffee. But the longer he stared, the harder he was going to be for me to explain away. With a subtle head-tilt, I directed him to join Bree-yark.

"No," I said at last.

"Looks a little like you," Jennifer remarked as Alec broke off his gaze and made his way toward the plush chairs.

"Think so? No, no children yet."

Jennifer's gaze lingered on her shadow's son as she drained her drink. She shook the cup, making the ice rattle, and set it down. "Well, this has been lovely, but I should probably get going. Dinner date tonight."

"Anything promising?"

"I'll know in a couple hours. Not getting my hopes up."

She stood and shouldered her purse, then kissed my cheek. "I'm glad you found me, even if it started off a little stalkerish. Thanks for the coffee."

"My pleasure. Great seeing you again, Jennifer."

As we hugged, I felt a strange release—maybe I *had* been holding onto a little guilt after all. Beyond her shoulder, Bree-yark and Alec were gesturing frantically for my attention. I turned up a hand behind Jennifer's back in question. Alec began to shake his head and make a thumbs-down gesture. Meanwhile, Bree-yark was pointing at his own head and miming a pair of scissors with his fingers.

Shit. Alec hadn't gotten any hairs from the apartment.

Jennifer gave me a final squeeze, and we separated. "Bye, Everson."

I searched the shoulders of her shirt for a strand I might casually pick away, but I couldn't see anything against the dark fabric.

Do I just ask her?

She reached for her cup. With a lunge, I beat her to it, shifting it out of her reach. "Oh, ah, I'll take care of that."

"Okaaay. Thanks." She left me with a strange smile and a parting wave. I waited until she was outside before lifting the cup, praying I'd seen what I thought I had. Bree-yark and Alec hustled over.

"I couldn't unlock the door," Alec said in a rushed whisper. "I tried every rune I could think of and nothing worked. I finally tried to barge through, but all I did was bruise my shoulder. Please tell me you got one."

"We're in luck," I said.

Jennifer had finger-combed her hair a couple times during our conversation, and now I pinched away a perfect strand from the condensation on her cup.

"Told you Everson had it covered," Bree-yark said, nudging Alec. He pushed the last of the cake into his wide mouth and dusted off his hands.

Alec sagged in relief. "Is she doing all right?"

"She is. She's doing really well."

I could tell he wanted to ask more, but he had his own mother to worry about. "What now?"

"We marinate this in some bonding potion," I said, placing the hair in a small bag holding the potion I'd distilled from the bottle of scotch that Eldred had used on his victims. "It should be ready for casting by the time we cross over. Do you have a good spot for transporting us other than that bush?"

"Not really."

18

"Thanks for the ride," Alec called from the backseat.

"Hey," Bree-yark barked before he could climb out. "Watch yourself over there. And listen to Everson, or I'll twist your ear the next time I see you." Having learned Alec was the son of my shadow, he was taking on the role of surrogate uncle. "Now get moving. I'll be waiting here when you get back."

"We appreciate the offer," I said, gathering my coat and cane, "but there's no telling when that'll be."

Before I could join Alec outside, Bree-yark grabbed my arm and lowered his voice. "Are you sure you can't get me over there?"

"Man, I wish there was a way."

I could have used his muscle, not to mention his company, but the only reason *I* could even make the journey was because I'd been peppered with Hermes magic a couple weeks earlier. I'd thought it was an accident at the time, but Arianna believed the Hermes essence had singled me out, much as it had chosen Alec.

"What's your strategy for when you get there?" Bree-yark asked.

"I don't know if you overheard my call home, but the goal is to find out where his mom's being held. If I think I can get her out safely, I will. If not, I'll pull back and reassess. Fortunately, we have some time." About six and a half hours, to be exact. Given how close I tended to cut things, that felt generous.

"Well, I want you to have something." Bree-yark leaned down and undid a sheath around his ankle.

"What's this?"

"What's it look like? I'm giving you my blade."

"Oh, that's not really necessary," I said, but he lifted my left leg by the pants and planted my foot on the seat.

"I know you've got your sword," he said, "but it's not really good for in close, is it? That's always bugged me about your kit." Bree-yark finished securing the leather sheath around my sock and straightened my pant leg over it. "Now if someone grabs you, you can introduce him to a half foot of goblin steel. It's a straight draw, nothing to fumble with. Be sure to give it a good twist once it's between his ribs."

Conventional weapons weren't really my thing, but when Bree-yark sat up, he was smiling with all of his teeth—a show of extreme pleasure. I returned a tight smile of my own and lowered my leg.

"Thanks..." I said, already feeling the discomfort of the concealed sheath.

"Well, I've got a heap of concrete to lay back at your place. Good luck over there."

As the Hummer pulled away, I joined Alec. Just inside the park, he nodded at the sizable eruption of bushes. "Entrance is around back, but maybe I should go in first so it doesn't look, you know, weird."

"Yeah, good idea."

I glanced around as Alec disappeared behind the foliage. It was late afternoon, the summer sun low enough to have drawn out the neighborhood walkers and bench-sitters. I waited a minute before following Alec's path, breaking through the brush to find myself in a small clearing at the center of the bushes.

"Not bad," I said, already drawing out the bag with Jennifer's hair.

I handed it to Alec to hold. From my satchel, I removed a polyethylene sheet with a premade casting circle, spread it on the ground, and placed the hair inside of it. Alec watched closely as I started into the hunting spell. Soon, the opal end of my cane was inhaling a purple wisp of smoke that climbed from the strand of hair.

"Did it work?" he asked as I drew the cane away.

"We won't know until we're over there. You ready?"

"Definitely."

With a self-conscious glance, he extended his arms toward me, and I clutched them in my own. The bushes blurred, my stomach dipped, and with my next breath, a harsh but familiar scent climbed my nostrils.

As Alec released me, I peered around. A layer of grit seemed to coat our surroundings, but it was an effect of the shadow realm, where *everything* appeared to be grit-coated. A premature dusk dimmed the hazy sky, while drug needles and scraps of old clothing littered the ground at our feet.

"We better get moving," Alec whispered. "This place can get sketchy late in the day." His dark eyes glimmered anxiously from a face that now blended with the growing dimness.

Refocusing on our task, I raised my cane and uttered, *"Seguire."*

The cane jerked in my grip, then drew me around in a half circle.

That can't be right, I thought.

I'd been using the tops of the surrounding buildings to orient myself, fully expecting the spell to draw us north, toward the Discovery Society. I'd been confident that was where the goons were holding Alec's mother. Instead, my cane was pointing in almost the exact opposite direction: southeast.

When I noticed Alec watching anxiously, I said, "I've got a hit."

"Okay, good," he breathed. "Should I go vague?"

I was about to tell him yes—I was already retrieving a stealth potion for myself—when I considered that we were all the way up at 52nd Street. There could be a lot of Manhattan between us and his mother.

"What's the taxi situation like here?" I asked.

"A little like Russian Roulette. Five out of six times they're fine, but there are rogue operators who take riders to some warehouse and hold them for ransom. Every year, a few bodies end up in the rivers that way. Most people call one of the companies and reserve their pickups in advance."

"You wouldn't happen to be carrying a phone?"

"We only have one, and it was with my mom."

"How about a payphone? Any around here?"

His brow furrowed. "A what?"

For whatever reason, those didn't exist in his reality. It looked like we were going to have to give the cylinder a spin. "Let's go with a taxi, then," I said, confident I could handle any rogues. "Lead the way."

I followed him from the bushes into the park. What had been a pleasant late-afternoon scene in my reality looked like a post-apocalyptic nightmare here. The neat arrangement of iron fencing and benches had been ripped out, replaced by heaps of garbage. All that remained of a large monument to a soldier was a fractured stone pedestal that had been sprayed with obscenities and a dire prophesy: HIS JUDGMENT COMETH!

"This way," Alec said, pointing to a beaten-down path through the refuse. Beyond, an occasional car droned down 11th Avenue. The forlorn sound conspired with the grittiness and decay to make me miss home. Even on a psychic level, the place reeked of misery. How did anyone endure here?

"Behind you!" Alec called.

I spun, a shield crackling into place moments before the snaps of small arms fire sounded. A pair of glancing rounds wobbled my protection—a good reminder that I needed to compensate for the shadowy energy I'd be channeling here. I concentrated, upping the shield's power. Beyond, men and women dressed in shabby camo seemed to be materializing from the dense growth.

"Grunts," Alec said.

"What?" I shouted.

"They camp in the parks. Sort of territorial."

Yeah, I'm starting to get that impression, I thought.

With a shouted, *"Respingere!"* I directed the power from my shield into their numbers.

Even using shadow energy, the explosive force felled

branches and knocked the "Grunts" around like paper dolls. An invocation that I'd once relied on to disorganize an attack could now put those same attacks down for good, especially mortal ones. The shooting stopped as suddenly as it had started.

I was turning to usher Alec from the park when a greenish comet grew from his hand and roared past me. The manifestation split into half a dozen fireballs, each one zeroing in on a downed Grunt, lighting them up in a succession of bright explosions. He was going to cook them alive.

"Entrapolare!" I bellowed.

The air around the thrashing Grunts hardened into spheres, and I drew out the available oxygen, reducing the geysers of flames to gushers of smoke. When I'd snuffed out the final fire, I spun on Alec.

"What in the hell are you doing?"

"Helping," he said, closing the hand onto which he'd drawn the fire rune.

"I already put them down," I said, looming over him. "They were no longer a threat. If we're going to find your mom, the last thing we need is a trail of burned bodies. Besides, do you really want that on your conscience?"

The anger gripping my mind was unlike anything I'd experienced because it came from a place of fear. Fear for this boy, the son of my shadow, for whom I'd assumed a huge responsibility. Whether the fire attack had been his idea or it had come from the Hermes essence, he was too young to be dealing in death. Defiance flashed in his eyes as I stared at him, but he quickly dropped his gaze.

"Sorry." It came out as if he'd wanted to add a small "geez" but refrained at the last moment.

"Look, I know they were shooting at us. Your adrenaline

kicked in, and your instinct was to protect us, but think about why we're here. We *cannot* draw attention to ourselves." I started to move past him when a disturbing thought occurred to me. "Have you ever attacked someone like that before?"

"Haven't had to." He tapped his thigh. "Vagueness rune."

"Good. Keep it that way until you've had more training. I also want you to warn me about any hazards like these Grunts from now on, even if they seem common to you. Remember, I'm not from here."

I could see his defiance wanting to reestablish itself, but he nodded.

I led the way from the park, the groans from the downed men and women fading behind us. At 11th Avenue, I watched for an approaching taxi. Alec stood several feet away, clearly wounded from the chastening. Having to dress him down hadn't been pleasant for me, either. My gentler nature wanted to assure him everything was fine, but I needed him to sit with what I'd told him—for his sake as well as mine.

When a taxi finally appeared, I flagged it down. The driver, a man with a smooth head and thick eyebrows, studied us in the rearview mirror. He was clearly sizing us up, though whether to determine our threat level or our value to him as hostages, I couldn't tell. I jumped slightly when the doors locked.

"Where to?" he asked.

"I don't have an address, but I know the route." I assessed the pull of my cane. "You'll start by taking Broadway south."

He grunted at my odd request but pulled out into the sporadic traffic. For the first mile, I watched to see that he was going the right way. His eyes kept reappearing in the rearview mirror. When he crossed Broadway instead of turning, he must have noticed my reaction because he said simply,

"Times Square." He wanted to avoid it for some reason. Sure enough, he rejoined Broadway several blocks later.

Reassured, I refocused on the pull of the hunting spell, which was more or less staying aligned with our southerly direction of travel.

Beside me, Alec was staring out his window at the gray façades. Though I recognized the buildings, most of the signage had changed and everything looked closed. Steel shutters faced block after block of empty sidewalks. We passed a disheveled man running headlong the other direction, one hand balling up the waist of his oversized pants, but I couldn't see what, if anything, he was fleeing. Maybe just the coming night.

Before long, Broadway straightened and we were driving through Greenwich Village, my neighborhood. Depressing only began to describe its abandoned look. As if on cue, it started to drizzle.

"You going downtown?" the driver asked as he snapped on the wipers. The droplets smeared like grease, streaking the windshield with dim lights. I looked at my cane, which had begun a slow pivot eastward.

"Not sure if you'd call it downtown," I hedged, "but it's not much farther."

"An extra fifty if I have to go through the checkpoint," he said.

"Checkpoint?"

Alec nudged me and nodded toward the windshield. Several blocks ahead, lights gleamed above concrete barricades and the silhouettes of armed guards. That was the start of a lot of New York's government buildings. Given the danger level in this version of the city, the checkpoint made sense, but still...

"Can you take a left at the next light?" I asked.

"Chinatown after dark?" he said. "Not on your life."

"How about here?"

The driver pulled over with what appeared relief, and I paid the fare. Alec and I got out and ducked into a doorway on Spring Street, where a metal awning kept the rain off us and helped conceal us from the street.

"Sorry I didn't mention the Canal Street checkpoints," Alec said as the taxi motored away.

"No biggie," I said, already softening my stance from earlier. "You have a lot on your mind. How long has it been there?"

"Ever since I can remember. You can't get through without a government ID or special permission. There's another security perimeter around the Financial District, a permanent wall, but I've never seen it."

I remembered the former wall from my own reality, installed to protect Arnaud Thorne and the vampire bankers of old. Fortunately, our mission didn't involve the Financial District, but that was small consolation.

"What is it?" Alec asked when I blew out my breath.

"The good news is that the hunting spell still has a lock on her." I paused to consult my cane again. "The not-so-good news is that she's somewhere behind the checkpoint. I have an idea where, but that puts us in bad-news territory."

"Where?" Alec asked nervously.

I squinted into the slanting drizzle, gauging the spell's pull to be sure.

"One Police Plaza," I said at last. "NYPD headquarters."

19

A lec slapped the wall with his hand. "They lied! They said I had until midnight!"

"All right, all right," I said, patting a hand toward the ground. "We have to play the cards we've been dealt."

"We're going to get her out, right?"

The security at NYPD headquarters was stout in my reality. Given the Canal Street checkpoints, I had to imagine that the stoutness went at least double here. "Yes, but not by force or stealth," I said. "Not unless you and your mom want to be on the run for the rest of your lives."

Alec was pacing back and forth now, hands balled into helpless fists. When a high hiccup sounded in his chest, I realized he was starting to break down again. Slotting my cane through my belt, I gripped him by the shoulders and lowered my head so I was looking directly into his eyes.

"I know this is hard, but I can't do this alone," I said firmly. "I need you."

He looked away and cycled through several shaky breaths.

"You have to keep it together for me," I said. "All right?"

He nodded. "Yeah. Sorry."

I squeezed his shoulders before releasing him. "I have a contact in the NYPD. It's not a slam dunk, but I think she'll be sympathetic enough to help."

His eyes grew large. "Not your wife."

"The *shadow* of my wife," I said. "And, yes, I know she shot you, but that was before she understood what was happening at the Discovery Society. I'm hoping it was enough to convince her we're the good guys."

"Hoping?"

"It's our best option."

"Color me skeptical," he said. "But Bree-yark did tell me to listen to you."

"And he takes that sort of thing very seriously, so you don't want me going back with a bad report."

When I winked, Alec allowed a tight smile. "Do you even know where Detective Vega is?"

"Fortunately, I had her in mind as a backup before we left." From my coat, I drew a plastic bag containing my wife's hair suspended in a shot of bonding potion.

While Alec took lookout, I repeated the ceremony I'd performed in the park, setting up my premade casting circle in the building's doorway. When my cane drew in my wife's essence while preserving Jennifer's, I gave myself a mental fist bump. Holding two hunting spells was something I couldn't have managed even a year earlier. I stood and moved the cane back and forth in search of a signal.

After several troubling moments that had me wondering whether I'd fist-bumped myself too soon, Alec asked, "Anything?" The question was just out of his mouth, when the cane spun me around toward the north.

"Got her," I whispered.

The only problem was that it was full dark now, and the traffic on Broadway had all but evaporated.

"What are our chances of catching another taxi?" I asked.

"To be honest, we were lucky to get the last one. Private companies take over after dark. Big, armored vehicles with armed escorts. They only work with trusted clients. Is she far away?"

I'd gotten good at gauging distances from my spell's pull. This one felt like it was in the eight to ten mile range. Accessing my mental map, I placed Vega somewhere between north Manhattan and the South Bronx.

"Too far to walk, but I have another idea," I said. "A much safer one."

And if I was lucky, it would also clue me into the magic situation here.

We arrived before a nondescript door in the side of a stone building, and I peered back the way we'd come. Even concealed by magic, I sensed threats around every corner. In the shadow present, fear hung heavy in the atmosphere, much like the ever-present grit, putting me on edge. Maybe that wasn't a bad thing.

"Is this it?" Alec asked, tamping down his vagueness rune enough to take spectral form.

"We'll see." I pulled out my keychain and inserted an odd-shaped key into the lock. It fit, but now came the moment of truth. When I twisted the key, the bolt held fast. I worked the key back and forth. Without warning, the bolt broke from what felt like a scab of rust and the door creaked ajar.

"I'll be damned," I murmured. "My key works here too."

Casting a ball of light ahead of us, I led the way down a short flight of steps. We were soon standing in a room snaked through with thick pipes and lined with old, bolted-down tanks. The smells of metal corrosion filled the air.

"It's an early pump station," I explained, growing the light out to ensure we had the space to ourselves. "In my New York, the Order has wards at strategic intersections of ley energy. The wards sift the energy for signs of intrusion from other realms, mostly nether, and triangulate their exact location."

"And you can hack into this ward?"

"I'm going to try. Need to find it first."

My plan would be to infuse the ward with my hunting spell. Once I had a location for Vega, we could flip to the actual present, take a cab there, and flip back, saving us a few hours and a lot of risk. But as I picked my way across the room, I wasn't sensing an active ward. At a dust-covered wall in back, I raised my cane.

"Rivelare!"

As the Word resounded around the concrete and metal, a large, elaborate sigil glimmered through the dust.

"Whoa," Alec said.

I stepped forward to inspect it, already not liking what I saw.

This ward had been drawn by Lich, a First Saint of my Order who'd been corrupted by an ancient being called Dhuul the Whisperer. Lich murdered his fellow saints, then spent the following centuries harvesting magic-users to create a portal to Dhuul. Indeed, one of the main functions of his wards had been to keep tabs on fellow magic-users.

After Lich's death, the Order in exile cleaned the wards of his influence and updated them. But this ward had been neither cleaned nor updated, suggesting the Order had never come out of exile. And the fact that this shadow world still existed meant Lich had never completed his portal to Dhuul, which didn't seem to follow.

My hand trembled as I reached toward the symbol. I could never recall that history without seeing my father plunge into the abyss to repel Dhuul. It was my final memory of him. Collecting myself, I drew a finger through the dust on the wall. Someone had idled these wards down long ago and hidden them.

Who, though? And why?

Noting my hesitance, Alec asked, "What's up?"

As I backed from the ward and cleaned my finger off on my coat, a vague paranoia gripped me. It may well have been caused by the same ambient fear I'd felt outside, but I was ready to leave.

"It's a no go," I said. "C'mon, we'll have to transport back and ballpark it."

Anything that got us closer in the actual present would mean less to traverse in the shadow, but as I eyed the ward a final time, something told me not to make the jump from down here.

I turned from the ward at the same moment a large gray hand appeared above one of the pipes near the steps leading out, talons scraping metal. A misshapen head followed, its lump of a nose sniffing wetly.

Crap, ghoul. Big one, too.

Motioning for Alec to stay behind me, I reached into a pocket for another stealth potion. The creature must have picked up our footfalls from a lower level and come up to investigate. I'd taken ghouls down before, but they were stubbornly death resistant. Pains in the asses, to be honest. The effort it would take to kill this thing would only alert the rest of its pack. Ghouls almost never hunted alone.

With a whispered Word, I ignited the tiny gems inside my stealth potion's suspension, activating its magic. The concrete enclosure amplified the hisses. I tried to muffle the sound with my coat, but the ghoul had already swung its head toward us. Yellow eyes flashed through the gloom, and an ungodly cry broke from its yawning mouth. A chorus of answering cries echoed from below.

Wonderful.

Returning the potion to my pocket, I shouted, *"Fuoco!"*

My sword's second rune glowed brightly, sending fire the length of the blade. The creature drew back.

"Stay behind me," I called to Alec, who had wisely activated his vagueness rune.

I side-stepped toward the exit, holding the sword before me. By the time we reached the pipes, the ghoul was crouched in a displaced section of flooring, cringing behind a scarred forearm. Though this one was easily four-hundred pounds, ghouls caught out alone had taut survival instincts, which usually meant flight.

I sensed Alec stopping behind me to stare.

"Keep moving," I told him as I held the fiery sword toward the creature.

The ghoul cowered lower from the roaring heat, but now sections of floor grating were clanging around us. Unaware of the fire threat, the rest of the pack was bursting from the lower level. With impressive speed and pack instincts, they scrambled to all sides of us. More ghouls emerged behind them. They remained back, wary of the fire, but they had numbers now—and fresh meat in front of them.

"Protezione!" I called.

As a wall of hardened air encircled us, Alec relaxed his vagueness rune.

"I would have warned you about them," he said, peering from one snarling face to another, "but I don't even know what these things are."

"Ghouls. When they're found in cities, it's going to be underground, so I don't want you going into any drainage systems or defunct subway tunnels." I didn't know why I was using this as a teaching moment—some combo of paternal and professional instincts—but now that I'd gotten started, I went ahead and finished. "They can only be killed by decapitation or extensive brain trauma. We eradicated our ghouls a couple years ago, but it appears you still have an infestation issue."

"Man, they're gruesome," he remarked.

One edged forward and swiped at my protection. As sparks tumbled from its own talons, the creature jumped back, but it was only a matter of time before they would grow bold enough to launch a full-scale assault. And as my brief encounter in the park reminded me, my shield wouldn't be up to it. I readied my sword to hose them with fire, drive them back into hiding, but another idea occurred to me.

"Those fireballs I lectured you about in the park earlier?" I said.

"Yeah?"

"Let 'em rip."

Alec hesitated. "Really?"

"These aren't people, and your fire won't kill them. It'll chase them off, though."

Bending over his open hand, he rendered a design on the palm with his silver-flecked grease pencil.

"It's ready," he said, his eyes bright with nerves.

With a Word, I released light and force from the shield, sending the giant-sized creatures staggering over pipes and into walls.

"Go," I said.

The green comet that burst from Alec's hand shot to the ceiling, where it pulsed like a beating heart. The scrambling ghouls stopped to stare, clearly not sure what to make of it. I was beginning to wonder if the manifestation was going to do anything but sit there when it began slinging fireballs. They roared around and exploded into the ghouls' gray hides, producing guttural cries of surprise and terror.

Soon the creatures were dashing in all directions, desperately trying to climb back down. My shielding shook from a ghoul's collision, but one by one, they disappeared below the floor. The comet continued to send fireballs after them until it exhausted itself and collapsed around a glimmer of emerald light.

"Nicely done," I said, not sure whether I was complimenting him or the Hermes essence. "Let's go."

We left the room, breaking through a wall of smoke as we climbed the steps and emerged onto the street. I locked the door, then sealed the frame with magic for good measure. It wouldn't last, but it would keep the ghouls from giving chase. I turned to Alec, unsure now of the wisdom of having encouraged him to channel the god's power. Had I overcompensated for my earlier strictness?

"You feel all right after that?" I asked casually.

"Are you kidding? I feel great! Did you see the way it tracked them down?"

"It was impressive," I admitted. "But that was an emergency situation, and we were dealing with ghouls."

I felt the tension of wanting Alec to exercise constraint,

but not wanting him to feel so constrained that he would hesitate to act in the face of danger. Especially since the danger here was so considerable.

Alec nodded, turning serious. "No, I get it."

I was tapping back into my hunting spell on Vega when the sound of a motorcycle's engine rose a block away. Several more followed, converging toward us. What now? I dug for the stealth potion I'd activated inside the pump station, only locating it as a bike roared around the corner, its headlight bearing down on us. More of the convoy appeared, thick tires skidding into blocking positions.

Dropping the potion, I redoubled my grip on my cane.

"Protection up," I told Alec.

20

The rest of the bikers arrived, all of them with thick beards, leathers built up like armor, and bearing an assortment of holstered firearms. The biggest of the group, the only one not in leathers, walked his Harley forward on boots that looked capable of stomping craters into the asphalt. Beneath a pair of wraparound shades, a thick red beard hung to his chest.

"Who are they?" I whispered to Alec from behind our shield.

"Don't know," he whispered back. "A lot of gangs operate in the city, but their territories are always shifting."

I swore inwardly. This version of New York was just not going to let us be subtle.

The lead biker stopped about fifteen feet in front of us, revved his engine hard once, then let it idle to a chop. Tatted arms stretched the sleeves of his black T, nearly splitting them. He stared at me from the voids of his shades as rain continued to slice down and drip from the end of his beard.

"What the fuck are you doing?" he demanded in a burly voice.

"We got caught out," I said. "We tried to find refuge behind that door, but there's something in there." I nodded to indicate the pump station. Though I'd used my wizard's voice, Red Beard smirked, and the rest of the bikers broke into laughter.

"Something funny?" I asked.

"*We* don't even go in there," he said.

"And you are...?"

I was pushing on purpose, trying to force their hand. Then I'd be able to react appropriately, which looked like it was either going to involve scattering them across the street or leaving for the actual present. Maybe both.

When Red Beard dropped his hand from his bike's grip, I braced for him to draw a weapon, but he tugged up the sleeve from his left shoulder. Amid the dark ink, a pale, medallion-sized symbol glowed into view. It depicted a skull wreathed in angel wings, while letters too distant to read cupped the bottom.

"Street Keepers," he said.

"Wait, I've heard of them," Alec whispered excitedly. "They're a volunteer group that patrols the city, but I've never seen them."

"Good guys?" I asked him from the side of my mouth.

"Supposed to be."

Red Beard's tattoo shimmered with what was clearly preternatural protection, no doubt what had blunted my voice a moment ago. I shifted to my wizard's senses. All the bikers were similarly marked, the protection bonding them in a soft light at odds with their muscle bikes and tough exteriors.

"Where you trying to get to?" Red Beard asked.

"Uptown," I said. "I don't have an address, but I know the way."

Red Beard glanced back at his gang. Hands eased from holstered grips, and a second biker walked his motorcycle forward.

"Hop on," Red Beard told us.

I looked at Alec in a way that asked whether he was absolutely sure about these guys. He gave a small shrug as if to say he hadn't heard anything bad and they were offering free rides. I tuned into my magic, but I couldn't get a hard answer there, either.

"Take the second bike," I told Alec. If things went sideways, I wanted the leader.

"I appreciate this," I said to Red Beard as I straddled the seat behind him and found places for my feet.

The broad back of his shirt was damp and smelled strongly of gasoline. Hoping he wasn't expecting me to bearhug him, I felt around, eventually finding a bar behind the seat. I gripped it one-handed, leaving my cane-hand free for the hunting spell and anything else I might have to cast in the event of an emergency.

"If we take Third Avenue north, we'll be good for a while," I said.

Red Beard grunted and gunned the bike from the curb with such force that I nearly toppled over backward. The other bikers followed, the collective firing of engines filling our urban canyon with a deafening blat. The rain remained a drizzle, but our increasing speed turned the slender droplets into needles. Several bikers spread onto parallel streets. I peered back to make sure Alec was still behind us, relaxing when I made out his hoodie flapping past the biker's right shoulder.

"Didn't want to say anything in front of your boy," Red Beard shouted above his engine, "but that was really fucking stupid. You don't go looking for refuge behind random doors. Good way to get yourself dead."

"I'm not from here," I shouted back. "Just arrived and got turned around."

"A brother Keeper heard some commotion and put out the call," he said, explaining how they'd found us. By the angle of his head, I could tell he was waiting for me to share what we'd encountered and how we'd escaped, but I held fast to my rule in these situations: listen more, say less. And I had plenty of questions of my own. Namely, what sort of supernatural was sponsoring these guys?

"It's great what you do," I said. "How did you get started?"

"Look around you. The city needs us."

"Do you work for someone?"

"We were called."

He must have abided by the same rule as me because he was clearly holding back.

"I imagine you've made a few enemies with what you do," I said, trying another approach. "Don't you feel vulnerable out here on your bikes?"

He hesitated before answering. "We've come to some understandings."

He raised a fist—something he'd done a couple times already—and I looked up in time to catch a figure in a passing window. A sentry, possibly for one of the gangs Alec had mentioned. If so, the Keepers had worked out truces for safe passage across their turfs. But what did they hold as leverage? The answer had to be connected to whoever had imbued their tattoos with protective magic.

Given the urgency with Alec's mom, I shouldn't have been this preoccupied with the question, but I was trying to get some sense of the magical landscape here. Maybe it would explain what had become of Lich and the other magic-users —and that included my own shadow, dead before Alec was three. I made one last-ditch attempt.

"Where did you get your Street Keeper tattoos?"

"Don't remember," he replied in a brusque tone that told me he was done answering questions.

We continued up 3rd Avenue, the bikes roaring in and out of different formations. A few times Red Beard cut from our course before rejoining it several blocks north, abiding by some territorial tapestry, invisible to me. At the southern end of Spanish Harlem, the pull of my spell began to angle westward. When it had almost completed a ninety-degree arc, I pointed past Red Beard.

"Left at the next light."

He nodded and turned onto 111th Street, which was nearly to East Harlem. The cane tugged savagely as we passed a depressing line of brownstones. I'd been wondering if the spell had caught Vega out on a case, but this looked like home. I had Red Beard take us up another block before pulling over.

"This is it," I said, climbing off. "I really appreciate your help."

He gripped my offered hand hard enough to shift the bones. "Don't let me catch you out at night again, especially with your boy." Though he meant it as a health-and-safety warning, the gravel in his voice made it sound threatening.

"Is there a way I can contact you?" I asked. "You know, just in case—"

"We're a volunteer patrol group," he said, cutting me off. "Not muscle for hire."

He took off. The rest of the Street Keepers merged behind him, the collective rip-roar like a parting notice to the neighborhood. The bikers careened from view, taking the secret of their supernatural ally with them.

"Man," Alec said, coming up beside me, "they're even more badass than I pictured."

I couldn't argue with him there, but we needed to get back to our objective—finding help for his mother. With a Word, I drew the shadows around us like a shroud and led the way toward Vega's apartment.

21

"She's alone," I whispered, pulling my ear from the wall as I dispersed the listening spell.

"You sure?" Alec asked.

"I know my wife's breathing, and hers is the only one inside."

We were in a dim corridor tagged with graffiti. If there had been any doubt about my hunting spell, or the sound of my wife's breaths, someone had sprayed MURDER PIGS across the door, the letters now faint and running from an attempt to remove them with a chemical solvent. And I'd thought Ricki's old apartment building in Brooklyn was grim. The shadow realm had a way of taking everything to another depressing level.

"Now what?" Alec asked.

I raised my fist and knocked. "We talk to her."

"Should I go vague?" he asked nervously.

"She won't shoot you."

"How do you know?"

Because I wanted to believe we'd connected in the basement of the Discovery Society and that, at her core, shadow Vega was the same beautiful, benevolent being as my wife. I hoped to hell I was right.

"Stay behind me," I said, just to be safe.

Beyond the door, a television went mute and footsteps approached. A sharp scrape followed—the sound of a privacy cover swiveling from the door's peephole. A point of light appeared momentarily before being blotted out.

"Who is it?" Vega asked.

I cleared my throat. "Everson Croft."

"Who's with you?"

"This is my son."

In my peripheral vision, I caught Alec looking over at me.

"What do you want?" she demanded.

"I need to talk to you."

"What about?"

"His mother is in police custody under a bogus pretext," I said. "Someone at the Society is trying to get to me. We need help."

"You shouldn't be here."

"I don't know anyone else. Please."

A moment of silence followed in which I could feel Alec's eyes cutting between me and the peephole. We were at a juncture with several directions things could go, most of them dire, some *really* dire. The fate of Alec's mother, as well as my own, hinged on what happened next.

Bolts turned. The door opened a pair of inches to reveal a wedge of shadow Vega backlit by the blue-gray glow of her television. Lines of distrust accented her one visible eye. Even though it was like seeing the twin of my wife—almost her, but not quite—my first reaction was profound concern for her wellbeing.

"How are you?" I asked.

She opened the door the rest of the way, and a bucket of ice dropped into my stomach. From her brow to her jawline, the left side of her face was a canvas of dark bruising. Her eye looked as if it were opening again after a period of complete swelling, the white shot through with old blood. She'd been seized and thrown by a shifter during the final showdown in the Discovery Society, but she hadn't looked like this.

"What happened?" I demanded. "Who did this to you?"

It just came out, my initial shock roaring up into a white-hot froth. Something seemed to kindle in the depths of her eyes—a reaction to the sincerity of my outrage, maybe—but it quickly dulled again.

"Car accident," she said.

Her words came out ponderously, and now I picked up the scent of liquor. She'd been drinking, probably why she'd opened the door. But her manner also suggested defeat, something I hadn't seen in her the last time either.

"Can we come in?" I asked, pushing a little power into my voice. It probably wasn't necessary. The disinterest on her face matched her loose T-shirt and gray sweatpants as she moved to one side.

Alec and I stepped into the living room, and she locked the door behind us. I recognized my wife's touch on the decor, but this Vega appeared to have given up on housekeeping. She limped past some tossed-off clothes to the couch where she'd been sitting. A small bottle of scotch and a glass with about a finger left sat on the coffee table. She was drinking it warm, no ice. As she sat heavily, the right cuff of her sweatpants drew up enough to reveal a plastic strap and what looked like a vintage pager.

Ankle monitor?

The wall above her was covered in framed photos. I recognized some of her brothers in the family shots, and there were a few of her wedding. Maybe it was an effect of the shadow realm, or maybe it was my own very obvious bias, but their faces looked cheerless. No children, either. I'd already had the pleasure of meeting her husband, a bruiser named Jag who led at least one Sup Squad unit here. Was he responsible for Vega's battered state? The idea set off another wave of fury, but I refused to believe she would have stayed with someone like that. My gaze fell back to her ankle monitor.

Unless she was forced to.

"Where did you disappear to?" she asked.

"You mean after the Discovery Society?" I took a seat at the other end of the couch, and Alec chose a chair, though I noticed it was the one farthest from Vega. "I called help for you, and then I went home."

"And where's home?"

"West Tenth Street."

"Bullshit," she said, though with no real care.

"Where did you go that night?" I asked, turning the questions on her. "What happened after I left?"

She waved a hand as if it were unimportant, but I was watching her expression. Beneath the heaviness were grooves of pain. She finished off the scotch in her glass, eyed the bottle as if to pour another, but left it. "How are you even alive?" she asked, setting her glass down. "I did background on you. You have a death certificate from twelve years ago."

That explained her reaction to our earlier encounter. "Where and from what?" I asked, leaning forward.

"Venice, Italy. The report just said 'accident.'"

So Alec's mom had told him the truth. But Venice?

"I saw some of the feats you pulled at the Society," Vega

said. "Was Venice just another magic act? Fake your death so your wife and son could collect the insurance?" Now she did pour herself another shot.

"It's a lot more complicated than that."

"I bet." She tipped the shot back. "Are you a Keeper now?"

"A Keeper?"

"I have ears. They were in the neighborhood right before you showed up, and you *do-gooders* seem a natural fit." She said "do-gooders" in a tone that was cynical at best. But though I had a lot of questions about the Street Keepers, they weren't our reason for coming. I angled my body toward her.

"I know we got off to a rocky start a few weeks ago, but I hope you understand now that we're on the same side."

She shrugged. "I'm off the force."

A charge went off in my chest. "What? Because of what happened at the Society?"

Her tight smile was all the answer I needed. She'd given her version of events to her higher ups, but it was the wrong version. It implicated Eldred, the leader of the Society of Cronus, who'd clearly had powerful ties in the city. When they tried to change her story, she stuck to her guns. That was the Ricki Vega I knew. They must have taken her badge and then arrested her to destroy her credibility. The defeat I saw on her wasn't from her injuries; it was from being denied her life's calling. That was what had broken her. It also explained why she'd let us in. She had nothing left to lose.

I wanted to close the three feet between us, wrap her in a protective embrace, tell her it would be all right, and then wreak mass destruction on the responsible parties. But with me being a stranger, the first part wouldn't go over very well.

"I'm sorry," I murmured, not knowing whether she heard me.

"So, yeah," she said. "There's nothing I can really do for you."

"What about your husband?" I asked. "Is he still on the force?"

"It's complicated."

"Where is he now?"

"Night duty."

"Hey, uh, can I have a glass of ice water?" Alec asked.

I started to shake my head to tell him that now wasn't the time and Vega was in no condition to be playing host, but an insistence in his eyes stopped me.

"Sure," Vega said, laboring to stand. I had to resist helping her. "Want anything?" she asked me tiredly.

"No, thanks."

As she limped toward the kitchen, Alec waved me over.

"That's him," he whispered, pointing at a framed photo of shadow Vega and her husband on the end table beside him.

Who? I mouthed.

Alec waited until the tap in the kitchen turned on before whispering, "The one who grabbed me, who told me to bring you in."

More charges went off in my chest. "Her husband? Are you sure?"

But it explained how he'd been able to pick up Alec's mother on suspicion. It explained how she could be charged at midnight. And it definitely explained why she was being held at 1 Police Plaza. But did Vega know?

"I think we should get out of here," Alec whispered.

The tap shut off. I was peering toward her returning foot-steps when the front door broke open and something went off with an ear-splitting bang. I staggered backward, half blind, as a cacophony of shouting sounded.

22

I shoved Alec back with an invocation, toppling his chair. The recoil sent me over the top of the couch, and I landed in a narrow alley between couch and wall. I pawed around for my cane, still half-blind and mostly deaf from the flash-bang grenade. Smoke burned my lungs as thudding boots entered the apartment. Instincts had gotten me to this point, but getting out was going to require clearer thinking.

Recovering my cane, I murmured, *"Protezione."*

The air around me wobbled into a shield, and I peeked over the top of the couch. Beyond the smoke, a team of armored men was spreading into the room. Aiming my cane at Alec, who was still down, I yanked him into an adjoining room and sealed the door. Vega must have retreated into the kitchen because I couldn't see her. I still didn't know her role, but I fashioned a wall of hardened air over the doorway to keep her safe.

Now for the goon squad.

A barrel pivoted toward me. I ducked a moment before gunfire chewed away the top of the couch. These guys weren't screwing around. I kicked myself to the couch's edge and aimed at the shooter's lower half.

"Vigore!"

The force invocation took out his legs, flipping him into the air. I directed another force at his neighbor, slamming him in the chest, sending his armored body into a wall. Photos and plaster spilled down around him.

Gunfire from the other goons tracked me. Rounds punched through the couch, a couple caroming off my shield, wobbling it. I was digging desperately inside a coat pocket, my brain still too rattled to recall my storage system, when cold glass numbed my fingertips. Not the potion I'd wanted, but it would do.

"Ghiaccio!" I cried.

The cap blew from the tube and a hoary cone roared into the living room. The subzero assault met the shooters, petering out their gunfire. Two men toppled over, one against a wall and another to the floor, ice shattering from the joints of his suit. I rose, directing the attack at the shooters I'd dropped a moment earlier.

As the pluming frost storm petered out, only one man remained standing. The final one to breach the apartment, he'd entered in a wide stance, giving his large frame an ample base of support. I directed the remaining attack at him, ensuring he was thoroughly coated, before tossing off the empty tube.

The apartment fell preternaturally still. I emerged from behind the couch, my breath sending up large plumes, and limped through the wreckage until I was in front of the standing man. I didn't have to see the face beyond the encrusted visor to know it was Vega's husband, Jag. The rest of his armor was coated in thick frost.

"Croft?" a faint voice called.

I looked over to see Vega behind the protective wall I'd fashioned. She was staring around the apartment, crossed arms hugging her shoulders. Had she been party to this? Had she alerted her husband I was here?

A hiss sounded, and I turned back to where Jag had been frozen. In his place was a gushing column of steam. *Son of a—*
A rifle butt thrust out and caught my shielded jaw, knocking me into a side stagger. I garbled out an invocation sufficient to summon a sphere of hardened air around him.

Snaps sounded from Jag's position, like an automatic weapon dry firing, and the enclosure I'd summoned crumbled to sparks. The big man stalked from the dissipating vapors, his suit beaded with moisture. Clearly not the standard-issue body armor the others were wearing. The same was no doubt true of his weapon, which he was leveling at my chest. I willed more energy into my protection as another series of snaps sounded. A jackhammer-like force met my shield, shaking me to my mental prism.

"A Pulser," Jag gloated. "Built for the fae, but seems to work pretty good on you too."

That must have been what he'd used to take Alec down outside the Discovery Society, because even braced against the assault, I could feel my muscles spasming. Just as suddenly as it started, though, the snapping stopped. It seemed this *Pulser* needed to recharge between bursts. I sagged, acting as if I were about to face-plant. Jag stepped forward.

Sucker.

I drove the end of my cane into his gut. My magic was still short of optimum strength, but the discharging force was enough to lift him from his feet and thrust him into a plant stand in the corner. Leaves and potting soil flew everywhere as he crashed down. A second force blast knocked the Pulser from his grip. He started to reach for it, then pivoted his fist toward me. From a small nozzle above his wrist, a plume of fire spewed out, bathing my shielded face in flames.

So his suit is more than a giant defroster, I thought, sidestepping to where I could see him again. The bottom of my knee slammed into the coffee table, and I stumbled for balance. Jag's fist broke through the fire and crushed my chin. I was down before realizing I'd fallen. All three-hundred pounds of Jag's armored body landed on top of me.

"Thought you'd go after my wife, you lowlife piece of shit?" he said, closing his gloved hand around my throat.

"And grabbing Alec's mom wasn't a dick move?" I grunted back.

I dug under his fingers while seizing his throat with my other hand. Though I'd lost my cane, I could still use my body as a conduit. Incanting, I pushed power into my hand, crushing his neck protection. Though shielding defended my own airway, I could feel a current pulsing through his glove, disrupting my magic's cohesion. It didn't help when he started punching me in the side of the head.

But each blow only made me angrier as I pictured him doing the same thing to Vega. I willed more power through my grip, further collapsing his throat protection. Beyond Jag's visor, his face reddened and the whites of his gritting teeth grew into view. I set my own jaw as I drew in every joule of available energy. It was magic versus technology and a question of which would yield first.

"Let him go!" Vega shouted.

In summoning the surrounding energy, I'd dissolved the manifestation walling her off in the kitchen. She appeared in

the living room now, a pistol in her two-handed grip. I didn't
have the power to repel bullets. Everything was going into
crushing her husband's throat before he could crush mine.
His eyes cut over, then stuck in a strange way that made me
look too. Vega's weapon was aimed at him.

"I mean it!" she said.

Jag didn't believe her, evidently, because his grip tightened, and my shield wobbled beneath the disruptive current
in his glove. Fortunately, I had an overprotective goblin for a
friend.

I released the hand squeezing my neck, drew the blade
from my ankle sheath, and swung it into the box-shaped pack
on Jag's back. Goblin steel punched through the outer casing
in an explosive burst, and I gave the blade a violent twist.

The grip around my throat suddenly relented, and my
shielding hardened. A torrent of smoke rose from Jag's back.
I'd disabled his power source. With an adrenaline-fueled
invocation, I drove him onto his back and raised my fist,
intent on driving it through his visor and into his shocked
face.

"You too!" Vega shifted her aim to me. "Back off!"

I knew that tone from the actual Vega—she wasn't
kidding. I released Jag's throat and moved away, panting hard.
Her weapon tracked me until I was sufficiently back, then cut
to my left.

A door opened, and Alec emerged from the room I'd
sealed him inside. His wide eyes took in the scene: armored
bodies covered in ice, smashed furniture, heaps of frost.
When he spotted Vega, he flinched. But she moved her
weapon back to me as her husband pushed himself to a
sitting position.

"What the hell are you doing?" he rasped at her.

"Me?" she said. "What the hell are *you* doing? Kidnapping? Ransom?"

"Yeah, to catch him." He thrust a finger at me. "He's a wanted man."

The rounds littering the floor were a nonlethal variety, I realized.

"We talked about that," she seethed.

He lowered his voice. "I'm doing it for you, baby."

"Did I ask you to?"

Jag looked over at me, nostrils flaring from our combat. He thrust himself to his feet—or attempted to. With the power source disabled, the suit was too cumbersome and he stumbled for balance.

"Stop!" Vega shouted.

She slammed her palm against the breast of his suit, sending him against the wall at his back. Her dark eyes blazed, the anger having burned off the alcohol and defeat in her system. It seemed absurd now that I'd ever thought she would allow her husband to hit her. The injuries had clearly come from somewhere else.

"Are you cool?" she demanded.

"Yeah, babe," He showed a hand. "I'm cool." He adjusted his footing so he was no longer dependent on the wall to stay upright. "But what're we gonna do about him?"

"First, you're going to release the boy's mother," she said. "Then they're going to walk."

I moved over to where Alec was standing, hope kindling inside me. Jag looked from us to his downed men. The ice encasing their armor was just starting to glisten, and a couple of the men rocked back and forth.

At last he shook his head. "I can't do that."

"You *will* do that," she said, "and you'll do it now."

He took her hands gently. "You don't understand. I called the Iron Guard already. They're on their way."

Jerking her hands free, she thrust her chin up at him. "You did *what?*"

I raised a finger. "Can I ask who the Iron Guard are and why that's a problem?"

Vega paced toward me and held out her hand. "Your knife?"

I was still holding Bree-yark's blade, I realized. Though I had no idea how she planned to use it, I knew better than to question her. I turned it around, hilt in the offering position. She took it, wedged the blade under the plastic strap at her ankle, and severed it cleanly. The monitor dropped to the floor.

"Thank you," she said, returning the knife.

"What are you doing?" Jag asked. "I just told you the Iron Guard were coming."

"Fuck the Iron Guard," she said.

Vega disappeared into a back room. Jag tried to follow, but she slammed and locked the door in his face. He peered back at us, lips thin with frustration, and removed his helmet. He spoke softly into the doorframe.

"Can we at least talk about this?" he asked.

"Any idea who the Iron Guard are?" I asked Alec.

He shook his head tightly, clearly nervous about being in the same apartment with the woman who'd shot him and the man who'd interrogated him, but no doubt more concerned for his mom. His gaze moved from the fallen men to me. "But I have a feeling they're going to be worse than these guys."

I didn't say it, but so did I.

23

When Vega emerged a couple minutes later, she looked like a different person. She'd swapped the T-shirt and sweats for a black tactical vest and pants and pulled her hair into the all-business ponytail I was used to. A sidearm was holstered at her hip, while the bulky duffle bag over her shoulder suggested more weaponry. It banged against the doorframe as she shoved her way past Jag.

"Where are you going?" he asked.

She turned to me and Alec. "I'll see what I can do about releasing your mom—I still have a couple honorable contacts inside the NYPD—but first we have to get someplace safe. Seems my apartment fails that test."

The small military pack on Vega's back looked like the bug-out kind. Wherever she was going, she wasn't coming back anytime soon.

Jag watched helplessly. "I just don't get why you're doing this."

"Because I'm out of booze to drink and fucks to give. Join

us if you want, but the train's leaving. Before your *friends* get here," she added sharply.

"All they want is this guy!" He jabbed a finger at me as if I were an inanimate object. "They'll release the mom, and you'll be reinstated. Everything goes back to the way it was. You're going to throw that away?"

When Vega spun on him, storms flashed in her eyes. "Throw *what* away? A life of lies and—and thuggery? Of ruining innocent lives because someone tells us it's our duty? I didn't sign up for this shit."

He looked like he was ready to shout, but he clamped his mouth and started again. "Just think about what you're doing, babe," he said softly.

I instinctively tensed at the *babe*, but I was trying to keep up with the rapid developments.

"How about you think about what you're doing," Vega told him. "What you've already done."

She made eye contact with me as she strode from the apartment. I motioned for Alec to follow and took up the rear. At the doorway, I peered back. Jag was standing among his downed men, smoke still leaking from his battery pack. His face was a clumped-up mass of emotions, but he made no move to follow us.

"I didn't know he was involved in the abduction," Vega said curtly. "I'm sorry."

She opened the door onto a stairwell and started down, her strength and purpose seeming to return with every step. Three floors down, we emerged into a small garage crowded with civilian vehicles. Vega looked around before veering toward a burgundy-colored SUV. She removed a small device from her pocket and waved it back and forth until the vehicle's alarm chirped and the doors unlocked.

"Get in," she said.

I climbed into the passenger seat and Alec the back. She repeated the ceremony, this time waving the device over the ignition button. When the button glowed to life, she thumbed it and gunned the engine.

"I'm borrowing it," she explained of our ride. "Mine's over there, but it's going to be tracked."

She threw the SUV into reverse, nearly taking out half the row of cars behind us before slamming the brakes. As we squealed to a stop, I caught her glancing toward the door to the stairwell. She was looking to see if Jag was coming. The door didn't budge, and she didn't wait. She slotted the vehicle into drive and accelerated toward a ramp, the metal door to the street already clanking upward.

Heavy rainfall slammed the rooftop as we emerged. Vega studied the street in both directions. I could all but see her mind calculating the most probable route the Iron Guard would arrive by. She took a hard right.

"The Iron Guard are a special security force for the city," she said. "To answer your earlier question."

"Special how?" I asked.

"If they're human, it's only barely. I've seen what you can do, but you don't want to mess with these guys." As she turned toward me, the bloodied eye and battered half of her face waxed into view. "Believe me."

Cold anger gripped my gut. So, it had been them. "What's the city's involvement in this?"

"All I know is someone up there wants you for the murders of Eldred and the organ-harvesting vics. Against all evidence." Her words cemented my theory that she'd stuck to her guns, even under physical coercion, and been fired and arrested as a consequence. Despite my feelings about her husband, it sounded from their exchange as if he may have been the reason she was released alive.

"You should have lied to them," I said.

"About what?"

"What you saw. I'm not worth your life."

"What I did wasn't out of concern for your wellbeing."

"Yeah, I know. You acted on principle, but my point still stands."

Shadow Vega looked over as if trying to gauge who I was and why I cared about her. She returned her attention to the road. "Well, they got what they wanted," she said, her wipers struggling to keep pace with the rain. It was falling hard enough to make rivers of the gutters, while pools grew around clogged storm drains.

"Where are we going?" I asked.

"Six months ago, I interviewed a suspect on a case. Drug smuggler out of east Midtown. He wasn't good for the murder, but I saw enough of his operation that I could have kicked him to Vice. I didn't, though. He wasn't big enough, and if he were, odds were Vice would have just shaken him down. The smuggler doesn't know that. Thinks he owes me a favor, and now I'm calling it in."

"Is his place safe?"

At the moment, I was more concerned for her. Alec and I could transport back to the actual present at any time, but she was stuck in this hellhole.

"Safe is relative in the city, but he's decent as far as dealers go." She raised her eyes to the rearview mirror. "How you doing back there?"

Alec, who had been listening quietly, scooted to the center of the backseat. "I'm fine."

"How's your shoulder?"

"It's all healed, thanks."

"That was fast," she remarked.

Though buried, I could hear the relief in her voice, which was a relief for me as well. At her core, she was the same person I'd come to love. The actual Vega would be relieved to know that, too.

"My dad healed me," Alec said, taking up the father-son ruse.

"In fact, once we get to where we're going," I said, "I'd be happy to address your injuries. I have spells that can repair damaged tissue." I'd been looking for an opening to offer my aid in a way that wouldn't come off as solicitous. Vega wouldn't have liked that, especially this edgier version of her.

"Let's worry about the 'getting to where we're going' part. The smuggler operates out of a building in the East Fifties, near the water."

As we drove through the Upper East Side, I noticed that she was avoiding the main avenues. The hammering rain reduced the passing buildings to dim spangles of light, while sinister shadows hunkered in the occasional doorway, some clearly inhuman. Vega had unhasped her sidearm, I noticed, and the duffle bag she'd stored beside her feet was open, gunmetal showing. Her eyes remained alert.

"Almost there," she said as she turned, the tires sending up a voluminous spray of water.

We were halfway down the block when two military-looking vehicles appeared through the rain, lights off, and barricaded the far end of the street. Swearing, Vega slammed the brakes. The SUV planed over the water and slammed into a curb gushing from the downpour. Our impact and the fast flow turned us around. At the other end of the block, from where we'd just come, two more vehicles rolled into view.

"Dammit," Vega seethed. She stomped the gas, but the tires only spun in place.

"Be ready to steer." I retracted my window and angled my cane down and back. *"Vigore!"*

The blast bore a hole through the downpour, hit the curb, and sent us forward. The tires caught asphalt, and we fishtailed back and forth before Vega gained control, accelerating back the way we'd come. The vehicles blocking the way were larger versions of Humvees. They appeared strange and alien, maybe because of their dim headlights. Beyond the windshields, I made out pale faces.

"Keep going!" I told Vega.

I swung my cane forward, the space ahead of it flashing and crackling into a wedge-shaped manifestation. I drove it between the Humvees and released its energy. The detonation turned the windows to snow and knocked one vehicle onto its side. The other teetered before returning to the street, bouncing on its large wheels. But Vega was already steering through the space I'd created, leaving both vehicles in her wake.

I peered back, but I could barely see anything through the rain.

"They must've spotted us from the air," she said. "It's not like there's a lot of traffic out in this weather." She hammered the steering wheel in frustration as she accelerated away from our destination.

"Are they behind us?" Alec asked, twisting around in his seat.

No sooner than the words were out of his mouth, a Humvee appeared in the glow of our taillights and rammed into the rear bumper. Our ride started to skid, then plane, but by some miracle Vega regained control.

I undid my seatbelt. "Open the sunroof!"

She searched until she located the controls beside the steering wheel. As the sunroof retracted, I summoned a shield and rose beneath it. I got my cane out just as the Humvee was coming in for a second ram.

"*Protezione!*" I shouted.

Thanks to the pounding rainfall and weak ambient energy, the manifestation—a slanted wall of hardened air— struggled to take form. But it was enough. The front of the Humvee caromed off it in a burst of sparks, jumped the curb, and leveled a bus stop before disappearing behind the wall of rain.

"They're just going to call in reinforcements!" Vega shouted.

Desperation was creeping into her voice, telling me just how dangerous these guys were.

I lurched as she pumped the brakes. Ahead, two Humvees were bearing down on us. She turned so suddenly that I pitched sideways, nearly losing my cane. The SUV slewed into a narrow alleyway. I quickly righted myself and began calling force invocations, pulling dumpsters into our wake. Seconds later, I heard the lead Humvee smash into one. The obstructions would slow them, but where could we go?

As Vega pulled out onto the street at the far end, I tossed a lightning grenade behind us, then squinted around to get our bearings. We were in Midtown, on a familiar street. We were just a couple blocks from—

"Midtown College," I said, ducking back into the vehicle.

"What?" Vega asked as she powered the sunroof closed.

"Go to Midtown College."

"It's infested. No one goes there."

"Exactly," I said, turning my head. *"Attivare!"*

The sky crackled and lightning seared down, lighting up the end of the alleyway where the grenade had landed. I'd timed it well. A bolt tore through the roof of the lead Humvee and it rolled dead. The trailing Humvee smashed into its rear. As the lightning faded again, the rain buried both vehicles from view.

"Can you render a self-driving rune?" I asked Alec.

I knew he'd never drawn one, but the Hermes essence would know how—just as it had known how to organize my classroom desks the week before. But was it smart to be giving the Hermes essence another excuse to cast through him? Alec blinked at me before something seemed to catch in his brain.

"Yeah, yeah, I think so," he said, pulling his pad and grease pencil from his pack.

My passenger window shattered. An arm plunged through and grabbed the front of my coat. *"What in the—?"* A man was clinging to the side of the SUV like a spider, and he was strong as hell. My seatbelt crushed my sternum as he tried to pull me out. With the belt's material ripping, I held up my cane.

"Illuminare," I grunted.

The opal lit up the man's face, gray and stony with an opaque visor over his eyes. He didn't even flinch from the flash. In his other hand, a blunt rod came into view. Dark red light squirmed around its end.

"Don't let it touch you!" Vega shouted in a voice that came close to terror.

Before I could figure out what the man was holding—or what he even was—Vega thrust her sidearm past my head and squeezed off a deafening series of shots into the being's face. Chunks of flesh broke more than blew from him, but he somehow redoubled his grip on me. Vega swerved as she retracted the weapon. A light pole rushed up. She corrected slightly, and the cement pole nailed the being, sending him tumbling away. The rear of our vehicle keened off the pole, and we bounced back onto the street.

"Iron Guard, I presume?" I asked.

Vega nodded, her face almost as ashen as the attacker's. "Are you all right?" she asked.

"Fine," I said, fixing my coat and chastising myself for letting my guard down. "Thanks for the assist."

"The college is coming up," she said. Ahead, the west wing loomed through the rain.

"Pull up beside it." I dug three stealth potions from a pocket, already incanting to activate them. "I need everyone to drink one." I uncapped them, took mine down in a single tilt, and passed around the others. Even though Alec had his vagueness rune, I wanted him focused on finishing the self-driving rendering.

Vega drank half of hers and grimaced. "This is horrible."

"It'll keep us hidden," I said, circling my hand quickly. "Keep going."

To her credit, she didn't question my claim and finished off the rest. Our ride rolled to a stop, wheels grinding against the curb. I turned to find that Alec had already shot his potion and returned to the rune.

"How we doing?" I asked.

"Done," he said, tearing the sheet from its pad.

"Leave the engine running and the lights on," I told Vega, lifting the duffle bag from her footwell. "I'll carry this."

She got out, the rain flattening her black hair to her head

before she'd even closed the door. Alec placed the rune on the driver seat and nodded that it was good to go. We hustled toward the college's west entrance, the storm that drenched us providing decent concealment.

By the time we were up the steps and huddled in the wedge of deep shadow outside the door, I could feel the stealth potion taking effect. On the street, the SUV we'd abandoned spun its wheels and shot forward, possessed now by Hermes magic. It was nearly to the end of the block when a line of Humvees shot past our position in pursuit.

I waited until the sounds of their motors faded before relaxing my grip on my cane. With any luck, the Hermes magic would elude them long enough to throw the Iron Guard off our scent. And if Vega's warnings were any indication, this was the last place they'd think to go looking for us.

I turned to find her inspecting her transparent-seeming hands. "Can I assume this is temporary?"

"You're not actually disappearing," Alec said. "Just becoming less noticeable. The magic's effect doesn't appear as absolute to us because we're all under its influence, but for everyone else, we're practically nonexistent." Like a good student, he was giving a layman's version of what I'd told him the week before.

"It peaks at twenty minutes before dwindling," I added. "Mine might be shorter since any casting I perform will burn through the magic."

Vega nodded absently, turning her hands over again. Beyond her, the door to the college was secured with chains and thick padlocks that appeared designed less to keep people out than something inside. Coming to terms with the potion, Vega followed my gaze to the door-turned-barricade.

"I still think this is a really bad idea," she said.

24

"Do either of you know what's actually inside?" I asked.

Vega was eyeing the chained entrance skeptically. Even Alec had backed away a couple steps, his sneakers squishing in the growing pond around our feet.

"Just that everyone knows to give it a wide berth," he said, before turning to the authority.

Vega pushed a strand of plastered hair from her brow. Though we were out of the rain, water continued to stream around her spectral face. "The vagrants moved in first, but something else followed. We found one of our street informants wandering the college grounds, his arm ripped clean from the socket. The NYPD sent a team in, but it was a massacre. This was before the Sup Squad. The surviving officers gave conflicting accounts of what they encountered, from hairy beasts to undead beings."

"Sounds like more than one type of creature in there," I said.

She nodded. "There's been talk of cleaning the place out, or demolishing it altogether, but it's not high on the city's list.

Their solution has been to keep it locked and hope they all kill each other."

"Are you sure about going inside?" Alec asked me.

"As counterintuitive as it seems, it'll be a good spot to hunker down. The stealth potion will cloak us until I can secure a room and ward it. The Iron Guard won't come looking, and the things inside won't know we're here."

Vega peered down the street. The rain had tapered slightly, increasing visibility. There was no sign of Humvees or Iron Guard, but it wouldn't be much longer before they discovered the SUV was driverless and retrace their route. She drew a shotgun from her duffle bag and slung the bag's strap over a shoulder.

"Can I trust you?" she asked.

"I believe you have it in you." That would have drawn a smirk from my wife, but she wasn't my wife—something I had to keep reminding myself. Before her frown could steepen, I nodded. "Yes."

"Then go ahead."

I faced the door, staff raised, and began incanting. Magic swirled, dropping chains and padlocks to the ground. When I tested the handle, it was still bolted. I started to dig for dragon sand but, recalling the pump station, fished out my keychain. The key for the college slid in the door and released the bolt.

"Stay close," I said.

The door creaked open on rusty hinges. I cast a ball of light ahead of us, drawing the corridor from its blackness. Graffiti-covered walls glowed into view along with streaks of what could have been old blood. I stopped to listen. An ominous series of low thumps sounded, followed by a wail, but both were far away.

I took lead, stepping onto a floor whose tiles had been raked down to cement in places. With Alec and Vega inside, I sealed the door with a force invocation and whispered, *"Fare."* Outside, chains and padlocks clanked back into place, covering our breach. Two large vehicles roared past, not stopping.

I released my breath and whispered, "This way."

Though the college was a nightmarish version of the one I taught in, the layout was the same. I could have made the turns in my sleep. The resident creatures didn't appear to be wandering the main floor at the moment, and the stealth potion kept our footfalls and scents from calling them up.

Every now and then, a concussion would reverberate from a lower level, causing the wing to shudder. I pictured something immense and grotesque shifting in its restless sleep.

With the final turn, I began counting doors. Several were hanging from hinges or absent altogether, but the one that corresponded with my classroom was intact. I turned the knob and eased it open.

My ball of light illuminated a space that had clearly been occupied by vagrants once, aligning with Vega's account. Several torn-up mattresses littered the space, along with scatterings of food packages, empty cans, and general refuse. The few desks left over from the now-defunct college were in shambles. I guided the light to the far wall, where some shredded sleeping bags lay in a pile.

When I spotted a shaggy head of hair, I swore in startlement. And here I'd just been thanking the stars we didn't have any corpses to deal with. Of course, I needed to ensure the corpse was actually dead first. Aiming my cane, I channeled a nudging force toward the lump. With my second nudge, the sleeping bags shook.

"Shit," I muttered, backpedaling.

The figure shot to its feet, way too fast to be a zombie. A pale humanoid stared at my hovering light, pupils shrinking to points inside his blood-red irises. As his gaze moved around the room, Vega raised her shotgun, but I eased the barrel back down. The creature's waxen skin pegged him as vampiric, and my grandfather's ring was pulsing with the power of the Brasov Pact, the medieval agreement between wizards and vampires. There were more efficient ways than buckshot to take out a bloodsucker.

I stepped forward, aiming my fist.

The vampire's slitted nostrils wrinkled and he swung toward us. My magic had burned through enough of my stealth potion that my scent was leaking out. Before he could launch himself, I shouted, *"Balaur!"*

The power of the Brasov Pact gathered in the ring's silver ingot and released with a ground-shaking whoomp. A storm of force and fire met the incoming vampire, slamming him against the far wall. He was apparently of weak stock, because he fell to his hands and knees, and then crumbled to dust. Or maybe his shadow was no match for an actual enchantment from an actual ring.

Either way... "All clear," I said, releasing my breath.

As I spoke a locking spell over the door, Vega crossed the room and swept a foot through the vampire's remains. Alec checked the window, pressing a hand to the welded metal that had been bolted to the outside. It was dented, as if something had pounded on it a few times, but it appeared solid enough.

"I need to start on the wards," I said.

Vega turned from the remains. "I'll call my contact in the NYPD. What's your mom's name, Alec, and when was she picked up?"

"Jennifer DeFazio," he replied. "They got her Friday afternoon or evening, I think. She's a nurse at New York General. Your husband said she'd been stealing narcotics to deal, but I swear she's never done anything like that in her life."

When Vega nodded, I picked up the cold anger in her eyes. She drew what was undoubtedly a burner phone from the small pocket of her pack and made a call. "It's Vega," she said. "I need something."

As she supplied her contact person the details, I produced my tungsten-carbide pen from a pocket and began sketching protective symbols on the door.

"Is there somewhere they can take her that's not obvious?" Vega asked Alec, moving the phone from her mouth.

"There's going to be a phone record of everyone she knows," he said, almost to himself. "Wait. There's an Italian restaurant on West Sixtieth we go to sometimes, or used to. It's called Toscano's. After my dad..." He glanced over at me. "When my mom was single, she used Mr. Toscano's wife as a babysitter of last resort. They lived in an apartment right above the restaurant. She was super friendly, they both were. They never let my mom pay them for babysitting. I'm sure they'd take her in."

Vega relayed the info to her contact and ended the call. "I have someone working on it," she told him. "They'll get back to me."

Alec exhaled. "Okay, good. What about you?"

"I should call 'Grizz.' That's the smuggler's street name," she said with an eyeroll.

When I peered over from my work, she was pressing her

phone to her chin and pacing the floor. I wondered if she was thinking about her husband. Having decided something, she walked to the back of the room to make her call. The content of the conversation was inaudible amid my scratches. I completed the final symbol and blasted copper filings into the grooves. When I stood back, I was surprised to find Vega beside me. Centering myself, I directed power into the copper until it began to glow.

As Vega watched, the radiance reflected beautifully from the rain on her face, but I sensed her thoughts were elsewhere.

"The wards are charging," I said. "How are you fixed for supplies?"

She blinked. "I have plenty in my bag, but I'm not leaving until I know his mother's safe." She angled her head toward Alec, who was sketching my ward designs into his pad. While he was being a keen student, I also suspected he was trying to take his mind off his mom. "I owe him that much," she finished quietly.

Alec closed his pad and joined us.

"Is there anything I can be doing?" he offered.

"There is, actually." I pulled my keys from my pocket and a twenty from my wallet. "There's a twenty-four-hour convenience store across the street. Grab some bottled water and snacks. These two keys will get you in and out of my classroom and the college." That was the reason I'd chosen my classroom among all the rooms on the large campus: access.

"Nothing's open now," Vega said.

"There will be where he's going," I replied.

Alec accepted the keys and cash, then stepped away from us. "Be back soon." In a flash of green light, he was gone.

Vega's gaze lingered on the spot where he'd been standing. "So that's how he got you off the street," she said, alluding to the night he'd foiled her best chance to arrest me. That was also the night she'd shot him.

"Out of the Discovery Society basement, too," I said. "I have some questions about that night."

"*You* have some questions?" She snorted dryly. "How did you know Eldred was behind the murders? Where in the hell did you even come from? And then there was that dinosaur thing," she added, meaning the shifter who had attacked her in the form of a hydra. "But I'm not even going to bother with him."

"How about I tell you while I take care of that." I gestured to the left side of my own face to indicate her injuries.

She peered at the door. "The room's secure?"

"It would take a wrecking ball to get in here. Not that anything's going to try. The symbols I drew also have cloaking features."

"Even with these potions wearing off?"

She may have accepted the supernatural, but like my wife, she maintained a healthy skepticism.

"Even then," I assured her. "Here." I removed my coat, folded it to pillow-sized proportions, and set it in the center of the room. "It's the least disgusting part of the floor."

She made a dubious face as she walked over and lowered herself onto her back. She adjusted my coat until it was cushioning her head in a nice, neutral position. "Do I need to do anything?" she asked.

"Besides relaxing, no."

I sat cross-legged behind her and flexed my fingers. I normally used my cane as a channel for healing magic, but the human-to-human contact felt important. Or maybe I knew it was the closest I would be able to come to comforting this Vega, who had been through so much. She tensed when I cupped the sides of her head, but then she adjusted her body, fingers interlacing across her stomach, and relaxed again.

"You're familiar with prisms, right?"

"Yeah?" she said.

"Well, that's basically what I do. I channel energies that are all around us and transform them into other things: force, light, the power to heal." I paused to incant softly. Warm energy coursed down my arms and emerged as a gauzy haze around my hands. The lines in Vega's face softened.

"I learned about Eldred through my magic," I said. "I tracked him to the Discovery Society, where he was using the organs he'd harvested for a god offering. That's what you walked into. The 'dinosaur' was a guardian in Eldred's service, a hydra. After it flung you, I destroyed the object, a scythe, that was giving Eldred and the guardian their power. I made sure you were safe, and then Alec pulled me out, to a parallel version of the city. A parallel version of reality, really. One where I didn't die. Your turn."

"That simple, huh?" she muttered.

The healing haze enveloped her head now, like swaddling. Her eyelids fluttered open, and she closed them again.

"I woke up in the basement," she managed. "Only I no longer had any injuries. Imagine that." One side of her mouth turned up—she understood that I'd healed her—but her smile straightened again.

"My husband wanted to take me to the hospital, but I started processing the scene. It took our chief showing up to get me to stop. Said we didn't have a warrant for the club's lower levels but that they were working on one. We both knew that was bullshit. By then it was clear what had happened down there. I told him about Eldred and that I no longer considered you a suspect. He had me write the report. That night, a pair of Iron Guards showed up." The lines across her brow deepened momentarily. "They asked if I wanted to change my report, then handed me a piece of paper that implicated you in Eldred's murder. There was a line for my signature. I told 'em to get bent. They kept pushing, kept pushing. Finally, they took me to City Hall. There's a new building they've been operating out of..." The skin around her eyes tensed. "They held me there for three days."

"Did Jag know where you were?" I asked.

"No. They brought him in on the third day. He wanted me to amend my report, pleaded with me. He wanted it all to go away. When I refused, the Iron Guard got me shit-canned from the force, charged with police corruption, and put on indefinite house arrest. They said they were giving me a break because of my husband's loyalty to the city. But if I ever brought up the case again, they'd show no leniency."

"I'm sorry," I said.

"Could have been anyone," she murmured.

I'd seen the Iron Guard up close and personal. Anyone else would have broken down and given them exactly what they wanted, but I didn't say that. Instead, I tried to make my hands as pliant as possible, finger pads pressing softly where the back of her head met her neck. I looked over her face. The bruising was in retreat along with the swelling, restoring the lovely angles of her cheek.

"How long has the Iron Guard been operating out of City Hall?" I asked.

"A couple years. Shortly after the last mayoral election. Why?"

"Because I don't think Eldred was working alone. Someone gave him the scythe as well as a potion he was using to bond his victims. That person also gave my name to him as the prime suspect in those murders. And the person is still obsessed with bringing me in, apparently." I'd looked into some candidates from Greek mythology, witches and sorcerers, but none of them felt right.

"Does the Iron Guard answer to the mayor?" I asked.

"On paper, but I doubt he's calling the shots."

"One of the deputy mayors, then?"

"Possibly. Pitts, if I had to guess. She's one power hungry bitch, and rumor is she and Lowder have a little something-something going on the side."

My hands stiffened. "Wait, Budge Lowder?"

"You know him?"

"Yeah, he's the mayor in my version of the city, too. I helped him get reelected." I didn't know any Pitts, though.

"I'm still not sure how I feel about this 'alternate version of New York' stuff," she said, "but it does explain some things about you. How do you know me over there?"

I hesitated. "Why do you ask?"

"That night at the Discovery Society, you mentioned my father and the reason I got into policing."

"Oh, right, right. I've, ah, worked with you a few times," I hedged. "In an official capacity."

"Explains your familiarity with police procedure. So, I'm a detective over there, huh?"

"The best I know. All done," I said, removing my hands.

Vega stretched her arms toward the ceiling. Symmetry had returned to her face, and the blood was gone from the white of her eye. She tested her left cheek with her fingers and worked her jaw around. Wonder softened her expression, but she seemed to catch herself. "It feels better," she said, sitting up. "Thank you."

As she stood, I rose along with her. "What did Grizz say? Or is that need-to-know?"

"If I can be at the pier near East Fifty-fifth at ten p.m. tomorrow night, he'll take me out of the city. But like I said, I'm not going anywhere until I know your kid's mother's safe."

"Did your NYPD contact say when that would be?"

"I'm supposed to call them at six in the morning for an update."

I'd promised Hoffman I would be back before the wererat was released. Tomorrow morning was going to be cutting it close, but my wards were the only things keeping us safe in this version of Midtown College. Alec reappeared bearing two loaded shopping bags.

"Mission accomplished," he announced, holding them up.

Vega walked over and pulled the receipt protruding from one of them. "Okay, I believe you about this parallel reality thing," she said after looking it over. "I can't say I understand it, but I also don't think you'd go through the trouble to fake a receipt."

She returned it to the bag, then froze as something large snuffed the doorframe. It stopped a moment later, only to be replaced by the sound of liquid striking the door—a werewolf marking its territory with what sounded like a hose. That went a long way toward explaining the ripeness of the place.

"So, what do we do now?" Alec whispered as the creature clicked away on its talons.

"We eat dinner and try to get some rest," I said. "I have a feeling tomorrow's going to be a full day."

25

As the night deepened, the college became a jungle. Savage barking, shrieks, and an occasional fit of laughter echoed from various sides. Things moved up and down the corridor. But the wards did their job. We slept in shifts, but I doubted any of us got much rest. I finally dozed off around five a.m., tumbling into a fragmented series of dreams.

In one, Alec was looking up at me with a grave expression. "I'm sorry," he was saying. "I can't help this." I tried to ask what he meant, but I couldn't talk. The dream changed to my apartment. My wife was walking into the living room holding our little girl's hand as she toddled beside her. She must have been about ten months old, just learning to walk. I smiled, my heart bursting with love, but then I noticed that the booties on our daughter's feet belonged to Emma, the missing girl. Fear seized me.

"Take them off!" I cried.

I had my voice, unlike in the Alec dream, but when I struggled to run toward them, to protect them, I couldn't move. My wife and daughter looked toward the window. Something was blotting out the sunlight that had been pouring through, casting the room in cold, heavy shadows. And then complete darkness.

Something hard nudged my side.

I squinted my eyes open to find myself curled up on the floor of my classroom, shirt soaked in sweat. Across the room, Alec was seated against the wall, drawn-in knees supporting his head. Shadow Vega stood over me, ready to nudge me with her foot again, but seeing I was awake, she withdrew.

"You were moaning," she said.

I scrubbed my eyes with a sleeve. "Weird dreams."

"Six a.m. Time to call my NYPD contact."

I sat up. By some circadian rhythm, the college had fallen quiet. I debated whether or not to awaken Alec before deciding to let him sleep. I stood and grabbed a water bottle, then joined Vega beside the covered window. While she punched in the number and brought the phone to her ear, I drank down half the bottle.

"No answer," she said.

"Should we be worried?"

"He might not have been able to talk."

"How risky is getting Alec's mother out of there?" I asked as she pocketed the phone.

"I don't know what the NYPD is like where you are, but it's a smoking mess here. The right hand hardly knows what the left is doing—or that there even *is* a left hand half the time. Getting her released shouldn't be too hard. My contact has rank."

"What about the Iron Guard? You don't think they're going to be watching?"

"I doubt my husband ever told them about Alec or that he

was holding his mom. He probably just said he could deliver you."

"Are you going to call him?"

She shook her head and started to turn away, then stopped. "Look, the big dummy meant well, believe it or not. Grabbing Alec's mom, delivering you to the Iron Guard—he was trying to restore my name and standing. It doesn't make it right, but..." Her exhausted look suggested she'd spent half the night going over his actions. "I'll wait to contact him when this is done and I'm out of the city."

I nodded in approval of the "when this is done" part. I didn't need him showing up again.

"We've talked about leaving before," she added with a despondent look that I completely understood.

"It's hard when the city feels like a part of you."

"Yeah," she agreed quietly. "No matter how effed up it is."

Alec stirred, making us both glance over, but he settled back down.

I can't help this, I heard him saying. Sometimes my magic spoke to me in dreams. Had it been trying to tell me something last night? Or was it just my own fear that no matter what I did, Alec would never be able to control what he was becoming? I thought about the next dream, my daughter in Emma's shoes.

"What's up?" Vega asked. "You look bothered."

"Oh." I let out my furrowed brow. "I'm on an NYPD task force for a bunch of disappearances, and I'm supposed to track someone today."

She suddenly dug into her pocket for her phone, which was vibrating. "Vega," she answered. "Okay." A long pause. "I owe you." Alec lifted his head, his eyes glinting from the shadow of his hoodie.

Vega nodded. "Your mom's safe."

My body unclenched, allowing in some relief.

"She's at Toscano's?" Alec said, pushing himself up. "Can I go see her?"

"I would wait until tomorrow. By then it should be safe for you and your mom to go back to your apartment." She turned to me. "You're free."

"I'm sorry?"

"The case you're working on. Things have settled down out there," she said, nodding at the door. "And I don't need to move till tonight. If your *wards* can last till then, I ask only that you come back and let me out."

"I don't like the idea of leaving," I said, adding a mental *you*.

"Yeah? And task forces are serious shit, so I'm not asking."

Hearing my wife's words almost verbatim made me want to smile and cry at the same time.

Alec stepped forward. "I'll stay with her." I liked that idea even less, but he pressed his case. "I can monitor the wards and deal with any emergencies that come up. Plus, I want to be here in case there are updates on my mom."

"Fine with me," Vega said.

I regarded the two of them: the son of my shadow and the shadow of my wife. And the longer I'd spent with the second, the more of my wife I could see in her—which was seriously screwing up my signals. Every instinct was telling me not to leave, and yet I had obligations in the actual present.

"I'll come back as soon as I can," I said at last.

Alec nodded importantly with his new responsibility, hitting me with another dose of paternal pride. He'd gone from fearing the detective who'd shot him to volunteering to help her. I gathered my things, said "bye for now" to Vega, and then clasped arms with Alec. In the next stomach-dipping moment, we were in my classroom in the actual present. I leaned a hand against my desk.

"You all right?" Alec asked.

"Yeah, just need a second to get my bearings. How about you?"

"I've taken these trips so many times, they don't bother me." He gave my back an awkward pat. "Thanks a lot for helping me over there, getting my mom out and everything. You took some big risks on our account."

"We're not out of the woods yet," I said. "When you go back, I want you to stay put and let Vega call the shots. No magic unless it's one hundred percent necessary, and don't go *anywhere* without me."

Maybe it was because of the dream, but my words came out stern-sounding. As Alec's face dipped, I sensed his gratitude souring into defiance. But he nodded, and that was what mattered right now.

"When do you think you'll be back?" he asked.

I ran a hand through my hair as I considered my schedule. Hunting spell to cast, wererat to follow, and I still had to prep for a battle with Mr. Funny, a being who could blow flesh from bone with a thought. It was going to be a packed morning. "How about I come back here at two, and we'll swap updates?"

"Sounds good," he said. "I'll see you then."

Before he could turn away, I gripped the back of his neck and pulled him in. "Hey, I'm really proud of the way you handled yourself over there. Keep it up, all right?"

"All right," he said, the corners of his mouth angling up.

"But if things take a bad turn, I want you to come back here."

His smile faltered. "What about Detective Vega? I wouldn't be able to take her with me."

She's a probability, I reminded myself. *A shadow.* But it didn't make what I had to say any easier.

"Just come back here," I repeated.

———

I turned my phone on, but it wasn't until I was outside that it finished booting up. Messages began arriving immediately— text alerts, voicemail alerts—one after another. I disregarded them and called my wife. Her voice was sleepy when she picked up.

"Welcome home," she said.

"Did I wake you?"

She laughed. "It's not like I've been able to sleep."

"Sorry about that. Well, I'm back now and feeling fine."

In fact, I felt better than fine. It didn't take much, apparently: blue skies, steady traffic in Midtown, and a college at my back that wasn't shuttered over and brimming with nightmares. Best of all, I was talking to my actual wife.

"How did it go?" she asked.

"With a lot of help from your shadow, we sprang Alec's mom and got her someplace safe. I'll fill in all the details later. Right now, I want you to play Sleeping Beauty. I'm heading home soon—I've got some prep work to do—but I'll be quiet as a mouse. In fact, go ahead and shut the bedroom door."

"Not without a kiss. You owe me that much."

I chuckled. "Then I'll be your Prince Charming."

"Your mixing up fairy tales, Mr. Mythology and Lore, but I'll take Prince Charming."

Though I'd spent the last twelve hours noting similarities between the two Vegas, my wife possessed a tenderness that shadow Vega would never attain in her city. That separation helped create some emotional distance with what I'd told Alec—to save himself, even at the expense of shadow Vega.

"How's she doing, anyway?" Ricki asked. "My shadow?"

And just like that, all my concerns for her came roaring back. I recalled the battered, hopeless state we'd found her in. And though she'd recovered her resolve, she was a wanted woman now, on the run.

"As well as can be expected," I said, which wasn't a lie. "I'm hailing a cab now, so expect me in about fifteen."

"Call Hoffman first. He's been looking for you since six this morning."

I'd already begun the cab-hailing process, but I stopped. "What about?"

"Didn't say, which tells me it's about the task force. And I know his moods. He's super stressed."

"All right," I sighed, knowing he was going to want me to come in. "I'll put that kiss on ice for now."

No sooner than we'd ended the call, my phone buzzed.

"Heard you've been looking for me," I answered.

"Where the hell are you?" Hoffman barked.

"I just got back. What's up?"

"Did you get my messages?"

"I was in a parallel realm, so no."

"We had another go missing last night. A hot case."

"Dammit," I muttered.

"And they already kicked Kriebel loose."

"The wererat? When?"

"Five this morning. Some non-profit is threatening to sue the city on behalf of everyone who's been booked without charges beyond the legal seventy-two. The DA wussed out and ordered them all released. The nightshift didn't call me or nothing, but that's not the worst part," he added darkly.

The ideas I'd begun assembling to track the wererat spilled like playing cards. "What?"

"They just found Kriebel under the Brooklyn Bridge," Hoffman said. "Dead."

26

I stepped out of the taxi and hustled toward the squad cars blocking traffic on Pearl Street. The knot of police activity was in the shadow of the Brooklyn Bridge's access ramp, its steel arches and towers of granite brick making the scene appear almost cathedral-like. Clearly, I was short on sleep.

"Son of a bitch OD'd," Hoffman told me as he lifted the police tape.

I ducked under and was soon peering down at Kriebel's draped figure. The wererat was seated at the edge of the sidewalk, scrawny legs splayed, back slumped against one of the bridge's support towers. I shifted to my wizard's senses, but other than the void of a recently departed soul, nothing stood out.

"He didn't go far," I said, noting that we were less than two blocks from NYPD headquarters.

"On release, he made straight for the coffee shop across the street," Hoffman said. "Ordered a cup of joe and a pastry bag filled with twenties. Mind control, I guess. Then he came here and blew the wad on something potent—opioids, judging from his blue fingernails. Lot of that crap circulating down here."

When Mayor Lowder relocated the homeless camps from the city's bridges a couple years ago, dealers crept into their wake, taking over the shadowy nooks. Almost overnight, the Brooklyn Bridge became opioid central—something Kriebel must have known. On the opposite sidewalk, a pair of dealers watched us furtively.

"Anyway, the medical examiner can tell us for sure," Hoffman said. "Anything magical you can do with him to help find Mr. Funny?"

"No, unfortunately. He did this to himself. Mr. Funny didn't touch him."

When Hoffman swore, I couldn't blame him. We'd just lost our best lead to the perp, the key to almost half the disappearances we'd been tasked with solving. That meant it was back to square one, which was precisely where I was with the thirty-odd disappearances that had ended in cold deaths.

"Did Mr. Funny do his set last night?" I asked.

Hoffman shook his head. "Place said he was a no show. Looks like you were right about him not wanting to take a stage without a guarantee of laughs. Probably gathering his new audience as we speak."

"Sorry I wasn't back here sooner," I said.

"Wasn't your fault," Hoffman grumbled. "DA's the one who went limp as a rag. It's what happens when you mix politics with public safety. The guy's up for reelection next year. Not that any of that's gonna matter to her."

I followed his squinting gaze to where Detective Rousseau was pacing toward us, the fierceness from two days earlier hot in her eyes.

"You called her this time, right?" I asked.

"That'd be a no," Hoffman said.

"You did promise, remember?"

He shrugged and dry-popped a pair of aspirin. "Forgot."

Rousseau came in like an arrow, glancing down at Kriebel's covered body as she arrived in front of us. "Can I talk to you two?"

Hoffman smacked the remains of his aspirin bitterly. "All ears."

"Privately," she said.

Hoffman sighed. "Yeah, yeah, we should have been on Kriebel like stink on shit, now he's dead, and it's all on us. Oh, and we should have called you the second we found out. Does that about cover it?"

I didn't care for his loose use of the pronoun "we," but when Rousseau's gaze cut to mine, what I'd mistaken for anger looked more like intense concern.

I stepped in front of Hoffman. "What's going on?"

"It's my partner," she said in a lowered voice. "Knowles. I'm pretty sure he's screwing with the data."

Twenty minutes later, we were sitting at a back booth in a downtown diner. Even though the coffee tasted burnt, I asked the waitress to leave the pot. Hurting for sleep, I wanted to be sharp for what Rousseau was telling us.

"Back up a second," I said. "When did you discover this?"

"Last night," she said. "When Hoffman called off the stakeout, I decided to review our data for the disappearances still unaccounted for. Wanted to make sure all of the last-known locations were up to date. So I had my spreadsheet open beside the latest map. Knowles coded it so the first fed into the second, but right away I saw that the jogger info was old. The map was still plotting his home address instead of the estimated point of disappearance. I was about to call Knowles to tell him about the glitch, but I decided to check the other locations. One after another, points had either reverted to old data or were completely off the mark. That's when I suspected it wasn't a glitch."

Hoffman usually interjected by now to assert his role as task force leader, but he was listening as intently as I was.

"My husband did some network engineering after college," Rousseau continued, "so I had him take a look." She frowned at me. "Yeah, I know—I broke my own rule about not talking about this stuff outside the task force."

"Well, given the circumstances..." I said. "What did your husband find?"

"It turns out the map wasn't reading from our shared data file, but another table altogether." She arched an eyebrow. "One none of the rest of us has access to."

"Yeah, but are we sure Knowles is behind it?" Hoffman asked. "Maybe someone hacked into the system."

"The file path leads to his computer," Rousseau said.

"Shit," Hoffman muttered and took a swallow of coffee.

"With the official map worthless, I went in and plotted all the data points manually." She opened her laptop. "When I was done, a much different picture emerged." She rotated the screen so we could see.

"Son of a gun," I whispered. The disappearances were still mostly in Lower Manhattan, but the pattern had changed. They were now concentrated along the water.

"Did you tell Knowles?" I asked her.

"No, I wanted to talk to you two first."

Hoffman, who'd begun massaging his fleshy brow, asked, "Any idea why he'd fudge the data?"

"None. In the four years I've worked with him, this is the first time something like this has happened."

"Far as you know," Hoffman said.

"Has he been acting differently lately?" I asked.

"Quieter, maybe, but it's hard to say. He was a strong, silent type to begin with."

I hadn't known Detective Knowles for very long, but sneaking around and data-manipulating seemed at odds somehow with his plodding frame, graying manbun, and stoic manner. Out of character.

"Must be working for someone," I said.

"Or being pressured by someone up the chain," Hoffman countered.

With tented fingers to lips, I considered how to phrase what I was about to say nicely. "I mean, I can understand hiding the surge in disappearances—that makes sense—but how does fudging the location data accomplish anything? It's only going to hinder us, and isn't the whole point of the task force to find and neutralize the cause of the surge? We do that, and the numbers fall back to their normal averages. Everyone from the mayor and police commissioner down is tickled pink."

"He has a point," Rousseau said.

"Yeah, he always does," Hoffman scowled.

"So, how should we handle this?" Rousseau asked nervously.

Though she'd been right to share what she knew, she was also courting blowback. Outing her partner could jeopardize her reputation in her department and alienate her from the other detectives.

Seeming to understand her dilemma, Hoffman nodded. "Before we go accusing your partner of anything, let's do a full workup on him. You can start by pulling his file and running his financials," he told her. "I'll go to my judge friend you love so much and see about a warrant for his cell data. If we find something, we'll go from there. In the meantime, no one mentions this to anyone. And don't start acting all hurt around him, Rousseau. I know how you women are about betrayal."

"I'll try to control myself," she said flatly.

"If this is tied to the perp somehow, it could be the break we need," Hoffman said. When he turned to me, his face pinched as if remembering my earlier counterpoint. "Is there anything you can do with this new location info?"

"I want to look at something first. Do you have that footage of the jogger handy?" I asked Rousseau.

Nodding, she tapped her screen until she accessed the video. I leaned forward, keeping a silent count as Demarcus Ward progressed across the screen in one-second intervals. At the far end of the frame, where he disappeared, the count was off. There should have been room for one final image of him. That's what had bugged me during our first viewing, I realized. The temporal inconsistency.

"Can you toggle between that final shot of him and the one right after?" I asked. "Okay, keep it there, where he's no longer visible." I studied the image until I found what I was looking for. "There."

"There, what?" Hoffman asked, squinting.

I pointed to a pattern of specks above the guard rail. "That's spray from the Hudson River. Something just yanked him into the water."

27

We watched the video several more times. Sure enough the spray only appeared in the final frame —the one where the victim, Demarcus Ward, should have been. Hoffman spent five minutes arguing for a wave slapping the seawall. I pointed out that it would have to be a hell of a wave given that the top of the railing was at least fifteen feet above the Hudson. It also wouldn't explain why Ward was missing from the final frame.

"All right, so what kind of creature can do that?" Hoffman challenged.

"Well, a host of supernaturals boast that kind of speed. Vampires, werewolves, demons. But you don't really hear about them taking their victims underwater. And whatever this is, it's taking them really damn deep."

"How would you know?" Rousseau asked.

I looked up from my coffee to find both her and Hoffman regarding me with puzzled expressions. In my mind, I replayed what I'd just said. The last part—about taking the victims deep—just came out. But those were the special category of victims I'd been compiling. From little Emma to the final name on my list, their deaths had carried a cold and sudden weight. Like they'd been dragged deep underwater.

"Those personal items I've been casting on?" I said. "Thirty-two of them pointed to submersions. I just didn't know it."

"Our new map shows thirty-four disappearances near water," Rousseau said.

I dug inside my satchel until I found my list. "How do they line up with these names?"

Rousseau took the paper and held it beside the spreadsheet on her laptop, eyes cutting between the two sets of data. After a minute, she nodded and handed it back. "A near-perfect match. I'm impressed."

I shook my head. "When I sent the list to your partner, he said 'no pattern.'"

"Jesus, Croft, were you going to say anything about this?" Hoffman asked, slapping my list.

"I just did. Can you get a team to drag both rivers around the Manhattan shoreline? They'll want to cover Twenty-third Street down to Battery Park. They'll be looking for human remains, the victims' personal items, and so on. If whatever grabbed the vics left a residue, I might be able to track it. The thing lives in the water, and it's feeding on humans. And judging from the rate it's consuming them, it's hungry."

"Last night's victim was last seen walking toward the Hudson River Greenway," Rousseau said ominously.

"I'll call the Harbor Unit," Hoffman said. "I'll also put a call into the Port Authority, see if there's been any weird shit in the water. But what does this have to do with wererats and that godawful comedian?"

"Maybe it doesn't," I said. "We could be looking at a second perp."

He made an incredulous face. "You mean there're *two* supernatural cases going on here?"

"It would explain the surge in disappearances," Rousseau put in, appearing relieved that the spike didn't indicate incompetence in her department. But her expression hardened again. "What about Knowles?"

"We keep him in the dark on this till we find out what he's up to," Hoffman said, a cruel smile curling his lower lip. "I'll give him a call in a bit. He's going to spend the day knocking on doors around those fake locations for potential witnesses. That'll teach the jerk to screw with my investigation."

"*Our* investigation," Rousseau corrected him.

Hoffman gulped down the rest of his coffee and wiped his mouth with his jacket sleeve. "Well, we've all got our assignments for the morning." He turned to me. "What are you going to be doing, hotshot?"

I looked up from the old bonding sigil that still showed faintly on the side of my right hand, below the thumb.

"I'm going to make a couple calls," I said. "Then I need to check in with Vega." I would pick up some flowers on the way home, too—the least I could do after spending the night in a parallel reality. "And since we lost our lead on Mr. Funny..."

I snuck a look at Rousseau. She looked back at Hoffman and me with a *you said it, not me* expression.

"...I'm going to do a crash course on any beings I might have overlooked," I finished. "Maybe I'll get lucky."

"Well, get lucky fast," Hoffman said, pushing himself up. "I don't wanna be on this task force for the rest of my career."

In the cab, I called Mayor Lowder's direct number.

"Everson!" he answered. "What've you got for me, buddy? Good news, I hope."

"A development. More than thirty of the disappearances happened along the rivers."

"From what?"

"Well, that's the next step—finding out—but I'm leaning toward it being something in the water. In the meantime, I need you to close the riverside parks and walkways from dusk to dawn. We may be dealing with a night feeder."

"Oh, Christ. Sure thing, you've got it. I'm going back to my grade-school math here, but once you stop this thing, we're good on the spike, right?" It was amazing how quickly his concerns turned political.

"It'll close the gap, but we have to find it first."

"Of course, of course. Well, I have faith in you, Everson."

Meaning you're counting on me to bail you out before the public learns about the spike. "Just be sure to follow up on the closures," I said. "It'll keep the spike from getting any bigger than it already is."

"I'm sending out the DOT crews now. We'll have a city alert up by noon."

I figured that would light a fire under him, but political animal or not, Budge was usually good about heeding my counsel.

"Much appreciated."

"That goes both ways," he said with a somber laugh. "Believe me."

When I returned to my apartment Tabitha was in a snoring heap on the divan—surprise, surprise—and the door to our bedroom was closed. I eased it open to find my wife in our bed, wearing a sleeping mask and earplugs, her body rising and falling with the profound breaths of the profoundly asleep.

Keeping my promise, I kissed her cheek, then placed her bouquet of fresh flowers in a vase, which I positioned on the nightstand in such a way that it would be the first thing she saw when she woke up.

My thoughts went to her shadow. If she was sleeping at all, it was in that nightmarish version of my classroom while she waited to be smuggled out of the city. I consulted my watch. Still a few hours before my check-in with Alec.

One shower and change of clothes later, I emerged from the bathroom feeling, if not like a new man, then a retread one. Tabitha had shifted on her divan, exposing the book I'd given her to read—something I'd all but forgotten. Not that it mattered. She was using the open book as a pillow.

When I saw drool glistening on one of the pages, I hurried over. "Oh, c'mon," I muttered, removing the book none-to-gently from under her big head.

"What the hell, darling?" she complained sleepily.

"I gave you this to read, not slobber all over."

"Well, it didn't have to be so tedious."

"Oh, so it's the book's fault?"

I brought my shirttail around to sponge off the drool—the book had been a rare find and was an important resource. A streak of her saliva had underlined one of the first entries: *Arimanius.* She'd barely even started. But when my gaze picked up a mention of rats, I went back to the top and read the entire entry.

"You—you found him," I stammered.

"Hmm?"

An obscure deity, Arimanius was the Greek interpretation of a Persian god of similar name. The dark twin to a god of light, Arimanius also lorded over rats—a detail the Greek version had added. *Explains why I missed him in my earlier search.* Nothing in the description explained the comedy part, but it more than explained the homicidal tendencies the late Stan Kriebel had described, not to mention his considerable power to command wererats. My magic nodded in agreement.

Mr. Funny was Arimanius.

"The god," I said. "You found him."

"Oh, yes, darling... I was just about to tell you."

Tabitha hadn't been about to tell me any such thing—she was merely reading the room—but that's how my magic worked sometimes. Arranging things in the background, ensuring I had what I needed. Tabitha had played her part, even if she hadn't known it. I gave the hair on her head a vigorous tousle, drawing a flat-eared scowl and some choice words, and hurried up to my library/lab.

"All right," I whispered, running my fingers across the book spines. "Now to *locate* you."

I drew out a Persian book on summoning and blew away the topping of dust. Though Arimanius was technically a Greek god, his Persian roots would make him snaggable, especially since he was local. Brimming with confidence, I flipped through the pages until I found the summoning ritual for the minor god. The ritual would need to be performed in a place where the "sun never shines."

Makes sense, god of darkness, I thought.

The ingredients were the leaf of a rare plant known as

omomi, which I would need to pound in a mortar and mix with...

My confidence faltered.

...the blood of a sacrificed wolf?

The plant and the dark space I could swing—I had a few candidates in mind for the second—but I liked wolves. In fact, a good friend of mine was a blue-haired variety of lupine. How in the hell was I going to *sacrifice* one?

I paced the room. The faint concussions in the walls told me Bree-yark was back at work in the basement. He'd made me promise to let him know if I needed another ride. I grabbed a few items from my lab, stuck a few others in my interplanar cubbyhole, and headed for the door to take him up on the offer.

I still hadn't solved the wolf dilemma, but if you wanted anything hard to acquire in this city, there was only one man to talk to.

28

M r. Han stared at me from behind the counter of his apothecary shop with a flat face and inscrutable eyes.

"Why need wolf's blood?" he asked.

"Not just wolf's blood," I clarified, "*sacrificial* wolf's blood. It's for locating someone, and it's an emergency."

Wolf's blood was still used in Mongolian folk medicine, and since there were a number of older Mongolians in Chinatown, I was praying Mr. Han knew a supplier. Whether their rituals for procuring wolf's blood would pass muster for the Arimanius summoning, I wasn't sure, but I wasn't about to start chanting in tongues while slitting a wolf's throat. I was shamelessly hoping someone else had already done that part.

A piercing shriek sounded behind me, making me jump.

"Hey!" Mr. Han called past me. "No opening *Qíngxù* jars!"

"Uh, yeah, sorry," Bree-yark said from behind one of the shelves. He grunted as if he were struggling to refasten a lid.

Judging from the sound, he'd opened one of the jars labeled INSANITY.

"Holy hell," I whispered, coaxing my heart back out of my throat.

"Sacrificial wolf's blood, hmm?" Mr. Han drummed his slender fingers against his smooth chin. Fortunately, he'd already located the *omomi* leaf for me and had a messenger running it over as we spoke. I was starting to lose hope on the wolf's blood, when he stopped drumming and thrust up a finger.

"Aha!"

Without explanation, he picked up the phone beside his register. Bree-yark, who'd been parking the Hummer while I entered, and apparently decided he'd explored enough of the shop, sauntered up beside me.

"How's it going?" he asked.

"Not sure yet," I said, pointing at Mr. Han.

He'd begun speaking into the phone in explosions of Chinese that sounded less as if he were inquiring after something and more like he was attacking someone through the receiver. Almost as suddenly as the conversation had begun, Mr. Han replaced the phone, his expression betraying nothing.

"Oh, hello, Bree-*hark*," he said.

"Hey, Mr. Han. Say, were you able to sell those things you made out of my hair and talons the last time?"

"Maybe you two can discuss that later?" I suggested.

"Oh, yes," Mr. Han replied. "They sell very quickly—how you say? Like hotcake?"

"In that case, can I interest you in some more hair?" Bree-yark asked, preening the few strands atop his head.

"Too short," Mr. Han decided. "Come back one month."

I cleared my throat. "So, about that wolf's blood..."

"Yes, I find somebody," Mr. Han said.

"Find or found?"

"Trang take you to him."

I looked around. "Who's Trang?"

At that moment, a sharp ring sounded—someone entering the shop—and a young Asian woman strode into view. She was wearing a white hoodie shirt, biker gloves, and baggy pants. She tossed her long, black hair from her face and dropped her backpack onto the counter in front of Mr. Han.

"Got your leaf," she said in perfect English. She dug inside the pack and withdrew a plastic-wrapped parcel. When Mr. Han reached for it, she drew it out of his reach and held open her other hand.

"Green for green," she said.

Mr. Han chuckled and turned to us. "She say, 'green for green.'"

He opened his register and produced a twenty. But she only looked at it and scoffed. "Really?"

Mr. Han said something in Chinese, and she responded in kind, the two going back and forth. At one point, Mr. Han nodded at Bree-yark and me, prompting the woman to register us for the first time. Her eyes were intelligent like Mr. Han's, but more shrewd. At last, she sighed and snatched the money from him.

"Very good," Mr. Han said. He placed the leaf package in a white paper bag and pushed it toward me. "Forty-two dollar."

"For the leaf and blood?"

"No, just for leaf. Blood separate."

Hell of a markup, I thought, but I was in no position to haggle.

"Do you know what the blood is going to cost me?" I asked as I paid him, thinking I might need to stop somewhere for cash.

"No, no," he said. "I take care. No money."

"Really?" I didn't know what to say. "Wow, thank you."

"Happy to help," he said. "Mr. Croft always very good customer."

As he placed my bills in the register, I made a mental note to ditch Midge's Medicinals in the West Village, whose prices had been ticking up anyway, and do all of my future business with this man.

"Trang take you to blood," he said, nodding at the young woman.

"Oh, hello, Trang," I said. "I'm Everson and this is Bree-yark."

She ignored our offered hands and swung her backpack over a shoulder.

"I'm on a bike," she said. "Try to keep up."

"Who in the blue blazes does she think she is?" Bree-yark barked, swerving onto the sidewalk to pass a slow-moving car. "Freaking Evel Knievel?"

Ahead, Trang was on a ten-speed, and not a very sophisticated-looking one. It reminded me of my silver Schwinn from junior high. But Bree-yark's observation was no exaggeration. She was commanding it like a pro, passing cars on the right and left, or else splitting them with bare inches to spare. Fortunately, the Hummer's height allowed us a good sightline on her streaming hair when she pulled ahead. And then she shot through an intersection just as the light turned red. Bree-yark braked hard.

"Mother thunder!" he shouted.

"It's cool," I said. "I'll keep an eye on her."

"She'll be a mile away before this thing changes," he seethed, releasing the brake.

"Hey, what are you—?"

The front of the Hummer nosed into pedestrians who'd begun to cross. Questioning murmurs turned to upset cries. One elderly woman began beating my side of the vehicle with a roasted duck. Hunched over the wheel, brow bent determinedly, Bree-yark wove through the blaring cross traffic, then angered the pedestrians on the other side until we were blessedly through the intersection.

"She turned left up there," I said.

Bree-yark accelerated, squalled into the turn, then slammed the brakes. The Hummer squealed to a standstill two feet before mowing down Trang, who'd stopped her bike in the middle of the alley and was peering at us over a shoulder.

"Park on the street and meet me back here," she called.

"You couldn't have told us that from the street?" Bree-yark muttered as he reversed through the smoke of his own tires.

We parked and hustled back to the alley before Trang could decide to take off again. But she'd dismounted and begun walking her bike to the alley's far end. We were at the back of a massive brick building that looked as if it had been a warehouse at one time. Trang stopped and nodded at a stone staircase leading down.

"Your wolf's blood is there," she said.

"What is this place?" I asked, picking up a sickly smell that seemed to be leaking around the wooden door below.

"Chinatown's Pleasure Palace," she said wryly.

"Doesn't look very palatial," I observed. *And underground to boot. Great.* "Well, thanks..."

"Yeah, thanks," Bree-yark muttered, clearly upset over the maneuvers he'd had to pull to follow her here.

Before we could descend, Trang thrust her bike into our path.

I squinted from the obstruction to her outstretched hand. "Um, I thought Mr. Han said no money."

"No money for the blood," she said. "But it's forty for my services."

"Your *services?*" Bree-yark repeated, incredulous. "Do you know how many times you nearly made me capsize?"

"You're here, aren't you?" she said.

"How much was that again?" I asked above Bree-yark's grumbling.

"Forty dollars."

"A little steep for five minute's work," I remarked.

"Not when you consider you're on Bashi's turf."

At mention of Chinatown's notorious mob boss, my gaze locked onto her white hoodie shirt. White Hand enforcer?

"Do you work for him?" I asked quietly.

She shrugged coyly and opened and closed her outstretched hand a couple times.

"Fine," I sighed, pulling out two twenties and slapping them into her palm.

She shouted something down the steps in Mandarin. A moment later, a voice answered from beyond the door.

"Your man is in back," she said and mounted her bike.

As she pedaled off, Bree-yark shouted, "Don't fall into any potholes and break your neck!"

At the bottom of the steps, a large man opened the door and looked us over. I was fully prepared for a pat down and an order to surrender our weapons, but he jerked his head for us to pass and closed the door at our backs. Darkness pressed in, squeezing my chest in a phobic clench. I was about to cast a ball of light when my eyes adjusted enough for the deep yellow of wall-mounted lanterns to glow into view.

Bree-yark, whose goblin eyes were accustomed to dark spaces, said, "Corridor leads to another room ahead."

"Okay, thanks."

With my cane in the ready position, I took lead. The odor I'd picked up outside, a sickly licorice scent, intensified, making my head swim. As we arrived at the bottom of a short set of steps and entered an open space, I saw why. In the sallow glow of more lanterns, a roomful of people were slung over armchairs, across couches, and sprawled on fine rugs. Some moaned, others laughed lazily, one man crooned, but they were all enveloped in the same languid smoke that they were dragging into their lungs.

The "Pleasure Palace" was an opium den.

"Mr. Han sends you to some interesting places," Bree-yark remarked, an allusion to our trip a couple weeks earlier to see the Gowdie sisters, a trio of swamp hags.

"No kidding," I replied, covering my mouth with a handkerchief. "Keep close."

Before long, I began to pick out the spectral forms of soul eaters among the mist. They turned from their helpless prey to peer at us with hollow eyes and yawning mouths. When several began to drift over, I pushed power into the protective amulet around my neck, the blue light warning them back.

"Up there," Bree-yark whispered.

I followed his nod toward the silhouette of a man seated on a dais, his erect figure a stark distinction from the sprawling populace he overlooked. And yet he was inhaling from his own pipe, the smoke encircling his head in thick tendrils. As we drew nearer, a large bird moved from one side of his shoulder to the other. Though Mr. Han hadn't given us a name, I knew we were looking at the contact.

"Mr. Croft," the man called down in a silky voice. "Welcome."

I continued past the final opium users and ascended the steps. The alcove in which the man sat was a small dispensary—a semi-circle of antique shelving and drawers, and a table with a vintage hanging scale. As the mist thinned, he resolved into a white-haired man with a horizontal mustache and heavy shadows under his eyes. Despite the moist heat of the den, he wore a thick robe. The bird staring at us from his shoulder wasn't a bird at all, I realized, but a black wyvern—a small dragon-like creature.

"Holy thunder," Bree-yark muttered of the wyvern, starting back.

"I'm here for the wolf's blood," I said, grabbing Bree-yark's arm before he could fall into a back-roll down the steps.

"Yesss," the man said, smiling. "I was told." Though his accent was Mongolian, he seemed to have added his own flair, as if he were on the verge of breaking into giggles at any moment.

He took a drag from his long pipe, not opium, but something that glowed faintly with magic. His pet wyvern watched us too, the natural set of its jaw resembling a grin, but its eyes cold as obsidian.

"Do you have it?" I pressed.

The less time we had to spend in here, the better.

"That depends," he said. "Are you prepared to make good on your payment?"

Here we go, I thought. *Everyone's got their frigging hand out.*

"I was under the impression that Mr. Han had taken care of that," I said stiffly.

The man's laughter finally broke through, releasing more tendrils of smoke. "He did, indeed. The wolf's blood for a favor."

Great, so Mr. Han hadn't paid for anything; he'd merely negotiated the terms of exchange.

Before I could respond, Bree-yark stepped forward with his chest thrust out. "Mr. Han didn't say nothing about no favor!"

The wyvern responded to his show of aggression by spreading its wings and hissing from a cocked neck, but the man only laughed some more. He spoke quietly to his pet and blew smoke in its face. The wyvern swooned slightly and folded its wings back in, but continued to watch Bree-yark crossly.

"I imagine there is much that Mr. Han does not say," the man replied mysteriously. "But for what you are asking, it is just."

"'Just,' my tuckus," Bree-yark grumbled.

The opiate mist drifting in from behind us was haloing my vision, my focus, making it hard to draw any kind of bead on the man. He wielded magic of some kind, and though it didn't strike me as particularly strong, swapping favors with a drug den operator didn't feel like a winning proposition.

"How about I just pay you?" I said.

He giggled. "Money is the last thing I want or need."

More opium smoke drifted in, this time accompanied by the moans of the users and soul eaters. I had to get us out of there.

"What's the favor?" I heard myself ask.

The man nodded as if to say, *That's more like it.* He moved his wyvern to the chair's armrest before loosening his robe and lowering it below his shoulders. He angled his back toward us—an invitation to look. I immediately wished I hadn't. In the flesh of his low back stood a gray boil the size of an inverted soup bowl.

"I need you to drain it."

I winced and swallowed. "I, ah, don't have experience with large cysts, unfortunately. Have you tried a doctor?"

"A doctor will lance it, yes, but what comes out will require the skill of a light-bearer."

As he said this, the wyvern hissed at the boil. Something was moving inside it, creating a faint squelching sound.

"Gods alive," Bree-yark muttered.

"Gods alive," I concurred.

29

The old man left the wyvern in charge of the den and led the way to a back room that looked like a monk's quarters, sparsely furnished with a large bed taking up much of the floor. Coals glowed from a small fireplace in back. Whistling a minor tune, the man removed his robe and hung it from a rack, leaving on only his swinging loincloth and a pair of calf-length socks. But my gaze barely moved from the boil.

I cleared my throat. "Can I ask what's going to come out of there?"

"I'm of the family Ragchaa, a looong line of shaman. We were always yellow shaman, the healers. That was until my great great grandfather, Gan Ragchaa, was seduced by a very bad spirit called a Chötgör. They made a deal, see? And he became a powerful black shaman as a result. Our family line has remained this way, down to me, Jargal. The Chötgör, he stays with us to see that we do not break the deal."

Bree-yark shuddered. "That's horrifying."

"Yes," Jargal agreed. "But it is a common story."

"I meant that growth," Bree-yark said, nodding at the boil.

"Why did you wait so long?" I asked him out of curiosity.

Jargal turned to face me. "Five years ago, my great grand-mother spoke to me from the fire and told me that if I were patient, a light-bearer would come. And it's about damn time. Sitting out there day and night dispensing opium, watching people wither away. It's a major downer, man. Ridding the Chötgör will change that. Bashi will not like that I am retir-ing, but it is a bridge I must cross."

"You work for Bashi?"

He released a high laugh. "Do you think I could distribute opium in Chinatown otherwise? This is his building. Many of the men and women out there are people he deems danger-ous. So he gives them opium, and they are much less danger-ous, see? No one pays here, officially—but they pay plenty."

I sized up the dumpling-shaped man. I'd feared some sort of Faustian exchange, like the one I'd gone through with the Gowdie sisters, but this seemed straightforward. He wanted to take his life in a new direction, and he needed this Chötgör banished before that could happen. Revolting, maybe, but straightforward.

"What's the story on your little dragon?" Bree-yark asked.

"Ahh, she has been in my family for maaany generations," he said, as if that were explanation enough. "I call her 'Pretty.'"

The boil shifted as he climbed onto his bed and lay on his side. For a brief moment, I thought I saw an eye peer through the translucent skin.

"Everything you need is beside the fire," Jargal said. "I have a circle under my bed for protection against lesser spir-its, but I am sure you can adapt it for your work."

Lowering myself to my hands and knees, I studied the

circle he'd rendered on the floor with yellow paste. A light mist lifted from it as I tested the circle with a small charge. The protection would keep out soul eaters, but for the kind of creature lurking inside the boil, it was going to take more energy.

I walked to the fireplace, where Jargal had set a ceramic bowl and a slender lance, the pointed end buried inside the coals. I wasn't sure whether to be more impressed by his preparation or his blind faith in me.

"You're really doing this?" Bree-yark whispered.

Though it felt dodgy as hell, my magic was unquestionably urging me on, and I nodded along with it.

"In fact, I could use a hand," I said. "Would you mind doing the lancing?"

The folds of his leathery face bunched up. "Oh, man. I am not good with that stuff."

"It won't be anything you haven't seen in the goblin army. Except maybe for the evil spirit."

"I'm fine with blood and gashes," he said. "The guy who used to march in front of me had a wedge taken out of his neck in battle, and I had to stare at that thing for a month till it healed. But pus? That's a whole 'nother ballgame."

"The thing is, Chötgörs are vicious little critters," I said. "And fast. The moment it's free, I'm going to need both hands to deal with it."

"I'm ready," Jargal called before biting down on a rolled-up washcloth.

Bree-yark looked from the cumbersome boil to me and sighed. "Only 'cause you're a friend."

While he stalked around, placing the bowl under the boil and several towels within reach, I tapped into the protective circle under the bed and infused it with my own energy. Bree-yark drew the lance from the fire, its tip glowing a healthy orange, and held it near the jiggling boil.

"Just tell me when," he grumbled.

Sword drawn, I spoke into the blade's rune for banishment until clear white light circled the smooth engraving.

"Go," I said.

Squinting, Bree-yark sunk the lance into the bottom of the boil. Jargal screamed around his washcloth. A jet of liquid shot from the cyst, nailing Bree-yark in the chest. With a shout, he went crashing into the dresser. I looked back at Jargal in time to see the Chötgör burst from the sagging boil and take form.

He was a hideous spirit with a goat's head, bat wings, and two enormous fangs bracketing his lower jaw. He was also livid, banging from one side of the column of hardened air to the other, clawing furiously at the protection. He released a series of bleats that felt like barbed wire lashing my brain.

As Bree-yark struggled, swearing, to stand from the destroyed dresser, I shifted from one foot to the other, poised to strike. I only needed the Chötgör to face me.

"Hey!" I shouted over his fresh bleats. "Goat boy!"

The evil spirit oriented to my voice, but before I could drive the blade home, something batted me into a side stumble. Jargal's damned wyvern had flown into the room and was trying to get at the Chötgör.

"Would you get out of the way?" I shouted in frustration.

When I tried to nudge the wyvern with my cane, she twisted her neck around and shot steam from her mouth. I invoked a shield before the blistering-hot vapors enveloped me. God, she was touchy.

Bree-yark was up now and shaking off a robe he'd

become entangled in. "What do you want me to do?" he shouted.

He'd kept ahold of the lance and was using it now to parry the wyvern's tail whenever it whipped past his face. She had returned to her faceoff with the Chötgör, the two fantastical creatures hissing and bleating as they struggled to attack the other through the protective field, which I labored to sustain through my broken focus. It didn't help when Jargal began shouting at his wyvern to return to her post.

If the noise wasn't enough, the small room was crowded and about to become even more so. The commotion was attracting soul eaters, several of them staring through the open door.

"Stay down!" I told Bree-yark.

With a Word, I fashioned a tunnel of air between the doorway and wyvern, upping the pressure until I created a vacuum that sucked her inside. She went tumbling down the tunnel and bowled through the gathered soul eaters. The apparitions scattered from the door as the very pissed-off wyvern pursued them.

The Chötgör glared after his former combatant long enough for me to step forward and drive my blade through his middle. He choked on a bleat, wings batting desperately, goat's eyes going bulbous.

"Disfare!" I shouted.

The light of banishment detonated from my blade's first rune, blowing holes through the spirit. The holes spread and joined, scattering the Chötgör into microparticles.

Withdrawing the blade, I dispersed the protective circle and waved at the lingering smoke, relieved to be rid of the horrid thing. The cyst that had been on Jargal's back began to crinkle and draw in on itself. Bree-yark stole forward for a better look. The wyvern returned too, vapor drifting from her nostrils as she flapped just above us. She began to whimper.

"Hey, Everson?" Bree-yark said. "I don't think Jargal's breathing."

Indeed, his body wasn't rising and falling. The washcloth he'd bitten down on hung loose from his mouth. Had the exorcism killed him? I was readying my cane for healing magic, when the shaman drew a heaving breath and shot upright. He stared from his wyvern to Bree-yark and finally to me.

"Is it gone?" he asked.

He reached around and pawed the spot where the boil had been. The loose skin had drawn all the way against his back and begun smoothing out. I hadn't even had to apply any magic.

"It-it's gone!" he stammered. "The Ragchaa line is clean!" he cried jubilantly.

Despite just having flatlined, he jumped from the bed and pranced around the room. He hooked my arm in his and danced me in a circle, his wyvern flapping excitedly over-head. Even Bree-yark had to stifle a smile. The shadows I'd first seen over Jargal's face were thinning, and light gleamed from his eyes.

He began to talk a mile a minute. "I'm sorry if I came off as creepy when you entered, smiling and talking funny and all of that, but when Mr. Han called me, I thought, 'Finally the light-bearer has come to rid me of this curse!' I couldn't stop smiling, couldn't stop talking that way, and by the grace of Tengri you did it!" He danced me in another circle before stopping suddenly and tugging me toward him. "Your blood."

It took me a moment to realize he was referring to the terms of our exchange. Releasing me, he scampered from the room, not bothering to pull a robe on over his barely working loincloth. When he returned, he was holding a small plastic bag that had been knotted at the neck. Something dark red sloshed inside: the wolf's blood.

"Thank you," I said, accepting the bag.

"But it's not enough," he said fervently. "Not *nearly* enough for what you've done. My first act as a yellow shaman will be to assist you with your spell."

He selected a light-colored robe from the mass that had erupted from the ruined dresser and began pulling it on. I was about to politely decline his offer, but time was of the essence, and I could use a sous-mage.

"I need to cast it in a space where 'the sun never shines,'" I said, quoting from the summoning literature.

Jargal laughed without humor. "You've come to the right place, my friend."

He tied off his robe and collected his ancestral staff from a closet. His wyvern settled on his shoulder but gave her master's neck a few exploratory sniffs as if checking to ensure it was still him. She sensed the change, too. Jargal led us from his room and down a short corridor that ended at a wooden door. When he opened it, two steps descended into a small space that smelled like—

"Death," he announced.

"The ones who overdose," I said in understanding. "You store them here."

"Until they can be removed, which is always done at night. You will find few places less sunny."

I couldn't argue with him there, and it would hopefully make up for any shortcomings in the blood.

"Let's get started, then," I said.

30

U sing a stone pestle, I scraped the pungent mixture of wolf's blood and crushed leaf from the mortar into a bowl I'd placed in the center of the casting circle. Jargal finished lighting the candles around the perimeter.

"It's ready," I announced.

He nodded and shook out his match. "These are good circles."

I looked over the design a final time before joining him inside the protective circle near the door. We were standing close enough together for his wyvern to nuzzle the angle of my jaw before nipping my ear.

"*Pretty,*" Jargal said sternly. "Outside."

The wyvern made a pouting noise, then turned and scratched at the door where, on the other side, Bree-yark was standing guard. He let her out, so it was only the shaman and me. If everything went according to plan, we'd have company soon: a Greek version of a Persian god who had a penchant for killing. Stage name, "Mr. Funny."

"All right," I said, pushing power into our protective circle.

"I'm going to get this going, but your job, your *one* job," I stressed, "will be feeding the circle around our feet. Let me worry about the spell."

"Yes, you can count on me," he said, his face suffused with his new mission in life.

With that reassurance, I closed the casting circle and focused on the bowl with the spell ingredients. I started into the summoning, a short Greek mantra. By the third recitation, the candle flames trembled and steam began rising from the bowl. The spell's power thrummed from my tongue. I became aware that I was shouting, and then the energy I'd been building up collapsed toward the bowl.

"Everson," someone whispered, shaking my shoulder. *"Everson."*

My right cheek smarted and the ribs on the same side felt bruised. I'd gone down. I was on the floor. I thought my eyes were closed, but it was just that the room was so dark. I grasped Jargal's hand.

"What happened?"

"Shh," he said. "Listen."

Across the room from us, something seemed to be dragging itself over the floor, accompanied by an oscillating whine, high and wet. Had I screwed up the spell and summoned a nether creature? And after all the times I'd lectured amateurs, dammit.

Finding my cane, I thrust it up and whispered, *"Illuminare."*

A ball of light lifted from the opal and hovered under the ceiling of the makeshift morgue. In the casting circle, beside the toppled bowl, a being was dragging himself in a circle and pawing at his confinement. I grew the light out. The being, it turned out, was a rotund middle-aged man. A grimy shirttail spilled over a pair of dress pants.

Had I actually landed our god?

His hair was the same color as the comic's at the club, but it was in disarray. "Arimanius?" I asked, to be sure.

He stopped pawing and peered at me over a shoulder, tears streaming down his fleshy cheeks. His breath caught once, and then he resumed whining—the high, wet sound I'd heard a moment earlier.

It *was* him.

I rose cautiously, ready to repel any attempts to strip my flesh, but the god only dropped his head and fell into a deeper fit of sobbing. It seemed I'd caught him at a low point, which was lucky. Stepping from the protective circle, I flipped open my phone, surprised to find a bar of signal. I called Trevor, leader of the Sup Squad.

"Can you bring a van and full restraint system to Chinatown?" I asked when he answered. "We've got a sup to book."

I peered through the window at Arimanius. He was restrained and sitting in the same cell the late Stan Kriebel had occupied earlier that morning. The wererat had taken his own life rather than face the wrath of a god who'd just put up zero resistance and was staring morosely at the floor like he'd lost his mother.

"You actually collared the son of a bitch," Hoffman said, arriving beside me and punching my shoulder. "Way to fucking go."

"I summoned him in Chinatown with the help of a

Mongolian shaman. Long story," I added when he raised his eyebrows.

Our farewell with Jargal and his wyvern had been necessarily hasty, but I wished him luck and told him how to reach me. I hoped we could at least keep in touch. Besides being a sweet man, he knew the ins and outs of Chinatown, which could be helpful. Not that Mr. Han wasn't, but I'd never quite figured out his allegiances. After a round of hugs with the shaman, I rode in the police wagon with Arimanius while Bree-yark headed home to shower before returning to work on my basement unit.

"What's he told you?" Hoffman asked.

"Nothing yet," I said. "He only just stopped crying."

"Let's see if we can change that. Safe to go in?"

I nodded. "The cell's wards are neutralizing his powers, but I'm keeping the restraints on just in case."

"I think you just earned yourself a nickname, Croft. 'Double-wrap.'"

"Don't," I warned.

He signaled to the armed members of the Sup Squad and opened the door. Arimanius didn't even raise his head. Back at the opium den, he'd been pliant as putty when I'd secured the restraints on him, and dead weight when Trevor and I half-dragged, half-carried him to the van. Same when we got him here.

"I'm Detective Hoffman, and this is Everson Croft," he said as the door locked behind us. "Why don't you start by telling us about the people you had the wererats kidnap. Your 'guests,' I think you called them?"

The god kept his head hung.

"Look, we know what you did," Hoffman said, "so there's

no point in playing mute. Was the whole scheme to get laughs?"

Arimanius peered up at us. The tears had mostly dried, but his eyes were the color of tombstones and just as hard. The look was less menacing than nihilistic, though—like he didn't care about anyone or anything. I supposed that was his default. He was a god of darkness, after all. But, like Hoffman, I still couldn't figure out why he'd been fooling around with comedy. A thought occurred to me.

"Hey, we caught your show the other night," I said, forcing a laugh. "That was some funny stuff."

"It was?" Hoffman muttered.

I elbowed him in the side. "Remember that bit about marriage and toilet seats?"

"Oh, yeah." Hoffman managed a grunt-chuckle that wasn't at all convincing. "I nearly asphyxiated."

"I'm telling you, Ari—I mean, Mr. Funny. I can't wait to see where your career goes from here."

The god dropped his head again. When he began to shudder, I realized he'd gone right back to sobbing. Crap. I pressed on with the rest of what I was going to say—about how we needed his help to understand what had happened, how his cooperation would ensure his quicker return to the stage—but the waterworks continued.

Hoffman sighed. "How about we let him sit for a while?"

"Is there anything we can get for you, Mr. Funny?" I asked as Hoffman signaled to a guard to let us back out. "A slide whistle, maybe?"

The god's crying intensified.

"Man, that guy's depressing," Hoffman muttered when we were back outside. "Think he'll talk?"

"Do we still have seventy-two hours?"

His mouth bent into a grimace. "Until the DA tells us otherwise. We were only able to pick him up 'cause of the wererat's statement. The minute his office learns the wererat is too dead to testify, they'll order him released. Nothing connects Mr. Funny to the crime right now. No evidence from the Farm, kidnapping victims never saw him, his nest of rat accomplices are all history. Forget about 'beyond a reasonable doubt;' we don't even have 'probable cause' anymore—unless he talks." Hoffman looked at me sidelong. "Have you considered just smoking him?"

The thought had crossed my mind. Not "smoking him," per se, but sending him back to wherever he'd come from and sealing the hole in his wake. But there was a reason my magic had urged me to summon him, and it wasn't that. His connection to Greek mythology wasn't lost on me, either.

"Let's see how he looks in a couple hours," I said. "At least we know he won't be assembling any more guest lists in the meantime. How are we doing with the water threat?"

"The Harbor Unit is out there now. I gave them the info on the disappeared. They're going to do some aerial sweeps too. They told us not to get our hopes up, though. Helluva big search area."

"Any updates on Knowles?" I asked. "If we can figure out who he's adjusting the data for, we might be able to narrow the search."

"I'm still waiting to hear back from the judge on that warrant for his cell. Maybe Rules found something."

"She did," Rousseau announced, crossing the floor of the holding area.

I'd called her upon leaving Chinatown and left her a message about Arimanius. It was time I could have spent getting the god to talk, but counting on Hoffman to call her would have been a mistake. I updated her as she peered into his cell. Hoffman turned fidgety until he couldn't contain himself.

"What did you find?" he blurted out.

Rousseau glanced around before raising her eyes to indicate we needed to talk in the task force room.

A lead, she mouthed.

31

We arrived in the task force room, Hoffman locking the door behind us.

"Don't worry," he said to Rousseau. "Your partner's gonna be out till after dark, at least. So, what do you got?"

She sat at the table, pulled several folders from her shoulder bag, and stacked them in a neat pile as if to compose herself. Hoffman and I sat across from her as she held up the top folder.

"His police file came back clean. A couple minor write-ups when he was rank-and-file, but nothing in the last fifteen years. One more year and he retires with a full pension."

"Doesn't mean much," Hoffman muttered, no doubt thinking of his own recent checkered past.

"His financials," she said, holding up the next file. "I had someone in Commercial Crimes take a look. No red flags in his accounts. If someone's paying him, it's in cash, and he's stuffing it under a mattress."

"Lot of good that does us," Hoffman said. "Where's this big lead you promised?"

"I never said 'big,' but here. Cell records on his private phone." She pushed the final folder toward him as if anxious to be rid of something dirty. She'd done the right thing, but she'd still gone digging on her partner.

"How in the hell did you get a warrant so fast?" Hoffman asked her.

She returned a smug smile. "Told you I knew a judge."

He frowned as he began thumbing through the file.

"Those are all the calls my partner made and received in the last month," she said. "A lot of what you'd expect—calls to me, various departments, friends and family. But note the highlighted rows. Twenty calls to the same mystery number."

"And the mystery number belongs to...?" Hoffman said, circling a hand for her to get to the point.

"A burner. But it's a number of interest now," she said when he started grumbling, "which means I can start working it. Get a general location, see if it's communicated with any numbers besides my partner's..."

"How long's that going to take?" I asked.

"I should know something by tomorrow."

I thought about last night's disappearance. Even with Budge closing the waterfronts—an alert had gone out to New Yorkers' phones around noon, citing the restricted hours—a determined enough predator could adapt.

"We might not have that long," I said. "Maybe it's time we confronted Knowles."

Hoffman and Rousseau exchanged looks before he turned to me. "We understand where you're coming from, Croft, and we know you're married to a cop, but you've gotta be in the club to really get this. It looks bad for him, yeah. But the bar for throwing an accusation like this in a cop's face is about as high as Knowles is tall. For all we know, the burner could be an informant he's working."

Rousseau nodded in agreement, probably thinking of the personal stakes if the accusation turned out to be false. Even being right would earn her flak. When a knock sounded on the door, she looked over apprehensively.

"Who's there?" Hoffman called.

"Harbor Patrol," a woman's voice answered.

Rousseau relaxed as Hoffman opened the door. The stocky officer was dressed in uniform pants and a blue NYPD T-shirt and cap.

"You told us to deliver anything on your priority list." When Hoffman opened the door further, she raised a large black plastic bag. "Found it butting up against the wall near the East River Promenade."

"Let's take a look," Hoffman said, waving her in.

I walked over as the officer set the bag on the floor and began unfastening one side. Rousseau turned the white boards with privileged info around before joining us. The bag opened to reveal a canvas stroller.

Hoffman grunted. "One of the items Mr. Crain reported missing when his wife and daughter disappeared." He turned to me. "This belonged to Emma."

As I eyed the stroller, I pictured her little white shoes kicking against the foot rest. It wasn't even the whole stroller. The back quarter, including the wheels had been torn away, and there were deep slashes in the fabric. Had that happened after it had been in the water or *while* it was being pulled in?

A deep chill told me the second.

"Thanks," Hoffman told the officer. "We'll hold onto this."

After she'd nodded and left the room, he turned to me. "What do you think?"

"See the way these slashes spiral down the plastic?" I said, indicating the guardrail. "Could have been inflicted by whatever grabbed them." But damned if I knew what kind of creature that would be.

"Anything on here you can track?" he asked.

I looked the stroller over again. It was saturated with saltwater and had been floating out there long enough to have been washed clean. "If forensics can locate any organic material, I'll cast a hunting spell."

"I'll have them pick it up, then," he said. "I'll ask them to look at the slashes too."

"I'm also bringing in an outside consultant," I said, studying the pulsing sigil on my thumb. "If that's all right with you guys."

"Fine with me," Hoffman said.

"Who is it?" Rousseau asked warily.

"An underwater expert who's intimately familiar with these waters. If there's something in the rivers or Upper Bay, she'll find it." When Rousseau made a hesitant face, I said, "Hey, you brought in your husband, remember?"

She pursed her lips before acceding. "Go ahead."

"Good. Because it just so happens she's already here."

A hole opened in the far wall, and a torrent of bright green water gushed out. I jumped back, but the liquid evaporated as it hit the floor, along with an interesting assortment of small marine life. Gorgantha was the exception. The large muscle-bound mermaid emerged from the hole and landed on her tail.

"You made it!" I said.

She splayed her webbed hands against the floor and stared around with orb-like eyes to get her bearings. When she spotted me, her tail swished, and she swept her dank hair from her face. I expected a joyful reunion—I hadn't seen her since my wedding—but she thrust herself to her feet with a scowl.

"Why'd you send that old fool to bring me?"

"Because I needed you here ASAP. Where is he, anyway?"

Gorgantha searched the floor, then peered back at the hole. "Oh, crap. Hold on."

She took two running steps and, legs flexing powerfully, dove against the outpour back into the portal.

"What in the hell is going on?" Rousseau cried.

She'd retreated to the far side of the room, a laptop under each arm to rescue them from water damage. Even Hoffman, who'd seen some wild stuff in my company, was staring around, stupefied.

Gorgantha reappeared a few moments later, landing on her feet this time. She was dragging Claudius behind her, one hand clutching the scruff of his black robe. His shades had remained in place somehow, but the eyes beyond the blue-tinted lenses were closed, and his body showed all the life of a wet noodle.

"Hey!" Gorgantha said, jerking him back and forth.

Claudius sputtered, the green water that erupted from his mouth also evaporating against the floor. He hacked for a moment, clutching Gorgantha's arm for support. When he noticed the open portal, he said, "Goodness me!" and made a busy series of hand motions. The portal closed, leaving no evidence of it or the few thousand gallons of liquid it had just deposited into the task force meeting room.

"Do I need to call the biohazard unit?" Hoffman asked.

"I'm, ah, pretty sure it was harmless," I replied, having no actual idea.

Claudius blinked to one side then the other, his hands wringing out his silk robe before realizing it was dry.

"Oh, yes, yes," he muttered. He cleared his throat and tucked his curtains of dyed-black hair behind his ears. "Sorry I'm late, Everson. I tried a new route, one I thought your friend would enjoy." Claudius's ability to translocate involved interplanar travel, and his route-finding tended toward adventurous.

"Enjoy?" Gorgantha said, a fist to her cocked hip. "For your information, that *wasn't* water. I damn near drowned in that mess."

"So did I," he said brightly, as if having that in common were a positive.

"Well, look, I'm just glad you're both here," I said. "And, Gorgantha, it's really wonderful to see you again."

It had been almost a year since I'd worked with the Upholders, but our bonding sigils remained operative, and I couldn't think of anyone more qualified to give us the skinny on the waters around Manhattan than the mer who'd once called those waters home. She was off the coast of Maine now, so after receiving her okay that she could come, I arranged for Claudius to meet her and bring her here.

She gave Claudius a final sidelong look before cracking me a smile. "Come 'ere, dawg," she said, lifting me under the arms, turning me once, and pulling me into a full-body hug. She was as affectionate as she was powerful. When she set me down again, I introduced her to Hoffman and Rousseau. While they shook hands, I went over to Claudius, who'd moseyed up to the white boards and was craning his neck behind them.

"I really appreciate the help," I said. "So... where are you heading now?"

Completely missing the hint, he replied, "Oh, I don't mind hanging around. It's been a little slow."

"So, what's the dealio?" Gorgantha called over to me.

I patted Claudius's back and signaled to Hoffman and Rousseau that he was fine before walking over.

"We think there's something in the waters around Lower Manhattan," I told her. "Something that's been grabbing people from the waterfronts. The victim count is at thirty-four, and those are just the ones we know about. NYPD pulled this stroller from the water earlier today. It belonged to two of the victims—a mother and her daughter."

Gorgantha hunkered down, the fin along her back glistening under the fluorescents, and looked the slashed and mangled stroller over. Hoffman and Rousseau watched silently, seeming to marvel over the idea that mermaids not only existed but looked like the muscle-bound creature before them.

"That's messed up," Gorgantha said at last.

I stepped up beside her. "Have you ever encountered anything that could grab its prey from land and inflict this kind of damage?"

"I've heard stories," she said, straightening. "But I thought they were just that—stories."

"What kind of stories?"

"Gohalo, our gramps, used to talk about the 'Sunken Ones.' Old creatures that ruled the deep places before our god, Leviathan, supposedly put them out of business. They were some nasty ass pimps."

"So you think our perp is a god?" Hoffman asked.

"I said 'creature,' not 'god,'" Gorgantha said. "And they're called the 'Sunken Ones' for a reason. They're sunk."

My knowledge of mer folklore was scant, but I'd been

around the block enough times to know that ancient creatures didn't always stay down. "Could something have possibly, I don't know, *disturbed* a Sunken One?"

She shrugged. "Like I said, I always considered them
stories."

Hoffman's face screwed up in thought. "You know, I heard
back from someone at the Port Authority earlier. Could be
nothing, but what you just said about disturbing one of these
creatures jogged something. The official said that the only
unusual activity was a big cleanup project in Dead Horse
Bay."

"Oh, that stank-ass place," Gorgantha remarked.

That about summed it up. A deep body of water off
southern Brooklyn, Dead Horse Bay had once served as a
landfill. I had never visited, but why would I? Even the
most diehard beachcombers avoided it without hazmat
suits.

"Yeah, it got out of hand, apparently," Hoffman continued.
"They were dropping charges to knock loose all the garbage
and crap packed at the bottom of the bay. It created a gusher
that bloomed into this big toxic mess, so they're steering
ships wide until they can get it all cleaned up."

A gusher because they blew open an underground pocket?

I pictured something monstrous stirring from its sunken
state and slouching forth to feed. Fortunately, we now had
someone on the team built for water and deep dives.
Gorgantha caught me watching her.

"I don't like that look, Everson," she said.

"Only if it's safe. And only if you want to, of course."

She sighed. "Only because it's you. After I've scoped the
waters around the lower tip, I'll head there. But I'm gonna be
holding my breath, which'll give me fifteen minutes of look-

ing, twenty tops. These gills don't need to be filtering that crap."

"Understood," I said. "And super appreciated." I turned to Hoffman. "Can someone give her a ride to the pier?"

"Might want to get a big coat and hat on me, too," Gorgantha said. "I know this is New York, but mers still aren't an everyday thing."

"Knowles keeps a trench coat in his locker," Rousseau said. "He's about your size. I'll grab it and give you a lift."

"Good, because I'm starting to flake," Gorgantha said, looking over her dry arms.

"Be safe out there," I said. "And if you find something, don't engage. This is just info gathering."

"Ten-four, Everson. *Ciao* for now."

She included Claudius in her farewell wave, but he was passed out in a chair, his slippered feet propped on the table. The door had barely closed behind Rousseau and Gorgantha when the task force phone rang. Claudius didn't even stir.

"Hello?" I answered.

"It's the Basement," a guard said. "You might want to come down here."

"What's happening?" I asked, my mind already going to worst-case scenarios. The last time we'd been summoned, our two wererats had just self-administered deadly poison.

"Just come down," he said.

32

Hoffman and I arrived in the Basement to find guards clustered around the cell—a scene not unlike yesterday morning's. There was a major difference, though. When Hoffman started shouldering past them, they were grinning.

I pressed forward in his wake and peered through the cell window. Far from being down and foaming at the mouth, Arimanius was pacing. With his arms restrained, he was making frenetic gestures with his head. The mic was on, against orders, and I could hear him talking to himself in a rapid mutter.

"'There was a baby standing on the corner,'" he recited. "'A baby standing on the corner.' But why a baby? Why not a poodle, or, or a pink chair? Why is the baby important? Why does that make them *laugh*? 'There was a baby standing on the corner,'" he repeated. "'A baby standing on the corner...'"

It was a punchline in a classic standup bit, and Arimanius sounded hellbent on figuring it out. He was failing miserably.

Hoffman muttered, "No wonder this guy had to kidnap his laughs."

He signaled for the Sup Squad to man the door as we entered. Arimanius glanced over, but never stopped muttering. He shook his head aggressively. It was as if he were trying to solve an unsolvable riddle.

"Do you want to know why it's funny?" I said. "Because it tells you just how bad that neighborhood is, but in a surprising way. It's a comic image by itself—a baby standing on a street corner at three a.m.—but a lot of the laughter comes from the pent-up anticipation of what the comedian's about to reveal."

I wasn't sure he was listening until he stopped suddenly and wheeled toward me. He repeated the punchline, nodding slowly now as a light of understanding illuminated the backs of his dead eyes.

"Does that make sense?" I asked.

He stopped nodding and slumped his shoulders. "No."

Arimanius actually had an amusing look about him, like a gloomier Jon Lovitz, and his high voice carried comic potential. I almost tried explaining the punchline another way before reminding myself he lorded over darkness and ignorance. Humor was as foreign to him as being an obscure god would have been to me.

"Why does this stuff even interest you?" Hoffman asked gruffly.

He shrugged his shoulders. "I got bored here. There are only so many hours of streaming television one can watch in a day. When I couldn't stand it anymore, I went for a long walk. It was late at night, rainy, nothing happening on the streets. But up ahead, there was this one lit window, and every once in a while I could hear a noise coming from inside, like a roar. When I reached the window, I saw a woman talking to a crowd. And when she said certain things, it made the people happy, and they laughed, all together." The memory glimmered faintly in his eyes. "It was the most amazing thing I'd ever seen. I asked some questions, and I learned there's a name for it: comedy. I wanted to be able to do that to people, too. I wanted to be a comedian. So I started watching videos of the best ones. I took notes, I practiced, I booked a few of these open-mic nights—"

"And when you bombed, you terrorized some wererats into kidnapping an audience," Hoffman cut in. "Is that the long and short of it?"

Arimanius nodded. "Until someone killed my rats and the audience disappeared."

The god had no idea he was confessing to a crime—or that he even understood it as a crime in the first place. He seemed equally clueless that most of the wererats had died in a police raid and his audience had been rescued. Hoffman picked up on that too.

"Is this guy even worth trying to build a case against?" he whispered to me.

"You mentioned being bored," I said to Arimanius. "How long have you been here?"

He shrugged again. "Weeks? It doesn't matter," he decided glumly. He started back into the "baby on the corner" bit, but there was no urgency behind it now. When his voice trailed off, I was afraid he was going to start crying again.

"If you're so bored," I asked, "what are you still doing here?"

"I didn't choose to come. I was brought and then abandoned."

"Who brought you?" Hoffman grunted.

"Hermes," he replied.

An icy fist seized my heart. "Hermes? Why?"

"He said I was being recruited for a war and to wait here until he called me."

In my peripheral vision, Hoffman's perplexed face turned toward me, but I remained staring at Arimanius.

"What did he look like?" I asked.

"Like you," he said matter-of-factly. "But with darker eyes. And he was younger."

Alec, I thought.

Urgency gripping me, I looked at my watch. Dammit. It was two o'clock—our prearranged meeting time at the college. Even if I left at that moment in a squalling police cruiser, I was still fifteen minutes out.

"I've gotta be somewhere," I said to Hoffman.

As he followed me from the cell, he asked, "What the hell was that Hermes talk about?"

I was about to say that I'd explain everything on the way to Midtown College, when Claudius came strolling in. He was whistling a tune, hands clasped behind his low back, as if he were in a park. He started when he saw me speeding toward him, then straightened, the eyes behind his shades sharpening in recognition.

"Oh, hello, Everson," he said. "What brings you here?"

"I need a portal."

"This is it, right?" Claudius asked.

Though we'd arrived several seconds earlier, I was still clutching Claudius's arm, bracing for the worst. It took a moment for me to accept that the rows of desks were features of my classroom and not some stopping-off point en route.

"We're done?" I asked, to be sure.

"Oh, yes, yes. I found a direct line." He tittered. "That happens sometimes."

I released him, barely having felt the transition, and checked my watch. Five after two, but no Alec.

He's just a little late, I told myself. *Nothing to freak out over.*

But I was plenty freaked. Arimanius had just told me that Hermes had operated through Alec to summon him as a recruit for a war. Had he done the same with other gods? Was he storing them here, in the actual present, much like the ancient cult who'd worshipped Hermes had stored their loot in the shadow present? Either way, it explained why Hermes remained attached to Alec: he wasn't done with whatever he was doing.

"Everson, you might want to take a gander at this," Claudius said.

He had moseyed over to my desk and was reading from a piece of paper that I recognized as having come from Alec's notepad. When I rushed over, he handed it to me, eyebrows raised above his shades.

I read the hasty script:

It's a little before 1:00 and something's happening at the main doors. Like someone's trying to break them down. If I'm not here at 2:00, it means we've moved.

Alec

"*Shit,*" I spat.

Claudius, who had been reading over my shoulder asked, "What's he apologizing for?"

"He was over there with my wife's shadow. I told him if anything happened, to come back, even if it meant leaving her."

"Hmm," he said, rereading the letter. "Sounds like his father's son."

Claudius knew too? Regardless, that wasn't what I wanted to hear, probably because it was too on point—I wouldn't have been able to leave her, either. But it didn't change the fact that Alec was over there while someone or something was attempting to break into the college, and I was stuck here, unable to help.

Had the Iron Guard found them?

"Is there any way you can get me over there?" I blurted out.

"To the shadow present?" Claudius asked in surprise. "Oh, no, no, no. I don't have that kind of magic in me."

"But I do."

In ancient times, Hermes had become Mercury, and during the Holy Roman Empire, he was briefly identified with Saint Michael, the line from which my magic came. According to Arianna, the Tablet of Hermes sensed a kindred spirit in me. It had deliberately peppered me with its magic, a magic I'd managed to tap into during my confrontation with Eldred, giving me Hermes-like speed. Not wanting to encourage the god essence, I hadn't tapped into it since, or even tried.

But that was then.

"If I access the magic," I said, "can you translocate me?"

Claudius propped his chin on his fist and looked me over.

"I suppose I can try," he said in a way that inspired zero confidence. "Could be dangerous, though."

That went without saying. Claudius's standard translocations were dangerous enough. I thought about Alec—and yes, shadow Vega. Also, Arimanius's talk of a war suggested Hermes was up to something, and the Order had assigned me to his case. I double-checked with my magic for confirmation. It wasn't saying no.

"Send me," I decided.

"All right, well, let's see now..." Claudius walked a couple circles around me, eyes gleaming with the anticipation of getting to try something new. Small charges broke out over me as he explored the spots of Hermes magic.

He clapped his hands together as he returned in front of me. "I had to get a little creative in my thinking, but I believe I've discovered a solution. If it doesn't work, you'll simply return here."

"Alive?" I asked.

"You'll return here," he repeated noncommittally. Before I could press him further, he added, "But if it *does* work, I won't be able to bring you back. You'll need to locate Alec for that."

Which meant that if, God forbid, something had happened to Alec, I would be stuck there. Slipping Alec's note into a coat pocket, I recalled something Arianna had told me the last time we talked: *Your magic will never mislead you.*

I nodded. "Understood."

"Bring it in, then," he said. I secured my coat and cane, then grasped his lanky arms. "That's right, good and tight."

When he leaned his head in, I mirrored the gesture until our foreheads were touching.

"Now listen to me," he whispered, sounding knowing and

serious for the first time. "You're going somewhere that the rest of the Order cannot. But you can still call on the power of the collective."

Before I could respond, a violent charge detonated from my core, and I burst into billions of particles.

33

I was as scattered as a rotating galaxy. A dizzying sensation of disorder inside of order, and with it came a roaring omniscience. I was intuiting anything and everything, and it all fit together in ways so obvious I was dumbfounded I'd never made the connections before. But it was also familiar. It was my magic—no, *I* was my magic. Instead of channeling it, I had *become* it, and the experience was as horrifying as it was wondrous.

What did Claudius do to me?

With that distant thought, I fell back together again and toppled to the ground like a stone statue. It was as if someone had filled me with quick-drying cement. Nothing beat or moved. Solid through and through. Then my heart flopped, and a breath scratched my lungs, and the whole pumping cycle of life started up again.

Holy hell.

I lay in the darkness for several moments, inhaling and exhaling, making sure I was truly back. I was, the last bit of my expanded mind dwindling to Everson-sized proportions.

The state of omniscience lingered briefly, but then it too was gone.

But I'm still with you, a retreating voice seemed to whisper. *If you listen... If you surrender...*

My nostrils contracted around familiar, foul smells. Whatever Claudius had done had worked. I was back in the shadow present.

Pulling my cane from my belt, I rasped a Word, and a ball of gathered light rose to the ceiling. I pushed myself to a knee. The classroom was in the same wrecked state we'd found it in the night before, only now there was no Alec or shadow Vega.

And the door was open.

Not bothering to test my legs, I stood and staggered toward the opening. A quick scan showed that the protective magic I'd installed was scattered now, its final remnants squiggling off into astral space. As my ball of light caught up with me, it cast a bar out into the corridor, revealing recent blood spatter.

I forced myself to stop and breathe, to remind myself that the danger level was significantly higher here. As if on cue, a beastly cry sounded from one floor up and was answered by several others throughout the college.

See?

I activated and downed a stealth potion before reaching into the special compartment in my coat's inner pocket. The tube I removed glimmered with gold light. A lot of time and expense had gone into its prep, but if there was a moment to down it, every instinct told me it was now. I tipped the tube back and waited for the potion to settle warmly in my stomach before venturing into the corridor.

I'd only seen the edge of the blood spatter, it turned out.

The corridor leading away was a blood bath, red pools littered with hair and random chunks—none of it human-looking, thank God. Burn marks scored the pocked walls, cooking the blood black in places, while a constellation of spent bullet shells littered the floor. By all appearances, Alec and Vega had fought their way out of the college, but to escape what?

No shoe prints tracked through the blood, suggesting they had been backing away from whatever they'd mowed down—likely creatures from deeper in the college—but I could follow the path of Vega's spent shells. They led toward the west doors, the ones we'd entered through. Consistent with Alec's note, the main doors had been broken down, the locks and chains scattered across the gray light pouring in from outside.

I imagined a scenario in which the Iron Guard had entered. They ventured deeper into the college. When Vega and Alec thought the coast clear, they left the classroom, only to be pursued by were creatures, from the looks of it. They made for the battered west doors, but had they escaped?

I'll have to hunt them to find out.

A check of my cane showed that the spell I'd cast on my wife's hair yesterday was spent. Reaching into a pocket, I drew out Alec's folded note. Given its urgency, I was betting on there being enough emotional residue to tap into.

Back in the classroom, I spread out my premade casting circle and placed the note inside. I spun the hunting spell. Dark vapors drifted up from the ink and into the opal. When the cane kicked in my grip, I exhaled.

He's alive.

The strength of the pull also told me he was close.

Back at the west doors, I stepped out into the city. On the

surface, midday in the shadow present looked like a much less busy version of the actual present. But that was before you factored in its smoggy, washed-out quality as well as the disturbing dearth of pedestrians—*sane-looking* pedestrians, I amended. There were a couple of the other kind shambling around, one of them screaming at a lamp post.

The spell drew me west, onto less trafficked streets. Before long, my eyes began to sting from a miasma of burning fuel. I spotted pillars of black smoke shortly, climbing from beyond the next corner—the same direction as the spell's pull. Powered by potent combustions of love and fear, I broke into a sprint, determined to beat the sounds of converging sirens. When I arrived, I pulled up hard.

Holy hell!

The sight of the two hulking vehicles ablaze was more shocking in some ways than the bloody scene back in the corridor. I recognized them immediately. They were the same model Humvee that had chased us the night before, and they were what I'd been afraid of—Iron Guard.

Several of their bodies were splayed among the wreckage. Remnants of powerful magic scored the air. More shells littered the street. In the cracked concrete on the far sidewalk I spotted a hastily drawn circle, enhanced with the sharp angles I'd come to know. A protection from which Alec had cast a fire assault.

But Alec or Hermes? I asked myself. *The son of my shadow or the Greek god and gatherer of conscripts for his war?*

I focused into my cane, but the same swirling chaos of fire and magic that batted my coat was also disorganizing the hunting spell. I picked a direction and moved off. The sirens were getting too close for comfort.

Before I could clear the scene, one of the Iron Guard

pushed himself up from the street. As if tapping into secondary power sources, the other two followed. They wore dark-gray military pants and armored vests, but no shirts, revealing emaciated arms the color and texture of stone. Helmets with opaque visors hugged their narrow heads, while their feet were bare. There was something both modern and ancient-looking about them. As far as the type of being, golems sprang to mind, but if they'd been rendered from clay, it had been by an extraordinarily powerful hand. More likely, they'd been human once.

One guard's visor had broken in half, and from deep inside his stony socket, his exposed eye exuded dark red light. It fixed on me as he drew a rod from a side holster, one end sputtering with energy the same color as his eye and that had so alarmed Vega last night. Impervious to the fiery maelstrom around them, the other two guards retrieved rifles from the ground and leveled them at my head.

"Submit," one of them ordered in a voice as stone-like as his flesh.

Somehow, they were seeing past my stealth potion. "No, thanks," I replied, hitting him with a force blast to the chest.

As he went into a back roll, I called up a shield. Shots rattled from the other's rifle, eerie for its silence. The rounds broke against my protection in crimson splatters. I swung my cane around and released a second force blast, sending the shooter airborne. With the long-range attackers out, I focused on the guard with the cracked visor. He'd broken into a charge, the red light squirming from the end of his rod.

"*Entrapolare!*" I bellowed.

He paused as an orb of hardened air encircled his head, but then powered on.

Resistant to fire and blunt-force trauma, these guys didn't

seem to have much use for oxygen, either. I upped the pressure, just as I'd done to the wererat a couple nights earlier. But whereas I'd inflicted immediate brain hemorrhaging on the rat, the Iron Guard didn't blink. He continued his advance.

Looks like this is going to take more syllables.

I spoke quickly, sending out a series of force invocations that took out his legs and heaved a portion of the flaming wreckage onto his back. I was turning to run again when I staggered and fell to my hands and knees. My heartrate had jumped, and I could barely catch my breath. It felt as if I'd been crammed into a too-small coffin and buried.

Some delayed reaction to whatever the rounds had released? If so, no wonder Vega had warned me not to let the rod touch me last night. This was a level of claustrophobia I'd never suffered before.

With fingernails scratching the insides of my skull and my cane-hand clutched to my stricken chest, I peered over a shoulder. The two shooters were back up, and the rod guy was climbing from the wreckage. His helmet had come off, and beneath a shorn head, his eyes bore into mine. I winced away, his stare seeming to twist the screws tighter on my claustrophobia.

Around me, Humvees rushed in and blocked the streets. More Iron Guard appeared from them, leading with their weapons. They advanced on stone feet, drawing their ring ever tighter around me.

"*Submit,*" they said in unison.

34

As the ring of Iron Guards came closer, so did the feeling of being buried. I couldn't have put two invocations together to save my life. Thankfully, I had a very powerful potion inside me. I tapped into it now, willing everything into the latent magic.

C'mon, baby...

Electric currents coursed through me, restoring my breath, my sense of space, then burst from my body in an aura of golden light. Even with their visors, the Iron Guard shied back, forearms to faces.

The potion pushed me upright as the aura spread into great boot-like enclosures around my legs. The same light swelled over my torso, extended down my arms, pulsed around my fists, and formed a protective dome over my head. By the time the golden light settled, I was encased in a massive, magical battle suit.

The Iron Guard recovered and opened fire. But with six months to age, the potion giving life to the suit was almost as powerful as my wards back home. It reduced the rounds to harmless dispersions of vapor.

With a shout, I willed the suit into an airborne thrust. Because a potion this powerful would burn out quickly, prudence told me to jet from the scene. But crippling their force now could pay dividends later. And I couldn't forget what they'd done to Vega. It was time to crack open some whoop-ass.

I aimed an open hand at one of the shooters and fired. The shaft of gold energy that shot from my palm exploded into him, knocking him to the ground. He began to jitter, the potent magic seeming to grapple with whatever dark energy sustained him. Fissures spread down his exposed arms, and he began beating divots into the asphalt with his bare heels. The repeated shocks caused him to crumble. I cut sharply around and strafed the others, pulses colliding into one shooter after another.

They'd messed with the wrong dude's wife's shadow.

Weapons clattered and bodies went sprawling into jerking fits. Four, six, a dozen. I was cutting around for another attack when my suit sputtered.

Already?

I glided low and slowed, hitting the street at a run. I had dropped the lion's share of the Iron Guard, but I'd only dealt glancing blows to several, and several more I'd yet to hit. I put the wreckage between myself and them as they resumed shooting. Though the potion was petering out, it had restored my energy and then some. Getting struck by another round would be a major setback.

I used the last of the potion to send several pulses through the flames, taking down a couple more of the Guard.

I then drew my cane from my belt and tapped into the hunting spell. I was far enough from the chaotic scene now for it to give me a direction: straight, then right. Ahead, an enormous figure turned the corner.

You've got to be freaking kidding me.

I recognized the man's bulky battle suit and rifle. It was Vega's husband, Jag. When he spotted me, he stopped and swung his rifle to his shoulder. But he was batting the air aside with his other hand.

"Move!" he shouted.

I veered left and he opened fire. With rounds ripping past, I turned to see an Iron Guard's top quarter being blown away at the shoulder. It was one of the ones I'd damaged. Jag had just finished the job. He switched aim and took down another member of the Guard. From there, he laid suppressive fire.

"Take a right," he shouted as I ran past him.

I turned the corner, not knowing what was going on, but the direction was the same as the spell's pull. Partway down the empty block, a section of sidewalk had been opened, revealing a hole.

Emergency hatch to the subway line.

My cane pointed at it and angled downward.

And Alec is inside!

"Hurry," Jag panted, catching up to me. "Gotta get out of sight before they see us."

He reached the hole just ahead of me and all but crammed me down a set of rebar rungs. He climbed in after me, pulled the lid of concrete back into place, and secured the hatch. A pair of runes to either side of the hatch glowed briefly—more protections, courtesy of Alec/Hermes—then subterranean darkness engulfed us. After the effects I'd just suffered from the Iron Guard, being underground didn't feel so bad now.

"Keep going," Jag panted above me.

After about twenty feet, my right foot touched concrete and a dim light glowed from the walls.

"Are you hurt?"

I turned to find shadow Vega's eyes penetrating the gloom. She was holding a tactical shotgun over one shoulder, while a small flashlight hung from her other hand. Still shaken by the rapid-fire events that had delivered me here, I had to remind myself that she wasn't my wife. But I was still relieved to see her. Damned relieved. It wasn't until she raised an eyebrow that her question registered.

"Oh, yeah, I'm fine," I said.

As my eyes adjusted, I made out Alec standing behind her.

"Hey," he said quietly, chin angled down as if bracing for a reprimand.

He'd defied my order by not returning to the actual present, and then there was the question of whether he'd kept Hermes's activities from me. But at that moment, it was all I could do to not rush up and bear-hug him. I moved forward so I could see him better. "Are you all right?" I asked, stooping to peer at his face.

He nodded.

"Are you sure?"

He nodded some more. "Yeah. I'm not hurt."

I turned back to Vega, conscious that Jag was behind me. He'd completed his descent and was covering the hatch with his weapon. *How in the hell is he involved in this? Did she call him?* The thought sent a squirm of jealousy through my gut.

Irrational, maybe, but she was still the shadow of the woman I loved.

Before Jag could join us, I asked her, "You're okay, too?"

She nodded once, all business. "We found a secure room. We'll fill you in there."

"Coast is clear," Jag said, joining us.

It was Alec who led the way down a narrow corridor and into what looked like an old control room. He'd already warded the space, combining what he'd seen me do in the college with enhancements from the god essence he carried in his pack. Vega's duffle bag rested in one corner. The larger bag beside it must have belonged to Jag. As he pulled the door closed, a cry echoed from one of the lines deeper down. Ghouls. The door clanged home, and Jag turned a wheel, locking us in.

"I saw the scene back at the college," I said to Alec and Vega. "I'm assuming the Iron Guard found you?"

"Not exactly," Vega said, peering past me.

"Yeah, that was my bad," Jag said, stepping around. His suit sported a new battery pack, and he'd patched the rupture I'd inflicted on the casing. "When I released Alec a couple days ago, I put a device in his backpack to track him. Never thought I'd be using it to track my own wife. When I picked up the signal this morning and saw it was coming from the college, I lost it. How the hell was I supposed to know she was hiding in there?"

"That was you who beat the door down?" I asked.

"Yeah, our department has special battering equipment." It came out sounding apologetic. "Woke up half the damned building, though."

I could only imagine the surge of creatures.

"When I realized it was him," Vega said, "I came out of

hiding. Almost didn't." She shot her husband a dark look that I'd received a few times myself. "I told your son to go back, but he's not a very good listener."

"All that shooting alerted a passing Iron Guard patrol," Jag continued. "We got out ahead of them, but reinforcements cut us off back there." He raised his chin to indicate the street we'd just been on. "If it hadn't been for your son, there's a good chance we'd be in their custody right now, or worse."

Alec's eyes seemed to shine green before he glanced away.

"He was also the one who suggested we come down here," Vega said.

"Only because you warned me about the abandoned lines," Alec added, alluding to our conversation in the pump house. "If going somewhere infested worked with the college, I thought it could work again."

I nodded, allowing that it had been good thinking. Risky, but good thinking.

"Luckily, we were only a half block from one of the old escape climbs," Vega said. "And here we are."

"So, what's the plan?" I asked the room.

Jag started to answer, but Vega cleared her throat at him.

"Oh, right," he said, becoming interested in his weapon as he angled his body toward me. "I want to apologize for all the business with trying to bring you in. I got people involved I shouldn't have. Alec... his mother... It's just that I didn't know the whole story. I should have listened to my wife."

"Damn right," Vega muttered.

Even though Jag had risked his life to find her, she hadn't entirely forgiven him. I selfishly hoped she would hold out at least until I left.

Jag surprised me by extending a gloved hand. "We cool?"

I kept my own hand down. "Let's hold off on the making-up part until this is all fixed. What's the plan?" I repeated.

As Jag dropped his arm, he glowered at me, but not enough for Vega to notice.

"We were actually in the middle of planning when we picked up the commotion outside," she said. "Alec said it was you—he wanted to go out himself, but Jag volunteered." Jag's look said, *That's right, you ingrate.*

"The Iron Guard is going to lock down the area," Vega continued. "They don't have the manpower, so the mayor will lean on the NYPD. Helos, stepped-up patrols, and building-to-building searches. At a minimum. The point is, we can't risk the streets."

She pulled a square of paper from her pocket, sat down, and unfolded it over the floor. She had already made some lines with a pen, and now she resumed drawing. "We're here," she said, making an X. "Right above the Sixth Avenue line. The plan is to take this route to here. That'll put us about two blocks from tonight's pickup."

"If Grizz doesn't flake out," Jag muttered.

Now his packed duffle bag became clearer. He was going with her. They were leaving the city together. As Vega looked up, I forced the conflicting emotions from my eyes.

"The pickup location is still in the search radius," I pointed out.

"Let us worry about that," Vega said. "You and your son have helped us enough."

I dragged a hand through my hair. "Look, the journey through the tunnels alone is going to be—"

"We're armed for sups," she cut in.

"Maybe for a few," I said, "but we're talking hundreds, most of them ghouls."

Alec stepped forward with a look of resolve that belied his youth. "We started this together. Let's finish this together."

When Vega's gaze shifted back to mine, her eyebrow arched in amusement.

"Can I have a word with you?" I asked Alec.

35

A lec followed me to the far corner of the control room, not exactly out of earshot, but we'd be hard to hear if we spoke low. Out of courtesy, Vega stood and began consulting with her husband about something.

"I'm sorry," Alec said.

It recalled my dream of him from the night before: *I'm sorry. I can't help this.*

In this case, he was apologizing for not transporting himself back from the college like I'd told him. But how could I lay blame? Even Jag admitted that he and Vega had only made it this far because of him.

"You did what I would have done," I said. "But are you really all right? Not just physically, but... with what we talked about?"

"He helped," Alec said, referring to the Hermes essence, "but it's still me."

In my wizard's senses, the bonds between him and the tablet remained clear, but I couldn't tell whether they'd strengthened. I didn't trust myself to be objective, anyway. He claimed he was himself, but when I considered the destruction I'd just walked through, I wasn't sure I could trust his objectivity either.

"I know it gets tiresome," I said, "me asking you all the time."

"It does, I won't lie." He grinned before turning serious. "But I'd rather you be concerned than not care. I appreciate that. When this is over, I'll back off the Hermes stuff. I promise. We'll focus on my own magic."

But could he?

"Does the name Arimanius mean anything to you?" I asked.

"Arimanius," he repeated, squinting in thought.

"He was a Persian god of darkness whom the Greeks basically adopted. He didn't play a part in their mythos. In fact, he's largely been forgotten—only a couple mentions in the literature, though it doesn't mean there wasn't a cult or two devoted to his worship." I caught myself slipping into professorial mode and corrected course. "In addition to the darkness and ignorance, he was a god of rats. Ring a bell?"

"Vaguely," Alec said slowly. "But I don't know why."

"We apprehended him earlier today. He was involved in a kidnapping ring." I didn't know how to put what followed delicately, so I decided to just say it. "When I asked him where he'd come from, he said Hermes summoned him to serve in a war. His description of Hermes was a spot-on match to you. I'm not accusing you of anything," I quickly added. "I just want to know if any of this sounds familiar. Even if it was something you dreamt."

He watched me intensely, and for a moment I didn't know whether I was looking at Alec or Hermes.

"I've had dreams," he said at last. "They don't make a lot

of sense, which is why I've never said anything, but that might explain it."

"What do you remember?"

"They're not vivid like some of the others I've had. In them I'm stocking a chest, like I'm preparing for something. A long winter, maybe. And just before I close the chest door, I realize they're living beings."

Stocking gods in the actual present, I thought. *In a war chest.*

"Can you remember any of the beings?" I asked. "Think hard."

He shook his head. "Like I said, the dreams aren't at all vivid. They're more like impressions or foggy memories."

"Have you experienced any missing time? Woken up in the middle of the night out of bed, not sure how you got there?"

"No, nothing like that."

I considered the information. According to a legend, Hermes had stolen pieces of universal knowledge from his aunts and uncles, the major gods of Olympus, and put them on a sacred tablet. Alec was carrying a fragment of that tablet in his pack. But was it so powerful that it could summon shadow gods and then have them piggyback off Alec when he transferred over to the actual present?

For a moment I burned to destroy the tablet and box for what it was doing to him. But then Arianna's calmly spoken words returned to me:

It's chosen him. This we mustn't question. And through him, it's also chosen you. Its essence is determined to prevent Cronus's return, but don't compel it to speak, and certainly don't attempt to force the lid. What's inside can no longer be looked upon with mortal eyes. Let it talk to you, when and where it chooses. Remem-

ber, you're dealing with a god essence, and they're often capricious. Few more than Hermes.

But I was through playing Hermes's game.

I stared into Alec's eyes until I locked onto the green lights that had been flitting in and out. "If we're going to help you," I said thickly. "Maybe it's time you stopped fucking around and tell us exactly what you want."

The green lights wavered, as if in a mocking dance, then disappeared.

"What?" Alec said, blinking. "I didn't catch all of that."

I unclenched my fists and shook my head. "Nothing."

"Are we going with them?" he asked.

I followed his gaze to where shadow Vega and Jag were organizing their bags. I had to remind myself that my Vega was safe at home and hopefully resting. Still, allowing shadow Vega to make the journey alone, even with her well-armed husband, would be tantamount to sending her to her death.

I couldn't do that.

"I'll take them," I said. "I want you to go back and go to my place. You got them this far, which is huge, but you've done enough casting for one day. Even as magic-users, our bodies can only channel so much."

"I won't harm him."

I was still watching Vega and her husband, so it took a moment for his words to register. I turned back to find the green lights alive in his eyes. The shadows they cast transformed his face in a way that made him appear impish and older without altering the structure. It was Alec, but it was Hermes.

"What do you want?" I growled.

"You have to let me accompany you."

"Through him? No way. He's just a kid."

"There's something you need to see," he said in a voice that managed to sound both authoritative and taunting, "and you won't see it without me."

"Then I won't see it."

He smiled. "There's a reason your *Order* doesn't want me destroyed. We're on the same side, amigo."

"Then tell me what you're doing."

"All in good time. All in good time."

"You realize Arimanius is causing havoc in my city?

He laughed. "I thought I sensed a kindred spirit. I do hope you're taking good care of him over there."

I pictured Hermes placing him in the war chest in Alec's dream.

"Why him?" I asked. "Why not a god who's better known or more powerful?"

"When one's circumstances are as fraught as ours, one can't afford to be choosy."

"How are our circumstances 'fraught'?"

"That's what I need to show you."

"You can't just tell me?"

He tapped a finger to his chin. "No," he decided, and then he was gone.

"Are we going with them?" Alec repeated, as if the last minute of conversation hadn't just happened. The green lights had dwindled back into the wells of his dark eyes, becoming Jennifer DeFazio's once more. I peered into them, considering what Hermes had just told me.

"Yes," I said at last. "But on my terms."

I spent the next couple hours hunkered over my amulet, installing a complex network of spells. I needed them to cast a stealth aura large enough to conceal the four of us as well as provide protections in the event anything sensed us.

I talked Alec through the layered process, and he watched, wholly absorbed, taking occasional notes. I could see his keenness to assist, but he didn't ask and I didn't offer. Even if it was his own magic, I was serious about him resting. There would be time to practice when we got back to our training.

For those two hours, Hermes stayed away. Maybe we'd come to an understanding, but probably not. Greek gods had a long and storied history of acting in their own interests, trickster gods especially. At last I straightened, cracking the small of my back, and lifted the amulet from the casting circle.

"Ready for a test drive?" I asked Alec.

He nodded and tucked his notepad back into his pack. I placed the amulet around his neck, backed away, and cycled through each spell I'd installed. When I finished, I gave him a thumbs-up.

"Good to go," I said, taking the amulet back and clapping his shoulder.

Jag watched from the far side of the room, where he'd taken a seat and powered down his suit to save battery power. Vega was napping in the corner, using his duffle bag as a pillow, no doubt catching up on lost sleep from the night before. Though they'd finalized their prep together, she'd remained cool with him.

"How's it going?" Jag asked quietly.

"We're ready when you guys are," I said.

He turned on his suit via a compartment on his left forearm. A high whine went up, barely audible, and then the suit gave a small shudder. He rose, glanced over at his wife, and crossed to where we were standing.

"I get that you don't like me," he said. "And probably for good reason."

You have no idea, buddy, I thought, conscious of Vega's sleeping form beyond his left hip.

"But if we're going to do this together, we need to establish the chain of command. In other words, who's calling the shots." He was posturing in a way that suggested the role should go to him.

"As long as I'm casting the spells," I said. "It's me."

His lips twisted into an arrogant smirk. "You ever led a unit before?"

"I trained the unit that eradicated the ghouls in our city. Something your squad seems to be struggling with." I cocked my head toward the door to indicate the shitshow on the lower levels.

"Maybe because we never got orders," he shot back.

"Croft's leading," Vega announced.

We looked over to find her drawing her pack on and making sharp adjustments to the straps. Tired lines scored her face, as if the nap had only deepened her fatigue. Jag gave me a final defiant look, then skulked over to retrieve the duffle bags. With her help, he secured them to the back of his suit.

Alec raised his eyebrows as if to say, *I guess that settles it.*

"When we move out, we need to stay close," I announced. "Imagine a ten-foot radius around me. It's the only way to keep everyone concealed. We can talk, but we'll need to keep our voices down. Vega will guide, and Jag will cover the rear."

Vega nodded for both of them. Jag unfastened the door,

and Vega took lead with her shotgun. I waved for Alec to move in behind her, and I went next. Jag emerged last, panning the surrounding space with his bulky rifle. We had nearly two miles of infested subway lines to traverse, and it was my job to ensure we did so undetected.

I drew a steadying breath and let it out slowly. With a few softly spoken words, a warm force emanated from the amulet, covering the four of us. To anything on the outside, we had become a silent, scentless blob of nothing. I waited for the interior light to kick in, pushing out a faint halo to see by.

"All set," I said.

36

Vega led us down a metal staircase to a line that was still in use but few rode anymore. We hurried along the tracks until we arrived at a platform at 47th Street. From there, we climbed a barricade and took a staircase down another level to the defunct line. The platform here was completely walled off. Fortunately, Vega had spent time on subway patrol in her rookie days and knew the tunnels throughout Midtown.

"This way," she said, veering toward a metal door set in the tiled wall. "Maintenance passage."

She yanked the handle, confirming it was locked. Drawing out a vial of dragon sand, I stepped forward and inserted a pair of granules into the keyhole. I then uttered a Word, *"fuoco,"* igniting the granules in a white hiss. With the melted bolt dribbling from the bore, the door yielded and swung open.

At the far end of the maintenance passage, the Metropolitan Transportation Authority had gone one step further. Not only was the door locked, but its edges had been blowtorched, fusing it to the frame.

"This could take a few minutes," I said, waving everyone back.

As my blade glowed to life, I wedged the tip between door and frame, softening the surrounding metal. When I'd finished working the blade along the seam, I pressed an ear to the door. Nothing. Another dragon-sand treatment later, and the door came open with a scrape, felt more than heard. A wave of damp air gusted in, the stench alone strong enough to knock me back.

"Jesus," Jag muttered from inside his helmet.

Vega retook lead, and we filed down a narrow set of steps to a line of tracks that looked like the floor of a condemned slaughterhouse. Some of the putrid remains were probably human, but ghouls weren't above eating their own. They also procreated like rabbits, so food was rarely in short supply. Grunts and cries bounced along the stone walls now, several of them originating from close by.

"Sounds like a group ahead," I whispered. "Tight single file."

We hugged the far side of the tracks until we arrived at a platform. The ghouls were a small pack whose members looked teenaged. They were picking over old bones, snapping them open and crunching them down.

I peered back to find Jag staring at them. Despite his role in the Sup Squad, I doubted he'd ever seen this many ghouls up close. His barrel had shifted from down ready to low ready, and his finger was warming the trigger.

"Stay cool and keep going," I whispered.

He scowled but extended his finger back to the guard.

When we drew even with the ghouls, one of them

lumbered to the edge of the platform and began scanning the tracks for anything else he might scavenge. He was close enough that I could have poked him in the forehead with my cane.

I checked to make sure Jag wasn't thinking the same about his bullets, but his barrel was pressed firmly to his thigh to maximize the distance between himself and the creature.

We cleared the pack and were soon approaching the end of the platform. The four ghouls looked up simultaneously. I placed a protective hand on Alec's shoulder. Had they heard us? I was checking my amulet when a distant whine grew in my hearing, and the tunnel began to shake. One level up, a train was approaching. Feeling exposed, the ghouls jumped from the platform and began stampeding toward us.

Crap.

Gunfire belched from the end of Jag's barrel, chewing into the lead ghoul.

Having built our protection with incidental contact in mind, I pushed a hand frantically toward the ground to get him to stop. Vega lunged past me and punched his shoulder. Only then did Jag break off.

We peered through the dissipating smoke to see just how much damage he'd inflicted. Only massive brain destruction would drop a ghoul, and I'd made a special point of telling Jag that the far better strategy was to not engage in the first place. One of the ghouls had gone down, but the remaining pack was creeping forward again, eyes squinting from cocked heads in search of their attacker.

"Hold fire, dammit," Vega hissed when Jag's rifle came up again.

He did, thank God. After another moment of sensing

nothing, the approaching ghouls spooked and bolted the other way.

"Hey, they were *charging,*" Jag said when they'd left.

"Yeah," I said, "and I built in protections for that. What do you think I was doing up there for the last two hours?"

"Let's go," Vega said in disgust. "We're gonna need to up our speed now."

She was right. If the ghoul pack didn't return with reinforcements, the downed ghoul was going to attract another pack in search of an easy meal. We left the scene, and before too much longer, Vega was navigating us through an exchange that would take us east, marking the one-quarter point.

We passed two more packs and a handful of loners, emaciated and skittish. I checked Jag each time. Unwilling to court Vega's wrath again, he maintained weapon discipline. I caught myself wondering what she saw in him before smothering the thought. It was a pointless exercise, and it was unfair to her. I mean, hell, I'd married someone else in this reality too. Not to mention gotten myself killed.

Fifteen minutes later, we reached an exchange at Lexington Avenue that had us climbing a level and then dropping down two before continuing along a new set of dark tracks. I'd expected members of the Iron Guard to be posted at the exchange, but there were no signs that anyone was monitoring the subway lines. We'd been walking for several minutes when Vega stopped suddenly.

"What is it?" I whispered.

"I don't think this is the right way."

We backtracked toward the Lexington Avenue station, but the return trip seemed to be taking longer than it had to arrive. Ahead, the track kept curving out of sight.

Vega stopped again. "What the hell is going on?"

She turned around and walked back up the track, this time scanning the walls for any service doors. I was with her —something felt off. I'd thought it was an effect of being underground or under the prolonged influence of my own magic, but the disorientation was coming from somewhere else. And for all the ghoul activity so far, we hadn't encountered a single creature along this stretch.

We arrived at an intersecting track that I knew for sure hadn't been there a few moments before. Or had it? Vega stopped and looked up and down the new line, her expression equal parts bafflement and anger.

"Can you give me a bearing?" she asked.

Jag consulted the panel on his suit's forearm. "Damned thing's gone haywire."

I turned to Alec, half hoping and half dreading I'd see Hermes peering back at me. "Any idea what's going on?"

He shook his head. "Do you want me to try to cast something?"

"No," I replied, intent on him remaining idle. I wanted Claudius to take a look at him after this, too.

"All these lines are supposed to have a climb to an emergency exit spaced about a city block apart," Vega said, "but I'm not seeing anything. All right if we explore this way?"

"Lead on," I told her.

As we followed her down an intersecting track, I shifted to my wizard's senses. Astral energies moved around us in perplexing patterns. Ahead, another intersection of tracks appeared. We explored it in one direction, which only led to more options. When we backtracked, new routes seemed to appear. And still no ghouls. When I consulted my wizard's senses this time, I picked up impressions of walls folding in on themselves, all paths leading to a central room, where something was waiting.

"Stop," I said, louder than I meant to.

The astral realm thinned from my vision, replaced by Vega's consternated face.

"I'm not sure what's going on," I whispered, "but there's some sort of magic at work down here, and not the good kind."

"Glad it's not just me," she said.

"I need to relax our concealment for just a moment," I said. I squeezed off the power I'd been channeling into my amulet. I wasn't sure about the others, but as the magic retreated, I felt as vulnerable as a newborn.

I wasted no time. *"Rivelare!"*

The Word reverberated off the walls and boomed down the tunnels. If there was illusory magic operating, the invocation would have dissolved it. But even though I'd released a strong one, the feeling of disorientation—and the sense we were in a maze—didn't so much as flicker. We were still lost.

"Did you see that?" Vega asked.

I screwed up my eyes as the amulet concealed us again. "See what?"

"What you just did gave off a burst of light, and the track ahead almost seemed to end at a roundabout. I know that doesn't make any sense."

"It makes too much sense," I said.

She turned her face to me. "What do you mean?"

"We're in a labyrinth, and not just any labyrinth." Ahead, a deep snort sounded, as if something were awakening. "I have a feeling that's a Minotaur."

"Head of a bull, body of a man?" she asked.

"And notoriously ill-tempered." I motioned everyone back.

"Well, what in the hell is it doing down here?" she demanded.

Is this what Hermes wanted me to see? I looked over at Alec, but there was no hint of the Greek god in his eyes. Just behind him, Jag had his rifle up, but he was using the sight to peer down the tracks.

"I'm not seeing anything with the night vision," he reported.

The mythical creature's grunts were interspersed with coarse intakes of breath. He was sniffing the air.

"Still not seeing anything," Jag said.

I switched back to my wizard's senses. About eighty yards down the tracks, I could just make out an immense humanoid. He was lumbering toward us, his horned head swinging side to side as he continued parsing smells. It was as though he were trying to take form in the shadow present but wasn't fully here yet. But the in-between state offered its own advantages, such as heightened astral perceptions. That made our concealment much less effective—and he could still wound or kill.

"Are you carrying salt rounds?" I asked Vega.

"Yeah," she answered. "It's part of the Sup Squad's kit."

"Salt?" Jag said skeptically.

The Minotaur released his loudest grunt yet and squared his head at us. He was hunkering low now, the thick muscles of his back bulging over his horns, the knuckles of his massive fists scraping the floor.

"Switch to salt," I whispered quickly. "Switch to salt."

As I balanced my vision between the astral and physical, Vega emptied the shells from her shotgun and pulled salt ones from her bag, which was still affixed to Jag's back. She passed a pair of salt magazines up to him. He hesitated before swapping his loaded mag for one and slotting it home.

"What are you seeing?" Vega asked me.

"Yeah, I'd like to know too," Jag said. "'Cause I'm not—"

He broke off as the Minotaur released a tunnel-rattling cry that we all heard.

And then the man-beast charged.

37

The Minotaur thundered toward us like an arriving train. The others could see him now too, though to them he would have appeared more shadow than substance.

"Move to the near wall!" I shouted.

The Minotaur had closed the distance with such horrifying speed that I was almost too slow. We arrived against the tunnel wall as the protection I'd built into the amulet released a pulse. It shoved the arriving Minotaur. With a furious head-lunge, the tip of one of his horns snagged the back of my coat, ripping it up to my waist line. Blessedly, his momentum carried him back out of range.

I checked to make sure Alec was all right before calling, "Shoot! Shoot!"

Vega unloaded a shotgun blast into the Minotaur's face as he wheeled around. Jag opened up with semi-automatic fire. The salt assault tore through the creature, becoming dark flames, and he staggered back, arms batting the air as if trying to fend off a swarm of bees. When his heel met a rail, he tripped and landed on his back.

"Get some!" Jag yelled, pouring more salt rounds into him.

But while their assault was keeping the Minotaur off us, it wasn't going to disperse him. That would require a high volume of salt over a large surface area hitting him repeatedly. I pulled the sheet with the casting circle from my satchel, spread it over the ground, and emptied half a bag of gray salt onto its center.

When I signaled a *hold fire,* Vega complied, but it took Jag emptying the rest of his magazine to follow suit.

"We need to put him in the circle," I said. "Use your gunfire strategically to slow his advance. *Strategically,*" I emphasized to Jag.

The Minotaur thrust himself to his feet and released a furious bellow that sent froth flying from his muzzle. We'd already started backing away, placing the circle between us and him, and now I drew my sword from my staff, adjusting my grip on both with slick palms. I'd read plenty of Minotaur legends, but nothing had prepared me for staring down the horns of one. It wasn't just the size of his towering bull head or the ridiculous thickness of his body. It was his fury. It blasted off him like a force of nature and with such violence that a younger me would have been reduced to jelly knees.

Though the others were only perceiving a shadow, it was clear they felt his fury too.

The Minotaur charged again. Jag's weapon erupted first, followed by another pair of shotgun blasts from Vega. The attack slowed the creature but also caused it to veer. I summoned a wall of hardened air to angle him back toward the circle, but it wasn't enough. In a jag of sparks, his horn tore through the manifestation, and his foot landed on the edge of the circle as he stampeded past it.

Shit.

We moved in concert, pivoting from his charge—all except for Jag, who'd remained firing from the center of the tracks, determined to mow him down. I spoke above Vega's shouting, manifesting a barricade of hardened air in front of Jag, but before the protection could take form, the Minotaur's head battered through it. The energy rushed back into me with enough force to steal my breath.

Jag, realizing his mistake too late, tried to dive out of the way, but the horns caught him and whipped him the other direction. Even in his bulky suit, Jag flew through the air like a rag doll. He landed in a disjointed series of rolls that sent up small explosions and made him lose his weapon.

The Minotaur rounded toward him, putting his back to us. Miraculously, Jag was still conscious. One of the horns had pierced his suit, and blood was leaking from his right shoulder, but he was dragging himself away from the Minotaur. Vega raised her shotgun.

"Wait," I said.

"I have to do *something*," she hissed.

"Just wait," I said. "Trust me. Trust *him*."

Jag had landed near the circle, and understanding he was the red cape, had begun crawling to its far side.

"Oh, shit," Vega said, getting his plan now.

The seconds must have felt like minutes for her, but her husband finally reached the opposite side of the circle ahead of the Minotaur and shoved himself onto his back. As he pushed with his heels, he made small adjustments, guiding the stalking creature closer and closer to the salt-loaded circle.

"Careful, babe," Vega whispered. "Careful..."

Salt crunched under the creature's lead heel.

"Cerrare!" I shouted.

The symbol around the Minotaur's planted foot glowed, and a column of gold-hued light shot up around him, halting his progress. He beat on it with his fists and released another furious bellow that I felt in my bones.

"Attivare!" I cried.

The salt jumped from the circle and began whipping around the Minotaur. I fed it power, propelling the salt faster. By the time dark flames began breaking from the creature, the salt had achieved whirlwind velocity. Grunts and bellows erupted from inside the storm as the Minotaur gashed his horns back and forth. I upped the power to sandblaster strength, and the creature began to come apart. Within moments, all that was spinning inside the column was salt and smoke. But I wanted to be absolutely sure.

"Cover your eyes!" I called.

I cranked up the pressure until it overwhelmed the column, and the whole thing detonated in a crack of light. A wave of salt and blue fire washed over us, and then the tunnel fell silent. I peered out to find my sheet of casting circle fluttering back down, coming to a rest on a single stretch of track.

Both Minotaur and labyrinth were gone.

"Whoa," Alec said. "That was intense."

Salt spilled from Vega's hair as she ran over to Jag. I had to hand it to him—doing what he'd done had taken a pair to rival the Minotaur's. By the time she reached him, he was already pushing himself up.

"I'm all right," he assured her as I joined them. "Son of a bitch nicked my armpit, but I'm not gonna bleed out or anything."

"Way to think on your back," I said. "Nice job."

"Not bad for a bulked-up meathead, huh?" But his wincing grin was friendly.

"The suit's coming off when we get to the other end," Vega told him. "I want to take a look at this so-called 'nick.'"

"Hey, you're the boss," he said.

Vega peered around. "I know where we are." She checked her watch, then pushed the cuff of my coat sleeve from mine. "That can't be right, can it?"

Somehow, we'd lost more than four hours in the labyrinth, severely shrinking our window to reach the pier.

"A consequence of the disorientation magic," I said. "Unfortunately."

"Can we expect anything like this ahead?" It almost came out an accusation, as if I'd neglected to mention it during planning.

"If so, I'll be as surprised as anyone. But, yes, we should expect anything."

There'd been no time for me to consider the Minotaur's origins, only how to destroy it, but I had two working theories now. I was already leaning toward the first—that a powerful adversary had placed him in our path. But maybe that was because I wasn't ready to consider the implications of the second.

"If Jag's okay to walk," I said, "we should keep going."

He assured us that he was and heaved himself into an ungainly limp. As we assumed our prior positions, I caught myself watching Alec's shifting backpack, which carried the Hermes box and tablet.

Could the Minotaur have come from them?

38

There were no surprises the rest of the way. Just more ghouls that lacked the astral acuity of the Minotaur and whom we easily bypassed. When we were nearly to where the line plunged under the East River, Vega located another escape climb, and we took it all the way to another small control room.

Inside, I warded the door and Vega began helping Jag out of his suit.

"Since we're pressed for time," I said to Vega, "I should finish the climb and take a peek. See what conditions are like out there." Even though we'd journeyed almost two miles through ghoul-infested subway lines, the two blocks to the pier felt like the greater challenge.

"Be careful," she replied without turning from her work. "We've already got one casualty."

"Oh, c'mon, it's nothing," Jag assured her, but with his helmet off, his face looked splotchy and shadows hung heavy under his eyes.

"Want me to come with you?" Alec asked me.

I half expected to find Hermes's taunting visage peering back at me. He'd seen me struggle with the Minotaur and may even have sensed that I had exhausted the enchantments I'd woven into the amulet. But in his earnest eyes, I saw only a boy who wanted to accompany his father.

"I'll just be gone a minute," I said, punching his shoulder companionably. I moved past him before he could see my eyes starting to water.

Outside the room, I finished the climb and unfastened the old hatch. When it cracked open, I breathed in a slip of fresh air—fresh for the shadow present, anyway. It was full night, and I could already tell there was too much traffic on the streets. I ducked down as a Humvee sped past followed by a pair of police cruisers. Overhead, I picked up the sound of helicopters droning back and forth, as if performing sweeps. Hours after the battle on the street, the city remained in full search mode.

"It's a hive's nest out there," I said when I returned to the others.

As I described the scene to them, Jag watched soberly from his seat against the wall, where Vega had just finished dressing his wound. Already, blood was striking through the center of the thick bandages.

"How close were the helicopters?" Jag asked.

"Several blocks to the west. They were coming closer, so I didn't hang around."

"If they're searching in grids, they'll be moving off soon," he said. "We need to be ready to go when they do."

He started to push himself up, but Vega stopped him and turned to me. "Can you do to Jag what you did to me earlier?"

"The healing?"

"I told you I'm fine," he complained.

"Not as long as you're bleeding you're not," she shot back.

The red point of strike-through had already grown to the size of a half dollar. "She's right," I said, thinking that the last thing we needed was for him to faint en route to the pier. "It won't take long."

"The pickup's at ten," he said. "We don't have *time*."

I arrived above him. "I'm in charge, remember? Now get comfortable."

He looked over at Vega, but she gave him a tight-lipped nod and arranged a duffle bag under his head. "While he's doing that," she said, "I'll get everything ready." She pecked him on the lips and moved off.

Jag sighed as he settled down. "I don't win a lot of arguments with her."

"Join the club," I muttered, drawing a strange look. "It's probably better if you close your eyes." He complied for two seconds before peeking at the cane I was bringing to his shoulder. "Don't worry," I said. "It won't hurt."

"It's not that. I've just never had anyone do magic on me."

"Well, I've never done this on someone who was gored by a Minotaur, so this is a first for both of us."

He sniggered. "You're all right, Croft."

As much as I hated to admit it, I nodded back. "You're growing on me, too. Now let's get you closed up, huh?"

I incanted until light haloed the opal end of the cane and settled over the wound. Jag made a low noise of interest as his punctured tissue began to heal. By the time I drew the cane away, Vega had come up beside me, my soft light reflecting faintly from her strong face.

"It's done," I told Jag, "but I need you to stay here for a few minutes."

Still under the magic's influence, he murmured something unintelligible.

Thank you, Vega mouthed to me.

I nodded and squeezed her upper arm—I'd done it as
much for her as anyone—and walked over to where Alec was
looking through his notebook of runes and spell notes. He
closed it when he saw me coming.

"Time to go?" he asked.

"Just about," I said. "Look, I've been thinking. Once we get
them safely to the boat, you should come back and stay with
us. Your mom's safe where she is, but you're not. Not here, not
for a while."

"Are you worried about me...?" He held up his pack. "Or
this?"

"Both," I answered honestly. "But mostly you."

When the sides of his mouth drew in, I sensed several
conflicts going on in his very active young mind, but the main
one may well have been his having to choose between his
mom and his dad.

"Can I think about it?" he asked at last.

"Of course."

When the few minutes were up, Vega began helping Jag
back into his body armor. The blood on his bandage had
dried, and some color had returned to his face. By the time he
was fully kitted, he looked ready for battle. I checked my
amulet. I'd used up most of the magic I'd woven into it, and I
hadn't the time or energy to restore it. The extra minutes
down here had tightened our window further.

"Let's go, let's go," Jag called.

He took lead up the rungs. With the most experience on
the street, he wanted to be the one to assess conditions. I

surprised myself by agreeing. At the hatch, he peered out for several moments before reporting down.

"Helos are moving off again," he whispered. "Coast is clear."

He pushed the hatch the rest of the way open, climbed out, and gave us each an assist as we crested the top rung before carefully setting the hatch back into the sidewalk. We hurried into the dark recess of the nearest doorway, where I spoke an invocation to draw the shadows around us. It was a poor man's cover, but I only needed it to work for the next couple blocks, and Vega knew a low-traffic route.

We waited to ensure no vehicles were coming before moving off. At the next block, a police cruiser blew past but didn't stop. Like with the choppers, the ground search appeared to have thinned out here. We arrived at a corner where East 55th crossed a major avenue and then dead-ended at a parking garage.

"The garage extends over FDR highway," Vega panted. "A staircase in back drops down to the piers."

It was two minutes till ten.

We were preparing to move when a vehicle's high beams glinted into view. We drew back into the shadows of a cornice, and I incanted again to deepen our cover. Seconds later, an armored car shot past—one of the night ride services. I released my breath. With the way clear again, we crossed.

A crack sounded, almost too high to register, and I staggered to my knees with an unflattering *"Ungh!"*

The pain arrived a moment later—like something hot and bright lancing my heart. I had no time to consider what had happened before a swarm of engines roared up, beams cutting through my shadow cover and surrounding us. I clutched my cane to my chest and shielded my eyes with a forearm.

The beams belonged to motorcycles. Their brawny riders aimed barrels at Vega, Jag, and Alec, while the foremost rider stopped in front of me. He sported a familiar beard and wraparound shades. Red Beard, leader of the Street Keepers.

In his left hand he was carrying what looked like a tactical whip—a handle and short length of steel cable. Was that what had put me down? The sensation continued to smolder in my chest. Whatever it was, the attack had also disorganized my casting prism to the extent that I couldn't channel anything.

"Apologies, Everson," he said in his burly voice. "But you're not supposed to exist."

Vega scoffed as she stepped up beside me. "Well, you're not the law."

Red Beard considered her for a moment. "Man's law, no," he said at last. "We answer to a higher power."

"Well, tough shit," she said, "because he's with us."

"And as I understand it," he continued over her, "you're not the law now either."

"We still have friends," Vega said portentously. "You sure you want to cross that line?"

I was picking up a long-standing tension between the NYPD and Street Keepers, but that was low on my list of concerns right now. *Not supposed to exist? Higher power?* Whoever these guys were working for, it wasn't the city. My gaze went to Red Beard's shoulder, where white light from his tattoo was pulsing through his black sleeve.

He scooted forward on his ride to make room behind him, like he'd done the last time. "C'mon, Everson. Your boy, too.

We don't have any beef with your lady friend or the suit. They can go their own way."

As strange as it may have seemed, I believed him. The code he lived by was baked into him, and his word was his word. He didn't care about Vega and Jag. He would allow them to complete their escape and never breathe a word. Jag must have been thinking the same thing because he'd fallen uncharacteristically quiet. I didn't blame him. In the skies, the helicopters were working their way back toward us, growing louder.

What it all added up to was that if there was a time for Alec and me to transport back to the actual present, it was now.

I stood slowly and peered over at Alec. But though only a couple of paces behind me, he made no move to come forward. In fact, he retreated a step. When he smirked at me, green lights danced in his eyes.

Hermes.

"What are you doing?" I asked him through gritted teeth.

"This is the last time I'm going to ask nicely," Red Beard said, switching the whip to his right hand. "You and your boy are coming with us."

"What the hell part of 'no' don't you understand?" Vega said. "He's not going anywhere but with us."

"It's all right," I told her. "You and Jag go ahead."

She trained her intense stare on me. "Forget it."

I expected Jag to take my cue and usher her toward the parking garage, but he appeared more interested in the surrounding streets. When he cracked a smile, I noticed the incoming headlights. The Street Keepers saw them too. The vehicles were machine-gun-mounted personnel carriers, and when they braked into positions around the bikers, Jag pumped a fist. He'd called in the Sup Squad.

"The boys are here!" he announced, heaving his assault rifle back to his shoulder.

"What's going on?" Vega demanded.

"Had 'em lurking nearby in case of trouble. They might be NYPD in name, but they still answer to the big dog."

"We should've discussed this," she said sternly.

"We should've." He slid her a smile. "But aren't you glad we didn't?"

Murmurs rose among the bearded bikers as they tried to decide where to aim their weapons. But when armored Sup Squad members started pouring from their vehicles, it was quickly evident that, preternatural protections or not, the Street Keepers were outgunned.

"That's right, ladies," Jag said to the bikers. "Put 'em down."

"Our business with Everson doesn't involve you or the NYPD," Red Beard said.

"It does now," Jag replied. "So why don't you fire up your little bicycles and ride away."

Red Beard remained staring at me. He gave the whip a few contemplative flicks, then slipped it inside his leather vest.

"Nothing personal, Everson," he said. "But we will hunt you down."

"Looking forward to it," I replied tiredly.

When he motioned for his gang to ride out, Jag nodded to the Sup Squad to allow them to pass. Before anyone could move, though, a helicopter swept in. It was soon joined by a second. Spotlights glared down on our position.

"STAY WHERE YOU ARE," an amplified voice ordered. "WEAPONS DOWN."

Shooters took aim from the helicopters' bay doors. Even from my distance, I could make them out as Iron Guard.

"You've gotta be kidding me," I muttered sickly.

New engines were roaring in now, large military-style vehicles with their lights off. They arrived around the Sup Squad carriers and deposited enough armed Iron Guards onto the street to turn the rest of us into a shooting gallery if they wanted. And here I thought I'd crippled their numbers.

My gaze panned from them to the Sup Squad to the Street Keepers to Vega and Jag, all of whom had lowered their weapons, some setting them on the street. Alec had moved to my other side, still smirking while those green lights danced in his eyes. But I was the only one who seemed to notice.

"Care to clue me in?" I asked him.

"Keep watching," he said.

He pointed to where two of the Iron Guard were pushing their way through the concentric layers, using their supernatural strength to force people and even vehicles aside. They then stood guard at the opening they'd created, about twenty feet ahead of us. Though Vega remained beside me, I sensed how badly she wanted to draw back. I was also keenly aware that her opportunity to leave had closed.

My instinct was to cast, to get us out of there, but my prism was still disorganized from whatever Red Beard had hit me with. Meanwhile, Hermes appeared content for us all to remain in jeopardy.

What the hell is he doing?

For that matter, what in the hell was going on?

A black armored SUV was now rolling through the lane the Iron Guard had just opened. It emerged between the sentry and turned so its passenger side was facing us. One of the sentry opened the back door. The short, trim man who climbed out was dressed in an expensive evening suit, his hair slicked back in the style of a power player, but I would have recognized his boyish face anywhere.

When Mayor Lowder spotted me, he opened his hands.

"Everson, baby!"

39

The mayor strode toward me in the confident and chummy manner of his parallel in the actual present. He was flanked by a pair of Iron Guards, who used their charged rods to warn Vega, Jag, and Alec back until it was just me and Budge. But this wasn't the Budge I knew, so how in the hell did he know me?

"Put it there, champ," he said, extending a hand glistening with rings.

"I'm sorry," I said in utter confusion. "Have we met before?"

"Well, not formally, but I applaud anyone who can cheat death. Maybe you can teach me that trick sometime." He tipped me a conspiratorial wink, suggesting he knew exactly how I'd managed to reappear in a reality where I'd lost my life twelve years earlier. He thrust his offered hand further forward.

"What do you want?" I said.

"Listen, buddy." He dropped his voice for my ears only. "This is all a big, fat misunderstanding. I mean, would you take a look at this shitshow?" He chuckled as he swept his offered hand to indicate the layers of armed factions, then slipped it deftly into his front pocket as if I hadn't left it hanging.

"So hunting me was a 'misunderstanding,'" I said.

"All right, maybe not the hunting part. You got me there. But we had to land you any way we could. The fact is…" He blew out his breath and gave me his most disarming look. "We need your help, Everson."

"My help," I repeated.

As he edged nearer, I looked him over. There were few places in his tightly tailored suit to stash a weapon. The Iron Guard, who continued to cover me from all sides, served that function. But surely they wouldn't risk a shot with him standing two feet away. Could I turn that to my advantage?

For a moment, I imagined seizing the mayor and holding Bree-yark's ankle knife to his throat. But now I sensed a protection flowing around him, a strange blend of light and darkness, and I canned the thought.

"Look, you destroying that scythe," he said. "You taking down the Society of Cronus. Those were *good things*. Between you and me, we tried to work with them at first. You know, keep your enemies close? But the Society was amassing power and influence in ways we never anticipated. Lord knows what would've happened had that wacko Eldred brought his plans to fruition. Now we need you to destroy something else."

"And what's that?" I asked, already knowing.

He glanced past me to where Alec stood beside Vega and Jag.

"That thing your boy's carrying. The tablet, or whatever the hell it is. It was never meant to come here—it's too powerful—and now it's drawing all kinds of things to it. Gods, monsters, you name it. As if I don't have enough going on in my city," he added ruefully. "Destroy it, and all that stuff goes away."

When he looked Alec's way again, I picked up two things. First, that he feared the Hermes tablet, and second, that he truly did need me to destroy it. Why else would the Sup Squad have given it back to Alec when they released him? Why else would Budge be standing here now, trying to flatter me?

"You'll also get your boy back," he added.

The Budge in my city had a natural gift of gab that veiled his shrewd political instincts, but this Budge had taken that gift to another level. I felt power exuding from his voice. Power that rivaled my own wizard's voice.

"Don't you want your boy back?" he pressed.

I nodded before I realized I was even doing it.

"You see?" he leapt. "And all I want is my city back. We work together on this, and we both get what we want." At some point, he'd put his arm over my shoulder as if we were at neighboring stools at the local bar. "Right, Everson?"

"Win-win," I said, not sure whether I meant it or not.

"Exactly!"

When he shook me companionably, I felt his influence growing stronger. I searched his eyes. He wasn't enchanted. He *believed* what he was telling me, but only because someone had manipulated him. The same someone who had enhanced the mayor's powers of persuasion and surrounded his office with Iron Guard soldiers. The same someone who'd helped Eldred at the Discovery Society, supplying him bonding potions, a shifter guardian, and the Scythe of Cronus. The same someone who now wanted Hermes out of the way. But for some reason, he or she couldn't do the deed himself.

"So what do you say we put this to bed, huh?" Budge suggested, practically in my ear. "Everyone wins, and you go back to doing whatever it is you do."

Though I had enough wherewithal to keep my head, he was speaking to some of my very real doubts. About the Tablet of Hermes, its hold over Alec. I was also feeling a growing urgency to get back to the actual present to help Gorgantha and the NYPD with the hunt. My leaving them felt irresponsible now. Grossly irresponsible. And that was to say nothing of abandoning my pregnant wife.

"You'll restore Detective Vega and her husband?" I asked him.

"Restore them? Hell, I'll see to it that they're promoted! I have the authority, you know."

I nodded, but not at him. That was what I'd needed to shake his hold over me—a statement I knew to be blatantly false. As long as Vega held onto the truth about the Discovery Society, she was dangerous to the mayor and whomever was standing behind him. Budge responded to my nodding with a back clap.

"Attaboy!" he said.

But how to get out of this? My mind went to what Claudius had said before sending me: *You're going somewhere that the rest of the Order cannot. But you can still call on the power of the collective.*

I called on it now. I didn't know what to expect—or if I should even be attempting it. I would be drawing power from the senior members, power they might need. But something assured me that if they could spare it, they would provide it. My mind expanded to that now-familiar space that was my magic, the magic of the collective. I couldn't hold onto it, though, and an instant later, I was back. Spent and powerless.

But something *had* happened.

A wave was bending slowly through the shadow reality. Could anyone else feel it? Budge was still gripping my shoulder and smiling, while everyone else looked on this strange scene of the mayor getting palsy-walsy with New York's most wanted.

When the wave reached the helicopters, one of them pitched suddenly. The second one veered from its path, but too slowly. The diving chopper chewed the gunman in half and gashed out plates of metal.

"Hey!" Budge shouted as his body guards pulled him toward safety.

He stretched his hand back, a fervent look on his face as if he expected me to grab hold and go with him. And then the guards turned him around and, with arms over his stooped back, hustled him through the raining debris.

The first chopper broke off the second's tail rotor. Its rudder swung into the bay door, taking out another gunman, and the two choppers became interlocked. An explosion followed, raining chunks of flaming metal now.

At the mayor's SUV, the Iron Guard had opened the back door and were shoving Budge inside. For a moment, I saw another figure in the backseat, a beautiful young woman with pomegranate colored lips and luminous eyes. She moved a scepter to her other side, and then the door slammed closed.

The SUV roared around and several Iron Guard vehicles swung into its wake, knocking over Street Keepers. The two helicopters plummeted, scattering everyone still amassed across the intersection.

"We can go now," Hermes as Alec said from my shoulder.

When he tugged me into a run, I realized that *he'd* been the one to send out the wave, not me. But the power of the collective had restored my casting prism, and not a moment too soon.

I aimed my cane past Vega and Jag at a rolldown steel door to the garage. Driving a wedge of hardened air under it, I expanded the wedge rapidly. The door rattled up, depositing a mess of metal parts. Behind us, more explosions erupted as the helicopters crashed to the street. We ducked under the door, the enclosed garage muting the pandemonium at our backs.

With the beam of her flashlight bouncing from the taillights of parked cars, Vega led us down a ramp and then slammed into a push bar at the back of the parking garage. The door flung open onto a final set of steel steps that zigzagged down to a narrow access road running along the East River.

"There!" she said, pointing out a small pier where a thirty-foot fishing boat was moored.

"Grizz actually came," Jag said in surprise.

We hit the road at the same moment the chopping of a motor sounded behind us. It was Red Beard. He'd followed us from the chaos and was now jouncing his bike down the steps at the back of the garage. And he was carrying that damned whip.

Jag turned and began squeezing off shots, but the rounds burst harmlessly against some sort of protective field. Red Beard was so focused on navigating his cumbersome bike around each turn, he never looked up.

"Keep going," I panted, ducking behind a cement bollard. "I've got him."

Jag fired a few more times before running to catch up with Vega and Alec, whom I'd waved onward.

I listened as the tires rattled down the final steps, engine gunning violently as the bike reached the road. I spoke quickly, gathering power, fixing my hands into a batter's grip around my cane. Believing me to be somewhere ahead, Red Beard sped up. I waited until the bike was almost to me before standing.

"*Forza*"—I swung the cane with all my strength—"*DURA!*"

The concentrated force that came off the cane collided into his protection at face level in a blast of white light. The concussion knocked him from his bike, which continued riderless, veering off the seawall and into the East River. Red Beard landed on his back hard enough to knock the shades from his head and the whip from his hand. When he struggled to sit up, blood spilled from his nose into his beard, and he collapsed down again. He watched my approach with crossed, unfocused eyes.

"Nothing personal," I said, stooping to retrieve the whip.

I caught up with the others, who'd stopped to watch, and we ran the rest of the way to the pier. Though the boat was a little lopsided and flaking paint, it sported a powerful four-engine configuration. Homely, maybe, but engineered for speed. As we made our way down the pier, a burly shadow shuffled from the cabin.

"Took you long enough," he grunted.

"Yeah, well, we got held up," Vega said.

"Yeah, well, I almost took off without you," Grizz retorted, pulling on the mooring rope to bring the boat flush against the pier.

Vega cocked her head for Jag to climb aboard, but I

gripped the thick arm of his battle suit and extended my right hand.

"You've more than earned it," I said.

I braced for a bone-breaking squeeze, but he responded with a respectful grasp and shake. "We'll have to do it again sometime," he joked before turning to Alec. "No hard feelings, I hope."

"We're good," Alec said.

Jag gave him a thumbs-up. "Best of luck, you two."

The boat rocked beneath his weight, leaving Vega alone with us on the pier.

"I just wanted to say thank you," she said. "You didn't have to get me here."

I took that to mean not just to the boat, but to a place where she felt like herself again.

"You helped us," I said. "Not only that, you're... Well, you're a good person. It was the least we could do."

She started to extend her hand but then moved in for a hug. The gesture was tense, almost formal, but when I held the back of her head, she yielded, allowing the hug to become something more familiar.

"C'mon, c'mon," Grizz muttered. "I don't got all night."

Vega separated from me and shook Alec's hand. "Take care of yourselves."

"You, too," I said.

I watched her climb aboard. Grizz unlooped the mooring lines from the wooden piling and snarled at us before returning to the cabin. A black beanie covered his head, but I recognized the lumpy face, and only then did his New York accent fall into place. Grizz, the small-time drug smuggler, was Hoffman's shadow.

I snorted. *Son of a gun.*

The engines started up and the boat pulled from the pier. Hoffman turned up the East River, where he reared the boat into high speed. I could just make out Vega and Jag waving from the back. By the time I raised my hand, they were practically out of sight.

"You all right?"

When I turned, I wasn't sure whether I would find Alec or Hermes, but it was Alec. He was asking how I felt about having to say goodbye to my wife's shadow.

"It was harder than I thought it'd be," I admitted. "But yeah. I'm fine."

When he nodded, I understood that this was how he must have felt seeing me with someone who wasn't his mother.

On the road, Red Beard was still down. Above us, several blocks away, the aftermath of the helicopter crash raged on.

"Let's ditch this place, huh?" I said.

40

W e arrived at the actual present on a construction site above the East River. There were no makeshift piers here, just a view of the Queensborough Bridge, its lights reflected beautifully from the water. It took climbing over a concrete partition and waving my arms crazily at the edge of FDR Drive to get a cab to stop. As Alec and I climbed in, dozens of drivers laid on their horns and shouted at us for blocking traffic.

It was good to be back.

"West Tenth Street," I told the cabbie.

"You got it, man," he said in a friendly Moroccan accent.

"Your place?" Alec asked me, his pack jostling on his lap.

"I'm going to have to run as soon as we get there, but my wife will set you up. I want you to take the night to think about what I proposed. I really want you to stay with us, at least for a little while. Your mom is safe," I reminded him.

He nodded pensively and looked out his window. In the glass's reflection, I watched the green lights take hold in his eyes.

"The woman in the backseat," I said. "That's who you wanted me to see."

Hermes turned his impish face toward me. "Do you know who she was?"

I'd looked into Greek witches and sorcerers, but those had been the wrong places. The scepter had been the first hint, the color of the woman's lips, the second. But it was her eyes that had cemented it for me. Eyes that balanced the darkness of the underworld, where Hades had forced her into queenhood, and the light and bounty of the living world, where she was allowed to return each spring.

"Persephone," I replied.

"Very good. Now you see what we're up against."

"A Greek god."

A *major* Greek god, more accurately—daughter of Zeus, half-sister of Hermes. But by most accounts, she was gentle and forbearing, a god of fertility. She was also an Olympian. Why would she want to bring about the return of Cronus and the Titans?

Seeing my perplexed expression, Hermes said, "Persephone has many aspects. To those who worshipped this aspect of her, the one you saw, she is a wronged god. A vengeful god. Kidnapped, forced into marriage to Hades— with our father's full knowledge, I should add—and tricked into eating the pomegranate seed that would bind her to that wretched underworld for the rest of her eternal existence. Is it any wonder she would seek to relitigate the Titanomachy and put her lot in with the Titans?"

I saw his point. It also fit with what I'd seen in the Discovery Society. Even as an unwilling queen of the under-world, she would have had access to dark potions, mythic creatures, and Cronus's scythe, the last via a portal to Tartarus. But she couldn't release Cronus into the shadow present herself. A god of his stature required human worship and sacrifice—something the Discovery Society turned Society of Cronus had provided in spades.

"Why didn't she strike us down back there?" I asked in a lowered voice.

"Don't worry about our driver," Hermes laughed. "Everything we're saying sounds Greek to his ears, because I've made it so. As for your question, she doesn't have the power. Or rather, I've become too powerful. When she got into that business at the Discovery Society, I was a tablet inside of a box. My interference was the least of her worries. But then I called to Alec, and through him, I called to you. She didn't count on that. And by the time you thwarted her efforts, I had achieved enough strength to balance against her."

"Then why didn't you destroy *her* back there?"

"I said 'balance against,' not 'overwhelm.' I haven't the power any more than she does."

"Or is it because you still have feelings for her?"

Hermes's unrequited love for Persephone was all over the myths. He had been the one to retrieve her from the underworld before Hades deceived her into eating the pomegranate seed that bound her to his kingdom.

He smiled wistfully. "I won't deny it. You saw her. She's perfect, right? But I value human existence more than my love for her."

I thought back to my argument with Alec about the definition of a trickster. He had disagreed with my use of Prometheus as an example, arguing that his deceptions were intended to benefit humankind, making him a cultural hero.

Pure tricksters, on the other hand, were amoral, indifferent to humans. Where did Hermes fall, I wondered? Particularly this version, who'd been worshipped by a thieves guild?

"Is that why you're stashing gods like Arimanius here?" I asked. "You're in an arms race with Persephone?"

"They're insurance, in case it does come to war. I can't summon all of the original Olympians any more than Persephone can summon all of the original Titans. So we gather what allies we can, those for whom there are objects that hold the old worship for them. But I trust it won't come to war. You saw her scepter. This is the artifact that holds the old worship for *her*. Destroy it, and she ceases to exist."

"And everything goes back to the way it was," I said, repeating Budge's claim about destroying the Tablet of Hermes.

"Not quite. I still have work to do. The mayor was correct about the tablet." Using his knee, he bounced the pack up and down. "It was stored in the shadow present for safekeeping, but it was never meant to remain for centuries. After so much time, it has awakened several objects of worship from the old world, and drawn them to the city that boasts some of the most powerful ley energy anywhere. Some years ago, for example, an antique coin honoring the Minotaur was lost in the subways." His eyes twinkled with mischief. "But the most powerful of these is Persephone's scepter. Once it's destroyed, I can deal with the others. And once this is done, I will ask you to open the box."

"The Box of Hermes?"

"It's what preserves the tablet, preserves *me,* but the group that constructed the box is no more. I serve no one now."

"You would erase yourself like that?" I asked skeptically.

"To preserve my father's world and for the good of humankind, yes."

Would a cultural hero actually say that, or just a trickster pretending to be one?

"And you'll release Alec? He's just a boy," I reminded him. "He didn't ask for this."

"Of course," he replied, not breaking eye contact. "But we're getting ahead of ourselves. First, we must destroy the scepter."

"How?"

"In due time, in due time. But I warn you. Just as you have seen Persephone this night, she has seen you. She knows our plans, and she will do everything in her power to stop them and bring about Cronus's return. As you've correctly deduced, Cronus will replace humankind with a worshipping race, one that will grow his power manifold. He'll lay claim to the entire Universe, including this one." Hermes gestured around us. "Far better if we destroy the scepter before that happens, no?"

"That could be a problem," I said.

When Hermes's eyebrows drew together, I pulled the tactical whip from my coat pocket and turned over the blunt handle.

"Do you know what it is?" I asked.

"It's beyond my ken, I'm afraid, but I saw what it did to you."

"Yeah, and I *felt* what it did to me. Those Street Keepers didn't just happen to show up when we were making our final run for the garage. My magic alerted them. I don't know what kind of being empowered them, not yet, but anything I do in the shadow present is going to register, including attempting to destroy Persephone's scepter."

Hermes appeared to be losing interest. "I trust you'll figure it out. In the meantime, I have my own figuring out to do."

"Wait!" I grabbed his arm before the light could vanish from his eyes. "When you say you'll release Alec..." I felt my tone turn harsh in my throat. "You mean intact, as he was. No harm done, right?"

Hermes's eyes narrowed as they peered into mine. "This care for your son," he said mysteriously, "hold onto it." The green lights dwindled into the depths of Alec's dark irises. He blinked twice, then nodded at me as if his gaze had merely wandered before he returned it out the window.

I watched him, weighing Hermes's final words, then powered my phone on. The messenger god had just dropped a lot of info, but right now I had obligations here. Alerts began arriving on my phone.

I pressed the final one, which took me to my voicemail.

"Croft, it's Hoffman again," his recorded voice said. *"Gorgantha's out of surgery at General."* I straightened, my stomach drawing into a sick knot. *"Dr. Nnamdi is seeing her—she's worked with sups before. Says she's stable, but they don't exactly have mer blood to give her, so they're keeping her volume up with saline. I know you're away, but the sooner you can get over there, the better."*

"Change of plans," I told the driver. "I need to stop at New York General."

Alec turned toward me. "What's up?"

"It's that case I'm working on. Someone was hurt." I prayed it wasn't badly. I would never forgive myself if Gorgantha had answered my call and been hurt badly. "I'll have the driver take you on to my place."

"Yes, no problem, man," the driver assured me.

I called my wife to tell her what was happening, then followed it with a call to Hoffman to let him know I was on the way.

41

Gorgantha's bed at New York General was a steel whirlpool tank that had been filled with saltwater. Otherwise, the space looked like a hospital room with IVs and monitor lines running into her large body. She was supine in the tank, eyes closed, head supported by a thick pad affixed to one end.

"We had to put her back under sedation," Dr. Nnamdi explained. Younger than I'd pictured, the doctor had a copper pixie cut and intense eyes that blinked a lot. "She was delirious when she started to awaken earlier. Lashed out a few times."

I noticed the mitts on Gorgantha's taloned hands. "How bad were her wounds?"

"She came in with multiple deep lacerations across her thorax and down both legs. We repaired two ruptured vessels and sutured her more severe cuts. We managed to stop the bleeding, but she lost a lot of fluid."

The creature grabbed her like it grabbed the others, I thought, *but Gorgantha got away.*

"I was told you might be able to help with that?" Dr. Nnamdi prompted.

"Is there a way to get her out of the tank without hurting her? What I do doesn't mix well with saltwater."

"There's a harness under her. I'll have a tech come in and lift her out. Is there anything else you need?"

"That should do it."

To her credit, Dr. Nnamdi didn't ask what type of work I planned to perform, or even what a mermaid was doing in her hospital. I would have to be sure to get her number for future emergencies.

The tech arrived shortly, a muscular young man who wheeled a lift over to the tank, attached the harness to the lift's cradle, and put his shoulder into a crank handle until Gorgantha was suspended, water spilling off her. He told me to hit the call button when she was ready to go back in and left.

No sooner had the door closed than I started into my healing mantra. I usually applied it to a specific wound or area, but for Gorgantha, I bathed her entire body in the gauzy white light, willing everything I had into the spell. Throughout the process, I picked up flashes of sharp pain, churning water, panic.

By the time I finished, I sensed that Gorgantha had fallen into a deeper, more restorative sleep. I withdrew on weak legs and leaned against the wall, spots dancing in my vision.

"Welcome back," a gruff voice said. "How is she?"

Hoffman had entered the room at some point. He dragged a chair over now and angled it for me to sit down, which I did gratefully. As the spots receded, it was hard to reconcile this version of him, a homicide detective in a suit, with the drug smuggler captaining a boat in the shadow present, but he'd made different choices in this reality. Or, more likely, this reality had offered him better options.

"Between surgery and the healing spell, she should recover," I said. "But she's going to be out for a while."

Hoffman eyed her suspended, light-haloed body.

"Would you mind hitting that button for the tech?" I said. "Do you know what happened to her?"

"She swam the rivers like you asked," he replied, going over and pressing the call light in the wall. "We had a helicopter following her. Worked it out so she'd come up at designated points and signal 'nothing' or 'something.'"

"Good thinking," I said, feeling slightly better about having abandoned the search.

"When she finished with the Hudson and East, she headed over to Dead Horse Bay. She didn't stay long on account of the mess. After another 'nothing' signal, she indicated that she wanted to check out something else. I don't know if she was on the trail of something or what, but she headed back toward Upper Bay. Just past Governor's Island, she dove down. When she surfaced ten minutes later, it was like this." He gestured toward her. "The helicopter crew scooped her up and flew her here."

"Did the crew see anything?"

He shook his head as the tech returned. We waited for him to lower Gorgantha back into the tank and remove the lift from her harness. She came to a floating rest in her natural medium, a serene look on her face.

"Anyway," Hoffman continued when the tech left, "we took a look at the most recent sonar readings around Upper Bay. Turns out there's a deep depression right where Gorgantha went down. I'm thinking she tracked the thing there."

"The charges drove it out of Dead Horse Bay," I said, musing aloud, "and it went and found the next deepest spot. Only it's awake now, and hungry. It's been going to the Manhattan waterfront for nighttime feedings."

"Aren't there enough fish out there?"

"Some of the ancient creatures acquired appetites for souls."

"Sweet Jesus. Well, thanks to your friend, we know where it's laired. Question now is, how do we kill the damned thing?"

As I considered the problem, his phone rang.

"Hoffman," he answered. "Hey, Croft's back, let me put you on speaker. Oh, and before you start, I haven't told him about Mr. Funny yet." Then to me: "We got an exemption on account of him being a supernatural. The DA agreed to a two-week hold so they can figure out whether he's worth charging." He pointed to the phone and mouthed *Rules*, as if I hadn't already guessed. "All right, what's going on?"

"Harbor Patrol is continuing aerial sweeps of the lower rivers," Detective Rousseau said. "They're not reporting anything in the water, but they say Pier 16 is lit up like a Christmas tree. Looks like a big party going on down there."

"Can't they break it up?" Hoffman asked.

"Negative," Rousseau replied. "It's sanctioned by the city. Apparently, Mayor Lowder is in attendance."

I stood from the chair. "How many people?"

"At least a hundred."

"Dammit," I seethed. "And right after he promised he was shutting everything down." Apparently he'd made an exception for himself. I grabbed my phone and scrolled for the mayor's direct number. When I punched it, the call went to a full mailbox.

"What do you want to do?" Rousseau asked.

I stuffed my phone back into a pocket. "We're heading there now."

Hoffman, who usually didn't like me infringing on his authority, surprised me by nodding. "Direct any officers you can over there," he added. "I don't care if he is the mayor, we're gonna bust this thing up—by force if we have to. The last thing our task force needs is more freaking disappeared."

As Hoffman sped us toward Lower Manhattan, I kept trying to reach Budge. After the fourth failed attempt, I suspected he was screening me.

"Will you take a look at that?" Hoffman muttered as we neared the piers that jutted into the East River. After the Crash, the piers had fallen into disuse, then disrepair. Ferry services and a circle line ran from one, but the rest were closed to the public pending improvements that never seemed to come. Now, though, Pier 16 was festooned with colorful lights and strobes that flashed in time to a thumping beat.

Hoffman veered off South Street and onto a walkway beneath FDR Drive. He parked near the pier's entrance, which was being manned by private security, and we jumped from his sedan.

"Hey, you can't park here!" one of the guards shouted.

"Oh, yeah?" Hoffman said as the smallest one ran up. "And which one of you rent-a-cops is gonna stop me?"

Flustered, the guard jogged beside us. "Well, you can't get in without an invite. This is a private event. VIP only."

"Then what are *you* doing here?" Hoffman said.

"I'm working security," he replied, the dig wasted on him.

"Well, here's my invite." Hoffman flashed his badge. "We've got actual police business."

The guard stammered, "W-well, what about him?"

"He's with me," Hoffman said. "Now tell your knuckle-heads to make like the Red Sea before we go Moses on your sorry asses."

The guard turned to me as if I might be more reasonable, but there wasn't time for this crap. "Do it," I warned, readying my cane for a force invocation. Fortunately, it didn't come to that. The guard waved to his crew.

"It's fine, they're NYPD," he called. Then, to save face: "I said they could go in."

Hoffman barked a laugh as he limped past the guards on his ortho boot. "Sure he did."

The pier was a crush of fashionably dressed bodies holding drinks and, judging from their bright faces, scintillating conversations. At the far end, a crowd bounced to the techno music being spun by a DJ. Attendance must have grown since Detective Rousseau talked to Harbor Patrol because it was at least two-hundred strong now.

"I'm gonna tell the DJ to shut it down!" Hoffman shouted above the noise.

"Keep your eye out for the mayor!" I shouted back.

I followed Hoffman as he shoved and shouldered his way through the crowd. With its unobstructed view of the Brooklyn Bridge, the pier made a fantastic nighttime venue —if not for the monster laired nearby. Something I'd warned Budge about, and yet here we were. As I searched for him, I was acutely aware of the dark waters lapping the pilings on three sides of us and how puny the guard rails looked. Worse, the security posted along the pier's perimeter was facing the wrong way—inward instead of out.

Hoffman and I passed under a covered area at the pier's center with drink bars on either end, the servers wearing tuxedos. No sign of Budge here, either. I grabbed the arm of an older man with a regal coat and snow-white hair, the kind of person who looked moneyed enough to know Budge personally.

"Have you seen the mayor?" I shouted.

He shook his head in annoyance and returned to his circle of conversation, where a woman was touting Centurion United as a solid long-term investment. "They do *everything*," she crowed, "even monster-hunting now!"

By the time I caught up to Hoffman, he was climbing to the DJ's stage. He showed his badge, and shouted something. The DJ, who had half a headset pressed to his far ear, never stopped bopping to the music. Hoffman leaned in and shouted some more, but the DJ only shook his head as if to say, *my stage, my show.*

Hoffman's face knotted up, and he began grasping for wires. The DJ blocked him, and a hand-wrestling contest ensued.

I'd seen enough.

"Disfare!" I shouted, releasing a cone of pure energy from my cane.

It swallowed the DJ's setup, setting off several small explosions. The music squawked, then collapsed into an electrical hum that had everyone covering their ears. Finally, it cut out entirely. Hoffman was poised to backhand the DJ, who was staring dumbstruck at his ruined equipment, but then gave me a thumbs-up. As he cupped his palms to the sides of his mouth, I joined him on stage.

"Party's over!" he shouted. "Everyone needs to leave!"

Boos sounded, first from the dance floor, but they quickly spread the length of the pier. "Turn the music back on!" someone complained.

"The pier is officially shut down!" Hoffman continued. "Order of the NYPD!"

Projectiles started to arrive. A skewered shrimp sailed past us, followed by chunks of sushi, and then a plate of prosciutto and cheese. When a cream tartlet stuck to Hoffman's forehead, he wiped it away aggressively and turned to me.

"Can you do something to get them moving?"

I reached into my coat and palmed a pair of lightning grenades. *A too-close-for-comfort strike in the water should do the trick without setting off a stampede.*

But before I could hurl one, I saw that the covered area we'd walked under supported a rooftop deck. Mayor Lowder was up there, waving for my attention. When he saw he'd succeeded, he made an urgent beckoning motion for me to join him.

Screams sounded.

They came from the crowd on the dance floor. I followed their stricken faces and pointing fingers to the security guards lining the end of the pier. Where one had just been standing was a noticeable gap.

42

The crowd on the dance floor began backing from the end of the pier. I waved at the remaining guards, who were oblivious to what had happened.

"Get away from the water!" I shouted, angling for a better view.

A guard turned toward me just as something dark and ragged tethered his neck. A burst of blood sprayed the deck, and he disappeared in a backflip. The crowd began surging toward the other end of the pier. Seeing the panic, but still puzzled, the remaining guards pulled pistols and panned the water. Another ragged tendril swallowed a guard's weapon and spiraled up his arms to his shoulders. He didn't have time to fire or cry out before he too was yanked over the side.

"*Vigore!*" I shouted.

The force invocation split from my cane and seized the remaining guards. I jerked my cane forward, and they sprawled from the railing. As they began pushing themselves up, Hoffman was there to grab them by the scruffs of their uniforms.

"Clear the pier!" he hollered as he shoved them toward the receding crowd.

My next invocation sent walls of hardened air glimmering around the sides of the pier, boxing us in.

Hoffman came panting up beside me. "Backup's on the way to help with the crowd."

"Call the Sup Squad," I said. "Tell them to come armed with flamethrowers and to pack extra fuel."

"We gonna cook this thing?"

"For starters. But first I have to get it out of the water."

Thanks to tidal currents, the East River was mostly salt—a crappy medium when it came to concentrating energy into manifestations. I wasn't going to be able to pluck the creature from its habitat, and I damned sure wasn't going to be able to plunge in after it. I'd have to figure out another way.

As the screams receded behind us, Hoffman called the Sup Squad. I peered around. Nothing was attacking my protections, but I could hear a hill of water passing underneath us, as if something very large were paralleling the pier just below the surface.

"Squad's a few minutes out," Hoffman said when he got off his phone.

"There were people up on the deck earlier, including the mayor," I said. "Check to make sure they cleared out, then set up a cordon at least two hundred feet from the water. Tell me when the Sup Squad gets here."

"You're staying out on this thing?" he asked, incredulous.

"I can't let the creature go back out again. We need to end this tonight."

"Just so long as it doesn't end *you*."

A hill of water moved under the pier from the other side now. I could feel the creature's nearness in my gut, a rocking, nauseating sensation. Hoffman must have felt it too because his face soured as he swallowed.

"All right, I'm going up," he said. "Stay safe."

With a parting back-clap, he headed toward the deck.

As I continued listening into the water, the germ of an idea was taking hold. I took stock of myself. The last two days had been long, sleepless, stressful, and had cost me a crap-ton of energy. If Thelonious weren't in the equivalent of a convalescent home, my incubus would have visited two or three times. My call to the collective had replenished me, but I could feel the indicator needle sliding down again.

Still, I believed I was up to the task.

"Deck's clear!" Hoffman called behind me. "And the Squad's pulling up!"

I turned to find that the pier had completely emptied out. Beyond, beams from two personnel carriers cut through the silhouettes of rubber-neckers and the security guards who'd been manning the entrance. To the latter's credit, they were keeping everyone back.

It took me a moment to notice that the sound of moving water had stopped. I stepped forward cautiously and searched the water beyond the end of the pier. A large swell was diminishing as it moved away.

No!

Sparks crashed around me as I allowed the pier's shielding to collapse. I ran toward the guard rail, waving my arms overhead.

"Hey!" I shouted. "Get back here!"

"What the hell are you doing?" Hoffman called down from the deck.

The swell continued to diminish, then stopped suddenly and reversed direction. In the space of a second, desperation turned to hope to an electric fear. The creature was surging toward the pier again—and fast. As the swell of water grew, I retreated until I was about fifty feet from the end of the pier.

That should do it.

I stopped and whispered, *"Protezione."*

The air around me shimmered and hardened into a form-fitting shield.

"Stay up there!" I called to Hoffman, sensing this was going to be my one good chance. "When I tell you, move the Squad into position!"

If he answered, I couldn't hear him. I was sending bands of energy from my shielding to the pillars supporting the deck behind me. I wrapped the pillars low, then sent another band from my right leg down between the pier's boards, anchoring it to a thick metal cross-section. The pier had been structurally reinforced for the party, and I hoped it would be enough now. Who knew how large a creature we were dealing with?

I tested my harnessing system to ensure I was secure, then leveled the guard rail at the end of the pier with a force blast. It fell into the water, leaving only exposed planking.

"Make the first move, you—"

The tendril arrived like a whip, wrapping my neck just as it had the security guard's. But as it contracted, my protection, as well as the system securing me to the pier, held. The appendage looked like a thick belt of seaweed. Every several inches, jagged ridges protruded from its underside, not unlike the bladed edges of oyster shells. I thought of Emma's torn-up stroller and Gorgantha's wounds.

Two more tendrils arrived, wrapping my waist from opposite sides.

"That's right," I grunted as I reinforced my protection. "Keep 'em coming, big boy."

As if obliging me, a host of encircling tendrils swarmed in, enough, I calculated, for me to proceed to step two. I spoke, invoking another layer of shielding around the first. The tendrils crunched and flattened as I pressed the layers together.

The creature may have had me, but now I had it too.

I cranked the bands I'd secured to the pillars behind me. The force pulled me into a backward step. Releasing the anchor from my right leg, I fashioned a new one around my left, fastening it below the pier.

I was planning to land this son of a bitch.

Through its insistent tugging, I felt the creature's immense hunger, its greed for human flesh and soul. I continued cranking, continued moving back one step at a time, continued anchoring my rear leg to the pier. The thing felt like it weighed a couple tons, but I was also fighting the weight of the water above it.

At last, I heard what I'd been listening for: the sound of cascading water. The creature had broken the surface.

Hoffman, who had a better angle than me, spoke in a pale, backing-away voice: "Holy shit, Croft. Holy shit."

With my next two steps, a mound of seaweed crested beyond the pier's end, then fell again. I paused, breathing hard. Without a ramp to guide it up, this was going to be the biggest challenge—getting it onto the pier.

"The Squad's in firing range!" Hoffman shouted.

More tendrils lashed in—and past me. I was afraid they were going for Hoffman or the Squad, but they were wrapping the pillars. When they tugged, more of the massive seaweed mound appeared.

It's giving itself a boost.

But where I had lashed myself low to the pillars, the creature had seized them high. Behind me, the entire deck groaned. Hoffman shouted, and I heard his uneven footfalls beating down the far steps.

More tendrils snaked in, wrapping the pier's planks now. As if working in concert, the creature and I heaved together. At least half of its body rose into view. The volume of seaweed made it look like the matted head of a sea giant. That was what sitting at the bottom of Dead Horse Bay for a few millennia would do.

But beyond the layers of growth, I could make out two columns of eyes. Possessed of a disturbing intelligence, they angled inward as they ascended toward a ridged crown.

The creature teetered at the pier's end. I strained with everything I had to bring it over the edge, while it remained just as intent on feeding. I pictured more than saw the Sup Squad arrayed behind me, itching to light up the thing with their flamethrowers. But if that happened, there was a good chance I'd lose it.

"Not yet..." I grunted, taking another backward step. "Not yet..."

A pair of deep snaps sounded from the pillars behind me, and then the creature seemed to arrive all at once, splashing onto the end of the pier like a displaced mountain top. It fixed its dozen eyes at me and began squelching forward on a mass of tendrils.

A chorus of muttered swears erupted behind me.

"Not yet!" I repeated, showing the Sup Squad a hand this time.

Below the creature's eyes, the seaweed parted and a small cavern opened. The dangling vegetation obscured most of it, but I glimpsed hooks for snagging prey and concentric muscles to crush and compress its victims to its center. And because I wasn't coming to it, the mouth was coming to me.

Sweat poured down my face as the creature squelched closer.

"The hell are you waiting for?" Hoffman shouted. "A written invite?"

I eyeballed the creature's distance to the end of the pier, to the water. The closer it came, the longer its path to safety. When it was fifteen feet away, I decided that was close enough.

"*Now!*" I shouted.

Flames jetted from nozzles in a collective whoosh, billowing as they impacted the creature. Its feeding mouth contracted, emitting an awful gargling noise. The ragged tendrils recoiled en masse, releasing me. Predictably, the creature began reversing toward the water, fleeing the thousand-degree jets of fuel.

Have to work fast...

With a shouted series of invocations, I dispersed the anchoring system around me and refashioned the walls of hardened air to box in the pier again. The creature, which had been picking up speed, collided into the far wall in a burst of flames and steam. Its burning tendrils scrambled up and down the confinement, then reached over to try the left side of the pier. I focused into my blade's second rune.

"*Fuoco!*" I bellowed.

Elemental fire circled the rune and shot the length of the blade and into the creature. Its body shuddered in a way that suggested pain. Understanding it had nowhere to go, the creature turned to confront its attackers. Blanketed in flames now and sending up billowing clouds of vapor, it was becoming harder to see.

"Back up everyone!" I shouted. "Get back!"

The tendrils that lashed out now weren't meant to grab, but slash and sever. One landed across my face. Even shielded, I felt the raw score it left. More lashed against my body, the charred seaweed falling away now to reveal gray, mottled appendages, each with a jagged ridge along its underside. But the ridge wasn't part of the creature, I realized. It consisted of actual oysters that had colonized its natural grooves. The shells, made brittle by the intense heat, were fragmenting and spilling to the pier.

I willed more power into the fire rune. My intention was to burn off the rest of the seaweed, expose the creature, and then drive my blade through whatever soul-hungry heart sustained it. When a giant husk of charred vegetation split and fell from its hide, the creature looked half the size as when it had first arrived.

Its lashes slowed. Its dozen eyes canted down. When several sharp snaps sounded, I saw it was ripping out the planking, attempting to escape by dropping through the pier's floor. I responded with a base layer of hardened air.

"You're mine, bud."

With a gurgling cry that could only be interpreted as frustration, the creature shot its remaining tentacles past me and seized the pillars once more. Already damaged from the creature's earlier effort to heave itself onto the pier, the pillars snapped like gunshots, and the entire deck collapsed toward me.

"*Protezione!*" I cried.

I drew all my power around me as the structure broke over my back. I fell to the deck, stunned, buried, but my shielding had held. Outside, shouts sounded. Footsteps beat toward me. I felt debris being heaved aside. Soon, Sup Squad helmets were peering down at me. They all clamored at once, asking if I was all right.

"The creature," I said, pushing myself up from the wreckage.

I followed their gazes to where a thick column of steam stood beyond the end of the torn-up pier.

No, dammit.

I ran and looked over the edge. Beneath a flotsam of charcoal, I made out a pulsating, pinkish glow. The core of the creature, sinking away. I pictured the creature dragging itself out to sea and burying itself in the floor. Then years, or perhaps decades later, it would emerge, fully recovered, ready to feed again.

I shed my coat, and with shouts trailing me, I dove in.

43

As bubbles stormed around my icy plunge, I had two thoughts. The first was of Emma's father. There was no way in hell I could stand before the man who had lost his wife and little girl and tell him that I'd allowed their killer to get away. Not when I would have my own wife, and soon my own daughter, to go home to.

The second thought was of my father, who'd leapt into an abyss to repel an ancient being of death and destruction. And he'd done so without hesitation.

It was with this resolve that I began kicking after the creature, my father's sword extended ahead of me. In my blurred vision, I spotted the pink glow. It was angling farther into the East River as it sank down.

Drawn to the depths.

If it knew I was following it, it gave no indication. More likely, it was too preoccupied with its own survival. I kicked harder, pushing myself deeper. The glow grew by degrees, but could I reach it before I gave out? Already the pressure was swelling inside my ears and compressing my aching lungs.

Emma's father. My father.

I thought of them in turn, each one providing a fresh jolt of resolve. The creature was the size of a small bus by the time I arrived above it. Still large, but manageable. My eardrums had gone numb by this point, and my oxygen-starved chest was convulsing.

Now or never.

Aiming for the glow, I thrust my sword. The tip met resistance at the skin before plunging inside a softer center. My entire arm followed. A gurgle erupted, and the tendrils writhed, but their direction was aimless.

I'd severed the creature's core.

Pink glow leaked from the wound, but I needed to disperse the core entirely. Could I even shape energy while submerged under tons of saltwater? I summoned what I could, but it was disorganized, not nearly enough. Though I hadn't been able to hold on the last time, I turned to the power of the collective again and signed with the fingers of my right hand.

Disfare.

The word emerged as a weak glug, jiggling the creature's core, but nothing else.

I felt my consciousness stagger, but I couldn't bring myself to pull the sword free, not without trying one more time. I focused past the pain and pressure and my body's desperate need for air. And then I let go.

DISFARE!

The power arrived at once, flashing from my blade in a minor nova. The pink core erupted, shooting off in all directions. The creature's tendrils convulsed, and its mouth lunged for me, but both suddenly sagged. Around my sunken arm, the creature's form began to separate into large chunks, and then to dissolve.

I turned my blade upward and began kicking toward the surface. I didn't know how far down we'd gone, but I had seconds to emerge, if that. Shadows crowded my vision, and then strange, shifting colors. They coalesced into the face of my father. He was smiling and telling me how proud he was. I reached forward to hold him, to hug him, and that was when my head broke the surface.

A ragged breath shocked my lungs, and I began to hack. The colors receded from my vision. I was nearly to the middle of the river. Back toward the pier, an NYPD helicopter was searching the waters along the shore.

How long was I down there?

I tried to channel enough power into the sword to make it glow, but I was spent. Nothing in the tank, not even fumes. I waved the sword overhead once before my arm shook and splashed down again.

I rolled onto my back and began to kick. One way or another, I was going to reach the shore. Around me, remnants of the creature's core were floating to the surface, luminous and pink. I was wondering how something so beautiful could come from something so horrid when I realized they were aspects of the souls it had devoured, freed now. I found peace in that, in their company, but they didn't linger.

One by one, they lifted from the water, streaking the night sky.

I'd almost forgotten about the helicopter when it turned

suddenly and bathed me in a shaft of searchlight. As I bobbed in the East River, awaiting rescue, the final soul lifted off like the burbling laugh of a little girl.

"Good night, sweetie," I called after her.

44

I slept fourteen hours that night, not dreaming or awakening once. By the time I opened my eyes, it was mid-afternoon. I stretched my arms and cracked my neck side to side, then rotated my hips, sending the satisfying pops up my back.

God, I needed that, I thought of the night's sleep.

"How are you feeling?" Ricki called from the kitchen.

"After a shower and a kiss," I croaked, "I'll feel like a million bucks."

"Start with the shower. I'll have your breakfast ready when you come out. Then we'll see about that kiss."

My shower was long and hot and did wonders for my aching muscles. I spent a full ten minutes letting it pound my sore back.

After hoisting me from the water last night, the helicopter crew delivered me to a waiting ambulance. I huddled in a blanket, teeth chattering, while a pair of medics checked me out. My temperature was low, but not dangerously so, and the cuts and welts I'd suffered from the creature were minor. But the medics remained concerned. By various accounts I'd been underwater anywhere from twelve to fifteen minutes. They wanted to take me to a hospital for observation. I tried to argue, but I was too exhausted. It was Hoffman who came to my rescue and drove me home.

When we arrived, Ricki met us at the door with one of my healing potions, which I promptly downed. The last thing I heard was Hoffman saying, "Your man landed the biggest damned fish I've ever seen tonight," and then I was out.

I emerged from the bathroom to a full breakfast spread: pancakes, scrambled eggs, fried potatoes with onions and green peppers, and several strips of bacon. From the divan, Tabitha looked on hungrily, but because begging would be akin to complimenting my wife's cooking, she turned her irritation on me.

"Well, look who decided to get up," she said.

"If you're worried about being outslept, there are still a few hours left in the day."

I grinned, but she wasn't amused.

My wife was at the coffee maker when I walked up behind her and slipped my arms around her. The hardest part of working with her shadow had been having to refrain from these natural gestures of affection. "If I wasn't already married to you," I said, kissing the side of her neck, "I just might leave my wife."

Tabitha let out a dreary "ugh" from the next room.

"Not sure how I feel about the 'might' part," Ricki said, "but welcome back." She turned and gave me a long kiss, something I'd been missing as well. "There. We didn't get to do that properly last night."

"No, we didn't," I laughed. "I'm surprised I was even able to crawl into bed."

"You had help," she assured me, placing a steaming mug of Colombian dark roast in my hands. "Go. Start eating before everything gets cold."

I did as she said, cleaning my plates, including seconds on the pancakes. I couldn't remember the last time I'd eaten so much in one sitting. My wife took the seat opposite me, nursing a chamomile tea.

"Is Alec still here?" I asked.

Her eyes dipped. "He didn't show up last night."

"Not at all?"

"Your taxi driver did." As she said this, I recalled the friendly Moroccan. "He gave me this to give to you. It's from Alec."

She produced a folded page from his notepad and handed it to me.

It read:

Everson,

Thanks for the invitation to stay with your family. It means a lot to me, more than you know, but there are some things I need to take care of. This isn't goodbye – I'll see you again. I just didn't want you to worry.

Best,
Alec

When I read it again, the words blurred. I sniffed softly, reminding myself that I'd given him a choice and that he'd been responsible enough to let me know his decision. If he decided to come and stay, he would come and stay. I had to accept that. But it didn't mean I wouldn't worry about him, wouldn't miss him.

"I'm sorry," Ricki said, grasping my forearm.

I folded the note back and patted it. "I'll be all right."

She rubbed my arm. "Well, Hoffman filled me in on last night."

"What happened to task force confidentiality?" I teased.

"Hey, he was the one flapping his gums, and he's the leader of the thing. I just happened to be within hearing range. If I didn't know better, I'd say you have a new fan."

"Hoffman?"

"Well, for this week, anyway. You know his moods."

"Right," I chuckled.

"Then again, it's not every day you get to see someone pull a two-ton creature from the East River."

"Yeah, well, I hope to God it was a one-off. I'm not sure I have the back to pull in another one."

Or the lungs to go swimming after it, I thought.

"And you're sure you're all right?" she asked, giving me her critical face.

I tested myself with a cough. Save for a specter of aching, my chest felt fine, and I said as much. I wasn't sure if Hoffman had told her how long I was under. Something told me he hadn't. Did I have the collective to thank for those twelve to fifteen minutes? My magic? Or was it just one of those extraordinary instances where an ability inherent in all humans had been spurred into action?

I'd probably never know.

"So I guess that wraps up the task force, then," she said.

"Almost."

"Oh, no."

"Yeah, there's one more thing I need to do." I checked my

watch. "In fact, I should do it now. Do you want me to tell you?"

"Not if it's task-force related."

"Oh, so we're back to that?" I leaned over the table and kissed her smile. "Fair enough. Leave the dishes. I'll wash them when I get back."

As I stood, I made eye contact with Tabitha and cut my gaze toward the bacon fragments and puddle of grease I'd left on my plate. She thumped down from her divan before I was even out the door.

Because I hadn't called ahead, I was surprised when Mayor Lowder's secretary said he was expecting me. He was already standing behind his desk when I entered his office at City Hall. Last night, he'd evacuated the pier along with everyone else and hadn't stuck around. Now he wore a look of contrition.

"I know, I know," he said. "Everything you say, I deserve."

"You endangered a lot of lives last night. A *lot* of lives. And for what?"

"Hey, I'm agreeing with you, but I'm going to ask you to look at things from my angle for just a second." As he came from behind his desk, he wiped his cowlick from his brow. "What you do is straightforward. Identify the threat, find the bad guy—or thing—and stop it. Not to mention you're the very best at it. I'd give anything to be in your shoes. But I can't. I'm a politician, a city steward. I wear leather oxfords. I have to balance those kinds of threats against the interests of New York."

He may not have had a Greek god backing him here, but

he still had an absurd talent for making someone feel like his privileged confidant.

"Last night's party, for example," he went on. "I scheduled that six months ago. I couldn't just cancel it on, what, two days' notice—we're talking some of the biggest names in music." He lowered his voice. "This thing is still under major wraps, but since I trust you, Everson..." He lowered his voice further. "I'm planning a big event for next spring. 'Manhattan's River to River Festival,' we're calling it. Four days, top acts, piers turned into stages, a hundred-thousand-plus attendees. What better way to announce the triumphant return of New York's waterfront! Can't you see it?"

"After last night?" I said. "No."

"Yeah, well, that's gonna take a little PR to fix, but the coverage a concert event like that would bring the city—"

"Mayor," I said sternly. "People *died* last night."

"Yeah, I know." His face turned sober. "I thought I'd done enough, I really did. I paid top dollar for that security—you saw 'em. But you're right. The buck stops with me. Like I said, it's about having to balance threats with the city's interests."

"Is that why you told Detective Knowles to change the data?"

His brow creased in a look of confusion. "Is that what he told you?"

The mayor may have been a gifted bullshitter, but he'd hesitated just long enough.

"He didn't have to. You just supplied the motive. Who else would have wanted to keep the waterfront attacks on the down low? I don't know. Maybe someone with a vested interest in promoting a major waterfront concert?"

Detective Hoffman had been right—the order had come from up the chain. The top link, in fact.

"C'mon, Everson," he said. "Don't I always shoot straight with you?"

I pulled my phone out and hit the call button. The data hadn't come back on the number in Knowles's phone records yet, but it didn't have to now. A chime sounded from the mayor's breast pocket.

He drew out a small phone and checked the display.

"You *used* to shoot straight," I replied. "That's me, by the way."

Putting two and two together, Budge said, "Oh, that. Yeah, I've been calling him for updates. Kept me from bothering you and Hoffman. Figured he was the guy with the easiest access to the info."

"Calling him on a burner phone?" I said. "All right, let's cut the crap. How did you leverage him? Did it have to do with this being his final year till retirement? Did you tell him that you'd hate to have to cut loose a detective so close to earning his full pension, but the budget being what it is...?"

I'd known Budge long enough to know his threats were often subtle and just as often effective.

"Look," he said, showing his hands. "It was just until you came through, which I never had any doubts about. You're my wizard, my ace in the hole, my—"

"You crippled us," I cut in through gritted teeth. "Had we known half the cases were along the rivers, we could have closed down the parks and walks sooner. Lives could have been saved. New Yorkers. Your people."

"C'mon, Everson." He gave me an aggrieved look that said, *We just went over what it's like being someone in my position.*

But I was seeing little Emma in her stroller. I was seeing Demarcus Ward jogging along the Hudson. I was seeing all of the other victims who had been going about their lives before being yanked into the maw of an abomination.

"No," I growled. "You're going to shut up and listen for a change. First, Detective Knowles is getting a demotion to a desk, but he serves out his final year and earns a full pension." I couldn't gloss over what the detective had done, but he'd done it under duress, and he had children from a prior marriage depending on him.

"Second, if you *ever* pull a stunt like this with me or the city again, it's over." I motioned between us. "Not only that, but the papers are going to hear about what happened, how you sacrificed common New Yorkers for a million-dollar party. How do you think that'll go over with your voters, most of them still working their way back from the Crash? Are we on the same page so far?"

"Yeah. Sure, sure," he said anxiously, but I could tell by his expression he thought he was getting off easy. Maybe he was, but I had a final condition that was perhaps the most important of all.

"Third," I said. "Have you had any blackouts?"

His face bunched up in confusion. "Like from drinking too much?"

"Any kind of blackout. Falling asleep at your desk, collapsing out of nowhere, losing twenty minutes or a couple hours without an explanation for what happened to the time. Anything like that?"

He shook his head. "Just the occasional afternoon nap, but I have a couch."

I believed him, but I needed to make sure. It went back to something we'd learned with Eldred at the Discovery Society. If you existed in one present but not the other, you traveled back and forth as you were, as was the case with Alec and me.

However, if you existed in both, you shifted from one *form* to the other. Persephone, who now controlled shadow Budge, could send him into the good mayor here at any time.

"If it's happened or it starts to happen in the future," I said, "tell me right away. It means your life is in danger, and I'm the only one who's going to be able to save you."

Though Budge lavished concern on his city, I knew his true weakness, and that's where I'd chosen to hit him.

"S-save me?" he stammered. "Where is this coming from, Everson? What are you talking about?"

"Remember the conditions," I said, holding up three fingers as I backed away.

Then I turned and left.

45

One week later

Ricki and I finally hosted the dinner party we'd been talking about. With her being just a few weeks shy of her due date, I'd insisted we order from a caterer. We chose a surf-and-turf spread, which seemed to please everyone.

Mae and Bree-yark joined us, along with Hoffman (who brought several bottles of startlingly good wine), his wife Kay, and their two boys. Claudius made a surprise appearance. He didn't remember half the messages I left him, so I was dubious that he'd remember the invitation. The prospect of food helped, apparently. He spent the evening eating happily and lavishing attention on the women.

Gorgantha joined us as well. She'd made a full recovery, save for some faint scarring, but she assured me she never thought twice about coming to help and would wear her new scars like badges of honor. Hoffman's theory had been correct. She'd followed a trail from the muck at the bottom of Dead Horse Bay into the deep depression in Upper Bay.

There, her echo location hit on something big, and she went down to check it out. What she'd thought was a massive plant came to life and seized her with its razor-sharp appendages. She escaped by sending a high-frequency burst into it. When she told the story to the table, she managed to make it funny, which few but Gorgantha could have managed.

"That's the last time I'm picking a fight with a plant," she finished with an exaggerated huff. "That's for *damn* sure."

We all laughed, Bree-yark watching her with hero-worship in his eyes, something he'd acquired during our journey through the time catches. It was no slight on Mae, who was just as impressed with the giant mermaid.

Tabitha just watched her hungrily.

"Here," I said, forking the rest of my salmon steak onto her plate. "It'll taste better."

"You think you're *so* clever," Tabitha muttered, but dug in greedily while shooting me the occasional side-eye.

"So what's this I hear about you fixing to tie the knot?" Gorgantha asked Bree-yark. "You trying to break a mermaid's heart?"

As he stammered, she winked at Mae, who laughed.

"If you knew half of what I had to go through just to get him to ask," Mae said, "you'd thank me for saving you the trouble."

"It was that way with Percy," Hoffman's wife said.

"Oh, c'mon, no one wants to hear this," he said, his cheeks turning the color of apples.

I'd never heard Hoffman's first name spoken before—and it was an odd fit—but I was more interested in the story.

"He took me out to Arby's for lunch," she continued with a mischievous smile. "It was the middle of summer, and he was sweating and pushing roast beef sandwiches into his mouth like they were going out of style, not saying a word to me. I'd been waiting months for him to propose, and now I'm getting angry, thinking, 'Great, now I have to dump this jerk.' Turns out he was just really nervous, because once we got in the car, he pulled out the ring and popped the question."

"Yeah," Hoffman took up. "And right at that moment, some dummy decides to back up his delivery truck."

"We joke that that's our song," Kay said.

"Beep-beep-beep," they intoned together, which had us all laughing again.

Though it was wonderful being surrounded by friends—and, yeah, even Hoffman was starting to fit that moniker—I was conscious of the empty place setting beside me. I'd left a note for Alec in his bush at Dewitt Clinton Park, inviting him to come tonight in the off-chance he saw it, but he must not have.

When Ricki began clearing plates, I stopped her and took over. In the living room, Tony was showing Hoffman's boys his winning design in that day's egg-drop contest. I paused to listen, as proud of him as if he were my own. Bree-yark arrived beside me, carrying another stack of dishware, probably at Mae's prompting.

"Kid's a heck of an engineer," he said. "Sure he doesn't have goblin in his blood?"

"Not that we're aware of, but you never know. Speaking of which, am I ever going to get to see the basement unit? You've been down there all week."

Bree-yark peered from side to side, then surprised me by saying, "All right. But just so you understand, there's still a little left to be done."

We set the plates in the kitchen, and I made the be-right-back gesture to my wife. She made the hurry-it-up gesture and pointed at Claudius. Not wanting to be outdone, he was telling the table about his proposal to his fourth wife, but kept getting it mixed up with his first three and was having to backtrack repeatedly.

As we descended toward the basement, Bree-yark's unusual silence upped my nervousness. He'd never provided me a spare key for the padlock like he'd promised. Something told me that "a little left to be done" was code for "a big mess."

"All right, Everson," he said anxiously when we arrived before the door. He'd straightened up the corridor, anyway. "Here goes."

He removed the padlock, pushed open the door, and hit the light switch.

I stepped inside and stared around for several moments. There were a few materials and tools lying about, as well as several debris piles, but they were peripheral. I was staring at the wall of handsome shelving, the cupboards for storage, the iron-topped island for preparing spells, the floor space for casting. And by raising the ceiling a couple feet, he'd made the constricted square footage feel expansive.

"What do you think?" he asked.

"Do you want me to be honest? It's perfect."

"Yeah?" His eyes brightened. "You're not just saying that?"

I walked around now, running my hands over surfaces, testing their solidity. "No," I said at last. "This is exactly what I asked for. More, actually."

Bree-yark smiled with all of his teeth, the surest expression of a goblin's pleasure. Then his eyes slanted roguishly.

"What?" I asked.

"You haven't seen the best part."

I looked around again. "Best part?"

He walked to a section of bare wall between the bathroom and kitchenette. "I put a hole through here by mistake. Turned out it gives onto a storage area that'd been sealed off. Place hadn't been touched in fifty years. So, a little goblin ingenuity, and..." He depressed a false light switch and pulled. "Ta-da!"

One side of the wall separated and swung out on an unseen hinge. The light glowed into what first appeared to be a cave. I soon realized that was exactly what it was. A man cave. Two reclining chairs with cup holders and food trays faced a large wall-mounted flatscreen. A mini poker table sat off to one side. He'd even installed a glass-topped bar in the corner, with a small keg tub and fridge.

"I'm still working on the wiring, and someone's supposed to hook us up with satellite," he said. "Had to go a little over budget, of course."

"Of course," I echoed.

"You mad?"

I looked down at him. "Just be sure to make a duplicate key for yourself."

He barked out a laugh, then jumped up to high-five me. "Yes!" he exclaimed as our hands smacked.

Loyal friends like Bree-yark only came along once or twice in a lifetime, and given everything he'd done for me, including lancing the shaman's boil, it was the least I could do in return.

"Not to cut the party short," I said, "but I promised my wife I'd be right back."

"I'll be behind you in a couple," he said, moving the hidden wall back and forth. "I'm picking up a slight rub that I want to plane out."

I took a final look around my new casting/storage area

and returned upstairs, shaking my head. To think I'd ever doubted Bree-yark and his goblin engineering.

I was almost back to the apartment when I heard footsteps jogging up the stairs behind me. I waited, expecting to see Bree-yark emerging into the corridor, saying the job could wait, but it was Alec.

"Hey," I said, stunned. "Did you get my message?"

"Yeah, just now as I was coming through." He dug the envelope from a pocket and held it up. I noticed he was also pulling a small suitcase behind him. When he saw me looking at it, he said, "Is this still cool? Me staying here?"

I clasped his hand and pulled him into a powerful hug. "Of course it is. It's really good to see you again." My voice caught on the last word.

His return hug rivaled mine. "You, too."

We clapped the other's back at the same time and separated.

"Yeah, sorry it took me so long," he said. "I wanted to check on Mom and sort of fill her in on what was going on." My paternal instincts for worry fired up at the idea of him spending time in the shadow present after what had happened, but if Hermes was to be believed, he couldn't afford to expose Alec to harm.

"How did she take it?" I asked.

"Learning her son can do actual magic?" he shrugged. "About as well as can be expected."

"Where does she think you are?" My heart was suddenly thudding in my chest. Had he told her about me?

"I said I'd be training with someone she didn't know, but who she could trust. Not exactly a lie."

"No," I agreed, marveling at how much he sounded like me. "Not exactly."

Laughter erupted beyond the door, and he eyed it hesitantly. "And you're sure about this?"

Before I could respond, Bree-yark arrived at the top of the steps. "Alec!" he exclaimed, charging toward him. "Where in thunder have you been? You had Everson and me worried sick! Get over here, you little pipsqueak." He play-wrestled him against a wall and scrubbed his hair, making Alec chuckle.

"C'mon, you two hooligans," I said, opening the door and pulling Alec's suitcase inside.

He separated from Bree-yark quickly and smoothed his hair back in place as everyone at the table turned to look.

"This is Alec," I announced to the room. "The son of my shadow—or 'my son,' for short."

I took him around to everyone. He exchanged handshakes and accepted kisses from Mae as well as Claudius. By the time he reached my wife, she'd already set a plate of food at the place we'd saved for him. Whether it was conscious or not, she patted the shoulder where her shadow's bullet had gone through and gave him a hug.

"I want you to make yourself at home here," she said, her eyes soft and warm. "You can start by cleaning your plate."

"That's an order," I warned. "Don't let her friendliness fool you."

Alec smiled as he lowered himself and began to dig in. I went into the kitchen to prepare the coffee and desserts. As the laughter and conversation picked up again, the dinner party felt complete.

Everyone was here now.

46

I joined Ricki in our bed late that night, the dishes rinsed and loaded in the dishwasher, two large garbage bags tied off and waiting beside the front door to be taken down in the morning. The mattress squeaked under my weight, and she stirred.

"Is he settled in?" she asked, meaning Alec.

"I think he was asleep the second his head hit the pillow."

As the party wound down, Claudius remained long enough to look him over. He pronounced that although the bonds between him and the tablet were stronger, they didn't appear to be doing any harm. That was a huge relief. To be safe, I had Mae coax the bonds looser like she'd done the last time.

I then set Alec up in the guest bedroom, part of the renovations I'd undertaken at the start of the summer to make this our family home. I could never have guessed that it would be housing my shadow's son.

While I cleaned up post-party, my thoughts turned from

my concern for Alec to the standoff between Hermes and Persephone. I trusted that when Hermes had something to say about the scepter or the gods he was gathering, he would talk. That was an extra benefit of having Alec stay here. It would have to be soon, though. Arimanius, aka Mr. Funny, was scheduled to be released next week, barring another extension.

I wiped down the table more aggressively than I meant to. Though this had all started only a few weeks earlier when I'd found the box in the landfill, I was beyond ready to be done with the Greek gods.

My thoughts turned to Red Beard. The tactical whip I'd lifted from him was stashed in a salt bag inside a protective circle, which I would be relocating to my new unit shortly. Claudius hadn't recognized the strange energy that lingered in the steel cable; Arianna was occupied in other realms; and in the midst of winding down the task force, catching up with my classes, and checking on Gorgantha, I hadn't had time to investigate it myself. But I couldn't shake the feeling that it was connected to the absence of magic-users over there, as well as to why the city-wide wards were disabled and hidden.

You're not supposed to exist, Red Beard had told me.

And I couldn't shake a feeling that went to a deeper and darker place. Much as the cleanup project had awakened the ancient creature in Dead Horse Bay, I feared that my shadow had awakened something just as horrible on that trip to Venice that had deprived Alec of a father when he was three.

"I'm proud of you," Ricki said.

"Huh?" I jerked. I'd started to drift off, and it took me a moment to understand she was referring to Alec.

"For taking him in," she said, "looking after him."

"I'm glad I was able to spend some time with him first."

"To get to know him?"

"That, but it forced me to confront my ideas around being a father. With our daughter, I've been nervous. All right, scared. I don't talk about it much because I know you'll be here to show me the ropes, and I'll figure out the rest as she grows. But then suddenly, here's this fifteen-year-old boy—a magic-user, no less—and it was like the learning curve for being a father got ridiculously compressed. I started worrying about how I acted around him, how I didn't act, what I said, how I said it. Finally, I realized that all you can do as a parent is the best you can, accepting that it won't be perfect."

"You just saved yourself eighteen years of guilt," she murmured, scooting her head onto my shoulder.

As I stroked her hair, I considered the parallels to magic-using, where becoming adept meant letting go to an extent—much as I'd done in the depths of the East River the week before, when I had nothing left.

"What am I like over there?" she asked.

Her question surprised me. Every time that week that I'd brought up my collaboration with her shadow, she had deftly changed the subject. I thought it was because the whole idea still weirded her out, but now I sensed concern over what it would reveal about her.

"Well, let's see," I said. "You're tough, but tender-hearted. Cool under pressure, but hot when you see someone being wronged. And you're one of the most amazing people I've ever met. A close second, in fact, to the woman I married." I thought that would reassure her, but I could still feel her concern.

"Everson, there's something I never told you." She lifted her head so she could look into my eyes. "I almost shot you."

"What? When?"

"The first time I saw you."

"I made that much of an impression, huh?"

"I'm being serious."

I thought back to that encounter, more than four years ago now. An amateur conjuring case in Hell's Kitchen. By the time I reached the conjurer's apartment, his creation was feeding on his remains. I expended all my power banishing the thing, then failed to flee the scene before Thelonious took over. I didn't remember Ricki arriving or arresting me, but I'd seen my blood-covered mug shot, a boozy smile slanting my lips. I cringed now, imagining the kinds of things my incubus had said.

"Well, think about it," I chuckled. "It's what any reasonable person would have done."

"You can laugh, but I keep thinking about what I would have lost."

No wonder she'd been so preoccupied with her shadow shooting Alec. It also explained why she'd teared up when I told her about my own shadow's death.

"But you didn't," I stressed, turning serious. "This you, the one I'm holding, navigated all of those probabilities to arrive here, married to me—whom you *didn't* shoot—and now we're going to be parents. If that's not kismet, I don't know what is." I kissed her gently. "And this me couldn't be more grateful."

She kissed me back, a long, devoted kiss. "Thank you," she whispered.

When her head returned to my shoulder, her tension had melted. She snuggled closer, her belly nestling into the curve of my waist. I followed her example, letting everything go but our immediacy. The rest of the world, actual and probable, could wait. And that was how we fell asleep.

THE END

But keep reading to learn what's coming...

GODLY WARS
PROF CROFT BOOK 11

The gods are definitely crazy

I'm in deeper with the Greeks than ever, and I don't mean my cat's recent yogurt binge.

Hermes insists he can stop Persephone from opening a deadly chasm to the underworld. The catch? He needs me to steal her scepter from the shadow present, a realm where I've nearly met my maker twice now.

Can I trust the trickster? He's using my shadow's son as a vessel, effectively holding him hostage. He's also stockpiling deities and mythic beings in Midtown. But with dread Persephone gaining strength, spilling fresh horrors into our world, I don't see a way out, not with a baby girl on the way.

That is unless I can pull off a herculean feat of savvy and spell-casting to smite *both* gods. But first I'll need to decrypt a hag's prophecy that's been haunting my dreams.

One that warns of my demise in an upcoming war...

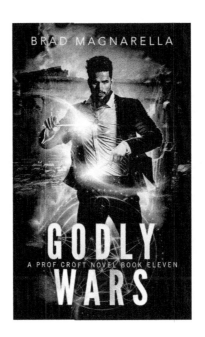

Godly Wars
(Prof Croft, Book II)

AUTHOR'S NOTES

Thus ends the second book of the third Prof Croft quadrilogy —Alec's mother and shadow Vega safe, the mission of the special task force accomplished, and Alec settling in with the Crofts. Whew. Now we just have to hope the conflict between Hermes and Persephone doesn't escalate.

Some years ago, I caught an interview with an author of a book on the Greek myths. She talked about the challenges of deciding which stories to include and which to leave out, as there are many, many stories of the major gods, often times painting conflicting portraits. Ultimately, the author had to choose which versions of the gods she would present to the reader.

That's more or less been my approach to dealing with gods in the Prof Croft series. Not as fully formed archetypes, but unique expressions depending on which version of the god was worshipped.

When I started looking into Hermes, for example, I discovered he was a god of a lot of things: merchants, shepherds, thieves, orators, boundaries, contracts, fertility—you name it. But because the Hermes artifact that Everson found (or found him) was worshipped by a thieves' guild, our Hermes skews toward that aspect of the god.

How much and to the detriment of his more humane qualities? Something tells me, one way or another, Everson is going to find out.

Another mystery to unpackage is what became of the magic-users in the shadow present and why Everson "shouldn't exist." This will take Everson to some interesting places and could well play out as a major story as well as a major threat...

Unless, of course, Everson attempts to put Tabitha on a diet.

One of my favorite parts of writing the Prof Croft series is researching New York City locations. Google maps and YouTube vids are wonderful visual resources. "The Hole" in Brooklyn, site of the wererat compound, is an actual sunken neighborhood and even had a horse farm until recently. Dead Horse Bay is undergoing environmental cleanup as I type. Pier 16 in Lower Manhattan also exists, though I took some liberties with its dimensions and use. To my knowledge, it's never been attacked by an ancient sea creature, but I could be wrong.

I have several people to thank for their help in bringing Shadow Deep into the world.

Thank you to the team at Damonza.com for designing another stellar cover. Kudos to my beta and advanced readers, including Beverly Collie, Mark Denman, Bob Singer, Linda Ash, Erin Halbmaier, Susie Johnson, Mark Mendez, and Larissa Thompson, who all provided valuable feedback during the writing process. And thanks to Sharlene

Magnarella and Donna Rich for taking on the painstaking task of final proofing. Naturally, any errors that remain are this author's alone.

I also want to give a shout out to James Patrick Cronin, who brings all the books in the Croftverse to life through his gifted narration on the audio editions. Those books, including samples, can be found at Audible.com.

Writing on Prof Croft 10 began in Guanajuato, Mexico, continued in Florida, and finished in Venice, Italy, where I wrote the final 40% in under a month. Must be something in their coffee. This time, I have Caffè del Doge to thank for serving up primo caffeine while I brainstormed Everson's next disaster.

The expanding Croftverse wouldn't be possible without the Strange Brigade, my dedicated fan group whose enthusiasm serves as motivation jet fuel, book after book.

Last but not least, thank you, fearless reader, for taking another ride with the Prof.

Till the next one...

Best Wishes,

Brad Magnarella

P.S. Be sure to check out my website to learn more about the Croftverse, download a pair of free prequels, and find out what's coming! That's all at bradmagnarella.com

CROFTVERSE CATALOGUE

PROF CROFT PREQUELS

Book of Souls

Siren Call

MAIN SERIES

Demon Moon

Blood Deal

Purge City

Death Mage

Black Luck

Power Game

Druid Bond

Night Rune

Shadow Duel

Shadow Deep

Godly Wars

Angel Doom

SPIN-OFFS

Croft & Tabby

Croft & Wesson

BLUE WOLF

Blue Curse

Blue Shadow

Blue Howl

Blue Venom

Blue Blood

Blue Storm

SPIN-OFF

Legion Files

For the entire chronology go to bradmagnarella.com

ABOUT THE AUTHOR

Brad Magnarella writes urban fantasy for the same reason most read it...

To explore worlds where magic crackles from fingertips, vampires and shifters walk city streets, cats talk (some excessively), and good prevails against all odds. It's shamelessly fun.

His two main series, Prof Croft and Blue Wolf, make up the growing Croftverse, with over a quarter-million books sold to date and an Independent Audiobook Award nomination.

Hopelessly nomadic, Brad can be found in a rented room overseas or hiking America's backcountry.

Or just go to www.bradmagnarella.com

Printed in Great Britain
by Amazon

44968522R00209